C. S. LAUNDY

Elderflower

To Jess,
who breathed life into this world,
and resuscitated it each time
I pronounced it dead.

Prologue

A woman stood motionless in a sun-drenched wheat field. She stared vacantly, lost in a distant, dark memory. Though alone, she heard *something* and broke from her reverie to listen: the field rustled, flies buzzed, and crows croaked upon the roof of her lonely cottage. *It's nothing*, she decided, wiping her sweaty, hair-plastered brow. She heard it again. The field had whispered; it had called. It hadn't called in years.

She closed her stinging, sunburnt eyes. A goat bleated from the shade of a solitary maple. Chickens clucked. Crickets clicked. Even the blazing sun seemed to throb a steady beat. Straining, she listened again, but not with her ears this time. Beneath all those distractions, she could feel that ancient call, that gentle chorus—the field, of ten thousand wheat stalks singing in perfect harmony. She beckoned, and The Song responded. It swelled as it washed over and around her, spiralling like a slow and gentle whirlwind. She opened herself up, and it began to fill her. As familiar as it was ancient, The Song was beautiful, powerful, dangerous, and sweet. It was like the voice of a lover, like the smell of warm bread, like coming home after a lifetime abroad. She drew more. Intoxicated, her body thrummed until—

The cottage door slammed open, shocking a dozen crows

into screeching flight. Startled, The Song dissipated and became silent as the dead. A young girl had burst from the cottage, laughing as she ran. A boy of the same age chased her down the garden path and into the golden field that swayed above their little heads. The woman sighed in disappointment, but she couldn't help a smile. Her children were up to mischief—as always. Taunting, the girl vaulted a half-buried harrow plough—its spikes like the rusted teeth of some long-dead predator.

"Careful," said the woman. "Plough's dangerous."

Heedless, the boy dashed to grab the girl, but she spun away, shrieking with laughter, and sped towards the woman.

Witch! The word blared in the woman's ears, unbidden and intrusive. Searing images followed: an angry mob, a dark cell, and a terrible, world-ending fire. Closing her eyes, she slowed her breath to calm her galloping heart and push the images away. She had her bad days. *Not today*, she decided, jaw clenched. Today, her children thrived. Today, her crop flourished. Today was going to be a good day.

The woman flung out her arms, and the girl and boy launched into them. She tickled them, and they giggled and squirmed, half-heartedly trying to escape. They loved being loved, she knew, and their joy calmed the woman and helped her forget.

The boy beamed up at her with twinkling eyes, flecked with shards of bright silver.

Silver… The woman smiled wistfully; her poor boy had no idea the trouble his beautiful Caveborn eyes would cause him. "Shoo!" she said, and they shot away to chase each other once again.

"Not near the plough," said the woman.

Ignoring her, the girl ran around the spiked skeleton, the boy a whisker behind.

"I said, not near the plough. It's…" The woman saw it happen: first in her head, then with her eyes. The boy tripped and fell amid the rusted spikes, missing all but one. He screamed as four inches sank into his thigh, quick and easy as butter. As he hit the ground, the blade snapped off the plough but remained embedded in his leg.

With a gasp, the woman sprinted to his side. Blood was already drenching his shorts, blossoming like some grotesque, crimson flower. "You're okay, Ridian. You're okay." Trembling, the woman grasped the rusty blade, and the boy wailed and thrashed and tried to pull away. But the woman knelt upon him and held him firm, crushing his small, soft body into the ground. Feeling sick, she gripped the blade with forced calm and slid the spike out with a quick tug. The boy screamed anew, and blood—brilliant and wet—pooled in the dirt. "Rayna," said the woman, staunching the bleeding with her dress. "Go fetch my medicine box—quick."

The girl stared, motionless.

"Rayna, go—"

Inexplicably, the girl collapsed and began writhing on the ground. Her spine arched, her joints locked. Foam frothed from between her clenched teeth, and her face became a twisted, twitching nightmare. Then it happened—

In an ever-expanding circle, the golden crop began to wilt, turn brown, and die. Weeds perished in a flash. Moss shrivelled and turned grey. And as the sagging wheat stalks struck the ground, they dissolved into dust. The invisible wave of Death left their grazing goat unharmed but groped up the lonely maple tree. Bark peeled away, and leaves, starting from the bottom and then travelling up, crinkled and began to fall. And as the leaves drifted and twirled and fluttered downward, they disintegrated and covered the ground like ash.

The woman gazed in astonishment—not at the dead field nor the dying tree—at her son. His wound was *healing*, stitching itself closed with darting strands of flesh, right there before her eyes.

The girl writhed.

The boy healed.

And Death took the field.

Chapter 1

Ridian was running out of dark. He could tell by the smell. With no moon, stars alone bathed everything in a delicate silver light, but it was more than enough for Ridian to see by. He was, after all, a Caveborn.

Ridian swung his mattock one last time. It lodged in the sodden mining wall, and with a grunt, he yanked out a clod and dumped it in his wheelbarrow, packed with soggy, low-grade clay. Tendrils of steam rose from his skin, and he huffed out swirling ghosts of frosty air. All night, he'd worked his lean, seventeen-year-old body to the bone to finish before dawn. People rose with the sun, and he didn't want to deal with people. Not today. Not on Sunfall.

Finally finished, he dumped his mattock and zigzagged down the twenty-foot scaffold until his toes squelched in the mud below. Fighting to keep his rickety barrow from bogging, he followed the mining wall all the way home. Half a mile later, there it lay upon the outskirts of Mudwall, a shit-hole town on the edge of Arden. In fact, the very edge of the known world, for Mudwall lay upon the banks of The Mire—a vast, bleak, and perilous swampland. Those who entered died, and survivors—if any—told strange stories of demons, witches, giants, and other supernatural terrors.

And Ridian's home lay upon its shore, right beneath the sprawling, miles-long mining wall that gave Mudwall its name. Locals called this narrow strip of land The Edge. Far from ideal, but unfortunates always find themselves in unsavoury places. Between a mire and a mud wall, as the saying went.

Ridian upended the wheelbarrow near his home, upon the pile he'd worked on all night. Later, he would process the mud: sift, soak, strain, and then wrap the clay slurry in cloth and hang it to dry. Tedious, but it helped them scratch a meagre living.

He washed up in a murky bowl of freezing water, then crept inside. His home was austere: a wonky table, two rickety chairs, a fireplace that smoked more than heated, and ragged drapes that offered privacy to two tiny bedrooms. One for him, one for his sister, Rayna. The walls and roof were sod bricks. Rayna's idea, of course. With timber so expensive, Edge dwellers often lived in miserable mud holes cut into the mining wall that were forever cold, wet, and collapsing. Their home, by contrast, was dry, sturdy, and strangely still alive. The severed roots of the sod bricks had re-grown, making the walls strong and the roof lush with grass which absorbed the rain. Many locals tried imitating the design, but most failed. The grassy roof died, leaked, and inevitably collapsed.

Ridian tip-toed towards bed. Before he arrived, however, Rayna tore aside the curtain to her room and glared at him. Or at least in his direction. She squinted, evidently unable to see him in the darkness. But Ridian could see her, his keen eyes being what they were. She was cut from the same lean cloth as Ridian, though her hair was a rich harvest gold, while Ridian's was raven black. And she was more sun-kissed than Ridian, who remained milk-white year-round due to his nocturnal working habits.

"Sneaking out again?" said Rayna accusingly, hands on hips.

Ridian said nothing. What could he say?

"Ah, Ridian," said Rayna in a condescending tone. "You think you're so smart. But the sad truth is, I'm older. Older and infinitely wiser." It was true, at least about her age. His twin sister was older by a whole two hours—a fact which she was very fond of reminding him.

"Well…" Ridian began, not sure how to finish.

Rayna must have caught something in Ridian's voice; she often did. "Don't tell me you started without me." She fumbled about in the dark and eventually lit a candle. She held it in front of Ridian's face to scrutinise him. "If you've gone ahead and started without me, you're going to be in a lot of trouble, young man."

Ridian looked anywhere but into Rayna's sturdy eyes. They found the kitchen. It was a shambles: littered with vials, a filthy mortar and pestle, and numerous herbs in various states of being crushed, cut, hung, steeped, or steamed. Rayna was very messy, but her amateur apothecary—her 'herb hustle,' as she called it—was enough to keep them afloat. Mudwallers were forever getting sick. The common cold, the flu, morning sickness, constipation, incontinence, migraines, stomach bugs, hives, period pain, you name it—Rayna had a remedy for everything.

Rayna threw up her hands in exasperation. "You've started without me, haven't you? I can tell. It's written all over your big stupid face. Guilty as sin. How much have you done? And don't lie. I'm your bloody twin sister. We shared a womb together, remember? I can tell when you're lying."

"I couldn't sleep," said Ridian. "So, I thought I would work 'til I got tired. And well…"

Rayna pointed an accusatory finger. "Don't tell me you did more than half?"

Ridian swallowed.

"Two-thirds?"

"Well…"

"You finished without me," said Rayna in profound incredulity.

Ridian opened his mouth to form some incoherent argument. It was not forthcoming.

"Oh no," said Rayna, her accusatory finger transforming into a wagging admonishment. "Don't think you can talk your way out of this one. You're in serious trouble, young man."

"But you hate harvesting clay."

"That's not the point, and you know it. We both pitch in. That's how we get by."

Ridian changed tack, one closer to the truth. "I know, but it's Sunfall…"

Rayna's face softened as a tinge of fear entered her eyes. The day of Sunfall made everyone nervous. Still, Ridian felt guilty for using it against her.

"I'm stressed too, Ridian," said Rayna at last. "And I'm grateful you work so hard." But she shook her head, resolved. "But we both need to pull our weight. You can't keep pampering and protecting me."

Ridian took a deep breath. Cornered, he decided to tell

the truth. "But you haven't been well lately."

Rayna tried to keep her face impassive, but the frustration showed. "I'm fine," she said flatly.

"No, you're pretending to be fine. I can tell. We shared a womb, remember? No, don't roll your eyes at me. You know you don't look after yourself."

"Not this again."

"Yes, this again."

They glared at each other until Rayna sighed and seemed to deflate. "Ridian, look around." She gestured expansively at their tiny home. "I know we don't have much, but we're better off than most. People need us."

"No. People need you." Ridian stared at her, knowing he sounded bitter. But he wasn't, he was concerned. "Lost gods, Rayna, it's the same story every week. You hike halfway across town for some sick widow. You stay up half the night cooking a potion for some family. You tend some fevered child. You push yourself and push yourself, and lo and behold, you get sick. It happens every bloody time." Ridian snorted a mirthless laugh. "And the best part is, most of the scabs around here don't even pay you. They milk you dry. I just don't get it. You kill yourself trying to help everybody when nobody has ever helped us." Actually, Ridian *was* bitter, but freezing hell, it was the truth.

Rayna was just about to respond with some snappy comeback when a man called from outside in a harsh voice, "Message for Elderflower!"

They frowned at each other. They never got messages. "We'll talk about this later," said Rayna and she walked outside into the growing light of a cold dawn.

Holding his breath, Ridian crept to the hessian flap that

served as their front door and peered through a tiny hole, knowing he remained invisible: past Rayna's lush herb garden and a wicker fence was a rider. But not just a rider; he wore the red leather armour of a Sol soldier. Whatever this was, it was official business, and it made Ridian's heart flutter. A visit from a Sol soldier on the day of Sunfall did not bode well.

"You have a message for us?" asked Rayna, approaching the soldier.

The man frowned at her. "For Ridian Elderflower. Is he here?" He wheeled his horse around in a complete circle, eyes darting in all directions. His hand was on his sword hilt, loose in its sheath.

He's afraid, thought Ridian. *And no wonder.*

Behind the rider lurked The Mire with its rotting trees, reeking bogs, and deadly secrets that even the mighty Sol Empire had failed to probe. For though the Sol invasion of Arden had spread like wildfire, their expansion had come to an abrupt halt upon the mysterious, bleak swampland. With an impassable mountain range to the north, and an unforgiving desert to the south, the Sol Empire had chosen The Mire for safe passage west. However, every expedition ended in bloody disaster—one after another. Convoys came back depleted or not at all. And the *stories*… Tales of quicksand and poisonous bogs. Of witches, walking upon water and cursing with a whisper. Of spirits, possessing your body. Of giants. Of monsters. Of talking animals. Of Faery shapeshifters, who could take on the form of a naked woman, a distressed child, or a dead relative—anything to lure the foolish into their realm. They were just stories, of course. Outlandish, superstitious nonsense. But people did die upon The Mire, and at night, the stories would come back to you, making you shiver and check the window.

"Ridian's here," said Rayna, gesturing behind her.

The man's fevered eyes locked onto their tiny sod home, and he licked his lips nervously.

Oh, he's not afraid of The Mire, Ridian realised. *He's afraid of the silver-eyed freak.*

The rider handed something small to Rayna. "Make sure he gets this." Then he cracked his reins and sped off with all the nervous efficiency he'd arrived with.

Rayna stared at the thing in her hand. She didn't look back; she didn't even move.

Ridian left the safety of their home to sidle up beside her. "What is it?"

Rayna handed a small note over, her eyes shining with apprehension. At the top was the wax seal of Sword and Sun, and beneath ran the words, "Report to the Asylum before dusk."

"The Asylum?" said Ridian, his heart pelting along now. "Why?"

"It doesn't make sense," said Rayna. "Your scheduled appointment isn't for ages."

Ridian sighed with depressed resignation. "I'm a Caveborn. It doesn't have to make sense."

They looked at each other, both knowing Ridian's words to be true. Then, a tiny, egg-sized finch flew in from nowhere and landed on Rayna's shoulder.

"Chirpy!" cried Rayna in delight.

The bird, Chirpy, fluttered quick as thought onto her far shoulder and whistled a merry tune. Exceedingly friendly, Chirpy was a bird of strange habit. It would visit them for a day, then disappear for months and sometimes even years. They'd known the bird since they were children (which explained the uninspired name) and like everybody, the bird was especially fond of Rayna, barely leaving her side during his brief visits. Something about the bird heartened them. It was a good omen. Indeed, Rayna was beaming as the bird hopped along her extended arm.

"I'll make you a deal," said Rayna. "If you stop fussing and let me do an equal share of today's Sunfall jobs, I won't help anyone for three whole days."

Ridian considered. "Five days," he replied.

"Four."

"Fine, but as long as you promise to take your medicine. On time, I might add."

Rayna didn't like this addition; she frowned. "Fine, I promise."

Ridian narrowed his eyes. "Full dose?"

"Yes, full dose!" said Rayna, frustrated but smiling all the same. "Do we have a deal or not?"

"With Chirpy as our witness?" said Ridian. "Deal." As they shook hands, Ridian tightened his grip so she couldn't let go. "Providing you rest, and have early nights, and…"

But he couldn't say more before Rayna tore her hand free. "Had to add that, didn't you?" she said, shaking her head and laughing. "You just can't help yourself, can you? You fuss, and you fuss, and you fuss. You're worse than an old hen."

"An old hen?" said Ridian with mock offence.

"Yes, a horrible thing to say about hens, isn't it?"

Ridian tried to grab at her so he could poke her in the ribs, but she spun away with a laugh, flapping her elbows and clucking like a chicken.

***

A few hours later, Ridian and Rayna were trundling their handcart towards Mudwall. They were heading to the dreaded Asylum, yes, but they needed to run a few essential errands first. Ridian pushed the crossbar at the front, Rayna pushed from the back, and together, they heaved the lumbering cart forward. The cart was loaded with wet, processed clay, and it kept slipping into muddy ruts and getting bogged. Chirpy contented himself with perching on the pull-shaft and singing. The mining wall, pocketed with cavities and crawling with muddy scaffolds, loomed on their right. The Mire slunk past on their left. Though vast, The Mire was forever shrouded in a thick concealing mist, but occasionally, on very clear days, Ridian thought he could see the faint outline of distant mountains.

True to her word, Rayna had taken her medicine. It was obvious: she was expressionless and withdrawn; her face was blank as paper; her eyes vacant as the windows of an empty home. She did not smile. She did not laugh. Ridian hated it, but she needed her medicine. Without it, she had strange, inexplicable fits, which the doctors said could be lethal. Thankfully, she'd taken enough to last the day, but Ridian insisted she always carry extra, just in case. As Rayna walked, the little glass vials clinked reassuringly in her pocket.

Edge dwellers had emerged from their huts and hovels and were busy preparing for Sunfall. Though many waved to Rayna, everyone avoided Ridian's gaze or shot brief, anxious smiles. *Friendly but not too friendly*, their strained smiles seemed to indicate. *Don't want to give the wrong impression.*

As the next turn loomed, Ridian stared at the ground. He knew what was around that bend: as familiar as an old scar, Trystan's Well lay among a dozen dilapidated homes, all empty, all quiet. The opening of the well had been boarded up, and a plaque was affixed to the outer stone ring with the words:

We remember them

Trystan Caddock, the well's namesake, was a young brick-layer who lived on The Edge a few decades prior. Trystan was considered thoroughly unremarkable except for one singular oddity: silver-flecked eyes, a peculiarity of all Caveborns, which is to say, someone born in the notorious Fell Caves Prison. The Sun was a blessing for the righteous, darkness a punishment for the wicked. Or so the Priest and Priestesses of Sol taught. And so, Arden lawbreakers—including Trystan's mother—were imprisoned in those dark caverns. And though Trystan was innocent, he spent the first few years of his life underground.

Nonetheless, Trystan grew up well-adjusted. That is, until the age of eighteen, when he inexplicably killed all his neighbours in the dead of night. And not just killed. He was found eating his victims with a wild, ravenous hunger, like some starved, rabid beast.

The Caveborn Cannibal and the Mudwall Massacre, as Trystan and the story became known, sent ripples throughout all of Arden. "How did this happen?" everyone asked. Superstitious Edge dwellers pointed to The Mire, believing some spirit had possessed him. However, the official Sol investigation concluded the massacre was due to Trystan's time in darkness during his formative years. Darkness was a purifier of the guilty but a corrupter of the innocent, they said. Bricking the well, a place of darkness, must have been a regressive trigger. And from that day, special care was taken to ensure another Caveborn would never be. But, of course, someone made a mistake.

Ridian scrunched his silver-flecked eyes shut. He was a cracked pot, waiting to shatter and cut those around him. One day—sooner or later—he would snap. He needed to leave. He needed to get as far away from Rayna as possible. And yet he stayed, as selfish a prick as ever existed. But how could he leave Rayna? He couldn't bear the thought. For he well remembered the endless terror of being alone.

"Careful!" cried a man's voice.

Startled, Ridian looked up to see a deranged man shambling towards them. Ridian sighed with relief. It was just Willem; he didn't need to worry about him.

Willem pointed a shaky finger at The Mire, his eyes wide. "A demon is loose upon The Mire. Saw it we did. Didn't we, Nancy?" Nancy was the chicken cradled in Willem's arms. He stroked the bird's comb affectionately and whispered something unintelligible in its ear. Willem had spent some time in the Fell Caves Prison as a teenager, and the visit had permanently addled him. Everyone knew he was crazy. Harmless but crazy.

"A demon?" asked Rayna in a lifeless voice.

Willem nodded vigorously. "Aye, a demon with sharp teeth and a furry hide. It even pinched one of my chickens!

But not Nancy, thank goodness, no! Snatched it and fled past the Gallows Tree, it did." He gestured at the nearby Gallows Tree, an ancient, long-dead elm where Sol authorities had traditionally hanged supposed witches, which is to say, anyone who deviated from Sol puritanism. The path leading out to it, for it stood upon The Mire itself, was called The Witch's Way: a narrow, winding, soggy thing, swamped on either side by dark, murky pools.

Ridian was not surprised by Willem's story. He had heard such things before, and not just from crazy crackpots like Willem. With the Sol Empire finding death and failure upon The Mire, strange sightings abounded.

Willem nuzzled Nancy to his cheek. "Thank goodness, it didn't take Nancy. I don't know what I would do if it took my Nancy." He abruptly turned and walked away. Nancy clucked, unfazed, and together, they disappeared into Willem's home, little more than a dark hole in the wall.

***

By early afternoon, Ridian and Rayna were approaching the town of Mudwall itself. Feeling squeamish, Ridian drew his hood over his tell-tale silver eyes and hoped to pass unnoticed.

All in all, Mudwall was just a big mud hole. Decades of excavation had cleared a vast expanse for homes, shops, potters, bakers, butchers, grocers, and more to rest within its walls. Planks connected every street, serving as bridges for carts and barrows that would otherwise flounder. And everything—from the streets to the buildings to the people— was covered in slick, wet mud.

The place was in a frenzy. Everyone was up and about, stomping along the planks and scampering up and down the complex scaffolding that clung to the clay wall. Barrow wheels creaked among the drone of voices, and children played, free from lessons and preoccupied parents. One group kicked a muddy ball. Another skipped rope while chanting an old nursery rhyme:

> *Lion, Liar, Minstrel, Flower,*
> *In truth, they're all the same.*
> *Up-jump Jack, make an attack,*
> *Soon you'll go insane.*
>
> *Come on, Lion, keep on tryin',*
> *Sing, Minstrel, sing.*
> *Come on, Flower, make your tower,*
> *Down with the King!*

Amidst the hustle and bustle, nobody paid Ridian or Rayna any heed, until one of the street kids kicked a ball underneath their cart.

"Sorry," said a grubby boy who dove between the muddy wheels, only to resurface dirtier than ever. His face fell when he met Ridian's eyes, and it was as if his father had come home, stinking drunk, belt in hand. The boy backed away slowly, then fled towards his friends, who clustered around him. They whispered conspiratorially and turned to peer at Ridian, their eyes full of mystery and fear. *Go ahead and stare,* thought Ridian. *It's not every day you get to see the silver-eyed freak.*

Not concentrating, Ridian steered the cart off the plank

and into the mud. Thankfully, Rayna managed to catch it before it capsized, and together, they pulled it back, but they had attracted attention. People laughed as they walked past, and a lounging gang of youths jeered.

One spotted Rayna, and his eyes followed her. He said something to his mates, and they grinned and slapped his arms and elbowed him as if to spur him on. Then he broke rank to strut towards Rayna, plucky as a rooster. "Hey, darlin'. How are you on this fine day?"

Rayna looked at him the same way she looked at everything whilst under the influence of her medication—blankly.

"Oh, come on," said the swaggering boy. "Don't be like that." He turned to grin at his mates, who couldn't believe he was actually doing it. That's when Ridian drew back his hood to glare at the boy.

The boy glanced fleetingly at Ridian, then his eyes snapped back, and his cocky bravado shriveled up like a leaf in a fire. He swallowed, mumbled something, and slunk back to the safety of his friends. Though his heart raced, Ridian pulled his hood back to hide a satisfied smile; his notoriety was good for something.

Ridian and Rayna passed a dozen blazing kilns and a dozen pottery shops before arriving at Daryll and Enid's Wagon. Daryll, a pleasant-looking man, sat hunched over a pottery wheel. He stuck out his tongue and frowned at the spinning blob of wet clay that seemed to defy his thick, clumsy fingers. His severe-looking wife, Enid, pinched her clay lump into shape as if wanting to inflict pain. Shoddy-looking bowls, plates, cups, and mugs were on display inside their wagon behind them.

"Rayna!" said Daryll heartily. "My favourite person in all the wide world. And that's including my dearest beloved." Daryll slapped his knee, leaving a muddy print.

Enid smiled. It looked like hard work. "So, are you buying today, or...?"

"Selling," said Rayna.

Enid's smile soured. "Oh." And she returned to torturing her clay.

This was how Ridian and Rayna made a living: selling processed clay. There were larger clay deposits in town, of course, but they were jealously guarded by rich locals who made lucrative deals with the major potters. That's why Ridian and Rayna serviced small fry like Enid and Daryll. Rayna's herb hustle was twice as profitable, but every little bit helped.

"Business has been a bit slow," said Daryll, by way of apology.

Rayna smiled weakly, her personality struggling to break through. "You'll get there."

No, you won't, thought Ridian. He'd heard all about Daryll and Enid. They were new to Mudwall, and had lived far away when they had the bright idea of a travelling pottery shop. "Quality and convenience," was their motto. Only they hadn't accounted for damaged goods on bumpy roads, overwhelming competition, and their own inferior stock. Simply put, they were doomed.

"Isn't this Sunfall business terrible," said Daryll conversationally. "Such a waste."

Enid swatted him across the arm. "Be quiet," she hissed. "The trouble you'll get us in."

"Would you relax?"

"I'll relax when you stop blabbering."

"I'm nurturing client relations. You should try it some-time."

They'd clearly been having this argument for years and would continue to have it until one of them was dead. Only they *did* stop due to a sudden hush falling over Mudwall. Ridian turned: a company of soldiers were marching down the street. They wore the boiled red leather armour that denoted the low-ranking, undisciplined rabble that usually garrisoned Mudwall, and from their appearance, were from all corners of the Sol Empire: there were golden-haired Tarks, bronze-skinned Altesians, burly Kermans, mahogany-skinned Sol natives, and races Ridian didn't even recognize. But no fair-skinned Ardens. No. All Arden conscripts had been shipped off to fight in distant lands. That was the Sol way: weaken the conquered; strengthen the conqueror. Consequently, none of these soldiers called Arden home, and so none of them gave two shits for it— never mind Mudwall. However, these soldiers showed none of their usual lazy swagger. They marched in lockstep, backs straight as the spears they held, brows sweaty as they glanced anxiously at the man who led them: a tall, imposing, mahogany-skinned man with black robes and a blazing, blood-red sun embroidered on his chest.

Freezing hell, thought Ridian. *A Sungazer!*

Rayna's blank face conveyed nothing, but her hands trembled. Everybody leapt off the path and into the mud to make way.

To say the Sungazers had a fearsome reputation was to say almost nothing. When the Sol Empire first landed on the shores of Arden some three hundred years ago, they sent

Priests to convert the people peacefully. But the stubborn Ardens clung to their pagan traditions. The second armada held soldiers, which the Ardens resisted. And so, the Sol Empire released their Sungazers. During the sweltering heat of one midsummer, half-a-dozen Sungazers baked their naked bodies under the sun by day and before a bonfire at night. On the third day, they rose with their god and summoned a giant firestorm that swept across the horizon, devastating the land and obliterating resistance.

As the Sungazer passed with his determined strides, he neither slowed nor looked aside. And soon, to everyone's relief, he and his soldiers passed out of sight. Adults returned to their duties, teenagers to their loitering, and children to their chanting of *Lion, Liar, Minstrel, Flower*. Chirpy twittered and flew around the wagon.

"What's a Sungazer doing in Mudwall?" asked Daryll, voicing everybody's thoughts.

"They must be after Tann," said Enid, who, in her astonishment, forgot to be surly. "It's there on the wall."

Sure enough, a poster was up for all to see:

Wanted

The outlaw Tann

Escaped the Fell Caves Prison on the 44th day of Winter, 311th Year of Wrath.

Appearance: mid-40s; 6'2; emaciated; unkempt black and white hair.

He is extremely dangerous.

Report any information to the Sol authorities

Tann was an illegal poacher who had employed Ridian off

the books a few months prior, just before his arrest. Nasty job, too—skinning the hides, soaking them in piss, scraping off the hair, rubbing them in dung, and then nailing them stretched out. All this on Tann's secret little hut just past the Gallows Tree. Ridian had only helped him once. It was too much risk, and he hated stepping onto The Mire. Even if it was 'close to shore.' Tann had treated Ridian well enough, but Ridian was no fool. Tann required help from a socially avoidant outcast who kept his mouth shut. Besides, Tann kept asking question after question about Rayna, and it ticked Ridian off.

"He escaped the Fell Caves?" said Rayna in disbelief. "Nobody escapes."

"Well, he did," said Daryll redundantly.

Enid pounded her lump of clay with her fist, looked up, then smiled her effortful smile. "Are you two going to make a deal or what?"

After some haggling, Ridian and Rayna traded a cart's worth of clay for a few copper pieces. They then stowed their cart and trudged over the wall and into rolling plains beyond, where tired farmers worked tired fields, until, at last, the Hill of Offering loomed. It was the highest hill in the district, and a long queue of locals trickled up the path. Nervous farmers checked their loads, craftsmen fussed over goods, swineherds drove pigs, and poultry farmers refastened cages. Rich and poor, Sol and Arden, everybody looked nervous—and for good reason. At tonight's Burning Ceremony, everyone was obliged to give an offering. Only there was no official standard of what was deemed an appropriate sacrifice. The Sol authorities had an inventory of people's assets, and from them, they made their calculations from which to derive a minimum contribution. These calculations were not shared with the populace, however, leaving people to fret. For if they did not give enough, consequences were swift and severe.

The giant pyre crested the hill like a castle of wood and produce. Celebrants climbed the ramp leading to the pyre's framework tip and upended carts, barrows, and baskets full of wheat, rye, sausages, herbs, pottery, potatoes, jewelry, coins, and more, while pigs, chickens, ducks, and geese were shoved into cramped cages at the base of the looming structure.

Soon enough, Ridian and Rayna stood before the Celebrants' makeshift desk: two barrels and a plank. Behind the desk, Celebrants scribbled furiously with quill pens. Behind them, Sol soldiers stood guard. Ridian was finding it hard to breathe. Celebrants held judiciary powers: one click of their fingers and they could apprehend possessions, make arrests, and even Exile someone to The Mire, which was tantamount to a death sentence. Every year they found someone to exile. Last year, it had been the beautiful Kaisy Prillan, whose only crime had been to snub the advances of a Celebrant. After she stepped onto The Mire, she was never seen or heard from again.

The line ended, and a gangling, sour-faced Celebrant by the name of Jakeer cried, *"Next!"* He sat expectantly, his greasy wisp of hair combed flat. Jakeer was an Arden-born Sol faithful: the demographic most despised by Arden natives. He even changed his Arden name to Jakeer to sound more Sol. He changed his name, but not his nature. "Name?" he asked curtly as they approached, without even a glance up. His quill hovered impatiently.

Rayna stepped forward. She was the personable one, after all. "Rayna and Ridian Elderflower, most Revered." Her response was crisp and alert; the personality-blunting effects of her medicine had evidently worn off.

As Jakeer's quill scampered along the paper, his mouth twitched into a smile. Jakeer wore the red robe and red tassel belt of an Ordinand—a priest in training—but Rayna had offered the more dignified title of a fully ordained, black-belted priest. Flattery was not lost on this pompous little up-and-coming, then.

This time Jakeer did look up, to find Rayna. First her eyes, then her lips, and then his nasty, greedy eyes scuttled all over her. He gave a greasy smile. "Let's see what you've brought me."

"Brought for the Burning, you mean," said Rayna flirtatiously.

Jakeer tittered and stared at Rayna's chest as she removed a purse from her satchel. Ridian's neck burned with anger, but he was powerless. And Jakeer knew it. He even managed to peel his eyes off Rayna to give Ridian a lavish, sneering grin. Jakeer feared Ridian like everybody else, of course. But not here. Not now. Not with soldiers at his beck and call.

Rayna upended the purse upon the desk, and coins tinkled out.

Jakeer whistled. "Very generous. Hard coin too. Most give mere produce. My, my… How does a young, attractive Edge dweller make so much? Or perhaps the unemployed brother brings home the butter?" His meaning was blatant: prostitution and theft. Both illegal.

Ridian's mind spun as Jakeer stared accusingly between

them. Then Jakeer brayed with laughter. "You should see your faces. It's too easy teasing you lot." He swiped the coins off the table and made a note in his register. "The acceptability of your offering will be made public tonight. Don't be late. I'll be keeping my eye out for you."

Chapter 2

After an hour of hiking, the Asylum appeared. It stood alone at a crossroads, surrounded by farmland. The perimeter wall was tall and topped with razor wire. As Ridian and Rayna made for the entrance, the wind-whipped clouds blazed red in the dying light. Sunfall was upon them.

Rayna banged on the wooden gate. "Hello?" she cried.

A small panel slid back, and scowling eyes appeared. "What do you want?" said a harsh voice.

"Ridian Elderflower is here for his—his summons."

The gate creaked open, then snapped shut behind them.

The grounds of the Asylum were pristine: plush lawns, tidy gardens, and cobbled paths lined with neat trees. A fountain splashed merrily in the courtyard. Only the patients spoiled the aesthetic. They littered the place even as they cleaned it—raking leaves, trimming hedges, weeding. Dirty and dishevelled, some lumbered with glacial slowness, while others sent their shackles jingling with nervous tics and frantic strides. Those that weren't groggy shot anxious glances at the patrolling wardens, whose batons rested ever ready at their hips.

The Asylum itself was an impressive four-story building with many windows. All barred, of course, and from the windows, faces stared: some gazes were empty, almost dead; some patients drooled; others swung off bars and hooted, while some scared-looking faces disappeared the moment Ridian looked at them.

Ridian loathed and feared this place. For as long as he could remember, he'd been summoned to sit opposite some nosy doctor. Ridian quickly learned to say no to all the questions:

Have you been hearing voices?

No.

Seen things others can't?

No.

Any thought of harming yourself?

No.

Thoughts of harming others?

No.

Any violent dreams?

No.

The questions went on and on. The doctor would scribble it down, and Ridian was free to go.

Ridian shook away the memories. *Just say no,* he told himself, and up the path and into the Asylum he and Rayna went. Chirpy left them at the door, fluttering into a friendlier sky. Wardens paced the foyer, while a clerk held the front desk, flicking through a stack of papers. "Can I help you?" she asked impatiently.

Rayna handed the summons. "Ridian Elderflower, here for—"

A door burst open, followed by a warden, wheeling a patient upon a bed. The patient thrashed against his leather restraints and screamed. A gag muffled the worst of it.

"Where's this one supposed to go?" said the warden who pushed the bed.

"How should I know?" said the clerk irritably. "He's the East Wing's problem, not mine."

The warden rolled the patient away, mouthing 'Bitch' once he'd turned his back.

"Sun in heaven," said the clerk, once the warden was out of earshot. "Some people." She frowned at Rayna and Ridian. "What did you want again?"

"Ridian Elderflower, here for—"

"Yeh, yeh. Come with me," she said, walking them briskly to a door. Somewhere, someone was crying. At the door, the clerk peered through a peephole. Satisfied, she produced a ring of keys, flicked through them, inserted one, twisted, and pushed. "In you go."

Ridian and Rayna obeyed, entering a grimy hallway with barred windows and dark cells. It stank of urine, faeces, and disinfectant. Patients wandered about or peered timidly from their cells.

"Feel free to wander around," said the clerk, as she closed the door. "General Selkyrie will see you when she's ready."

"Wait? What?" said Rayna, her hand shooting out to keep the door ajar. But the door thumped closed, and a lock clicked into place.

Ridian and Rayna looked at each other in alarm. General Selkyrie was one of the most celebrated war heroes in the Sol Empire. What was she doing in Mudwall, the most backwater district you could imagine? And what did she want with a nobody like Ridian?

"What did you do?" demanded Rayna, glaring at him.

"Nothing," said Ridian defensively, though it wasn't precisely true. Ridian had committed a few crimes. He'd mined someone else's portion of the wall, 'borrowed' a mattock when his one broke, and stolen a handful of firewood when Rayna was sick, to boil her a quick remedy. But these were all so petty. None of his crimes warranted a meeting with the Empire's most decorated soldier.

Rayna glowered at him. "You're hiding something."

"No, I swear. This is all some big mistake."

Rayna narrowed her eyes.

"Seriously," Ridian insisted. "I have nothing to say to the General. Nothing."

Rayna relaxed her shoulders. "Fine," she said reluctantly. "Well, we might as well say hi while we're here."

The Asylum had four wings. The East Wing restrained the most dangerous and deranged inpatients. It was a dark place with padded walls, said to release more screams per hour than patients per year. The North Wing housed those in early recovery, while the West Wing was home to the most functional. The ones tending the garden. And the South Wing—the one in which Ridian and Rayna now found themselves—held the long-timers and no-hopers. The crackpots, broken beyond repair.

A woman rushed at them, feverish with excitement, the corners of her mouth caked with saliva. "Look!" she cried. "Look!" And she tore a clump of her hair away with frenetic energy and held it out for them to see. "A bird's nest! See!" She went to rip again, though most of her frayed hair had already been pulled out long ago.

"Judith, no!" said Rayna, and she closed her hands around Judith's. "If you get another nest, all the eggs will fall out. We don't want that, do we?"

Judith squinted at Rayna for a long time, then, without a word, hastened away.

Ridian recognised others as they walked down the hall. There was Burton, who peered at his face with excruciating care in the dull reflection of a metal spoon. "Can't you see it? Can't you see it?" he said over and over and over. No one ever did. But he always asked: every day, all day, as he gazed at his spoon. There was Jayson, who was forever laughing behind his hands, but if you asked him what was so funny, he would only say you wouldn't get it. Miles babbled nonsense. Jacinta licked the walls. Fayden rocked in the corner, his hands clasped over his ears.

Ridian and Rayna passed them all until the hallway opened upon an open courtyard. A woman sat alone in the garden. She looked strikingly like Rayna.

"Mother?" said Rayna in her gentlest voice. "It's us… It's Ridian and Rayna."

Mother remained motionless. Indeed, her vacant eyes didn't even blink.

Chirpy flew in from the darkening twilight above and landed on Rayna's shoulder. It seemed to give her confidence, for she knelt and laid a soft hand upon Mother's knee. "Mother?" she asked again.

Mother said nothing, did nothing. Ridian held back. He wanted to come closer but couldn't; a lump was rising in his throat.

Rayna clasped Mother's limp, lifeless hand as if trying to draw out the soul lost within. But their mother remained as distant as a long-forgotten dream.

Ridian found his voice. "Rayna, she's not—"

"A black moon rises," said Mother, in an expressionless

voice. "A black moon with no face."

Rayna's mouth dropped open. "Yes, that's right! Tonight's a new moon." She turned to look at Ridian, her face alive with wonder and delight.

Mother's face remained blank as paper. "Moonflowers bloom but one night a year and then die come morning. Maybe tonight they will hear their mother's call?" Throughout the surrounding garden, dozens of Moonflowers stood to attention upon their long stems, though their petals remained bound up in a tight bud.

"Yes, Moonflowers!" Rayna cried. "But it's too early. They won't bloom for another month or so."

Mother said nothing, and the silence became profound.

"Mother?" said Rayna, gripping the unresponsive hand in earnest. "Tell me more about Moonflowers, please." But their mother had vanished. They were lucky to have heard as much. It was months and sometimes even years between words.

Chirpy twittered merrily, his bright, happy tone at odds with the moment.

Still, it made Rayna laugh. "What about a song then? You do love music." Rayna took a shaky breath and began a lilting folk song as old as the hills.

> *Before the first man, life given him,*
> *Before he fell, the black death grim,*
> *Before the world and the Great Unknowing,*
> *I heard the Song of Silent Growing.*
>
> *Slow but steady, the Song grew strong,*
> *And all could hear before very long,*

After fall and the spring harvest ripe,
I joined the song with the sickle swipe.

While the moon stood, oh sentinel true,
While the sun set and rose anew,
There was life within, the river flowing,
And I sang! I sang! Of the Silent Growing.

To Ridian's astonishment, Mother began to sing along. Her
tremulous voice was sweet and delicate, and to Ridian, it
was like the falling of summer rain.

Singing thus, our work divine,
Our Song gave life like grapes from a vine,
And through us all, our mother's kiss,
For those who listened, the reaping bliss.

But some men turned from actions just,
Blackened hearts and broken trust,
And so, we travelled and kept going,
To sing forever of the Silent Growing.

Song finished, Rayna's voice faded. But Mother, who
remained carved from stone, sang on, her voice sad and
full of longing.

Far from home, the Song murmured on,
Like the seasons we rely upon,
Until at last, the Song grew still,
And now we feel the winter chill.

Now the Song is all but dead,
Words never spoken, never said,
'til the last fall, I'll keep sowing,
To hear once more the Song of Silent Growing.

The Song of Silent Growing was a timeless classic sung in the fields and hearts of all Arden natives. Yet these last two verses were new. Ridian had never heard them before. Only, he had heard them. Long ago, as a toddler, playing in a cave. And unbidden, the memory played out before Ridian's eyes like a waking dream.

***

A thin shaft of slanting sunlight illuminated his tiny home. Enthralled, Ridian waved his small hands through the beam, trying to catch the uncatchable dust motes that swirled around his tiny palms. Mamma was sitting against the cave wall, singing her sad song again.

A drop of water fell from the ceiling onto his head. *"Water,"* Ridian cried. He knew so many words now: water, cup, night, day, big door, little door, mushroom, milk –

"Milk!" he cried, waddling over to her.

Mamma smiled. "Greedy boy!" And Ridian suckled from her bosom.

When he finished, they sat cuddling in the perfect dark. Only it wasn't perfectly dark. A small, silver orb glowed upon the ceiling. How curious! He'd never seen a glowing mushroom before.

"Mushroom!" He pointed eagerly at it. They'd eaten mushrooms yesterday, and Ridian was very proud he'd learnt that word so quickly.

"Are you being silly?" Mamma teased.

"Mushroom," Ridian insisted.

"But it's dark. You can't see any mushrooms."

But there it was. He could see it. "Mushroom!"

They heard a loud bang from big door. "Dinner!" shouted a gruff voice on the other side.

"Mushroom!" Ridian shouted again.

"Shhhhh… Not so loud." And Mamma trembled as she held him close.

But Ridian was frustrated. There was a mushroom. He could see it. "Mushroom! Mushroom! Mushroom!" he shouted.

Mamma clapped her hand over Ridian's mouth. "Shhhh… little door is opening. Remember, little voice for little door." She was scared, and it made Ridian scared.

Little door opened, and a bowl of slop slid inside.

Ridian lurched free of Mamma's grip and cried.

"What the…?" said the gruff voice.

A bolt slid and big door screeched open. It had never opened before. As it did, a great, burning, flickering, red light seared Ridian's eyes, blinding him, and the gruff voice shouted. "Oi! There's a kid in here!"

"What?" replied another voice.

"Seriously, have a look."

Mamma clung to Ridian. "No, no no…"

The second voice swore.

"I know," said the gruff voice.

"What should we do?"

"Not sure. But he can't stay here. Let's grab the little fella and let the bosses figure it out. They're the ones who get paid to deal with this sort of thing."

"Please," wailed Mamma. "Don't take my baby! Don't take my baby boy!"

Still blind, Ridian felt rough hands grab hold of his wrists. Mamma clung on desperately, but the cruel fingers tightened, and after a few violent jerks, he was pulled away. Overwhelmed with a world-ending terror, Ridian wailed, but they didn't listen. They carried him away, and Mamma's cries grew suddenly faint as big door slammed shut. Ridian kicked and thrashed and screamed for Mamma, but still, they carried him away.

And soon light and colour. A storm of burning colour. He scrunched his eyes shut and clasped his hands over his eyes. Still, they burned.

Time wore on: minutes, hours, days… impossible to tell. People gave him food. But he didn't eat. They gave him water. But he didn't drink. Mamma. He wanted Mamma. But she was gone—gone forever, and he knew nothing would ever be okay again. Then a pair of small arms hugged him, and a sweet voice said new words: Rayna, sister, and brother. The girl clung to him, and they cried, and the pain he thought would never go away, eased. And the girl called Rayna—his sister—gave him the courage to open his eyes…

***

The memory faded, and to Ridian's surprise, Mother was alert. Her song had somehow drawn her timid self out. Her eyes shone with clarity. She could *see*. Smiling with warm gentleness, Mother removed the necklace from around her neck and placed it affectionately in Rayna's hand. It was a simple necklace—a glossy black-rock pendant in the shape of a flower on the end of a tatty leather cord—but it was the family's last remaining keepsake. Beaming, Rayna held the necklace to her chest, and behold! All around them, all at once, the white-petal Moonflowers began to bloom. It was like all the buds were yawning and stretching after a long sleep. They opened and opened, and a moment later, the sweetest, strongest perfume filled the air.

How is this happening? Then, for the first time in many years, Mother looked at Ridian and actually *saw* him.

"Ridian Elderflower!" called a hard voice from behind Ridian, and Mother retreated back into herself in the blink of an eye.

Ridian whirled around to see a trio glaring at him: one woman and two men. The sight of them sent Ridian's insides into a sickening free fall. The woman had the sharp nose and piercing eyes of a hawk. The men were tall and powerfully built. All three had the mahogany skin of Sol Island natives and wore black Sungazer robes, though the colour of the Sun on their chests differed: green, white, and gold respectively. The woman's Sun was gold, which matched the gleaming irises of her eyes.

Ridian swallowed. "I'm Ridian Elderflower."

The woman gave a terse command in her native tongue, and the men peeled away without a word. She pinned Ridian with her golden, hawk like eyes—pinned him as a predator does its prey. "Do you know who I am?" she asked, in a rich exotic accent.

Ridian nodded. Who else but General Selkyrie?

"Well, an Edge-dwelling bastard like you shouldn't know," said General Selkyrie, full of contempt. "It means people whom I trusted have spoken. I will find out and punish them accordingly. The Sun Sees All." Gold glimmered here and there upon her person: hair beads, lips, fingernails, eyeliner, embroidery. Even swirls of burnt orange wove through her dreadlocked hair, evoking images of her basking in a distant Sun.

Selkyrie sauntered forward like a cat, lithe and athletic, and Ridian became painfully aware of the sheer, high walls surrounding them. "My sources tell me you have had dealings with the outlaw Tann. Tell me, where is he?"

Ridian was taken aback. *Tann? How should I know?* Then he pictured Tann's secret little island out on The Mire. He almost blurted it out. But he bit his tongue. Years of interrogation had made him cautious. No, he couldn't tell. Not without incriminating himself in Tann's crimes. "I have no idea, General."

"Don't lie. The Sun Sees All. I know your father abandoned you before birth. I know your mother is a reformed witch, gone insane. And I know your sister runs an unauthorised apothecary. Now, tell me: where is the outlaw Tann?"

Stammering, Ridian turned to Rayna for help. But she was pale and wide-eyed. Even Chirpy remained silent in the general's presence. Selkyrie advanced like a stalking predator.

Ridian stepped back. "I don't know where he is. I swear."

"Liar," said the General. She was very close now, and she smelled of foreign spices. "I know you are a Caveborn, a child of darkness, doomed to commit your own massacre one day. I could have you thrown in the Asylum for the rest of your miserable life. I could send your sister to the barracks as a comfort girl, to satisfy fifty men a day and a hundred men a night, to be utterly used and abused until she grew old and knew true despair."

Quick as a snake, General Selkyrie snatched Ridian's collar. As she did, her eyes—iris, pupil, and whites—turned a solid gold, and a blast of hot air blew from her as if from the sudden opening of a furnace. Panicked, Ridian tried to shy away from the heat radiating off her. But Selkyrie held him fast. "Tell me," she said, in a terrifying voice that sounded like ironed grating over stone. "Where is the outlaw Tann?"

"He doesn't know," Rayna cried.

"Silence!"

"Tann was a poacher," said Ridian, stalling as sweat dripped down his temples. "He always bragged he could find anything, anywhere, anytime."

"Yes, and…?"

"Well, he was always covered in black mud." Ridian's insinuation was obvious, but he said it anyway. "Maybe he's hiding on The Mire."

Selkyrie's eyes burned like molten gold, and the air around her shivered. "What else do you know?"

"Nothing."

General Selkyrie yanked Ridian's hair back, and he cried out in pain. When he opened his eyes, he found a sharp, gold-painted thumbnail hovering over one of them, ready to plunge. "Perhaps pain will loosen your tongue."

"Please!" shouted Rayna, stepping forward. "Let him go!"

To Ridian's utter surprise, the General obeyed. Her grip slackened, and the fire in her eyes dimmed, flickered, and then went out—human once more. At the same moment, the hot air radiating from her faded away. She looked lost and confused. "Fine. I believe your story." Then, blinking in bewilderment, she left.

Ridian was dumbfounded. Rayna looked equally surprised. But before they could make sense of it, the clerk who had locked them in earlier bustled into the courtyard and said, "You're free to go."

Not needing to be told twice, they left in all haste and soon found themselves breathless in a lonely field of winter rye overlooking the Asylum, with only the stars for light. *A black moon rises. A black moon with no face.*

"What the hell just happened?" asked Ridian. Despite their being alone, he felt compelled to whisper.

Rayna stared at the necklace in her palm: the thin strand of stained leather with its glossy, black rock pendant, carved in the shape of a simple flower. "She gave me the Elderflower," she said as if she couldn't believe it. "She gave it to me..." She looked up at Ridian. "Do you remember when we all lived together? You, Mum, and I? In that little cottage, out in that field?"

The image of a dead field and a dying tree flashed across Ridian's eyes. A dead field and a dying tree—the same image that haunted so many of his dreams. He didn't know why, but the image terrified him. *Don't go there,* some part of him warned, and Ridian, with considerable force of will, buried the image deep within himself, locking it away as he always did.

"Not really," he managed to say.

Rayna was too busy staring at the Elderflower necklace to notice Ridian's brief struggle. "Mum always said she would give me the Elderflower one day," she continued. "You would keep the Elderflower name; I would keep the flower. She said it would look prettier on me."

Besides the black-rock Elderflower sat a Moonflower. It was a gorgeous, many-petalled beauty, white as snow. But even as Ridian admired it, it began to wilt: the petals shrivelled and curled, their pristine whiteness fading to grey. In moments, the entire flower disintegrated into dust—as if a hundred years had passed.

Ridian's astonishment shattered as Rayna's hand snapped shut. Her eyes rolled back; her face contorted. Then she flung herself backwards, twitching and thrashing among the rye, gripped by a violent seizure.

She was dying.

Chapter 3

Ridian was paralysed with shock. He didn't know what to do. Rayna had always felt the seizures coming on and so had always self-administered her medication. "It warns me," she always said. "Stop fussing."

Chirpy fluttered across Ridian's face, and the tiny wing-beats startled him into action. He snatched at Rayna's coat pocket, the precious vials holding medicine clinking inside. But Rayna twisted away with a violent lurch, and kicked and flailed spasmodically, flattening rye stalks as she did. Again, Ridian fumbled for her pocket, but she rolled and he heard the dreaded sound—the tinkling of crushed glass.

"No!" Ridian cried.

Ridian managed to plunge his hand into Rayna's pocket and draw out a fistful of wet, shattered glass. Trembling, he examined the glass splinters under the scant starlight: one vial still had a small green sample. He steadied himself, then knelt on her chest to restrain her, but she continued to buck beneath him with incredible, mindless strength. And her jaw was locked shut. It was going to be impossible. But suddenly, she went limp as a boned eel, and Ridian poured the solution into her sagging mouth. And not a moment too soon; again, she writhed, and her teeth snapped shut like a trap.

"It's okay, Rayna," he said, not believing his words. "It's okay." Ridian clamped his hands over her foaming mouth to keep what little potion there was within her. Her nose was bleeding, and it covered his knuckles. He waited, and waited, and waited, until finally, after the longest, most dreadful minute, her seizure started to subside, then stopped altogether. Her breath steadied, though she remained unconscious.

She needs more medicine. It's not enough.

He looked at the gloomy Asylum. No help would come from there. Only one thing could. Ridian tore off his cloak and tucked it under Rayna's head for a pillow. "Don't worry," he said. "I'll be back soon." Then, with a parting glance at her pale, blood-smeared face, he sprinted home. And never had he run so fast. Rye stalks whipped past in a blur, and his eyes stung from the speed of his flight. A stone wall appeared, then vanished behind him. A stream was leapt. A hill was climbed. He had only one job: run. His legs burned. His lungs burned. A stitch stabbed his side. But he didn't slow down. Panic spurred him. He kept imagining Rayna: cold, rigid, and with bugs crawling over her eyes. *Just run,* he told himself. He took the road; he took the fields—whatever was quickest, through stream or over hill. He recalled the Moonflower dying on her palm. He shook his head. *Just run.*

At long last, panting furiously, he found himself atop the mining wall, above their little sod-brick home. The nearest scaffold was a hundred yards away. *Too far,* and he jumped. Falling, falling, then the lush grass roof caught him. He leapt down, dashed inside, and, after a frantic search, shot away with a fistful of vials. The muddy path sucked at his feet, slowing him. Twice he slipped and twice he was filled with the brief but intense horror of smashing the precious vials. His focus became absolute. The ground before his feet was everything. He climbed a scaffold and ran through fields, farms, rivers and streams until he arrived back at the field of winter rye where he'd left Rayna.

But she was gone. The stars alone kept him company. *Wrong spot?* No, there was his cloak in the centre of a flattened patch of rye. Legs and lungs screaming, he looked about the lonely waist-high field. At least she could walk. The medicine must be more potent than he'd thought. Still, she'd need another dose. And where had she gone? The answer came to him immediately: the Burning, of course. Everyone needed to be there; *he* needed to be there. Already, the new moon hung high in the sky. Tardiness would be deemed a sacrilege, and any sacrilege was a most grievous crime.

Better get going, thought Ridian wearily, and as he grabbed his cloak, a twinkle in the grass caught his eye: the Elderflower necklace. Ridian picked it up. As he did, rye stalks got trapped in his fingers and dissolved into ash. Then Ridian saw what he hadn't before: the trampled circle of rye wasn't just trampled—it was dead. Indeed, in a ten-foot radius, all was ash. Just as the Moonflower on Rayna's palm had withered, shrivelled and died, so too had this small patch of rye. Ridian scooped up another handful; dry flakes crumbled and blew away like dust. Another handful, the same. The surrounding field swayed, healthy and strong. Ridian's mind reeled. It didn't fit with anything he'd ever seen before. Then, for the second time that night, the image of a dead field and a dying tree flashed before his eyes. And again, as terrifying emotions rose within him, Ridian scrunched his eyes shut and pushed the image away, not knowing why, only that he needed to.

Whatever was happening, he needed to go. Standing around wouldn't solve any of tonight's riddles. Perhaps Rayna had the answers. So, he put the Elderflower necklace around his neck and left at a jog.

He was plodding along a gravel path when the Hill of Offering emerged. The pyre, bloated with wood and produce, crested the hill like an obscene crown, and numerous torches flickered around the hill, illuminating the crowd.

Of course, a bonfire at the winter solstice had originally been an Arden tradition. But who knew its original significance? The Sol Empire had purposefully lost its true meaning. That was the Sol way: conquer and erase. It wasn't enough to colonise; they *consumed*. Churches, libraries, playhouses, artworks, museums, songs—anything that held Arden's history or culture had been meticulously hunted down and destroyed centuries ago. A generation of scholars, writers, poets, and doctors—Arden's finest—had been exiled or executed. Nothing was allowed to be preserved. Only a few scraps, the odd song or story, survived. And any remaining traditions were appropriated. The Burning was a prime example. Sunfall was no longer an Arden custom but a ritual of sacrifice, meant to summon the Sun back to full strength.

"You're such a thick-headed lackwit!" cried a woman's shrill voice.

"Just shut up and lift!" replied a man.

It was Daryll and Enid. Their wagon, which held all their

futile hopes, lay lopsided. A wheel had fallen off, and they were straining to lift the cart to put it back on. Clay pots and crocks lay shattered upon the ground. Their mule chewed grass, unconcerned. They were anything but.

Ridian skidded to a stop. "Have you seen Rayna pass through here?"

"Oh, thank goodness!" said Enid. "Please help us! We're running late and we haven't even given our offering yet." Enid's eyes gave the impression of an animal sinking neck deep into mud.

But Ridian didn't have time for two ill-prepared strangers who didn't give a spit about him. Besides, they were already too late. It was almost midnight. The Burning was mere minutes away. "Have you seen Rayna?" he asked again, more forcefully.

Daryll set the corner of the wagon down with effort. "Aye, we have." He looked levelly at Ridian, a man on the brink of giving bad news. "Sorry son, she's gone."

Ridian frowned. "What?"

Daryll licked his lips nervously. "She's walking the Witch's Way."

Ridian pictured the path out to the Gallows Tree. "She's been exiled?" he asked in alarm.

Daryll shook his head. "Oh, no, nothing like that. She—she took herself. She was alone."

Ridian couldn't believe the nonsense coming out of this idiot's mouth. Enid was right, Daryll was a thick-headed lackwit. "You think that's funny? You think my sister walking The Mire is funny?" Ridian's voice was hard and cold as a frost-covered stone.

"I'm not joking," said Daryll. "We called to her. We tried

to stop her, but she—"

Ridian had heard enough. He turned to leave.

"Please!" cried Enid, grabbing Ridian's arm. "We need your help. If we don't get there in time, they'll—they'll…"

But Ridian didn't care what the Sol would do to them. "Help yourself," he said, and he shrugged Enid off and left her, Daryll, and their doomed little wagon at a run.

Enid's curses chased after him. Ridian ignored the pang of guilt rising within him. Why should he endanger himself in helping them? He'd worked tirelessly for weeks to prepare for Sunfall. They should have done the same. Besides, Rayna needed more medicine, and time was of the essence.

A minute later, Ridian approached Jakeer, who sat at his desk, quill at the ready.

"Ridian Elderflower," he said, panting.

"Ridian Elderflower," said Jakeer in a condescending tone. "Dear, dear. Tut-tut." He shook his head disapprovingly. "You're cutting it awfully fine, aren't you?" He scanned the ledger with a long, soft finger. "Yes, I remember you, though I remember your sister better." He peered down the hill Ridian had just climbed. "Where is she?"

Ridian's heart dropped. "She's not here?"

"No."

"Are you sure?"

With a look of utter contempt, Jakeer picked up his ledger and pointed at Rayna's name. "She's not here—*see.*" Jakeer shook his head. "Pity. Your sister's going to be in a lot of trouble."

Unreality washed over Ridian as he recalled Daryll's honest words: *Sorry son, she's gone… She's walking the Witch's Way.*

Then, from uphill, a voice cried, "All praise the Sun!" and the crowd echoed the words. Someone then lit the pyre, and the pigs, goats, and chickens squealed, bleated and squawked in their cages.

"They started without me," complained Jakeer, quickly collecting his things. "Typical."

Five figures approached the bonfire—black-robed, mahogany-skinned Sungazers. As they did, the fire roared as if fanned by a great wind, though the night was still. And as the fire grew in sudden vigour, the animals shrieked and bucked and stamped with growing panic.

In unison, the Sungazers extended their hands and cried, "All praise the Sun!" And the pyre roared like a hurricane and erupted into a dazzling, colossal flame—a pillar of fire, hundreds of feet high. A moment later, a blast of hot wind ruffled Ridian's clothes and dried his eyes. It smelled of bacon, manure, hay, and a hundred other offerings. And despite Ridian's distance from the fire, he shielded his face from the intense glare and growing heat. Indeed, the hill and surrounding fields were alight as if by a small sun. Awestruck, Ridian peeped from behind his forearm: the Sungazers were drawing closer to the bonfire, their robes billowing in the fiery wind. As they did, the pillar of fire shot even higher, sending burning debris fluttering far and wide from its pluming peak.

Now the flames were changing colour. Swirls of black, white, green, blue, and gold spiralled upward through the pillar of fire. A miracle. A beautiful, terrifying miracle.

Somewhere downhill, Ridian thought he heard Enid's wail of despair.

Chapter 4

It was all a dream, surely. It certainly didn't feel real. He felt no pain, no fatigue, no emotion. Nothing. He was floating.

Home—he needed to go home. Maybe Rayna went there. That was the most likely place. Not The Mire, certainly not there. He ran down the hill, and things flew past like leaves in a storm. At home, upon their table, a note waited for him. It was written in Rayna's careless hand:

> *Sorry to leave without a goodbye.*
> *I'm fine. Promise.*
> *Not sure when back. Please don't follow, and*
> *please don't fuss.*

Yes, this was all definitely a dream. Nonetheless, seemingly of their own accord, his legs led him to the Gallows Tree. There was nowhere else to go. Drawing close, the heavy mist parted to reveal the ancient tree, its dead trunk twisting into the night sky. A moss-covered noose dangled from a snapped branch—a relic from witch hunts of yesteryear. *How many necks had it snapped before the branch?*

He stepped over the gnarled roots and looked upon The Mire, upon black water, upon rotting trees, upon the edge of the world. Something slithered through the reeds and slipped into the water, while somewhere out in the mist, a bird gave a long, lonely cry. He shivered. The Mire was an evil, unforgiving place, and his body knew it. Sure, he'd been out here before with Tann, but not alone, and certainly not at night. All the nasty tall tales of witches, monsters, and demons he'd heard growing up flooded back. Even Willem's demon-chicken-thief didn't seem far-fetched.

Dread sat hot and heavy in his chest like oven-baked brick, but his concern for Rayna was paramount. He imagined her fainting, falling, disappearing into the mud… He shouted her name; The Mire answered with a long, chilly silence. Everything inside him told him to leave, to run. Then, a memory of long ago: of Rayna clinging to him, afraid of the dark. Ridian had never been afraid of the dark—darkness was an old friend—and so he comforted her. It was perhaps the only time she had needed him more than he needed her.

She needs me now. Then, steeling himself, he did the bravest thing he'd ever done: he took a step. His foot plunged into soggy, wet decay, sending sluggish ripples along the water. The disrupted muck stank, but nothing sinister rushed at him through the gloom. He took another sinking, squelching step. Then another. The Witch's Way was little more than a fragile strip of sodden ground, twisting through bogs and black pools. Clumps of tussock were good for stability, but he brushed past the Sword Reeds with care—they were extraordinarily sharp.

Ridian looked over his shoulder: Mudwall had vanished. The fog had swallowed him whole. He pressed forward, waiting for some nightmare to shamble towards him. What had possessed Rayna to come here? Her fit must have totally addled her. But her note, despite being ridiculous, seemed coherent enough.

The path split, each way disappearing into mist. Ridian checked for Rayna's footprints but only saw mud. "Rayna!" he cried, with no answer. He went left, but offshoots appeared—pathways going hither and thither. He took one way, only for it to vanish, forcing him to backtrack. He tried another path. It wound like a serpent only to end on the bank of a murky pool. Again, he backtracked. He looked around for reference and again saw only enclosing walls of mist. Frustration mounted. He didn't have time for this. Rayna was deluded, a drop of medicine sustaining her. He saw a sturdy-looking path on the other side of a six-foot bog. He tested the water, and his foot sank knee-deep. Reckless, he took another step and sank up to his crotch. Lost gods, he was stuck—and sinking. Already, he was up to his belly button.

He twisted around and clutched the only thing available— Sword Reeds. It was like clutching a bundle of sharp knives, but he couldn't let go; mud was climbing up to his armpits. He gritted his teeth and pulled. The razor-sharp reeds slipped through his grip, stinging his palms, but he made a few inches, and then a few inches more. It stank so much that it was hard to breathe. Then, with great effort, he wrestled his way onto solid ground, teeth chattering from cold. He checked his palms; they smarted from a dozen deep slits. He flexed his fingers and pain, cruel as laughter, lanced through his fingers.

He was being stupid. *Think, Ridian, think.* The Mire was a labyrinth of treacherous waterways. He couldn't find Rayna wandering like this. And what if he did? Could he get them back? No. They'd both be lost. He needed a guide. No, a tracker. Someone who could find anything, anywhere, anytime. *Tann! I need Tann!*

It was absurd but true. Ridian hadn't been lying to General Selkyrie about the black mud. Tann did hide and hunt upon The Mire. If he could track game, surely, he could track Rayna.

Decision made, Ridian made for Tann's secret little island. It wasn't far. From the Gallows Tree, he took a slender, twisting path towards a black lake, quiet as the new moon above. For some time, he searched among the reeds until he found what he was looking for—a smooth wooden spike hammered into the ground. A rope was looped around the spike, with both ends slinking into the murky water. Ignoring his stinging hands, he pulled the rope, which was slimy as an eel. There was resistance, but after a few dozen effortful pulls, a raft emerged through the gloom, which eventually touched the bank at Ridian's feet. Ridian boarded the half-rotten and unstable craft and tugged the rope on the other side of the spike, knowing it passed around a similar spike on Tann's Island. As he did, the raft glided slowly away from the shore and out into the lake. Algae covered the water like phlegm in a sick man's bowl—and the raft gathered little clumps as it passed.

Soon, the fog unveiled Tann's tiny island and his dilapidated shack: moss-covered, rotten, and leaning. Adrenaline coursed through Ridian. Tann could very well be insane from his time in the Fell Caves Prison—violent even. His wanted poster in town certainly said he was dangerous.

Nonetheless, he leapt ashore and approached Tann's hovel. The door was off its hinges, and, creeping forward, Ridian peered inside: empty. Ridian was equal parts relieved and disappointed. Only a rucksack hid in a mouldy corner. Ridian rummaged inside the rucksack and found a flint, water skin, blanket, salted meat, dried biscuits, and a rusty knife—perfect for a long journey or quick flight.

Ridian was deciding what to do when the waterlogged rope sprang to life and pulled the raft eerily into the gloom.

Tann was coming.

Chapter 5

As anxiety crawled up his spine, Ridian racked his brain. How was he supposed to persuade Tann to help? Ridian hadn't thought this far ahead. Tann was a competent poacher, so he didn't need food. Tann was a head taller and twelve inches broader, so Ridian couldn't threaten him with force. Tann already had the perfect hideout. And appealing to Tann's better nature seemed preposterous. Then an idea—blackmail. It would be a dangerous game; Tann was a desperate man. But Ridian was also desperate.

Ridian strained his eyes to see through the fog, waiting for the outlaw to appear. Then he did. Stooped low, Tann pulled the rope, quick and strong.

Ridian fought a powerful urge to scurry into the shack and hide. "Hello, Tann!" he cried. "It's me, Ridian."

Tann stopped pulling and stood upright. Fog obscured his features. "Ridian Elderflower?" His voice was hoarse, as if it hadn't been used in a while. "What a pleasant surprise. If I knew you were visiting, I would have tidied up and made the place more presentable."

Was Tann joking or was he nuts? "No, the place looks great," said Ridian awkwardly. He doubted a tidy-up would improve The Mire's appeal.

"You're too kind," said Tann, pleasant as a picnic. "Truthfully, I've let the place go. It's hard keeping on top of domestic duties when you're rotting in prison."

"So I've heard."

Tann chuckled. "Ridian, tell me…" Now his voice was hard. "What the hell are you doing here?"

Ridian steadied himself. "I need your help."

Again, Tann spoke in friendly tones. "I'm not in the business of helping people when I'm in sore need of it myself."

"Please, my sister. She's lost on The Mire. She's—she's sick. She could pass out at any moment."

"Nothing would warm my heart more than finding your dear, sweet sister, truly." Tann began to pull the rope again. "But unfortunately, the Sol Empire and I have had something of a falling out. I don't want to bore you with all the unpleasant details, but I'd rather avoid an awkward encounter if it's all the same to you. Now, throw me my rucksack. I'm in a hurry. I see you've taken a peek."

Ridian brandished the knife from Tann's bag. It was time to blackmail. "Listen, Tann," said Ridian. "If you don't promise to help me, I'll cut the rope."

Tann's raft continued to glide over the water. "So?" he said, calm as midnight, totally unperturbed.

"So, you'll be stranded."

Tann's laughter carried over the still water. "Ridian, think your threats through. If you cut the rope, *you* will be stranded."

"I have your food."

"Yes, but you'll eventually starve."

"If I must."

"And what about your sister? Sick and lost and soon to pass out." Tann was getting close now.

Ridian tried to grab the rope, to stop Tann, but the rope was evidently easier to pull than to hold firm. The slimy rope slipped through Ridian's lacerated hands like grease.

Tann finally came into view, but the muscular, athletic man Ridian remembered was unrecognisable. He was gaunt as a corpse and terribly unkempt. His cheeks were hollow behind a filthy beard, and rags hung off his thin frame. Only his distinctive hair remained more or less the same: jet black, with thick streaks of white.

The raft bumped against the shore and the fugitive leapt off, quiet as a shadow. Ridian raised the knife with one hand and clutched the rucksack with the other.

"You're brave, kid," said Tann, his sunken eyes boring into Ridian. "But stupid. And you're not the threatening type. Please, give me my things." The way he said 'please' implied that he didn't want to use force, but that he would.

"Just help me find my sister and I'll give you the bag."

Tann extended a sinewy arm. "I don't want any unpleasantries. Just hand it over."

"We can both get what we want."

"No, the best you can hope for is to leave this island unharmed."

The knife quivered in Ridian's hand. *What am I going to do? Stab him?* Ridian sighed and threw the bag.

Tann let the bag fall in a heap at his feet. He was glaring at Ridian, eyes wide, evidently stunned. "Show me that," he said at last with a strange, intense tone.

"Show you what?" said Ridian uncomfortably.

Tann pointed at Ridian with a profound sense of importance. *"That."*

"This?" said Ridian, touching the Elderflower pendant about his neck.

Tann nodded, though his eyes never left the thing. "Aye."

"It's a cheap family heirloom; it's worth nothing to you."

Without warning, Tann swatted the knife in Ridian's hand aside and snatched the necklace, breaking it free from its leather cord. He held the Elderflower necklace in his withered hand and gazed at it, enthralled. "This is yours?" he asked in disbelief.

Ridian nodded. "It's been in my family forever. But its worth is merely sentimental. Give it back." To Ridian's surprise, he did.

Tann gazed at the ground, deep in thought, looking almost dead if not for the strange fire that burned behind his sunken eyes. "It's very important that we find your sister," he said with sudden decisiveness.

"You'll help me?"

Tann grabbed his rucksack and leapt onto the raft. "Yes. Now stop wasting time."

Ridian jumped on board, and together they pulled the raft across the murky water. Ridian felt uncomfortable this close to Tann. Not only did he stink of urine and body odour, but Tann's behaviour was strange. He wasn't exactly insane—Ridian had seen enough madness at the Asylum to tell—but he was definitely odd. Why had the Elderflower necklace changed Tann's mind? He wanted to ask, but Tann radiated an intense energy and a purity of focus that inspired silence. Besides, it didn't matter right now. He could satisfy his curiosity after they found Rayna. They eventually landed and were soon standing before the

Gallows Tree.

"When did she leave?" asked Tann.

"A few hours ago."

Tann then scampered about, doubled over, inspecting every bent bit of grass, mud pocket, and flattened reed. Finally, after ten nerve-wracking minutes, he gave a cry. He went down on all fours, his face inches from a patch of moss. "There she is," he said with deep satisfaction.

"You sure?"

"There he is!" cried a voice through the mist.

Ridian whirled around to see Jakeer, pointing wildly, eyes shining in triumph. He held his precious robes out of the mud, exposing his pale ankles. "I knew that Caveborn bastard was up to something. I just knew it. Seize them." Four soldiers emerged from behind Jakeer and hemmed Ridian and Tann against the water's edge with their long, pointed spears.

Ridian's heart sank. They would be arrested, perhaps killed, and Rayna would never be found.

Tann smiled, not a care in the world. "Fellas," he said, as if greeting old friends. "You've done well to catch me, you have. I commend you."

"Shut up!" said a big one who looked to be in charge. He gestured at his companions. "You two, bind him."

Two soldiers advanced. One brutish-looking one stabbed his spear into the mud and plodded towards Tann, binding cord in hand. The other had a pointed, rat-like face. "No funny business now," he said, jabbing his spear in Tann's direction. "Or I'll spit you like a squealing pig."

The third soldier was little more than a boy. He fixed Ridian with a shaky spear. "Don't move," he said with hollow confidence.

"Kneel down and put your hands behind you," said the brute to Tann.

"Dear me," said Tann pleasantly. "Where are your manners?"

The brute clenched his jaw. "I said, kneel down and put your hands behind you."

"Would it kill you to ask nicely?" asked Tann.

"*Now*," said the brute with growing hostility.

Tann shook his head with grave disapproval. "My, my… your manners are atrocious. Is it so hard to say—"

The brute slammed a club-like fist into Tann's stomach, making the starved fugitive gasp and crumple to his knees. "Have I asked properly now?" asked the brute, walking to stand behind the groaning Tann.

Tann grimaced. "Not yet. Let me give you a clue. It starts with the letter *p*."

"Oh, very cute." A vein pulsed along the brute's temple. He raised his fist.

"Just bind him already," said the large commander. "This place gives me the creeps."

Ratface narrowed cruel eyes. "Let me give him a little tickle… just to make sure there's no funny business."

The large commander shook his head. "The orders were to keep him alive."

"Alive, but not unharmed," said Jakeer, with a nasty smile, still keeping his pristine robes out of the mud.

The commander looked appalled, but said nothing. Emboldened, Ratface aimed the spear at Tann's shoulder and jabbed—but it never landed. Quick as a blink, Tann snatched the spear shaft and buried the tip into the brute's thigh. The brute howled, and Ratface stared in confusion at his empty hands. Before another second had passed, Tann rolled onto his back and kicked the brute out into the water. He then swivelled and landed a swift heel into Ratface's kneecap, snapping it backwards. Tann flicked to his feet and ended Ratface's scream with a deadly right hook, knocking the soldier senseless. All of this happened with unbelievable, supernatural speed. Tann had moved almost as fast as sight itself. A streak in the night. A blur. And Ridian wondered with horror whether Tann was indeed possessed by some demon of The Mire.

The large commander rushed protectively in front of Jakeer, while the boy shuffled towards Tann, eyes bright with panic. He poked with a shaky, non-committal spear.

"Stab him!" said Jakeer, stumbling backwards.

Hands poised in front of him, Tann prowled like a half-starved predator, waiting for a weakness. He found it—a clumsy, overreaching thrust. Quick as silver, Tann grabbed the boy's spear, darted within reach, and drove his knee into the boy's stomach. As the boy pitched forward, Tann grabbed the young face and crunched it with a swift upward knee thrust.

The large commander roared, preparing to charge. But Tann hefted the boy's spear and hurled it at the large commander. The man looked very surprised at the spear shaft sprouting from his chest before he collapsed. Jakeer fled into the mist.

One of the soldiers was still conscious: the brute. He floundered, jaw-deep in mud. "Help me," he cried, neck craning to keep above the waterline. "Please!"

Tann smiled a satisfied smile. "Ah, *please...* you remembered your manners."

The brute's eyes widened in panic as mud gurgled over his mouth, then his nose, and then the brute vanished altogether. Disturbed algae coalesced where he had sunk, and it was as if he had never fallen in.

Ridian felt sick. He'd seen death before: at funeral processions, surrounded by mourners and the safety of rite and ritual. Never like this. He was stunned. Unarmed, Tann had taken out four soldiers with apparent ease. The way he moved: so fast, so impossibly fast. It was like watching Chirpy flit, here and there, almost too quick to see. Was Tann a supernatural product of The Mire? A demon? A fae? Some other accursed creature? Ridian backed away. He didn't want Tann's help after all.

"Don't worry," said Tann with genuine reassurance. "We still have your sister's prints. We'll find her soon enough. Yanala will be with us momentarily."

Ridian didn't ask. A Sungazer was striding through the mist towards them. His eyes were a solid, blazing green—as was the fire dancing above his empty palm. The Sungazer opened his other palm, and another green flame sprang from it, burning on nothing. "Surrender," said the Sungazer with the crushing voice of a god. Tann withered beneath the burning green eyes, his calm self-assurance and bravado gone.

Ridian knelt, hands up, and the Sungazer turned his oppressive gaze upon Ridian. "For missing the Burning and aiding a known felon, the penalty is death." And the Sungazer pointed his palm at Ridian and flexed. As he did, a brilliant ball of green fire exploded from his hand and grew larger and larger as it roared towards Ridian.

Ridian was going to die. As certain as sunset, this was it. He'd never faced death before, and the existential terror triggered something strange and inexplicable—

He tore free from his body.

His mind shot away like a slingshot, only to come to a sudden stop, hovering.

He saw nothing.

Felt nothing.

Heard nothing.

Everything was black.

Then he saw that it was not so. His translucent body, kneeling beneath him, was glowing with thousands of trickling rivulets of light. Every muscle, every fibre, every nerve shone with silky, vibrant light.

And it wasn't just him. Every living thing—reeds, grass, frogs, eels, Tann, and even the Sungazer—shone with the little streams of light. And what light? He'd never seen such colours before. Not with his eyes, anyway.

He was dead, surely.

Then Ridian shot back to his body.

Sight, sound, smell, taste, touch—the real world returned in a flash. So did the blazing fireball. It was still hurtling towards him. Almost no time had passed. Ridian leapt, and to his astonishment, he rolled away from the shooting fireball with an impossible, unnatural speed. He'd moved with the speed of a loosed arrow, and the roaring fireball zoomed past to sizzle into the water. He was vaguely aware he'd moved like Tann. Like a blur, almost too quick to see.

And he trembled all over. Not from fear. A strange supernatural energy thrummed through him. His hands vibrated. His veins pulsed. He was alive for the first time in his life. He could do anything. Everything. Nothing was impossible.

Ridian had moved so quickly the Sungazer hadn't noticed his escape. He was focused on Tann—and on the great ring of fire lassoed around the outlaw. The Sungazer curled his fingers, which seemed to constrict the fiery noose, trapping the cowering Tann inside the fiery vortex.

Ridian was contemplating what to do when he heard the patter of feet and saw something streak towards the Sungazer. It leapt, collided, and the tremendous green fire extinguished in a flash.

After-images floated where the fire had been, and it took a moment for Ridian's eyes to adjust. When they did, the Sungazer was clutching his throat… or what was left of it. It had been torn open, and blood gushed from the tattered hole. Panic shone in the Sungazer's eyes—human once more—as he gargled and spluttered. He fell to his knees, then flopped to the ground.

Then Ridian saw it—the snarling, four-legged demon. It lifted its bloody snout and shot towards Tann. In a heartbeat, it leapt, slamming him to the ground.

Horror held Ridian transfixed… then confusion.

Tann was laughing. "Stop it," he said good-humouredly, shoving the four-legged beast aside and getting to his feet. "You're covered in blood."

It was just a wolf. An ordinary wolf.

Ridian's mind swirled. "What just happened? What's happening to me?" He held his thrumming hands for Tann to see.

Tann's face was inscrutable. "You have been Awakened."

"What the hell does that mean?"

"It means you're a Soulcaster."

Then the supernatural energy pulsing through Ridian vanished, and he slumped to the ground, senseless.

Chapter 6

Ridian awoke: groggy, head pounding, sore all over. Had he overslept? Why hadn't Rayna woken him? Then he remembered and jolted upright.

Tann and his wolf sat on the other side of a campfire, gazing at an eel roasting above the flames. Ridian tried to stand, but his strength abandoned him, and he collapsed.

"Good morning," said Tann, though it was still dark. "Don't worry about Yanala. She's harmless."

Ridian found Tann's reassurance hard to believe. The lean, menacing wolf looked like a hundred and fifty pounds of sudden death. It yawned, exposing the teeth that had killed a Sungazer.

As Tann turned the skewered eel on its rotisserie, Ridian noticed he cradled his spare arm protectively. Blisters rippled along the forearm from a hideous burn. It was red, white, and weeping. "You're in luck," he said. "This sucker's almost ready."

The wolf whined.

"Patience," said Tann. "It's coming."

"What happened?" asked Ridian. "How long have I been asleep?" He looked around at sick trees, giant boulders, scissor reeds, and black pools. Nothing looked familiar.

"And where am I?"

"That's three questions. Which do you want first?" Tann poked the fire with a stick and sparks flew into the night sky.

Ridian tried shaking his head clear. He was so sore and bone tired, but he still had some wits. "Where's my sister?"

Tann's grin faltered. "I don't know," he said gravely. "We should have found her by now. But her trail keeps disappearing. We've been on the hunt for about three hours."

"Three hours?"

"You better believe it. I've been lugging you around this whole time." Tann must have misread the alarm in Ridian's eyes as he looked about for any sign of Rayna. "If you're worried about demons or witches or such, don't be. It's all nonsense. Just Sol propaganda."

"What?"

"With all their failures to cross The Mire, they needed to save face. I'm quite partial to the stories of faeries taking the form of naked women. Would certainly improve the view. At least until we crossed The Mire."

Cross The Mire? "We need to find my sister," said Ridian, and he tried and failed to rise to his feet; he was too weak.

"Easy," said Tann. "We'll be on the move soon. You're going to feel a bit rough."

Rough was putting it lightly. Drunks often complain of hangovers, but surely they never felt this bad, or they would never drink again. He dug his knuckles into his throbbing eyes, then licked his dry lips and realised he was thirsty.

"Here." Tann flung him a waterskin. "Don't worry, it's not Mire water. Can't have you exploding out both ends now, can we?"

Ridian tilted the waterskin and guzzled. Cold, sweet, delicious—it was unbelievably refreshing. Then he turned his attention to the eel, oozing and hissing fat. His mouth watered.

"Let's call it done," said Tann, grabbing the skewer. He then cut the head off the eel for Yanala to snap up, cut a six-inch portion for himself, and handed the rest to Ridian. "Dig in."

Ridian did. He burnt his tongue, but he didn't care. Even though it had a heavy, rancid taste, he moaned with satisfaction as grease dribbled down his chin.

Tann grinned. "Amazing how good terrible food can be when you're hungry."

Ridian ate every morsel, even licking the stick clean. When Tann handed Ridian some dried biscuits with his gaunt hand, Ridian's mistrust was rekindled. "Why are you helping me?" he asked warily, taking the biscuit all the same.

"I'm helping you so I don't have to carry you," said Tann lightly, looking away to scratch between Yanala's pointed ears.

It wasn't an answer; Tann was hiding something. But Ridian didn't push it. Tann was helping—that was all that mattered for now. And he wasn't immediately dangerous: he wouldn't have carried Ridian to safety otherwise. Still, as long as Tann withheld secrets, Ridian would remain on guard.

Then Ridian remembered leaving his body to shoot into a black place. And seeing all those twinkling, running lights, only to return and... "Wait," he said. "What...?"

"Happened to you?"

Ridian nodded.

"You Split from your body and entered the Astral Plane. And when you came back, you felt…" Tann struggled to find the right word.

Ridian found one first. "Invincible."

Tann gave a sad smile. "If only that were true."

"So, what does any of that mean?"

"Awakening a Soulcaster can take years of disciplined meditation and study." He shrugged. "Or a simple life-or-death situation can Awaken a Soulcaster in the blink of an eye. It's considered a latent defence mechanism. A good theory, in my opinion."

"What's a Soulcaster?" asked Ridian, who had never heard of such a thing.

"As the name implies, a Soulcaster casts their soul from their body to forge a unique connection with an animal Familiar. They can see what they see, feel what they feel, and importantly, draw supernatural strength from the bond." Tann leaned forward, firelight dancing in his eyes. "A Soulcaster is nothing without a Familiar. Remember that."

Ridian's head whirled. Cast your soul? Leave your body? Bond with animals? It was preposterous, but there was no arguing with how strong and fast he had become, or Tann for that matter. He looked from the lounging Tann to the wolf, crunching the eel's skull between its jaws. "You're a Soulcaster."

"And Yanala's my Familiar," Tann replied coolly.

"But I don't have a Familiar, and I did—what I did."

"An Awakening is a once-off. The release of a lifetime's supply of pent-up magical potential. That's why you passed out. You depleted yourself of Rava, and your body shut down."

Rava? This was all a lot to take in, and before Ridian could ask more, Tann stood and said, "We should go."

Ridian had more questions—lots more—but they could wait. They left quickly and marched quickly. Yanala dashed ahead, her snuffling nose rarely leaving the soggy ground. Tann's strides were swift and long, and Ridian struggled to keep up. Tired as he was, he kept slipping, stumbling, and occasionally falling elbow-deep into gurgling mud. There were frequent breaks though. Time and again, Yanala kept losing Rayna's trail. She would scamper about and whine impatiently. Tann even lost his cool. One time, he kicked a clump of moss and growled, "How do we keep losing her?" But eventually, Yanala would pick up the trail again—on the far side of some pool or barely visible pathway—and Tann would insist they were catching up.

"How's Rayna finding her way?" said Ridian. *Never mind why.*

"I was hoping you could tell me," said Tann with a curious sideways look.

As they trudged on through the miserable, murky mudland, Ridian mulled over the various mysteries: the blooming Moonflowers at the Asylum; Selkyrie inexplicably letting him go; the dying Moonflower on Rayna's palm; the dead rye where Rayna had lain; the reason why Rayna had disappeared; being a Soulcaster, whatever that meant; and of course, Tann's interest in the Elderflower necklace.

Eventually, the sun rose upon a bleak world, and still, Rayna's prints led them westward, ever deeper into the unknown. Ridian saw little through the gloom, only snatches of trees or boulders, ranging in size from watermelons to houses. The hours passed slowly—walking, walking, walking. Tired. Hungry. Thirsty. There's only so much a mouthful of water, a dirty eel, and a couple of dried biscuits can do, and Ridian began to lag. When they came upon a stretch of hot bubbling mud pools, the fumes made Ridian dizzy, and he would have fallen in had Tann not grabbed him.

"Where is she even going?" asked Ridian, delirium growing.

"To Mirecross Castle," Tann replied.

Too tired, Ridian didn't ask, and Tann said no more.

Rain fell, thick and icy cold, sending Ridian's teeth chattering and his limbs shivering. Exhaustion, hunger, and thirst were all. Only the desperate fire in his chest kept him moving.

The sun set. Lightning lashed the night sky. And still, they marched.

"There it is!" cried Tann at last, through the rain and howling wind.

Ridian looked up: through the downpour, an island rose high above The Mire. A strong stone wall encircled it, and, within its perimeter were row upon row of buildings, alleyways, and zig-zagging pathways. All rising. All made of stone. All cramped and seemingly stacked on top of each other. Ridian's astonished gaze wandered upward and he found a castle cresting the peak of the hilltop island. He couldn't believe his eyes. How was any of this possible?

"Is—is this the end of The Mire?" asked Ridian.

"No, we're only halfway," said Tann. "But all the paths lead through here. So, your sister must have—wait, look!" He pointed.

Upon the shore, before the perimeter wall, a young woman stood sobbing into her hands.

"Rayna!" cried Ridian, and he ran squelching towards her.

Rayna looked up—but it wasn't Rayna. Alarmed, the young woman went to flee. But she turned back to scan them with anxious, calculating eyes. After a moment's deliberation, she cried, "Please, save me from this hellish place." It was Kaisy Prillan. The girl who had been Exiled a whole year earlier.

Chapter 7

Miraculously, Kaisy Prillan was alive, but the year had not been kind to her. Considered a beauty back at Mudwall, her eyes were now deep-set and haunted, her hair lank and thin. She shivered as she hugged her now bony elbows and withered chest.

"Kaisy," said Tann. "Do you remember us?"

She glanced between them and nodded; evidently, outlaws and Caveborns were as well known as local beauties.

"Have you seen his sister?" asked Tann, pointing a thumb at Ridian.

Kaisy nodded. "She passed over the far side of the island about an hour ago. I tried calling to her, but she didn't hear me in the storm."

"Did Locke spot her?"

"Who's Locke?" asked Ridian.

"No, Locke's not here," said Kaisy, ignoring Ridian. "That's why it's the perfect time to escape. Why do you think I'm standing out here in the rain? I'm summoning the courage. Summoning the courage because he always catches me and when he does, he can be very cruel." She wrung her hands. Bruises covered her arms, and though she flinched as Yanala loped up and sniffed her, she stood her ground. "Please," she implored. "I want to go home."

Ridian was impressed by her courage—or her desperation—asking help from a Caveborn and an outlaw. But he didn't care about Kaisy or Locke, whoever he was. "Sorry," said Ridian. "But we need to find my sister first."

Tann nodded reluctantly. "I'm sorry. But he's right."

"No, please, don't leave." Kaisy grabbed Tann's burnt arm, and he recoiled in pain. The burn looked even worse. Blisters were popped and crawling with pus. Tann strode past Kaisy towards the island's impressive perimeter wall. Ridian and a reluctant Kaisy followed. The wall looked impregnable in Ridian's estimation if not for the missing gate. Its stone frame was charred black, and the rusted hinges were twisted as if by some great force. Whether bashed in or burnt to ash, the absent gate whispered of battle.

Once through the gate, they immediately began climbing a steep stairway of slick, wet rock, Kaisy pleading incessantly as they went. Tann was apologetic but resolved, and soon, he ignored her altogether. Flanking the stairs, stone buildings loomed tall and crowded, making use of every square inch. Narrow passageways twisted out of view, and gutters overflowed in the heavy rainfall.

Ridian marvelled. The Mire was supposed to be an empty wasteland. Mudwall was supposed to be the edge of the world, the final frontier. This shattered the narrative. "Tann? What is this place?"

"Mirecross Castle, an ancient Arden stronghold. All paths across The Mire converge here, making it the perfect defence point. All those ridiculous stories cooked up by the Sol—witches and demons and such—they all originate here.

But from the looks of things, the last fight was a bad one. They look damn near wiped out."

It was true. The streets were empty, and Ridian caught snatches of empty rooms, empty chairs, and empty beds through the rain-blurred windows. Untended rooftop gardens overflowed with dangling tomatoes and trailing pumpkins, and fruit trees littered the ground with piles of rotten fruit.

The stairs kept twisting and turning—up and up—until they crested the highest staircase and had sweeping views of the far side of the island. Tann swore loudly.

"What's wrong?" asked Ridian.

"The Mire's flooded. Look."

Westward, as far as the eye could see, was a veritable ocean. Not a path in sight.

"How we supposed to cross that?" asked Ridian.

"We can't," said Tann. "Not unless you feel like swimming."

"But Rayna—"

"Your bloody sister knows some secret way that we don't," snapped Tann. "I don't know how, but she somehow keeps eluding us and staying ahead, while we've been zig-zagging and dancing around behind her like a bunch of idiots."

"So, what do we do?"

"Wait for the water to drop."

"How long will that take?"

"I don't know. A few months."

"Months!"

Tann rounded on Ridian. "What do you want me to say?"

"So, will you help me now?" asked Kaisy, hands clasped imploringly.

Ridian glared at her and might have said something harsh,

when Yanala began barking eastward, back the way they had come.

"Everybody shut up," said Tann, and he crouched beside the wolf, laying a hand on the wolf's neck. "What is it, girl?"

Kaisy bit her nails. "Is it Locke? Is he back?"

Ridian strained his eyes. It was dark and thick with rain, and he saw nothing. Then lightning flashed, bathing The Mire in blue light. In the momentary glow, Ridian saw two distant figures walking towards them: a large man and a little girl. But that wasn't the strangest part; they seemed to be walking on water. No, a trick of the eye, surely. But lightning flashed again, and sure enough, the two figures were walking upon a wide pool with no apparent pathway beneath their feet.

"It's him!" cried Kaisy. "And he's captured another one."

Another child? Ridian felt disgusted.

But Tann grinned with satisfaction. "I think we've found your sister's secret pathway. Good girl." He scratched Yanala behind the ear, and she kicked a hind leg with pleasure. "I'll make you a deal," he said to Kaisy. "If you help me sneak up on Locke, I'll kill him for you."

Kaisy beamed, and for a moment, Ridian saw the pretty girl from Mudwall, not the broken woman she'd become. "Really?"

Tann pulled out his rusty knife and thumbed the edge. "Really."

Kaisy's eyes danced with some grand idea. "Follow me to the Great Hall. Quick." And she dashed through the rain towards the castle, Tann and Yanala sloshing along behind her.

"Wait!" said Ridian. "Kill Locke? Why? How does that

help us?" But they ignored him, and he was forced to follow.

The castle was a crumbling heap. One of its four towers had collapsed, shrubbery clung to cracks in the masonry, and the fire-scarred gatehouse was missing a gate. Across the empty bailey and through the enormous doors of the castle they went. They ran through the antechamber and then into the immense Great Hall. Wide and deep and tall, it was far and away the largest room Ridian had ever seen, but he didn't have time to appreciate it.

"Hurry," said Kaisy, and she shoved them inside a nearby storeroom. It was full of stacked furniture and stank of mould. Kaisy pointed at the ginormous double doors of the main entrance and whispered anxiously, "Locke will soon enter through there. He'll have dinner, excuse us, and then it'll just be him and the newcomer. That'll be your moment. Now hide." She closed the doors, only to wrench them open and fix Tann with a ferocious gaze. "Slit the bastard's throat."

Tann nodded, and Kaisy closed the doors, leaving them in darkness. Yanala began licking Ridian's fingers, and Ridian realised he was no longer afraid of the wolf—not while he remained on the right side of Tann, at least. Soon Ridian's eyes adjusted, and he leant forward and put his eye to the vertical gap in the door. A sadness hung over the Great Hall. Though massive, it preserved little of its former grandeur: the arched windows loomed broken and boarded; the minstrels' loft hung dangerously lopsided; the pretentiously large throne was stained; and the plastered walls resembled an aged woman masking her years with makeup. Only the giant longsword retained its splendour. It hung above the mantelpiece, eight feet of cold metal ending in a large, black pommel. Beneath the remarkable blade, a plaque ran thus:

Never shall the east touch the west

However, it was the tapestry that drew the eye. It stretched from wall to wall and was intricate in detail, though its colour had faded. In the background was a castle, but unlike any castle Ridian had ever heard of. It was made of trees. Not timber, trees—*living* trees. Dozens of them, all fused and moulded together into one colossal structure. The trunks made towers, the branches walkways, and beneath its overhanging boughs, a battle raged. And what a battle. Among the carnage, men and beasts fought alongside each other: eagles swooped, boars gored, wolves and great cats mauled each other, and even a bear charged through the chaos. It made Ridian think of Tann and Yanala. *Soulcasters? An army of Soulcasters?*

Ridian looked harder and was surprised to see that the men in the tapestry were eating each other. Amidst the fighting, they were biting into each other's skin, blood trailing down their chins. It disturbed him. It reminded him of Trystan Caddock, of the Caveborn Cannibal and the Mudwall Massacre. It reminded him of what he, Ridian, could become if he cracked... *when* he cracked.

The focal point of the tapestry, though, was the golden-haired Giant. Twice as tall as the rest, the Giant was cleaving a crowned man—perhaps a King— in two with an enormous sword—exactly like the black-pommelled blade above the mantelpiece. Nearby, a minstrel lay dead at the base of a tree, a sword run through his eye. Most interesting of all was the woman. She appeared to be summoning a large thorny bush into being. A bush that wrapped around like a wall, trapping the Giant, the King, the Minstrel, and herself within.

"Tann, what are we doing here?" whispered Ridian.

"We're finding your sister."

"How's killing this Locke gonna help?"

"Shhhh!"

The Great Hall doors groaned open, and Tann, Ridian and Yanala all jostled to peer through the gap in their storeroom door. Women poured inside—ten of them. One stoked the hearth fire into life; another added firewood. Others rushed to place cutlery and food upon a large oak table in the centre of the room, while another lit candles. Kaisy poured ale into goblets, her sunken eyes never so much as glancing at the storeroom. Jobs finished, the women stood silently in line, shoulder to shoulder, from the entrance to the table. The fire crackled, and everyone waited. The women fidgeted with their appearance—a smoothing of a dress here, a tuck of loose hair there. They were all young, good looking, and shared the same haunted look as Kaisy. And Ridian recognised them. They had all been Exiled from Mudwall at one time or another. What were they all doing here? Alive?

Finally, Locke—who else—entered the hall. He was massive. Approaching seven feet tall, he was broad of shoulder and deep of chest. Not quite a giant, but close. It made Ridian glance at the golden-haired Giant in the tapestry. *His ancestor?*

Locke took a hand towel from one of the women and dried himself—face, hair, arms, and the back of his meaty neck—

before strolling self-importantly down the hall. He had a curious limp—and not from an injury, but from a twisted, malformed leg. The women stood rigid, eyes riveted to the floor as he lumbered past.

To Ridian's immense surprise, Enid walked in. She looked like a scared, half-drowned rat, and tiny compared to Locke. Then it dawned on Ridian: she was the figure he had mistaken for a child earlier, her smallness exaggerated by Locke's immense size. *She must have been Exiled after I left her and Daryll upon the road,* Ridian realised. He pushed the guilt away. Enid, Daryll, and their stupid wagon would have been late regardless. But where was Daryll? Where were all the men Exiled in recent years?

An old woman entered last. She was all bony edges, sagging jowls, and loose skin. The corners of her mouth hung down in an inverted U. She scanned the women, one by one, as she hobbled past, dissecting them with cold eyes. Did they linger on Kaisy?

Locke, Enid, and the old woman found the table, and the rest of the women swarmed about them: pulling chairs, fluffing pillows, laying napkins, serving food. All in silence. Once finished, the women stood about the table, ready to serve.

Locke, his back to the storeroom, spoke. His voice was deep, resounding, and full of solemnity. "We remember Daegan, the Lion, who killed the Tyrant King and built this castle. Never shall the east touch the west!"

"Nor the west the east!" replied all the women in unison.

"Holy crow, I'm thirsty," bellowed Locke, dissipating the ritualistic atmosphere. And he downed his ale in a few greedy gulps, then slammed his goblet upon the table, making the women flinch. "Don't be skittish, darlings. I don't bite." He snapped his teeth together playfully and laughed. As Kaisy leaned over to refill his goblet, his giant hand crept out and groped her backside. No one seemed to notice, not even Kaisy. Goblet full, she shuffled back into line.

The old woman blew her steaming soup with thin, pursed lips. "Eat," she said to Enid.

Enid, who looked lost, shook her head. "No, thank you. No appetite."

"Eat," insisted the old woman, handing her a loaf of bread.

Enid smiled a tepid smile, took the loaf, and nibbled. This seemed to appease the old woman.

"Thank you for your hospitality," said Enid in a tremulous voice. "And thank you again for rescuing me. Without your grandson's guidance, I would have surely perished upon The Mire. But may I ask, who are you? And what is this place? Please, forgive my ignorance."

"Don't apologise," said Locke. "You can't help your ignorance. You're dining in Mirecross Castle. Built by Daegan himself." He pointed a bread-filled fist at the Giant in the tapestry. "And you have the pleasure of dining with Locke the Elderlion, Lord of Mirecross Castle, Defender of the Midland Realm. Along with my eternally beautiful grandmother." He nodded deferentially at the old woman, who took no notice.

Enid didn't seem to know what to do with all that information. "Pleasure, to be sure."

Locke chomped away on his bread. "For over four hundred years we've defended the Midlands—The Mire, as you would call it. We've kept Daegan's oath. Never shall the east touch the west!"

"Nor the west the east," chanted the women.

"Of course," continued Locke, between mouthfuls of food, "being the Lord of Mirecross Castle used to mean more. We Elderlions were legends! Now look at us." He gestured expansively. "Our great people on the brink of extinction, our castle in ruins, our defensive wall compromised."

"And no heir," said the old woman. Her voice was calm, but full of poison. She didn't look at Locke, the obvious target of her contempt, but simply slurped off her spoon with those thin, pursed lips of hers.

"Hang on…" said Locke, but the old woman's face snapped towards him, full of murderous anger. Locke wilted like a scolded, oversized child as a dreadful silence filled the Great Hall.

Cringing, Enid looked from the massive brute to the shrivelled old woman. "I'm sure a child will bless your fine house soon. But—but I was wondering if I could call upon your generosity once again, to guide me back to Mudwall. We came an awful long way, and I'm—well, I'm rather lost." She laughed nervously.

The old woman wiped her puckered mouth with the back of her spotted hand. "No."

Enid was taken aback. "Of course, I draw too deeply from the well of hospitality. Perhaps directions will suffice. And, of course, I'm happy to work hard to earn that favour."

"You can't leave," said the old woman.

Knowing looks darted between the other women.

Enid's discomfort mounted. "You're right, of course, I can't leave yet. My sentence lasts another six months. Then I can go home."

The old woman slammed her fist upon the table, her face twitching with fury. "Listen here, you little mud slut—this is your new home!"

Enid recoiled "But, but…"

The old woman locked Enid with her cold, cruel eyes. "You have eaten at our table and taken shelter under our roof. Your life, we saved. The Old Laws are clear—from head to heel and mind to marrow—we own you."

Horrified, Enid looked from one serving woman to another. None dared look back. Enid jumped to her feet, sending her chair toppling backwards with a clatter. She turned to run, but Locke reached across the table and clamped his hand around her wrist. She screamed and flailed but Locke held her with no apparent effort. He even reached down with his free hand and took another bite of his bread.

The old woman's voice rang through the hall. "Leave us."

Immediately, the serving women funnelled out, and Kaisy glared at the storeroom door. *Do it,* her eyes demanded.

"Hold her still," snapped the old woman. Locke obliged, pinning Enid face down across the table with brutish strength.

The old woman pulled twine from her pocket and began binding Enid's wrists with the routine efficiency of a spider. Ridian felt sick. It all made sense now. Sol Priests would Exile someone to The Mire, and Locke and this horrible old woman would 'save them'. And not the men—only the women.

The old woman yanked Enid's head back by the hair. "I can see a nasty, low-born defiance in you. But small folk like you are easy to break. You will learn obedience." The old woman looked at Locke with scorn. "And you, disgrace of the Elderlions, do your duty. Make me an heir." Then the old woman hobbled away, leaving Locke and the whimpering Enid alone.

But not for long. The moment the old woman left, Tann slipped silently out of the storeroom and crept towards Locke. Locke, too busy ripping the back of Enid's dress open, failed to see. Tann crept and crept until he stood directly behind Locke. Ridian's insides squirmed, and he held his breath. He waited for it: for the slice of the knife, for Locke to turn around in shock, for the neck to gape open like a large mouth and vomit blood.

"Good evening!" said Tann with sudden loud cheeriness.

Locke whirled around, blinking in bewilderment. "Who the hell are you!" Locke bellowed, chest and shoulders swelling, bracing to attack.

"Tannerion Sky is my name, and I wouldn't if I were you," said Tann, flashing the knife and a big smile.

Locke sized the filthy, skeletal Tann up. "You and that puny knife won't stop me."

"I believe you," said Tann. "But before you overpowered me, I would have stabbed you at least a couple of times. We'd both die—me fast, you slow. Besides…" Yanala shot from the storeroom to Tann's side and snarled. "A Soulcaster is never alone." Tann slid the blade into his belt and raised his hands. "I could have killed you, but I didn't."

Locke looked between Tann and Yanala with a mixture of fear and rage.

"Please, help me," whimpered Enid.

"Sorry, darl," said Tann. "I'm here to help myself, and Locke here, if he has any sense."

Enid whimpered. "Please…"

Locke remained tense as a bowstring. "What do you want?"

"To talk."

"Then talk!"

Tann smiled his irritating smile. "Let me be frank. We both have a problem. My problem…" Tann raised his wounded, festering arm for Locke to see. "…is that my arm will soon kill me if I don't get the medicine I need."

"And what's my problem?"

"Some of the women are plotting to kill you."

Ridian was gobsmacked: Tann was betraying Kaisy.

Locke snorted incredulously. "A likely story." But his eyes betrayed his doubt.

"No, it's true," said Tann. "I know it's hard to believe when you treat your women so kindly." He gestured at the tear-streaked Enid, her eyes glazed in shock.

Locke narrowed his eyes. "Prove it."

"I can't. But how do you think I was able to find that well-concealed storeroom? How was I able to catch you with your pants down? I had help. Help from the same women who want to cut you, neck to navel, and make a windchime with your innards."

"Who?" asked Locke. "I want names."

"Come now. That's not how this little game works."

"If there is a conspiracy, I can uncover it myself."

"Good luck sleeping tonight."

"I bar my chamber door every night."

"A woman's grudge is patient as spring," said Tann sweetly. "Eventually you'll let your guard down, take a nap, and they'll cut off your pecker."

Locke clenched his jaw. "What do you propose?"

"I tell you names, and you take me west, across The Mire to Tor. I can make my own way to Fidicia itself."

Tor? Fidicia? Ridian had never heard of such places.

Locke's eyes flicked to the motto above the mantlepiece. "You're asking me to break Daegan's oath."

"Please." Tann rolled his eyes. "Daegan made it, not you. And besides, that was a long, long time ago. You don't even know *why* he made the vow to stop people crossing The Mire."

Locke, clearly uncomfortable with the conversation, changed tack. "The penalty for trespassing is death, and you're trespassing."

Tann sighed with impatience and pinched the bridge of his nose. "Look. You've got a good thing going here. You've inherited or stolen the Lion's name—I don't know which, and I don't care. Either way, once you sire an heir, your position is assured. After that, you can inseminate your stolen Mudwall girls to your heart's content and make a nice little Lion army, just like the good old days. But you can't do that if you're dead."

"What's in it for you?"

"If you take me to the edge of Tor, I can hike it to Fidicia and get the best medicine the world has to offer."

Fidicia? There it was again.

"So, you tell me who the traitors are," said Locke slowly, "and I take you west."

"No. You take me west, *then* I tell you."

Locke hesitated, then said decidedly, "Then we have a deal."

"Wonderful!" said Tann with verve, clapping his hands

together. "Of course, you won't mind if my servant comes with me."

Locke bristled. "Your servant? There's more of you?"

"Easy," said Tann, arms raised as if reining in a wild stallion. "Just a little mud rat." Locke looked ready to kill, deal or no deal.

Tann called over his shoulder. "Ridian, it would be a good time to show your friendly face right about now."

Frozen with fear, Ridian stayed put.

"Ridian?" pleaded Tann. Yanala shot back to the storeroom and snatched Ridian's pants about the knee and tugged him out.

Locke puffed up like a toad. "Nice to know my home has become a bloody thoroughfare!" He rounded on Tann. "You ask too much. Maintaining the reputation of this place is everything. Surely you understand. The Ardens and their Sol masters—may they burn forever for what they've done— think The Mire is haunted, and so don't dare cross. The Torians in the west believe we are still the ruthless warrior class we once were—willing to kill anyone and everyone who trespassed upon our land. So, as it stands, we are left in peace. And yet, here you are, a couple of blabbermouths..."

"We're not going to talk."

"Why should I trust you?"

Tann stood tall. "I give my word."

Locke laughed. "Your word doesn't mean spit. You help me; I help you. Perhaps that's worth the risk." He glowered at Ridian. "But what does this little mud stain offer?"

Ridian shrunk; he had nothing to offer.

"Well?" said Locke.

Tann opened and closed his mouth, lost.

"Then your wolf stays," said Locke.

Tann looked stricken. "What?"

Locke's eyes gleamed. "You heard me. I could use a guard dog to keep an eye on these pesky girls of mine. Besides, I don't trust you. So why would I leave myself at the mercy of a Soulcaster and his Familiar? But two ordinary humans…" He snorted smugly. "I think I can handle that."

"Taking my wolf is like taking my daughter."

Locke shrugged. "I could let you die of infection, and then take the wolf."

"She won't obey you."

"We shall see. I have a knack for instilling obedience."

Ridian recalled Kaisy's bruised limbs and haunted eyes. *He always catches me,* she had said. *And when he does, he can be very cruel.*

Tann stroked Yanala between the ears, crestfallen.

"Do we have a deal?" demanded Locke.

Tann took a long time to answer, and when he did, it was with a sad, little nod.

Chapter 8

No matter how much Tann argued, Locke would not leave before dawn. "I'm wet and cold and I'm not leaving until morning," he'd roared, before storming off.

Tann reassured Ridian. "Don't worry. Rayna has to sleep as well. With Locke's help, we'll catch up."

Ridian wanted to ask Tann a hundred questions—what lay on the other side of The Mire, for one—but a large part of him wanted to curl up before the Great Hall fire and fall asleep. That part won.

As he slept, he kept having nightmares: Locke creeping down the minstrels' loft steps with his stunted leg; Selkyrie caging him with the animals in the Pyre; the Brute drowning in mud, only for Ridian to realise it wasn't the Brute, but Rayna. The nightmare that woke him, however, was the same nightmare he had most nights—of a dead field and a dying tree. Though he never understood the dream, it kept him awake for a long time. Tann's snores and the creaking of the castle didn't help.

Tann shook him awake at dawn. "Let's go."

Ridian scampered to his feet with a terrible sense of lost time, then he, Tann, and Locke descended the twisting, turning pathway down to the western Gate—an open, rectangular hole in the impressive stone wall. A bleak ocean lay beyond.

Locke flung a rope at Tann. "Tie her up."

Tann knelt before Yanala and looped the rope over her head. A knot was tied, then tightened. Yanala licked Tann's face happily, oblivious of her imminent abandonment. Tann was abandoning Kaisy as well. *Ridian* was also abandoning her. But she wasn't his problem—none of the women were. At least, he told himself so, but whenever he imagined what Locke might do to them, his chest filled with lead.

"Tie her to that post," said Locke.

"Can't we bring her with us for a little bit?"

"The wolf stays, or we go nowhere," said Locke impatiently.

Head down, Tann led Yanala to a nearby balcony post and fastened the rope. While Locke checked the knots thoroughly, Tann knelt before Yanala and stroked her head.

Satisfied, Locke scoffed and stormed out the gate. "Hurry up."

"Shut up and give me a minute," said Tann. Finally, when Locke called again from over the wall, Tann stood, turned, and walked away. When he didn't look back, Yanala cocked her head. When he was through the gate, she scratched and pawed the ground. When he turned the corner, she whined and strained against her leash. And when they were a hundred yards down the shoreline, skirting the perimeter wall, she howled. It made Ridian feel a little sad and, to his surprise, less safe.

Finally, at a nondescript spot, Locke kicked off his boots, exposing his malformed foot—a twisted, stunted, ugly thing. He shot hostile glances at them, as if daring them to jeer.

Ridian looked away as if Locke were naked. Tann looked too glum to care.

Feet squelching in mud, Locke limped to the water's edge, took a step, and then walked upon the very surface of the water. "Hurry up," he said irritably, as if he hadn't just performed a miracle.

Ridian's eyebrows shot up; the stories of witches walking on water were true.

Tann planted a cautious foot on the water, and it didn't sink. "Very clever," he said appreciatively, before following Locke.

Ridian approached the water's edge and tapped it with a toe, as if testing a sheet of ice. Sure enough, something solid rested just below the surface of the water. He knelt and brushed his fingers along what felt like rippling knots of wood. He flicked the water and caught a glimpse of tangled roots. But not tangled; the roots were entwined in an elegant pattern, precise and consistent as a braid, not with the randomness of nature. Ridian committed his whole weight. The roots sagged ever so slightly, like a taut suspension bridge, yet remained invisible to the naked eye. It was amazing.

"The Waterways were created by the Elderflower," said Locke. "They are a gift and a secret. So keep your mouths shut."

The Elderflower? Ridian went to ask *which one?* But Tann frowned at him severely. *Not now,* his glare seemed to say, leaving Ridian to ponder yet another mystery.

They marched along the secret Waterway at a cracking pace, straight as an arrow, quite unlike the twisted Witch's Way. It was tricky. The path was a couple of yards wide and had no markings and no points of reference. Just murky brown water stretching on forever, and yet Locke blustered along as if it were a highway. Following single file, Ridian and Tann did their best to imitate Locke's quirky, shuffling strides. However, as the hours passed, Tann began to lag. Bent over, he cradled his arm and dragged his feet.

A Soulcaster is nothing without a Familiar, Tann had said. And indeed, without his beast, the man was fading.

Ridian wanted to learn more about being a Soulcaster, but when he opened his mouth, even to whisper, Locke would whirl around and glare at him. Thus, nobody spoke, offering Ridian plenty of time to think. What the hell was Rayna doing out here? Why had she left? Where was she going? Why was Tann helping? Ridian also recalled his Awakening—the surge of energy, the limitless strength. He wondered if he could do it again, and what it would mean if he could. Power like that could grant Ridian a new life. No one would dare mess with him—or Rayna—again.

A few hours later, a small island emerged through the fog. When they arrived, it was a relief to get off the surreal, watery landscape and feel dry earth under one's sore, waterlogged feet. They pushed through some dense trees towards an inner clearing. Cabins littered the area, though overgrown grass and rampant ivy gave the place an air of abandonment. Locke cut straight through the waist-high grass, failing to see the recent pathway that led to one cabin—a tumbledown, with a tree bursting through the roof. The ivy-engulfed door stood ajar.

Tann looked meaningfully at Ridian. *Yes, Rayna was here,* his weary nod said.

Ridian was shocked by how much Tann had deteriorated.

He was pale and shivering, and his skin looked too big for him. He looked even more like a corpse, and Ridian wondered how he was even standing.

"Hurry up," barked Locke, pushing through to the far side of the island and back onto the secret Waterway. The man appeared footsore, his limp even more pronounced, and with each step, his apparent frustration mounted. There was something about his clenched jaw and the agitation in his stride that suggested an ever-growing discontent. He would steal menacing glances. Was he reconsidering the deal? Contemplating a double-cross? It was a terrifying thought. This near giant could drown Tann and Ridian, no problem. Probably enjoy it. *No. Locke wants names,* Ridian reassured himself. *Without them, we're safe.* Could Tann sense the poorly-masked fury radiating mere feet in front of him? Ridian doubted it. Hunched and quivering, Tann marched with a grim, bleary-eyed determination.

By mid-afternoon, the fog withered somewhat, and Ridian's breath was stolen by mountains—and what mountains they were. Sheer and sharp, they stretched across the horizon and into the sky. Ridian was enthralled. He'd heard many a story and even glimpsed them from time to time, but the tales and glimpses never did their beauty and grandeur justice. And they were close. Very soon, they would cross the uncrossable Mire, and be at their feet.

"What is this place?" Ridian whispered to Tann.

"Fidicia," said Tann blearily. "Capital of Tor."

Locke spun around. "Shut up!"

Not looking, Ridian misstepped, and his foot plunged into mud.

"And stop wasting time," said Locke, looking so vexed that

Ridian thought he might attack them there and then. But he huffed and puffed and hobbled on. "Can't believe I'm doing this," he muttered.

As the mountains grew taller and closer, the landscape changed: more trees, more boulders, less water. Then the secret Waterway vanished from beneath Ridian's feet, and he felt the comfort of solid ground.

Ridian's heart rate quickened. How would the bargain play out? But even as he thought it, he found out. Tann slipped out his knife, stumbled forward, and slashed across Locke's good calf. Ridian had a brief moment to see the gaping slit and the severed Achilles tendon shoot up the calf before Locke fell with a scream. He clutched his leg, his face a rictus of pain.

"Deal's a deal," said Tann, wiping the sweat from his brow. "You brought us to Fidicia, so now you get the names. I'm a man of my word, after all."

"I'm going to kill you!" roared Locke, spittle flying.

"I'll be brief," Tann continued. "All the women want to kill you. Well, besides your grandmother, though she's probably considered it. But you won't have to worry about the women anymore. Yanala is guiding them safely back to Mudwall as we speak. She's got a good nose; she'll get them back."

"You treacherous, lying bastard!"

"Apt," said Tann. "Though a pot may call a kettle black." Then, looking terrible, he staggered past the screaming Locke to climb the slope beyond. Ridian followed, giving Locke a wide berth. Even injured, Locke could snap Ridian in two.

Locke's curses faded as they climbed the foothills, thick

with naked beeches, birches, elms, and oaks. Tann dragged his feet. Twice, he tripped and almost fell. The third time, he did, and Ridian had to help him to his feet. Tann's skin burned, and he dripped with sweat. His infected arm was oozing pus and crawling with tentacles of black-green decay. It stank of death, and Ridian began to worry Tann would grow delirious before they found Rayna.

"There," said Tann, sometime later. "There she is." He pointed to something on the path before them—perhaps a snapped branch or a crushed leaf. Whatever it was, it was invisible to Ridian's untrained eyes. Still, it was reassuring.

The rise finally ended upon a clearing with dozens of ravens bobbing about in the knee-high grass. As Ridian and Tann neared the clearing's centre, the birds fluttered a short distance away, staring at them and squawking with extreme irritation.

Then Ridian saw the bodies… Strewn about the clearing, half-hidden in the grass, the mangled bodies lay in twisted, unnatural-looking positions. There were ten, twelve, thirteen, maybe more. There were wolves and a couple of cats— snow leopards, Ridian thought. None of the dead had eyes. All the eye sockets were ragged, gaping holes, pecked clean. Some were missing lips, exposing grotesque grins.

Acid rose in Ridian's throat, and he keeled over to vomit. Eyes watering, he looked again and retched again. Tann shooed the bolder ravens still feasting, but a violent coughing fit dropped him to his knees. The displaced ravens ruffled their feathers, disgruntled.

An unthinkable thought struck Ridian: *is Rayna among the dead?* From body to body he went, checking the leaking eye sockets and half-eaten faces. He found swords and spears—some covered with clotted blood—but Rayna was not among the fallen. He sighed, then saw the glimmer of glass—medicine vials spilling from a burlap sack and twinkling in the sunlight. They looked like Rayna's vials. He upended the sack, and a whole number of Rayna's things tumbled out.

"Tann!" said Ridian. "It's Rayna's stuff."

Tann did not appear to hear. Looking dazed, he rifled through the dead men's and women's packs until he produced a small bundle—an assortment of dried herbs, flowers, and roots. "Thank you, brother," he said to the man he'd just scavenged, and he plucked out a wad of herbs and began chewing it.

"Tann," Ridian tried again. "Rayna was here."

Tann peered through glazed, half-lidded eyes. "I know. But she's gone. Hector's disciples have her. You can see the tracks."

Even Ridian could see the trampled strip of soggy earth leading to the wood. "Who's Hector?"

Tann picked the chewed wad of herbs from his mouth and applied it gingerly to his stinking wound. "A cult leader."

"Leader of who?"

"Rebel Kyrosians."

"Kyrosians?" Ridian was sick of all these new, no-context names. "Who the hell are they?"

"Northern savages." And Tann laughed lazily at some private joke, though he looked delirious.

"Regardless, we need to go after them. There isn't a moment to lose."

"I'm sorry, I am. But your sister's gone."

"We have to do something," demanded Ridian.

Tann swayed and caught himself before falling. "Hector would have sent his best. Perhaps you can save her one day, or at least avenge her. But not now. I can barely stand. Find a flint. Get a fire going. There's medicine here that can save me. It's an involved process, but I can direct you."

"But Rayna…"

"You can't save her," snapped Tann. "Not today. But you can still save me."

Ridian looked at Tann, then at his sister's trail, growing colder with every minute. He imagined Rayna's panic as these 'northern savages' hauled her along.

"I'm sorry, Tann," said Ridian. "I'll be back as soon as I can."

Tann squinted at him, confused. "You don't understand. I'll die."

But Ridian did understand, and he turned his back on Tann and ran.

Chapter 9

Ridian plunged through the forest, leaves crackling under-foot. He'd left Tann. Just left him to die, to become raven food. He imagined Tann with his eyes pecked out, then forced it away. He'd made up his mind, and dwelling on that morbid thought would not help him.

Down a valley he went, his feet plunging into soft, rich earth and rotting leaves. The trail was easy to follow. Hector's disciples—whoever they were—cleaved an obvious path of snapped branches, flattened shrubs, and churned soil. About twenty of them, he guessed, but what did he know? Across a stream, stepping stones had been scraped clean of moss by careless footfalls. Speed, not stealth, had evidently been their priority.

What would he do once he caught up? Hector's disciples had killed a host of armed men and women, and their wolves and great cats. They were probably these magically infused Soulcasters—able to move with unnatural speed and strength. What could Ridian do, alone and unarmed? He had no answers, but he also had no choice.

He crested an exposed rocky ridge and took a moment to catch his breath. As he did, he felt the unmistakable sensation of being watched. Neck prickling, he glanced back into the valley. Sure enough, down below, a shadow slipped from tree to tree. His stomach lurched, but as he stared, he saw nothing more than swaying trees. *A trick of the eye,* he reassured himself. Surely it wasn't Tann shambling after him in the grip of a deadly fever. He shook his head clear of the crazy thought and continued his climb.

Breathless, legs trembling, he crested another ridgeline. Again, he felt the strange sensation of being watched. Again, he stole a glance. Something darted between the shadows, and his insides went cold, though the moment he looked was the moment it disappeared. But he was certain he saw something this time—and it was closer. He peered at the forest for a long time, but eventually, he tore his eyes away. Skin crawling, he scanned the forest as he ran and checked over his shoulder many times.

The path wound down through trees, stumps, and fallen trunks until it hit a dirt track at the base of a valley. *Which way? Left or right?*

Ridian was biting his lip with indecision when he heard a distinct *snap* behind him. He spun around: a bush quivered, but he saw nothing. Frantic, he looked about and saw nothing untoward. He held his breath and strained his ears: leaves rustled, branches creaked, trunks groaned, a bird squawked. Every sound seemed suspicious. Another *crack.* He whirled about, desperate to see something, hoping for nothing. *There's more than one thing out there,* instinct told him. He stooped to grab a branch for a weapon, and when he looked up, a wolf was staring at him—a mere ten feet away upon the path. It hadn't been there a moment before.

Ridian swung his stick wildly. "Get back!"

The beast growled as it crept slowly towards him. Instinct

told Ridian to look behind: another snarling wolf. Then there was a rustle on either side of the path, and two more wolves skulked towards him. One raised its snout and emitted an almighty howl. The other three joined in. A moment later, the forest was thick with the chilling harmony. Soon, a dozen or so wolves appeared from the surrounding thicket to form a ring around him. They moved in concert, hemming Ridian in, slow and deliberate. Ridian swung his stick in all directions to vainly ward off the constricting circle.

Suddenly, a man appeared from the forest the way an arrow does as it strikes its target: invisible, then visible in the blink of an eye. He was all lean muscle and had the bearing of one who could handle himself. Tunic, cloak, pants—all grey. A Soulcaster, surely.

He stood among the wolves, one of them. "Drop the stick," the Soulcaster said calmly, drawing a sword from the scabbard on his back. It was a graceful, curved thing with a long handle and a small, circular guard.

More men and women appeared, all wearing the same grey robes. Some drew swords. Some bows. All glowered at Ridian, seriously pissed off.

Ridian swallowed. "Please, I don't want any trouble."

"Drop the stick," said the first Soulcaster serenely, though the veins of his forearm bulged as he gripped his beautiful sword. "I won't ask again."

"Will you hurt me?"

"Not unless you make me."

Ridian hesitated, then dropped the stick. A moment later, iron-like hands twisted his arms, forcing him to his knees.

A young man—perhaps seventeen—marched up to Ridian. He had striking green eyes, high cheekbones, and a chiselled jaw. But his handsome face was twisted with rage. "Murderous little shit," he hissed, and he yanked Ridian's head back painfully by the hair and pressed a cold blade to his throat.

He's going to kill me. And he might have, had the first Soulcaster not said, "Lukas, stay that knife."

The young man, Lukas, exhaled in frustration and his breath wafted over Ridian's face. It stank of old eggs. "But Nawar, this prick deserves to die." He shook with suppressed fury, and for a moment, Ridian was certain he would feel the sharp burn of a quick slash across his neck.

"It's *Captain* Nawar," said the first Soulcaster. "And as such, I expect obedience, not insolence."

Lukas ground his teeth, but after a moment's deliberation, flicked the knife away and released Ridian's hair with a cruel tug. "Lucky bastard," he muttered.

Captain Nawar levelled his calm eyes upon Ridian. "Who are you?"

"Ridian from Mudwall, sir."

"Never heard of you or your Mudwall. What is your business here?"

"Well, I'm…" Ridian wasn't sure who these guys were, nor their allegiance, so he phrased his next words very carefully. "I'm following Hector's disciples."

"See!" spat Lukas, eyes flashing. "He's one of *them.* He even looks Kyrosian." Some of the others nodded their agreement.

They're no friend of Hector. That's something.

Nawar whistled, and a wolf padded up and sniffed Ridian all over. "Explain to us, Ridian of Mudwall, why your scent is all over the killing field yonder." Nawar nodded his head back the way Ridian had come.

"I had nothing to do with that," said Ridian. "They were already dead when I got there. And I'm not one of Hector's disciples. I'm trying to catch them. They've kidnapped my sister."

This sent Lukas into a frenzy. "Liar!" he shouted. "Tell the truth! Tell us how you ambushed them. Tell us!"

"Lukas," said Nawar, pinching the bridge of his nose, showing something other than perfect serenity for the first time. "You're a Fidician Knight, for Fidic's sake. Act like one."

Lukas looked wounded by these words.

"In fact," said Nawar. "You can do your duty by taking this Ridian of Mudwall hostage."

"Back to Fidicia?" asked Lukas, mortified. "I would prefer to be in the field."

"My orders supersede your preferences. Now shut your mouth and take him back to Fidicia, *safely*." He emphasised the last word.

Lukas stared at the ground, humiliated, but when he did look up, he glared at Ridian with murder in his eyes.

"Back to the hunt," said Nawar, then he and his party shot into the forest like loosed arrows, leaving Ridian with Lukas, the two men holding him, and three wolves, snapping at each other.

Lukas stared after them for a long moment, before smiling sickly sweet at Ridian. "Let's get you to Fidicia then, *safely*."

***

100

Safely did not mean pleasantly. Though Ridian's wrists were bound, Lukas drove him at a merciless pace, swatting him with a supple branch whenever he faltered. The whip blows burned as hot as a poker, and Ridian could feel Lukas' pleasure whenever he cried out in pain. "Hurry up, Kyrosian scum," Lukas would say after a stinging swat of his branch. "Have to get you back safely, don't we?" The other two Soulcasters and their wolves prowled alongside. None of them seemed to tire in the least, though Ridian panted and sweated like a pig.

The steep slopes and narrow valleys were as beautiful as they were exhausting. Streams cascaded into waterfalls, ranging from a babbling few inches to impressive fifty-foot drops. And as they climbed, the deciduous woodlands turned into pines, firs, and other evergreens. Up and down and around foothills and escarpments they went, taking a track that tended upward. Occasionally, Ridian saw farmhouses—nestled in a shallow valley, upon a bend in the river, or upon a balding hilltop with sweeping views. Cattle, sheep, and goats grazed in the meadows, while farmers tended their fields or wandered their orchards. Even with his exhaustion, it amazed Ridian to see them. Any life on this side of The Mire seemed like a miracle.

They turned a corner: up the empty, gradual slope was a towering mountain, far and away the biggest one he'd seen yet. Skyward it stretched, its stony peak covered in snow. Left and right, mountains of the same grandeur continued, seemingly forever. Surely these were the same mountains Ridian had glimpsed back in Mudwall, on those clear days with little fog.

A neat stone road ran towards the closest mountain.

Ridian and his escorts took it, and as they drew near, Ridian saw a slender canyon slicing through the mountain, and a fortified gate at the canyon base. Because they ran, the gate came and went, with Ridian only vaguely aware of an impressive stone gatehouse. The canyon was terrifically narrow—and dark. No more than ten feet across, its sheer walls shot up and up and up, allowing only a tiny slither of sunlight far above. It wound on and on until it turned a corner and opened upon a truly breathtaking view: a valley, but unlike any Ridian had seen before. It was many miles wide, and the immense circle of mountains enclosing it gave the impression of a colossal stone crown. A glittering silver river wound through the valley, with homes clustering along its banks. Most breathtaking of all—if Ridian had breath to take—were the trees. Autumn colours of spectacular brilliance blazed across the whole expanse. Bright yellow, fierce orange, vivid red—the trees were drenched in colour.

Lukas swatted Ridian across the back. "Welcome to Fidicia."

Down the valley and into the blazing, autumnal forest they went. The trees were ancient, gnarled, twisted things, yet the dazzling leaves were fresh as spring. Indeed, Ridian did not see a single fallen leaf. Not one. Some part of him—a part that wasn't keeping his legs pumping—registered this as odd. Lukas whipped him at a fork in the road, and they were soon striding up a steep uphill path. Homes lined this path. Quaint homes with gardens, windows, and chimneys. Ridian barely registered them. His legs burned with acid. His heart hammered in his ears. His chest swirled with molten lead.

"We should slow down," said one of the Soulcasters.

"We've punished him enough."

Lukas must have shot him a look, because the pace quickened, and the man said no more. At the top of the hill, nothing could have prepared Ridian for what he saw. The beautiful valley behind them was nothing compared to this. A wide meadow stretched out before them, and upon this meadow was a great semi-circular wall, its ends flush against the sheer mountain flank. What made the view remarkable, however, was the castle. It was made of *trees*. Enormous, living trees. Dozens of them, their trunks and boughs stretched and fused and moulded into one another, exactly like the tapestry at Mirecross Castle.

A stinging swat drove Ridian forward. They approached the stone wall, passed under the open gatehouse, and entered the bailey. A street ran straight towards the big tree castle (Ridian had no other words to describe it). Buildings lined either side. People roamed the street and stared as Ridian passed by.

The castle loomed. Already, its high, distant branches provided shade. At the front doors, Lukas jerked Ridian to a stop and he almost collapsed. His skin steamed, and he felt like throwing up.

Now inside: a big hall, full of people; now down a corridor; now up some winding stairs; now another corridor, now another. The floor was smooth, living wood. So were the walls. So was the ceiling. Now Ridian found himself in a dark, stone tunnel lined with flickering torches. The *Fell Caves Prison?* Ridian thought for one delirious second. No, they were far, far away. *I'm inside the mountain behind the tree castle.* Suddenly, Figures emerged from a dark alcove.

"Give our Kyrosian friend here our very best room," said

Lukas. "Spare no indulgences."

"Certainly," said one of the figures. "Always a pleasure hosting our northern neighbours." Ridian was too tired to argue and say he wasn't a Kyrosian, and they pulled him down a gloomy passageway. Keys tinkled, a lock turned, and Ridian was flung into a miserable place with iron-barred cells.

A dungeon.

Chapter 10

Ridian's cell reeked. His chamber pot had overflowed three bowel movements ago, and despite huddling in the furthest corner of his small cell, the stench was unbelievably potent.

Three bowel movements… that meant three days, right? Maybe two. Maybe four? With no daylight, it was impossible to keep track of time, though he had plenty of it. Plenty of time to wallow. Plenty of time to worry about Rayna. Plenty of time to imagine Tann's eyes being pecked out. Plenty of time to ponder why Rayna had left. Or where he was or what would happen to him…

Wardens had delivered a few bowls of slop, but they ignored his questions. Soldiers had come to interrogate him, but Ridian barely understood the questions, never mind the answers, and they had left, frustrated.

The dungeon was very dark. Not that it bothered him. Ridian only needed the smallest scrap of light to see by— a shard of moonlight, or a slither of starlight. And here, flickering torchlight illuminated every dark secret: tallies carved into the cold stone walls, unpleasant-looking stains upon his bed, fragments of broken fingernails, and the ever-expanding pool from his chamber pot. There were no more secrets to discover.

There were eight cells on either side of the dungeon hallway: four on the left, four on the right. Ridian was in one of the back cells, furthest from the door. And he was all alone. There had been another prisoner in an opposite cell when Ridian arrived. The man had swung on the bars, hollering and hooting, and called Ridian 'pretty boy'—among other things—and blew noisy kisses. There had been nowhere to hide from the drooling inmate, and Ridian was relieved to see him dragged off. Still, it was lonely.

Finally, after untold hours, the entrance opened with a screech. A cacophony of scuffling feet and curses filled the chamber. Ridian dashed to the bars to peep out, but, being in the back corner of the dungeon, caught only glimpses of guards wrestling unruly prisoners. Three cell doors shrieked open, then slammed closed.

"Those pricks left my chains on," whined a high, nasally voice once the guards had left.

"Well, I did headbutt one," said a deep, booming voice. "Think I broke his nose."

The nasally voice chortled. "I elbowed one in the eye."

From where Ridian stood, he could just see one of the prisoners. He was a tall, spindling man with a long, pointed nose at the end of a cunning-looking face. He poked it through the gap in the cell bars, his eyes glimmering with torchlight. "I kicked one in the privates," he said, his articulate voice cutting through the echoing chamber. "His balls must be flat as oatcakes." The other two laughed: one a high piping squeak, the other like the roaring of a bull.

"Geez… look where we are?" said the nasally voice. "Reminds me of your place, Basher."

"Whatever, Sneak," said the deep, booming voice. "You've never been to my place."

"Sure I have. All those midnight trips visiting your missus."

"Well, I was busy satisfying your mother."

More laughter bounced off the walls.

"Dear me…" said the spindling man with the articulate voice, recovering from his laugh. *The Father is good…*"

"*…to those who bleed for his sake*," said the other two in solemn unison, as if it were a prayer.

The spindling man poked his head as far through the bars as possible to scan the dungeon. Ridian hid before the man saw him, but Ridian caught a glimpse of the man's hair. It was prematurely streaked with thick strips of white—just like Tann's had been.

"Hello," called the spindling man politely. "Is anybody there? Anyone from home? From Kyrosia, I mean?"

Ridian held his breath.

"Don't be shy," said the prisoner. "We're all friendly. I'm Tinker."

"I'm Sneak," said the nasally voice.

"And I'm Basher," rumbled the deep voice.

Ridian remained quiet.

"No one's there, Tink," said Sneak. "Dungeon rats crave conversation. They'd be frothing at the bars for a little chit-chat."

"Really?" said Tinker. "I didn't realise someone who shits in their pants could be such an authority on human psychology."

Basher roared with laughter.

"It was one time!" said Sneak. "And I was sick! I've told

you a hundred times!"

"Okay, okay," said Tinker placatingly.

"No, seriously," said Sneak. "I'm tired of you guys always bringing that up. I'm not some kid to be bullied. Hector himself chose me—entrusted me—to help get the Elderflower girl."

"*Sneak!*" hissed Tinker. "Be quiet!"

"Why should I?"

"The less people know of Hector's plans, the better."

"But there's nobody here!"

Ridian's heart hammered at what he'd just heard: *Elderflower girl?* He was deciding whether to remain silent and hope they divulged more, or declare himself, when the dungeon entrance thumped open again. As it did, the prisoners whistled and hooted.

"Miss us already?"

"Did we hurt your feelings?"

"Want me to kiss your poor schnozzel better?"

Firelight grew until four guards appeared before Ridian's cell.

"Get him," said a hard voice.

They wrenched open the cell door, snapped shackles about Ridian's wrists, ankles, and neck, then yanked him along by a chain. As they passed Tinker's cell, Ridian called out, "What did you mean, 'Bring back the Elderflower girl?' What did you mean?!"

But Tinker just stared at him in alarm as the guards marched Ridian away—out the door, through twisting stone passageways, and up and down a few stairs. Finally, they came upon a door framed in sunlight, and when they opened the door and yanked him through, Ridian was dazzled.

When his eyes adjusted, he found himself in a large hall with about twenty people—

Everyone wore mono-colour grey, white, or black. Wolves, cats, foxes, wolverines, and other four-legged hunters sat by their sides, while birds of prey perched on human shoulders. The floor and terrifically tall walls were composed of a single piece of smooth, living wood. Ornate windows allowed diagonal shafts of rectangular light, though not a nail or saw mark could be seen. They had simply *grown* that way. And the ceiling was really a canopy of tree branches and shivering leaves. Ridian didn't have long to marvel, however.

"Prisoner for questioning," declared a guard.

Silence fell like an axe, and all eyes turned upon Ridian. He became powerfully aware of his filthy appearance and dropped his gaze to the timber floor—but not timber, wood—and the guards marched Ridian down the aisle of men, women, beasts, and birds. After a short walk, his chains and shackles jingling, he stood before a raised dais at the end of the hall.

Upon the dais, three people sat on three elaborate thrones. The centre person stood—a boy of perhaps eight. He glanced anxiously at the severe-looking man on his left and at an ancient-looking woman on his right. The boy wore white, the man grey, and the woman black. The ancient woman gave the boy a reassuring smile, creasing every part of her face.

The boy adjusted his tunic, straightened his shoulders, and addressed the hall in a rehearsed voice that made him seem even younger than he looked. "Accused, you stand trial before the Free Council of Fidicia: before I, Prince

Bevrik; before Commander Sevron; and before Mother Asarah. Together, we replace the Elder Three: Fidic, the Bard; Daegan, the Lion; and Valaria, the Flower."

Corresponding tapestries hung above each of them: a lute, a lion, and a flower respectively. Something about all this seemed oddly familiar, but Ridian was too muddled to make sense of it.

The boy stalled, eyes widening in panic. The ancient woman whispered a prompt, and he continued. "Accused, state your name and place of origin."

Ridian's mouth was dry as paper. "Ridian Elderflower, from Mudwall… in Arden."

Grumblings broke out. He turned to see people frowning and shaking their heads.

What did I say wrong? Had he conveyed disrespect? He bowed, hoping to undo the damage. "Your Highness."

The collective displeasure continued, however, until the boy raised his small hand. "You are charged with treason and first-degree murder, thirteen counts. How do you plead?"

Treason? Murder? Ridian felt cold. "Innocent. I'm innocent. I had nothing to—"

A guard pulled Ridian's neck chain, silencing him.

The ancient woman, Mother Asarah, gave young Bevrik an encouraging nod, and he sank into his chair, relieved. Mother Asarah then addressed the guards. "You may uncuff the prisoner."

"Wait," said Sevron, the formidable-looking man on Bevrik's left. He gazed down at Ridian with a single, angry eye. An eyepatch covered the other, and part of a raking scar that streaked down his face. His single eye was more than enough to intimidate Ridian, however, and so was the enormous wolf that sat by his side. Its hostile, hungry glare was almost identical to Sevron's. "With all due respect, Mother Asarah," said Sevron. "We have no idea what this Kyrosian is capable of." He said the word 'Kyrosian' with utter disdain.

Why do they keep thinking I'm Kyrosian?

"Suspicion alone cannot condemn," said Mother Asarah, returning Sevron's gaze. "Assume innocence until proof is provided. Those are Fidic's Sacred Words, are they not?" She gestured at Ridian with a spotted hand. "He is well guarded. Let us at least remove the burden from his neck to honour Fidic, upon whose wisdom this place is founded."

Sevron and Asarah glared at each other. Young Bevrik withered in his seat, trapped as he was between them. The guards, who wore the same grey uniform as Sevron, looked at each other awkwardly, unsure what to do. Finally, Sevron broke eye contact and gave the guards a curt nod. Ridian's neck shackle was removed, and he would have felt light as a feather if not for the terrible weight in his chest.

Mother Asarah, seemingly unaffected by the tension, addressed a man in the assembly. "Captain Nawar, please state the facts of the case."

Captain Nawar stood just as Ridian remembered him— calm and expressionless—his wolf at his heels. He stepped forward to address the hall. "My platoon and I were dispatched to the edge of the Great Waste to investigate the disappearance of our missing squad. We found them and all their Familiars dead. We then pursued the northbound suspects and soon apprehended the prisoner. He did not resist capture. His stated name was Ridian of Mudwall. He denied any involvement in the killings, though his scent was on the killing field. He claimed he was following Hector's disciples because they had captured his sister. We then continued the chase into the Wrathwolds, where we apprehended the three Kyrosians who refer to themselves as Sneak, Basher, and Tinker. They mocked us as we arrested them, saying we'd picked the wrong trail. They apparently served as a diversion. We subsequently backtracked and found the main trail, but not before the blizzard set in and blocked all passes through the Wrathwolds into Kyrosia. Despite our best efforts, we were unable to continue the pursuit, and all investigations will be impossible until the passes reopen in spring." Nawar hung his head. "I have disgraced myself."

"No, Captain," said Mother Asarah. "This was a well-coordinated, well-planned attack. You could not have done more."

Rayna's gone, then, thought Ridian with despair. *Out of reach beyond some frozen mountains. Who knows where she'll be by spring?*

"Could the hostiles have died in the blizzard?" asked Sevron.

Ridian's heart dropped.

Nawar shook his head. "Their lead was considerable. They likely passed through the Wrathwolds and into Kyrosia before the blizzard even hit."

Through the Wrathwolds and into Kyrosia. He didn't understand these directions, but he needed to remember them.

Nawar bowed and returned to his place.

Sevron's single eye glared at Ridian. "So, what's the

accused got to say for himself? Your scent was all over the dead and you were caught fleeing the scene in the exact same direction as a hostile alien force." He laughed, the furthest thing from amused. "And you're from Arden, eh? And you think you're the Elder Flower, huh?" His face scrunched up with contempt. "How dare you mock us, with our brothers and sisters' blood on your hands?" Sevron's wolf twitched a lip, the beginning of a snarl.

Ridian withered beneath Sevron's brutal gaze. What was the penalty for treason and thirteen counts of murder? It couldn't be good. "I'm telling the truth," said Ridian. "My name's Ridian Elderflower, and I'm from Mudwall. I'm an Arden. What do you want me to say?"

"This lying, little, Kyrosian turd is wasting our time," said Sevron, grinding his teeth so hard he might have chipped them. "Arden? What a load of—"

"He speaks truth," said a familiar voice that rang through the hall.

Ridian turned.

Tann stood in the doorway.

Chapter 11

Stunned silence greeted Tann, who, despite his wild white-streaked hair and beard, looked every bit like a grinning skeleton. "I have critical information pertaining to this case," he said, striding forward. "May I give witness?"

Sevron rallied first. "Who the hell is this? Guards!"

Grey-clad guards swarmed around Tann in a flash, swords unsheathed, wolves crouching by their side.

"Stop!" cried Mother Asarah, standing as tall as her old bent body would allow. The guards halted, but did not lower their swords.

"Master Tannerion," said Mother Asarah warmly. "Good to see you."

Tann bowed. "Always a pleasure."

"You know this—this Kyrosian?" asked Sevron.

"Yes," said Mother Asarah. "Now lower your swords."

"Wait!" Sevron twisted in his chair towards Mother Asarah. "Removing a shackle is one thing, but I cannot allow a Kyrosian outsider to wander free in this hall after what has transpired."

Mother Asarah pursed her lips and took an irritated, whistling breath through her nose to keep her composure. "Master Tannerion has served Fidicia for many years at great personal peril. He is one of the most decorated yet under-celebrated heroes of our nation. His reputation is beyond question, his word beyond reproach, and I personally hold him in the highest esteem. What's more…" She glanced at Prince Bevrik. "Our late King made him an honorary Fidician Knight, and I defy anyone to contest *his* decision." She glared at the room, daring someone to speak against her. No one did. Not even Sevron. It was only then that Ridian noticed the bear slumbering in the corner. It yawned itself awake, then lumbered over to Mother Asarah with heavy, plodding paws. It sat beside her and dwarfed her, a small mountain of fur.

"Unshackle the prisoner," said Mother Asarah. Immediately, guards obeyed, and Ridian rubbed his tender wrists. "And Master Tannerion?" Mother Asarah returned to her seat and stroked the enormous bear's flank. "You have information for us?"

"I do."

The guards let Tann pass, though their eyes remained fixed upon him.

Ridian's heart rattled against his ribs. What would Tann say? Ridian had left him to die and now he had the ear and respect of this Mother Asarah. Would Tann condemn Ridian in retribution?

Tann strolled past Ridian without so much as a glance in his direction. In fact, Tann had yet to look at him at all. "The accused is innocent of all crimes," he said simply.

Mother Asarah shrugged as if the matter were closed, and Ridian sighed with relief.

"On what evidence?" asked Sevron.

"My witness," said Tann.

Sevron snorted. "Right. And what about all that nonsense of him being The Elderflower? Is he insane?"

"As it turns out," said Tann. "He appears to be her distant relative."

Her distant relative? thought Ridian, but before he could ask, the hall broke out into mutterings of outrage. Even the bird squawks sounded indignant.

"This is ridiculous," someone cried.

"Someone get rid of this outlander," said another.

Mother Asarah rapped her walking cane on the floor. "Silence!" She got it. "Master Tannerion, forgive our waning hospitality. Many of us fear the outbreak of another Soulcaster War. Please, tell the Council what you know."

"The whole story?" said Tann warily.

"The time for secrecy is over," said Mother Asarah. "Tell all."

Tann bowed deferentially to Mother Asarah. "Very well. My name is Tannerion Sky, Kyrosian born, Wrathwoli raised. I have been working undercover for many years among various Kyrosian gangs and rebel factions, and I can tell you unequivocally that the attack was not made by Kyrosia herself, though some Kyrosians did the killing."

Sevron huffed. "A pointless distinction."

"No. Not pointless." Tann returned Sevron's displeasure tenfold. "A rogue, terrorist organisation committed this atrocity— not Kyrosia herself."

"How do you know?" asked Sevron.

"Six months ago," said Tann with forced calm, "I had successfully infiltrated The Six Knives, the largest of the Kyrosian crime rings. I was planning on inciting a mutiny and ensuring all capable leaders died in the bloody fallout when I learned a troubling secret: all the rival gangs of the Kyrosian underbelly were setting aside their differences and uniting."

"How is this possible?" asked Mother Asarah in astonishment. "The Kyrosian gangs have sworn to eradicate each other."

"How?" said Tann. "Through the charisma of one man: Hector, the supposed descendant of the fabled Kyros the Terrible."

The room swelled with silence.

Hector? Though Ridian. *The one who supposedly kidnapped Rayna.*

Mother Asarah cleared her throat. "Hector? The General who slaughtered the Wrathwoli during the Day of Windless Storm. The man who started The Last Soulcaster War." She shook her head, confused. "But…"

"But Hector died years ago," said Tann. "I know." A fierce light burned in Tann's eyes. "And yet, he's alive and well and calling the Kyrosians to rise and reclaim their stolen land."

Sevron went to argue, but Tann raised a gaunt hand. "I'm not here to debate the veracity of that claim. I'm merely trying to convey the situation. Hector is marshalling an army of young, impressionable criminals for a holy war. Think about it. They're the perfect recruits. You've stolen prized lands, crippled their economy with taxes, drove them into poverty, and all thanks to a war their absent fathers started. They are poor and starving and they blame you… and I don't blame them."

Someone called out. "We don't have to listen to the justifications of the enemy."

Tann rounded on him. "I'm not your enemy, you—"

"Master Tannerion," said Mother Asarah firmly. "How does the massacre fit into Hector's schemes?"

"It all revolves around his sister."

Ridian blinked at the finger Tann pointed at him. What did Rayna have to do with Hector? With some warlord half a world away?

"Whilst infiltrating The Six Knives, I heard rumours," Tann continued. "The living descendant of the Elder Flower lives, they said. A young woman in a place called Mudwall, beyond the Great Waste. They said she was the linchpin of all of Hector's plans—a secret weapon."

Secret weapon? Ridiculous. But even as Ridian thought it, he pictured the premature blooming of the Moonflowers, General Selkyrie's abrupt and inexplicable dismissal, and the dead patch of winter rye where she had lain. It filled him with unease.

"What kind of weapon?" asked Mother Asarah.

"I don't know," Tann admitted. "But I followed the party sent to retrieve her across the Great Waste, determined to find her before Hector could find and exploit her."

"Nobody has crossed the Great Waste in living memory," said Mother Asarah. "How did you survive when so many have perished?"

"Daegan's line has failed," said Tann, gesturing at the tapestry lion above Sevron's head. "Mirecross Castle lies in ruins, and his people are all but extinct. They can no longer uphold Daegan's Oath to stop all from crossing the Great Waste."

Great Waste? That's The Mire, Ridian surmised.

"And the Ardens?" asked a blonde, bespeckled man excitedly. "You actually found them?"

Tann smiled. "Yes, Theodor. I found them."

"Amazing!" Theodor beamed, oblivious or uncaring of the many frowns directed at him.

"But finding the girl proved difficult," Tann continued. "The Ardens are a broken people, oppressed by a foreign power that can wield fire. They've forgotten their history, their culture, even their magic. They don't even know who the Elder Flower was—never mind her descendant. I did find one girl who went by the surname Elderflower, but after some investigation, I concluded she was nothing special…" Tann sighed. "I then made a fatal error and was captured. The fire sorcerers wanted me to guide them across the Great Waste. I refused, of course, and paid the price for my recalcitrance dearly, as you can see by my famished appearance. Thankfully, I managed to escape— and yet, who should I run into but Ridian Elderflower, all in a fluster, claiming his sister had mysteriously disappeared into the Great Waste. And what's more, he wore this." Without warning, Tann snatched the leather cord that held the Elderflower necklace around Ridian's neck and yanked it off. He then strode to the wall and held it before an expansive portrait. "Look familiar?"

Three figures graced the painting: a golden-haired giant, a minstrel with an impish grin, and—Ridian's mouth dropped open—a beautiful young woman who looked an awful lot like Rayna. The pendant below her neck was black as midnight and shaped like a flower.

Ridian felt like he'd been struck by a swinging door. Two black, flower-shaped stones winked down at him, one from Tann's hand and the other from the portrait woman's neck, though her necklace chain was silver.

Hungry for answers, Ridian examined the rest of the canvas. Seated, the stoic giant towered above the other two who stood, his meaty hands resting upon the black-stone pommel of a longsword—identical to the one at Mirecross Castle. *That must be Daegan,* thought Ridian, *the so-called Elderlion who built Mirecross Castle.*

The minstrel was as different from the giant as night is to day. He was a thin wisp of a man with a wild shock of black hair. He grinned winningly, and his clever-looking fingers caressed a leaf-shaped lute carved from a single piece of wood. The minstrel's eyes gleamed knowingly, a trove of secrets. He wore a black-stone ring.

And the woman… upon second inspection, she was less like Rayna and more like their mother, he decided, though the artist had gone to great lengths to beautify her. Her hair was a burning autumn. Her eyes were the green of a longed-for spring. She was tall and proud and lithe and alluring. She was the secret desire of all men. She was fire: beautiful and dangerous and all-consuming. And she wore the Elderflower.

Ridian peeled his eyes away and found everyone staring at him in awe. Prince Bevrik gaped, enthralled in boyhood wonder. Ridian took to examining his shoes. They were caked in dry, cracked mud.

Sevron, who also gazed with astonishment, an odd expression on his harsh, one-eyed countenance, shook himself from the apparent spell. "It's a fake, surely."

Tann threw the necklace at the blond bespeckled man in the crowd. "Theodor, catch."

Theodor caught the necklace in a fluster, then gazed upon the black stone as if it were a newborn.

"You're the expert on these sorts of things," said Tann. "Authenticate it for our ever-sceptical Commander."

Theodor then spent a few minutes fussing over the stone pendant: he held it to a beam of light and scrutinized its reflection; he gazed into its depths; he shook the stone gently against his ear and listened; he compared the stone's weight to a coin in his pocket; bit it delicately; then tasted it with the tip of his tongue.

Finally, Theodor gave a conclusive nod. "It's a Fellstone, alright: its colour, weight and substance are all consistent. This stone fell from the heavens; I'd bet my life on it. What's more, Fellstones rust, but this has all the crispness of a freshly fallen star. Only Cedever Quan knew how to immortalise the Fellstones, and sadly, his method died with him centuries ago. This is, therefore, beyond a doubt, the same Fellstone worn by Valaria, the Elder Flower herself."

Valaria... the woman in the picture was supposed to be Ridian's ancestor. His head reeled.

Theodor approached Ridian, eyes sparkling with wonder. Then, with a gracious little bow, he handed back the Elderflower before retreating to his place. The room was very quiet. Self-conscious, Ridian placed the necklace over his head and tucked it under his tunic.

"Hang on," said Sevron. "I'm surprised as anyone to see the necklace. But it doesn't prove that *he's* her descendant. He just happens to have her necklace, that's all."

"This is true, Master Tannerion," said Mother Asarah.

Tann faltered. "Ah, well, Valaria and her brothers were supernaturally gifted, and Hector certainly believes his sister to be some sort of secret weapon."

"So you say," said Sevron coldly.

"Hector has gone to extraordinary lengths to acquire her," said Tann. "So yes, I do say."

"And Ridian?" Mother Asarah, laying her gentle eyes upon him. "Are you preternaturally gifted?"

"Um…" said Ridian.

"He is a Soulcaster," said Tann. "I witnessed his Awakening."

People raised eyebrows at this.

"An Arden and a Soulcaster?" said Mother Asarah thoughtfully. "That is a curious thing. The Elder Three were the only Ardens ever so blessed." Mother Asarah shook her head. "But it's not conclusive.

"Either way," said Sevron. "Thirteen of our own are dead and we must respond. The way I see it, the Kyrosians have been our natural enemies for centuries, and nothing's changed. If they're marshalling their forces against us, why wait for them to choose an hour that suits them? I say we marshal our own forces. I say we bring them war!"

Half the room erupted into hearty cries, the other half shook their heads. Mother Asarah frowned her hundred-wrinkle frown in concern, while Young Bevrik looked lost in his too-big chair.

A man cried out, "The Kyrosians have it coming!"

"Violence begets violence!" shouted a woman.

"They drew first blood!"

People broke into fierce debate, while even the animals got twitchy: a growl here and snap of the jaws there.

Again, Mother Asarah rapped her cane, and silence returned.

"We cannot permit such wanton slaughter," said Sevron. "We must strike back."

"No," said Mother Asarah, "Master Tannerion is right. The Kyrosians are innocent. It's Hector and his agitators who are responsible. You're talking about burning a forest because of one diseased tree, killing a pack because of one rabid dog."

"What do you propose, then?" asked Sevron.

"We kill Hector." Tann's voice found every corner of the room, and the room listened. "Without their charismatic leader," Tann continued, "the gangs will fracture and go back to killing each other. I propose that when the snows melt and the passes into Kyrosia are open, I lead a small team to assassinate Hector."

"Why you?" asked Sevron darkly.

"Who here has my distinctive Kyrosian hair?" said Tann. "Who knows the intricacies of the Kyrosian underbelly? Who has contacts and resources throughout all of Kyrosia whilst maintaining the trust of the distinguished Mother Asarah? Find another more suitable, and they may go."

Sevron glared, but he had nothing to say.

"You are confident Hector's death will disband the league he forged?" asked Mother Asarah.

Tann nodded. "I am."

"Assassinating one man while others were also culpable is not justice," said Sevron.

"There will be plenty of blood, I assure you," said Tann with distaste.

"And will the death of Hector foster peace or promote war between our nations?" asked Mother Asarah.

"Peace," said Tann.

"Are you sure?" she asked, with a hundred years of cautious wisdom.

"I am."

Mother Asarah and Commander Sevron looked thoughtfully at each other. Finally, they seemed to reach a silent agreement.

"Very well," said Mother Asarah. "It is decided."

Ridian's mind raced. Hector had Rayna, and Tann was leading a force directly to Hector.

"I will go with Tann," Ridian blurted.

Sevron scoffed, and even Mother Asarah shook her head solemnly.

"Sorry, kid," said Tann. "We can't have you screwing up a delicate operation. Besides, I need someone I can trust." Tann then looked at Ridian for the first time, and the shame of it made Ridian look away.

It was then that Young Bevrik sat up. "But they have his sister," he said in his high, childish voice.

"Your point, Prince Bevrik," asked Mother Asarah.

The hall was quiet as the boy rallied the confidence to speak more. "He has more cause than many to go. Besides, he's an Arden *and* a Soulcaster. Maybe he is Valaria's descendant. Maybe he has his own special gift like one of The Elder Three. Maybe *he* is a secret weapon, just like his sister. A weapon *we* can use." When Prince Bevrik piped down, he was very red in the face.

"True," said Tann. "But he's ignorant of both Soulcasting and his gift, if he has one."

"Then we train him in Soulcasting and help him find his gift," said Prince Bevrik, as if it were the most obvious thing in the world.

"Absolutely not," said Sevron. "He's an outsider, a stranger. He has not earned our trust. Besides, we don't have proof that he's anything but a nuisance."

Young Bevrik turned to Mother Asarah imploringly.

Mother Asarah considered Ridian with her hundred-year-old eyes. "Prince Bevrik is right. *A Soulcaster must learn Soulcasting... Fidic's Sacred Words.*"

"The Sacred Words do not apply to outsiders," said Sevron, to a murmuring of agreement. "Besides, a student needs a master, and we have none to spare. And I will be damned if we change our tradition of one master and one student. Not for this blow-in."

Mother Asarah considered for a moment. "There is one master without a student."

"Who?" demanded Sevron, looking about the room.

"Though he never wore The Grey, Master Tannerion *is* a Fidician Knight," said Mother Asarah to the assembly, before turning her gaze upon Tann. "Master Tannerion, would you take Ridian of Mudwall as your student?"

Tann looked more surprised than anyone. The room awaited his response. Tann went to say no, but then reconsidered. He studied Ridian with calculating eyes, thinking very hard.

Sevron rolled his eyes and muttered, "An outsider to train an outsider. How fitting."

This snarky comment seemed to sway Tann. "I accept," he said with the faintest smirk, which was clearly meant to annoy Sevron. "But only till spring. Once the snows melt, I will be committed to assassinating Hector. And I cannot promise him a place," added Tann hastily. "Not to a student."

"What if he passes the Trials and becomes a Fidician Knight?" asked Prince Bevrik.

"If he passes the Trials?" Tann snorted as if he doubted it.

"Maybe."

"Very well," declared Mother Asarah. "Master Tannerion shall train Ridian of Mudwall in the Secrets of Soulcasting until spring. If Ridian masters the Knightly Discipline and passes the Trials, then Tann, at his discretion, may take him to assassinate Hector. All here are sworn to secrecy. Not a word must be spoken of what transpired here today." Then Mother Asarah stood with an arthritic groan. "I've had enough," she said bluntly. Then without any decorum, she hobbled away, supported by her cane. Her bear yawned and padded after her.

Chapter 12

The crowd lingered and pretended not to stare at Ridian, though Young Bevrik gawped openly—and Sevron glowered. Tann turned on his heels, spoke briefly to the man called Theodor, and left without a glance.

Was Ridian supposed to follow Tann? The outlaw had just agreed to train him as a Soulcaster and *maybe* take Ridian to find Hector. It was a long shot, and it meant waiting until spring. Perhaps he was better off slipping away alone. *Through the Wrathwolds and into Kyrosia,* Nawar had said. The Captain might be unable to cross those frozen mountains, but he didn't have his sister's life on the line.

"An Arden!" cried an eager voice.

Ridian turned to see Theodor striding towards him, grinning with delighted disbelief, arms wide in an emphatic gesture of welcome. Like some in the room, he wore all white: tunic, pants, coat, cloak. He grabbed Ridian's hand and shook it as if it brought him luck. His spectacles slipped, and he slid them back up with a finger.

"An Arden," he cried again, saying the words as if he liked the sound of them. "Welcome, welcome. In all my long years, I never thought I would meet an *Arden.*" Theodor was forty-something, though youthful as a teenager. "My name is Theodor Thunderfall, humble physician and father of four."

"Hi," said Ridian, managing to remove his hand from Theodor's spirited grip. Ridian was not used to such friendliness. Mudwallers avoided Ridian like a diseased rat. Even friendly newcomers like Daryll were a rarity, but they soon learned who—and what—Ridian was. To Ridian's surprise, a red ferret with a white underbelly popped out from within Theodor's coat pocket, sniffed the air, then dove back inside. Theodor chuckled. "That was Felix. Gets a bit anxious in crowds. But don't worry, he'll perk up when we get home. Speaking of which, would you care to stay with me and my family while Tann trains you?"

"Ah…"

"Oh, but you must!" Theodor insisted. "Tann's idea, and besides, I would be jealous as a kid without a cupcake if you stayed with anybody else."

Ridian looked around; nobody else was offering. "Sure, okay."

"Excellent, excellent! Follow me." And Theodor led Ridian past gawking humans and staring animals to an arched door. As they left, the eyes of the giant, the minstrel, and the woman in the painting seemed to follow Ridian. The woman was Ridian's supposed ancestor. Who was she, and what was her magic? Ridian promised himself that he would find out.

The door opened upon a well-lit corridor. A man hobbled past with a bandage wrapped around his head, a teenager sauntered by with his arm in a cast, and a white-clad orderly pushed an empty bed with wheels. Once again, the floor, walls, and ceiling were made of smooth, living wood.

"Level five," said Theodor, gesturing up and down the corridor. "Day stay for minor wounds and injuries." Felix resurfaced from Theodor's coat pocket to twitch his whiskers and rub his nose.

"This level is a hospital?" asked Ridian uncertainly.

"This whole place is a hospital. Finest in the world. Us Stewards keep the place running."

"Stewards?"

"Ah, yes. The Fidician Order has three disciplines: Stewards, Clerics, and Knights. You would have noticed the three colours inside. Stewards don The White and run the hospital in remembrance of Fidic. Clerics don The Black. They study the Sacred Word after the fashion of Valaria. And Knights wear The Grey and defend our borders, as Daegan did long ago. Though between you and I, us Stewards do all the work around here." He winked and nudged Ridian with a playful elbow.

Ridian went to one of the windows lining the hallway. There was a lot to see. He was high up, gazing down upon the bailey, the meadow, the expansive valley, and the mountains beyond. But Ridian was intent upon seeing the hospital itself. He stuck his head out the window and looked up and down and side to side. He couldn't get a good look at it, but he saw massive branches swayed high above.

"The Living Fort," said Theodor. "Built by the Elderflower herself." His eyes darted to Ridian's neckline, to where the Elderflower necklace hid.

Valaria—my supposed ancestor—built this. But built was the wrong word. You didn't build fortifications like this. They were grown. Magic was involved. No wonder Ridian and the reappearance of the family necklace had caused such a stir. Ridian went to ask who Valaria was, but Theodor cut him off.

"Oh, look! There's my daughter." He pointed excitedly at the largest building in the bailey: a massive stone amphitheatre with enormous arched walls. Though it was far, Ridian could make out a small group sitting in a circle in the middle of the arena. They were watching a boy and a girl fight each other.

"Feya is the best Varki fighter in the whole program," said Theodor with unrestrained pride. "Watch! She'll drop him in no time."

Theodor was right. The boy did a quick shuffle and a kick, but the girl grabbed the swinging leg and swiped the boy's supporting leg from under him with her own swivelling kick.

"Ha!" cried Theodor. "Told you. Come, let's say hi." Ridian then followed the giddy Theodor as he dashed down a winding stairwell. They passed slit windows and an open corridor with each revolution until they came upon an expansive foyer full of people: clutching wounds, coughing, hugging stomachs, looking green, and generally looking miserable.

"Level 1. The Emergency Wing," said Theodor.

People queued before a desk where a plump woman sat. Given her all-white attire, Ridian presumed she must be a Steward.

"Aha—yes—I see. And how long have you had this itchy rash of yours?" said the plump Steward.

The man at the front of the line wrung his hands and whispered something.

"Two weeks," said the woman, writing it down. "Blast. I'm

out of ink. Ink please!" A crow hopped along the desk and flew to a nearby shelf to retrieve a bottle of ink. The woman took the bottle from the crow's extended claw and returned her attention to the patient. "And is the rash widespread or localised? Localised. Right. And where is this itchy rash or yours?" The man's face burned red as he gestured vaguely towards his nether region.

Past the sick and injured Theodor and Ridian went, then through the large front entrance. Outside, people were busy living their lives. Along the street was a smithy, a cobbler, a grocer, tailor, bookbinder, baker, dyer, glassblower, weaver… all the professions were at work. And amongst them and alongside them were various prey animals: wolves sleeping in doorways, wolverines fighting, foxes lurking, mountain lions licking their paws. Eagles and hawks perched on rooftops or wheeled overhead. Ridian braced himself.

Theodor chuckled. "Don't worry. Nothing will take a bite out of you. Hunting is expressly forbidden within Fidicia."

Not entirely reassured, Ridian turned to admire the hospital, and as he did, he realised 'hospital' was too banal a word for what stood before him. At first glance, it looked like a colossal tree, too big to believe, but no, it was the fusion of *dozens* of trees—stretched and moulded and warped into each other. There were windows and walkways, turrets and towers, stairs and staircases, bridges and balconies. And dappled sunlight shone through the distant leaves of the vast canopy.

"A wonder, isn't it?" said Theodor. "But if you're impressed now, wait till you meet my daughter." Then, depriving Ridian of the chance to gawk more, Theodor rushed them past ordinary timber-and-tile buildings towards the looming amphitheatre. Ridian struggled to keep up, dodging human and animal pedestrians alike.

Grand and imposing, the amphitheatre consisted of four rows of massive stone archways stacked on top of each other. The stonework looked flawless.

"The Lion's Den," said Theodor, gesturing towards the amphitheatre. "Built by the giant Daegan, who was a master mason as well as a warrior." They walked under an arch, across a brief arcade, and down a short tunnel that opened onto the circular arena. Row upon row of tiered seating rose skyward. The seats were empty, but brown-robed youths sat cross-legged in the sandy arena, watching another fight. A man in grey and his wolf looked on.

"That's her," whispered Theodor, pointing to a thin slip of a girl with wild brown hair. She faced a boy who stood head and shoulders above her, limbs long and muscular. The boy advanced with neat footwork and adder-quick jabs.

She's got no chance, thought Ridian.

"Watch this," said Theodor with a meaningful nod.

The boy jabbed twice; the girl slipped them both with the ease and fluidity of a dancer. The boy committed a cross punch, and the girl stepped inside and sank a fist into the boy's solar plexus. Then, even as the boy pitched forward with a groan, she leapt, nimble as a deer, and wrapped her legs around the boy's neck. The moment she latched on, she twisted and flung the boy to the ground. Still squeezing his windpipe between her thighs, she wrenched his outstretched arm back, locking it in place. The boy tapped her leg frantically, and the fight was over. It happened so fast. Not Soulcaster fast. Not magically fast.

But fast all the same. The girl popped to her feet and dusted the sand from her shoulders.

Theodor clapped with enthusiasm. He was the only one. Everyone turned to look, and his daughter's face burned red with embarrassment.

"May I borrow Feya for a moment?" asked Theodor.

The man in grey nodded. "You may. In fact, that's all for today. See you all tomorrow."

The youths dispersed in twos and threes, while Feya, who looked about Ridian's age, jogged light-footed towards them. She was petite as a hummingbird, and Ridian couldn't quite decide if she was pretty or not. Her most notable feature was easily her hair: thick and full and crinkly, it framed her head and shoulders in a giant halo, an immense brown storm. Coloured twine bound a coil here and there, and a feather was lodged deep within her mane, but Ridian wasn't sure whether she meant it to be there or not.

"Feya, meet Ridian," said Theodor. "The newest initiate to the Soulcaster Program." He wrapped his arm around Feya's shoulder and squeezed. "Ridian, meet my darling daughter, Feya. Apple of my eye."

Side by side, Ridian couldn't see the resemblance. Theodor was all receding blond hair and blue eyes; Feya was olive, with dark, monolid eyes that were almost black. And her hair was just so big.

Feya tried to squirm free. "Dad, *stop.*"

"I'm embarrassing you again, aren't I?" said Theodor, knowing he was, but not caring.

"*Yes.*"

Theodor let go and winked at Ridian. "Teenagers—never change. I was exactly the same at her age."

Feya looked like she died a little inside, but smiled valiantly as she shook Ridian's hand. She didn't flinch at his mud-stained fingers. Her own hand was small and bird-boned, but very strong.

"Aren't you supposed to be in surgery?" she said to Theodor.

Theodor slapped his forehead. "I totally forgot! Do you mind taking Ridian home? He's staying with us for a while."

Feya shrugged. "Sure."

"Now, Feya…" And Theodor frowned the way all parents do when they wish to dispense some wisdom upon their child, wanted or not. "Ridian's never been in Fidicia before, so be sure to answer all his questions. And don't pry," he added firmly. "You know the rules: no questions on the first day. Ridian has been through a terrible ordeal, and he needs true—no, don't roll your eyes at me. True…?"

Feya sighed the way all children do when forced to regurgitate some parental wisdom. "True Fidician kindness. I *know*."

Theodor grinned, his apparent default. "Ridian, it's been an absolute pleasure." And he left in a fluster.

"Ridian, huh?" said Feya.

"Yep. Feya, right?"

"That's right."

Ridian looked around for inspiration for something to say and found none.

Feya took in Ridian's filthy, mud-stained appearance with a genuine curiosity. "Hmmm… Street, orphanage, or foster home? I know I'm not supposed to ask, but I can still guess." She cocked her head as if sizing him up and tapped her chin thoughtfully. "I reckon you're a runaway foster kid."

"Um…" Ridian didn't know what to say. He had grown up in various foster homes—and run away once or twice. But that was back in Arden. This girl had no idea what she was talking about. Ridian's stomach growled.

"Hungry?" asked Feya—then, before Ridian could answer, "Me too. Let's grab some food."

Back on the street, nobody looked twice at Ridian or the brown-robed, wild-haired Feya. He, on the other hand, stared at it all: the Living Fort, swaying in the breeze; the impressive arches of The Lion's Den; the people, and, of course, the animals that loped along or circled overhead.

Ridian pointed at a cougar as it sauntered past. "Do you…?"

"Have a Familiar? Nah, I'm still a Novice, see?" She gestured at her brown tunic and pants. "Novices are not allowed to have Familiars until we've passed the Trials."

The Trials? Tann had said something about Ridian needing to pass them. "Trials?" he asked.

Feya looked at him in surprise. "Maybe you're not from a foster home after all. Perhaps an orphanage. Anyways, to join the Fidician Order, you need to demonstrate proficiency in one of the disciplines. Stewards must pass tests of medical knowledge. Clerics must memorise reams of religious doctrine. And Knights must win two out of three fights."

Ridian gulped. He'd just seen how effectively Feya had taken down her opponent. "What if you don't win two out of three fights?"

"You try again next year."

"Next year?" Ridian said in alarm.

"Yeah, the Fidician Festival is held every spring."

Every spring! Ridian couldn't wait another year. He was already waiting all of winter.

Feya purchased some apples from a grocer, which they quickly devoured. Ridian munched gratefully as they passed through the impressive outer wall, complete with crenelations, guard towers, and a fortified guard house. The lush grass of the meadow on the far side swayed from a pleasant-smelling breeze. Ridian closed his eyes and breathed deeply, enjoying the sunshine on his face. It definitely beat his faeces-infested cell.

After a time, the meadow sloped down into the expansive valley that was covered with vivid autumnal trees. Indeed, every shade of red, yellow, and orange saturated the basin.

"Leaves are late to fall," said Ridian around a mouthful of apple.

"The Firetrees?" said Feya. "They look like that year-round."

The Firetrees were aptly named. If you squinted, the whole valley looked ablaze.

"Valaria loved the Autumn colours," Feya continued. "So, she created the Firetrees to forever showcase them. Pretentious arseholes call Fidicia—" She put on an airy voice,"—the Valley of Eternal Fall."

Ridian had to ask. "Who was Valaria?"

Feya frowned. "The Elder Flower? Arden's most famous Druidess? Fidic's sister? Doesn't ring a bell?"

Ridian shook his head.

Feya scratched the back of her neck. "Geez... Where do I start? If you wait until we get home, you can ask my brother, Ollie. He'll talk your ear off about it."

"Hello!" cried an eager voice.

Ridian turned to see Theodor steering a horse-drawn cart. His whole face seemed to grin. "Got my days mixed up. Surgery's tomorrow."

Ridian and Feya leapt aboard, and the cart rattled down the hill, beneath the blazing canopy of Firetrees. With a loose one-handed hold on the reins, Theodor commented on things as they passed: the poor state of a bridge, and how someone should really fix it; his favourite tree, which looked like a bearded man; his favourite creek to catch tadpoles; his dream home, if only he could afford it; a cloud that looked like a pig one moment, then an eagle the next.

"When do I start training?" interrupted Ridian.

"Soulcaster training?" said Theodor. "Tomorrow. You'll be introduced to all three Disciplines, but Tann said he's got something special lined up for you. He's suspended your usual subjects—literacy, arithmetic, music, and history—so you can focus exclusively on the core competencies of Soulcasting." Theodor chuckled. "He's going to push you real hard, by the bye. I've known that man for a long time, and believe me when I say he doesn't mess around. No, sir. He's going to whip you into shape, that's for certain."

Whipped into shape by the man he'd abandoned to die. Ridian didn't like the sound of that. "How do you know Tann?" he asked.

Theodor's shoulders sagged, and a shadow crossed his face. "The war," he said flatly.

Feya, who was leaning on the rail and enjoying the wind on her face, glanced over.

They rattled on in silence until they stopped before a quaint two-story home, surrounded by Firetrees. "This is us. Feya, can you get the spare room ready?"

"Sure." Feya leapt deftly from the cart and went inside.

Theodor drove the cart into an adjacent stable, where he got the horse free of shaft, saddle, and bit. He stroked the horse's neck. "Good boy, good *boooooy*," he cooed. "How about a little treat, eh? It'll be our little secret." He glanced towards the door conspiratorially, then hand-fed the horse an apple with all the doting intensity of an indulgent grandmother.

Felix scampered along Theodor's arm and squeaked.

"Don't be jealous," Theodor teased, stroking the ferret's back.

Out the front of the house, the garden was overgrown with weeds, and the doormat was littered with shoes. Theodor looked embarrassed. "Pardon the mess. Been meaning to get on top of this place for ages." As he reached for the doorknob, a woman hurled the door open and shushed Theodor as if a dragon slumbered inside.

Theodor winced, shoulders hunched about his ears. "Sorry," he mouthed.

The woman braced herself as if for an earthquake. Theodor did too. Felix dove into Theodor's coat pocket. Nothing happened, and they both sighed with profound relief.

Dark bags circled the woman's eyes, yet they still twinkled when she smiled. "Welcome back," she said, giving Theodor a peck on the cheek.

"Big day?" asked Theodor.

The woman nodded wearily. "Big day."

"Kess, meet Ridian," said Theodor. "Fidicia's newest Novice. Ridian, meet Kessandra, key to my heart." He looked at her affectionately. "You don't mind if Ridian pinches the spare bed, do you?"

"Not at all," said Kess with hearty sincerity. "And please, call me Kess."

Then the dragon awoke in the form of a squalling infant, and Kess sagged as she released all the air from her lungs.

"My turn to look after her," said Theodor, dashing inside. "Show Ridian in."

Kess beckoned Ridian inside. It was a little messy, but nice. A crackling fire licked a simmering pot in the kitchen fireplace. Couches enclosed a cosy living room. Child-drawn pictures graced the walls. And a freckled redhead of about eight sat at the dining table, reading. He wore all brown, the same as Feya. "Hello," he said cheerily to Ridian, not getting up. "Did you know that apples, potatoes, and onions taste the same?" He pointed at a passage in his book and squinted at the page. "It says here that if you block your nose and close your eyes, you can't even tell the difference. Do you think that's true, Mum?"

"We should conduct an experiment," said Kess. "But first, come say hi to Ridian." The boy held his chin thoughtfully. "I do like experiments, but I think I could tell the difference. No matter what the book says."

Kess smiled. "Ollie, come say hi."

Ollie swapped the glasses on his face with a pair hidden in a pocket. Then he shuffled awkwardly off his chair and waddled over with a limping, lumbering gait. He clinked and clanked and squeaked with each step—the sound of metal braces and leather straps, straining to keep his bowed legs straight. "Pleased to meet you, Ridian," he said, gripping Ridian's hand spiritedly. "Oliver Thunderfell's my name, but everyone calls me Ollie. Oh, look at this." He opened his mouth and wiggled a loose tooth with his tongue. "My brother, Kai, keeps daring me to tie it to a door handle with a piece of string and slam the door. But that would hurt like crazy. Though probably not as much as when I did *this*." He parted his hair to reveal a rippling scar across his scalp. "I did this falling down those stairs. And *this*." He rolled up his sleeve to expose a scar-streaked elbow. "All I'll say is, don't play kickball on cobblestones. And this one…"

Theodor entered the room, bouncing a tear-streaked toddler. "Look Ella, a new friend."

Ella took one look at Ridian and began wailing again.

"Don't take it personally," said Theodor. "She's just tired."

Feya slid down the banister, landing with well-practised expertise. "Room's ready."

"Excellent," said Theodor. "Help your mum in the kitchen, would you? Ollie, take Ridian to his room."

Ollie tugged Ridian eagerly towards the staircase, where he plodded up with heavy help from the bannister. Upstairs was a corridor with a series of doors. They entered the farthest, a small, sparse bedroom with only a bed, desk, and cupboard. A dark piece of hardwood hung upon the wall. It had intricate little craters and ridges running all along it: tiny mountains, trees, and rivers carved with painstaking detail. The word 'Tor' was carved along the top frame. A topographical map, he realised, and he stared at the unfamiliar markings, intrigued.

"My older brother, Kai, made that." Ollie pointed to a tiny carved castle. "We're here in Fidicia, the capital of Tor, and if you look, you can see the Ring Mountains encircling the whole valley." Ollie's finger traced around a circle of mountains. He then gestured above Fidicia at a long stretch of mountains, running east to west. "And those mountains are the Wrathwolds, and north of the Wrathwolds is..."

"Kyrosia," said Ridian, remembering Nawar's instructions: *through the Wrathwolds and into Kyrosia.*

Ollie nodded like a teacher pleased with a student. "That's right."

Rayna was in Kyrosia, and these Wrathwold mountains were in the way. They looked an imposing obstacle, to say the least. They were proportionally tall and thick on the map, without any apparent way around them, and Nawar had declared them unpassable till spring. Ridian wasn't convinced.

"How do you cross the Wrathwolds?" asked Ridian.

"With great difficulty, but this is the best way." Ollie pointed at a dotted line that ran northward from Fidicia. That was good to know. If worse came to worst, Ridian could find Rayna on his own.

Ollie prattled on about some Horoc desert in the south and some great lake west, but Ridian wasn't listening. His attention was stolen by the eastern part of the map. It was smooth as a tabletop, without any markings except for the words: 'The Great Waste'.

The Mire, Ridian realised. *It's a mystery to them as well.*

"Knock, knock," said Theodor, darting in with a bowl of hot water, a sponge, a towel, and a change of clothes. "I brought you some Novitiate Browns. You'll need to wear these until you graduate and pick your own speciality."

"I'm going to become a Knight," said Ollie with verve.

"Oh, your brains would be wasted wearing the Grey," said Theodor. He held up the tunic and shook his head. "Can you believe these were mine, once upon a time? I was slimmer then, had a full head of hair, and two good knees. Had to beat the ladies off with a stick."

"*Dad*," said Ollie, scandalised.

Theodor chortled. "Let's leave Ridian to freshen up."

***

Washed and changed, Ridian admired himself in the vague reflection of the glass window. He wore brown from neck to wrist to ankle. The tunic and pants were well cut, allowing full range of motion without any unnecessary flap of material. The crinkled leather shoes fit poorly, so he wore his old ones, and it wasn't cold enough for the cloak or surcoat, so he left them on the bed.

He stared at the Firetree that swayed out the window, lost in thought. There was a lot to take in. He was in a strange land with wonders that shouldn't exist. A man named Hector had captured Rayna because he believed her to be a secret weapon. Some believed Ridian to be a weapon. And Tann had agreed to teach him Soulcasting, and *maybe* find Hector. All because his apparent ancestor—this Valaria—was some famous druidess who could shape trees into living castles. As he thought, he played absent-mindedly with the Elderflower pendant about his neck.

It was dark when the cry of *DINNER TIME* rang through the house. Ridian tucked the Elderflower necklace beneath his tunic and descended the stairs.

"There he is!" said Theodor. "Spick and span. A Fidician Novice indeed."

The family—Theodor, Kess, Feya, Ollie, Ella, and even Felix—sat at the dining table around a steaming pot of stew.

They all stared at him. Feeling awkward, Ridian went for the closest empty seat.

"Sit with me," said Ollie, tapping the seat next to him. Ridian did.

"Let's give thanks," said Theodor.

The family reached out and held hands. Ollie clasped Ridian's hand, unabashed. Ridian and Feya's eyes met, then ricocheted away. Somehow, their hands met and Ridian tried not to think how sweaty his palms were growing.

"Thanks be to Roki, who gifted himself, then, now, and always..." began the family in unison.

Meanwhile, Ollie sneered at the blushing Feya. There was a thump under the table; Ollie winced in pain, and Feya smiled, satisfied. Eyes closed, Theodor remained oblivious, though Kess peeped a disapproving eye. When the prayer finished, Ridian whipped his hand from Feya's and wiped his sweaty palms on his trousers.

Theodor ladled the stew, swimming with veggies and generous chunks of meat, into bowls. He handed the first bowl to Ridian. "It's good to have you with us, Ridian."

"Thank you." Ridian took the bowl and under Theodor's beaming, expectant gaze, took a sip. It was piping hot, and he burnt his tongue.

"So, what's with your eyes?" blurted Ollie, squinting up at him, his own eyes magnified behind his glasses.

Ridian's heart stopped. That was the wrong question—the wrong question. He stammered.

"Ollie," said Theodor in an admonishing tone. "You know the rules. First day, no questions. Ridian will share if and when he's ready."

"Yeah, Ollie," said Feya with all the reproachful authority

of an older sister. "You know the rules."

Ollie stuck out his tongue.

"Ollie," said Kess. "First warning."

"But—"

"No buts. Yes, Mum."

Ollie deflated. "Yes, Mum."

Feya hid her smirk behind a wild curtain of hair. Ridian was still undecided about whether she was pretty or not.

The front door opened, and to Ridian's surprise, in swooped a hawk. It soared across the room, and, after a brief flap of wings and a snapping of talons, perched upon a chair. Ridian was stunned. Everyone else seemed unfazed, all except Felix, who scurried into Theodor's robes with a squeak.

"Hello, Zeke," said Theodor to the hawk.

Zeke squawked.

A young man, perhaps a year older than Ridian, followed the hawk into the room. His skin was dark as a Sungazer, and he wore the all grey uniform of a Fidician Knight. He sauntered in with a winning smile. "What's for dinner? Smells amazing."

"Well, well, well… look who finally decided to show up," said Feya.

"Somebody's in trouble," sang Ollie.

The youth frowned. "What? What trouble?"

"Hello Kai," said Kess with false sweetness. "Can you explain why you failed to cook dinner? *Again.*"

The youth looked shocked—a great act, anyway. "It was my turn? You're joking!"

"The roster is above the mantlepiece, same as always," said Theodor.

"And I reminded you this morning," added Kess, folding her arms, unimpressed.

Kai clutched his head, squashing tight black curls. He knelt before Kess, hands clasped in a dramatic entreaty. "Please, Mother dear, can you find it in your generous, loving heart to forgive a mindless klutz like me—the world's worst son?"

Kai looked nothing like Kess, or Theodor, or anyone else for that matter. In fact, none of the family shared any resemblance. Theodor was a blue-eyed blonde, Kess a red-cheeked brunette. The wiry Feya was ivory-skinned, and had those dark, almost black eyes. Ollie was a freckled redhead. Ella was chocolate brown. And now Kai, his skin a dark mahogany. Ridian remembered Feya's comment about whether Ridian came from the street, an orphanage, or a foster home. *They're all adopted,* Ridian realised.

Kess turned away, full of affronted dignity. "No. This is the last straw. No more forgiveness. No mercy."

"Please don't make me beg," said Kai, already begging.

Kess peeped at him out of the corner of her eye. "Well, a decent hug and an apology might go a long way."

Kai leapt to his feet and wrapped his arms about her head in an extravagant embrace. "A thousand apologies my magnanimous mother! I simply don't deserve you."

"No, you don't," said Kess, behind his smothering arm. "And if you're truly repentant, you'll do the dishes."

"Shhhhh," said Kai. "Don't ruin a beautiful moment."

"Kai," said Theodor. "This is Ridian."

"Pleasure to meet you, Ridian." Kai went to sit, and Zeke—Kai's Familiar—burst into the rafters to make room. Then Kai plucked a piece of meat from his soup and flung it towards the ceiling, where the hawk snapped it up mid-air.

Nobody found this remarkable except the toddler, Ella. She clapped, eager for Kai to do it again.

"So, Kai, why exactly are you late?" asked Feya, insinuation thick in her voice.

Kai examined his spoon very carefully and didn't look at her. "Hmm…?"

"You heard me."

"Oh, you know." Kai waved his hand meaninglessly. "A quiet drink with the boys."

Everyone but Ridian and Ella chuckled at this.

Kai was the very picture of shocked innocence. "What's so funny?"

"A quiet drink with the boys?" said Feya with delighted incredulity. "You mean romancing Sabrina Crawford." She lay her hands over her heart, dramatic and earnest. "O Sabrina! My heart doth leap. O Sabrina! To kiss thy cheek." She pretended to swoon, the back of her hand resting against her forehead, and spoke in an unnaturally high-pitched tone. "O Kai… Thy words, they woo."

The family erupted into laughter, even Ella, though she didn't know why.

Kai glowered at Feya, though he also worked hard to suppress a grin. In fact, there was no malice between them. Despite the joke being at Kai's expense, it was clearly an affirmation of the bond between them.

Dinner continued in much the same fashion—some light conversation, some banter, and some jokes, mostly at each other's expense. Nothing cruel. The family genuinely liked each other. Ridian ate his soup in silence, his disquiet growing. The Thunderfells were too damn nice. It piqued his suspicion. What did they want from him? How were they going to use him? And what would they do once they found out he was a Caveborn, as they assuredly would? Cast him out, no doubt. What else would you do with someone who could snap at any moment and murder you in your sleep?

Dinner finished, the family scattered to attend to various chores, leaving Ridian alone with Ollie.

Ollie opened his mouth to talk.

"Who was Valaria Elderflower?" Ridian asked before Ollie could talk about his scars.

Ollie looked puzzled. "What do you mean?"

"I mean, who was she?"

Ollie's eyes narrowed. "Are you tricking me? Kai does this sometimes. He asks me stupid questions and then..."

"No, promise. I genuinely don't know. I keep hearing about her, but I know nothing."

"Nothing?"

"Nothing."

Ollie whistled. "Your orphanage must have been rough." Then he stomped over to a bookshelf and waddled back with a slim book. "The Tale of the Elder Three," he said. "Not exactly factual, but should serve as a good introduction."

Then, before Ollie could say another word, Ridian snatched the book and dashed upstairs, to read by the moonlight spilling through his bedroom window.

Chapter 13

The Tale of the Elder Three

A long time ago, when the Ardens enslaved our Tor ancestors, an Arden woman gave birth to children three: Daegan, destined to become a giant; Valaria, most gifted of the Arden Druids; and Fidic, who had no gift, yet became the greatest of the Three.

Though born together, the Three grew up and went their separate ways. Twice as tall and many times as strong as any man alive, Daegan became a mighty warrior. Beautiful and powerful, Valaria seduced the prince himself, while the ungifted Fidic ran away with nothing but his lute and his cunning.

Meanwhile, Kyros the Great—but not yet the Terrible— uncovered the secrets of Soulcasting. "Finally," he declared, "we have magic to match the Ardens." And he Awakened many Torian slaves from their Soulcaster slumber. Then Kyros the Great—but not yet the Terrible—with an army of slaves and wild animals, the likes of which the world had never seen, marched upon the Living City of Terillion.

When Daegan heard of the uprising, he rode out to confront the Soulcaster army. "Kyros!" he boomed across the battlefield. "Spare our men. Fight me alone, and let our swords decide the fates of our people."

Kyros accepted the giant's challenge with a sword in each hand. Twice as tall and many times as strong, Daegan's strikes were terrible to behold. But, quick as a hare, Kyros eluded the giant's blade but never struck back. After hours of fighting, Daegan's sword grew heavy, his stroke slow, and at sundown, Kyros positioned himself before the setting sun. And in that moment, when the giant was momentarily blind, Kyros unleashed his full Soulcaster strength. He struck Daegan's shield with the force of a thunderclap, shattering the shield and the arm that held it. The giant fled, and without their champion, the Arden army scattered like autumn leaves. Then Kyros the Great—but not yet the Terrible—with his army of freed slaves and wild animals, the likes of which the world had never seen, marched upon the Living City of Terillion.

Hearing of his brother's defeat, pride kindled in Fidic's heart, and he rode out to face the Soulcaster army. Upon a bridge, Fidic took lute and sang:

> *I cannot best you with strength of arm,*
> *But perhaps with magic's charm,*
> *One false step, and this bridge I'll blow,*
> *To water deep and flowing below.*

> *Riddles three you must unravel,*
> *Or cross this bridge, you cannot travel.*
> *One's broken and cannot be fixed,*
> *Two's the thing that cannot be,*
> *Three's the darkness in the light.*
> *Now tell me three answers right.*

> *Answer true, and I'll let you pass,*

Safely without alchemy blast,
But err in judgement, and you'll find,
Deadly magic, most unkind.

Then Fidic sparked strange potions from distant lands and made an explosion of many colours. Fireworks, as they were later called, were a new spectacle, and the Soulcaster army cowered.

Kyros answered with a smile:

Who seems right, but is so wrong,
Riddles, rhymes, and sings in song,
Who seems perfect, but is flawed,
The answer, of course, a fraud.

Bluff called, Fidic fled, and Kyros the Great—but not yet the Terrible—with an army of freed slaves and wild animals, the likes of which the world had never seen, marched upon the Living City of Terillion.

Meanwhile, Valaria poured forth her magic. With unmatched power, she walked around Terillion and grew a great living wall around the Living City. Day and night, she laboured until a spectacular wall soared into the heavens—a veritable mountain range of living wood. Exhausted by her great work, she collapsed and was thus asleep when Kyros the Great—but not yet the Terrible—stood before the Living City.

The Soulcaster army looked upon the living wall in dismay. But Kyros did not lose heart. With knives in hand, he scaled the unscalable living wall. All night he climbed, until at last, with the rising sun, he stood atop the living wall and cried:

Children! My Children! Rise from your beds!

A new day is dawning! It is yours!
For too long you have suffered!
For too long you have wept!
Now is the time! Our time!
Arise! Arise! Arise!

Fear held the Torian slaves within the city hostage. But at Kyros' cry, courage and rage fanned aflame within their hearts. The slaves rioted, fighting broke out in the streets, and the gutters ran red with Arden blood.

Valaria awoke to her people being slaughtered, trapped within the very walls she had made to protect them. Horrified, she carved a hole in the wall with her magic and fled.

And with the Ardens overthrown, the Torians crowned Kyros King—the First Free King—and had he stopped there, history would have remembered him as Kyros the Great. But Kyros was not satisfied with mere victory. He marched the surviving Ardens outside the walls of their beloved Living City and made them watch as he burnt it to the ground. For weeks, the great fire roared, and still Kyros made them watch. Then, with cruel irony, Kyros enslaved them, and their suffering was great.

Many Torians opposed the Arden mistreatment, for many Ardens had dealt kindly with their former slaves, treating them as servants, friends, and sometimes even family. They appealed to Kyros. "How can we foster lasting peace when we treat them so? Sooner or later, they will rise as we did."

"Your wisdom is sound," replied Kyros. "Therefore, upon the morn, every Arden man, woman, and child must die."

Many disavowed the monstrous decree and freed the Ardens before the slaughter could begin.

Kyros' wrath and retribution were terrible. Gathering his most trusted, he dragged suspected conspirators from their beds and had them executed. But his paranoia only grew. Everywhere, he saw snakes and knives and poison. Surely, there was a plot to kill him, and suspicion alone was damning. Without proof, many innocents received swift, unflinching justice. Death and torture reigned, and even when thousands had died, the hunt continued.

And while the world trembled, Daegan, Valaria, and Fidic sought refuge in the mountain caves of their home. Daegan was a broken man with a broken arm. The grief-stricken Valaria was a shadow of her former self, and Fidic, devoid of hope, climbed the highest peak to cast himself off. He cried to the Goddess Vel, Mother of the Ardens, to save her children. But Vel did not answer. Again, he cried, and again, she was silent.

But Roki, the wild god of Tor, heard Fidic's cries. He cast his spirit into a nearby Raven and cried, "Fidic. It is I, Roki, lord of Tor and the beasts that roam it. I have heard your prayers. I, too, am aggrieved. I, too, am angered. And though you are unworthy, you shall become my instrument of vengeance." Then Roki bound his soul with Fidic, making him the first Arden-born Soulcaster.

Fidic returned to the caves with the hallowed Raven upon his shoulder and, stretching forth his hand, released Roki's power, Awakening Daegan's soul. The giant's soul searched outward and bonded with a lion. Valaria's soul searched inward, and from that moment she could create new life—new flowers and plants yet unseen. And when Fidic laid his hands upon Daegan's arm, he felt compelled to sing. And singing thus, the arm healed, and they were all filled with wonder.

United at last, the Three forged the United Resistance. Fidic sent the talking Roki far and wide to gather Arden and Torian *refugees alike, Valaria grew the Living Fort to shelter them, and Daegan trained the new recruits in combat. The United Resistance grew, and Fidic—with his songs of healing and a god upon his shoulder—became their leader.*

But Kyros found and besieged the Living Fort. Though outnumbered ten to one, the United Resistance held firm. Daegan and his warriors defended the walls, Valaria grew food for all, and Fidic healed the wounded. But every day, some were killed. Numbers dwindled, and hope began to die.

In that grave hour, Fidic devised a plan. He ordered Daegan to redirect a mountain spring towards Kyros' camp. For six days and six nights, Kyros' troops drank freely and were replenished. But on the seventh day, Fidic directed Valaria to use her arts to poison the spring. Kyros' army drank, and the poison took effect. A terrible madness possessed them, and they became like rabid dogs. With a mindless rage, they attacked each other and consumed each other's flesh. And Kyros' army tore itself apart. But Kyros himself was spared. Forever paranoid, he only drank water of verified purity and was saved from the madness. But Kyros was a soldier before he was a king. Though overrun, he hacked his way through the deranged soldiers with his twin swords, and it seemed as if he would escape. Then Daegan, Valaria, and Fidic left the safety of the Living Fort and stormed out into the madness to attack Kyros. Daegan rained blows, and the formidable Kyros struck in return, drawing blood. But Fidic healed his brother with his divine voice. Seeing defeat, Kyros went to flee, but Valaria summoned a great, thorny hedge around them and cut off his retreat.

His doom at hand, Kyros hurled one of his twin swords with reckless abandon through Fidic's eye, pinning him to a tree. This break in concentration allowed Daegan to cleave the Tyrant King in two. And with Kyros dead, the United Resistance rose supreme. They drove Kyros' remaining armies north over the Wrathwolds and into a frozen land they named Kyrosia in homage to Kyros, the First Free King and Soulcaster. The United Resistance named their sanctuary Fidicia, after Fidic, their beloved leader and healer. And legend tells that Fidic's immortal soul passed into the Tree that he died upon, so he could watch over his beloved people for centuries to come.

Peace returned to Tor, but it was short-lived. The Torians remembered their enslavement, and the Ardens remembered the slaughter. And without Fidic's god-given wisdom, the country teetered on the brink of another war.

To avoid further bloodshed, Daegan and Valaria gathered the Ardens—every man, woman, and child—and travelled east, into permanent exile. Still, Torian resentment ran deep, and Soulcaster forces attacked the Ardens in their new home. Enraged, Valaria poisoned the land between the two peoples, creating the Great Waste, and Daegan built Mirecross Castle and swore that the east shall never Touch the west, vowing to safeguard the Ardens from Tor hostility.

With these deeds done, Valaria and Daegan left the light of history and passed into legend, but Fidic's legacy lives on. His Sacred Words are remembered still and will be cherished until the end of days.

Chapter 14

Ridian placed the book down, head whirling. 'The Tale of the Elder Three' read like a myth, like a fairy tale, but it was at least partly true. He'd seen the impossibility of the Living Fort, walked upon Valaria's Secret Waterway, beheld the Lion's Den, and admired Daegan's giant sword at Mirecross Castle. Did the man truly match the blade? And Fidic? They'd named this place after him. The Elder Three were a legend, and yet Ridian wore Valaria's pendant. Was she truly Ridian and Rayna's ancestor? If so, what did it mean? Did it mean they also possessed some secret power? And didn't Tann say Hector was Kyros' descendant? It all seemed so ridiculous, so fantastical, but he remembered the Moonflowers, Selkyrie's bizarre dismissal, and the dead rye sifting through his fingers where Rayna had lain. What if Rayna did have some extraordinary magical power? What if she was a weapon? How would Hector exploit her? How was he planning on using her?

Ridian also remembered why so much of this place and story had seemed familiar. He chanted the old nursery rhyme all Mudwall kids knew:

Lion, Liar, Minstrel, Flower,

In truth, they're all the same.
Up-jump Jack, make an attack,
Soon you'll go insane.

Come on, Lion, keep on tryin',
Sing, Minstrel, sing.
Come on, Flower, make your tower,
Down with the King!

The nonsensical verses made sense. They were whimsical fragments of Arden and Tor history, long forgotten and consciously erased by the Sol Empire.

Moon shone through the window. The curtains swayed from a lazy breeze. Outside, the Firetree creaked. Everything was peaceful—everything except Ridian. He tossed and turned in his bed. What were the chances Tann would take Ridian, an inexperienced nobody, on a high-stakes mission to kill Hector? None, surely. Ridian didn't know the first thing about Soulcasting. Even if he did, Ridian had left Tann to die, effectively destroying any goodwill the man might have had. And besides, why should Ridian sleep in a cosy bed with a full belly when Rayna was the captive plaything for the likes of Tinker, Basher, and Sneak?

Ridian slipped back into his old rags and stepped to the window. A branch snaked right beneath the windowsill. He poked his leg over the ledge and gave the branch an experimental shove with his foot. He committed more weight: it sank, but held. He then clambered onto the branch and down the tree. It was an easy climb, and he had the distinct feeling he wasn't the first to do this. He was wiping his hands on his pants and wondering which way to go when a voice said, "Where you off to?"

Ridian whirled around.

Feya was leaning against the house, wearing a wry smile. Her eyes shone with moonlight. *Pretty*, Ridian decided.

"The runaway foster kid," she said. "Such a cliché. But we've all been there."

Theodor evidently hadn't told her anything, as Ridian presumed he would. "What are you doing out here?" asked Ridian.

"I'm going to try talk sense into you."

Ridian collected himself. "I'm leaving. That's that."

"Just hear me out, okay?"

"Fine."

Feya rolled her eyes. "Look, I don't know where you're from or where you're thinking of going, but Theodor and Kess are the best thing that's ever going to happen to an unloved foster kid like you. No offence."

"None taken. But you don't understand. I can't stay. My sister's been kidnapped."

Feya looked genuinely surprised. "Kidnapped? By who?"

"By some Kyrosian called Hector."

"Hector?" said Feya, eyebrows arching. "The general? He's alive?"

"Apparently."

Feya blew out a sigh. "Well, shit."

"I know."

"What's your plan?"

Through the Wrathwold and into Kyrosia. Ridian pointed at the inky black outline of the northern mountains. "Well, Hector's in Kyrosia, and Kyrosia is north. So, I'll go north."

Feya looked as if that was the stupidest thing she'd ever

heard. "Wait. That's your plan? *Go north?*"

Ridian bristled. "Yeh, that's my plan. What of it?"

Feya shook her head and chuckled in amused disbelief. "I'm really glad I stopped you. *Go north.* Listen, you don't understand. Fidicia is probably the safest, most well-guarded place in the world. It's surrounded by sheer, impassable mountains on all sides, with only two gates in or out: one north, one east, both of which are heavily fortified and guarded by Soulcasters. They're not just going to let you stroll north into hostile territory. But say you did manage to sneak out. The Wrathwold Mountains are currently frozen solid. You'd be lost within an hour and dead within two. And even if you did cross the Wrathwolds without freezing to death, Hector and his men would be in hiding. And just say, miracle of miracles, you somehow found them, they would kill you on the spot." She reconsidered. "Well, maybe they'd torture you first. But regardless. You have no resources, no support, and no clue what you're doing. I get that you want to save your sister, anyone would, but *'go north'...* I'm sorry, but your idea is as naïve as it is stupid. Dying won't save her."

Hopelessness swelled within Ridian. His plan was dumb, and he knew it. "I can't just wait until spring for Tann to *maybe* take me," he said at last.

"Wait. Tann will take you?"

Ridian shrugged. "Maybe, depends."

Feya pinched the bridge of her nose. "I'm really, *really* glad I stopped you. Listen, Tann's an old pal of Dad's. He's been running secret missions for longer than we've been alive. He will have the means and the know-how to actually save your sister."

"But Tann's mission isn't to save my sister. It's to kill Hector."

"So you get to save your sister and kill the prick who took her? What's the problem?"

"But he probably won't take me. Depends on how my training goes."

Feya exhaled in frustration. "Then work your arse off and impress him. Use your brain for two seconds, and you'll realise I'm right." As she glared at him, Ridian saw that her face was a little too narrow. She also had a snaggle tooth, and her hair was just too big. Not pretty, after all. Even so, she was right. Whether he liked it or not, he was stuck in Fidicia for now. His best bet was to impress Tann, even if the man hated his guts.

Feya must have seen Ridian's change of heart, because she turned and began scaling the ivy-covered lattice to a bedroom window like it was her thousandth time. "Get some rest," she said, over her shoulder. "You have a big tomorrow."

"Wait," said Ridian. "Why help me? Why do you care?"

Feya paused at the windowsill. "Because us foster kids have enough crap to deal with." And with that, she slipped through the window and out of sight.

Ridian lingered for a while, but eventually he climbed back up the tree, went to bed, and soon fell into an uneasy sleep.

***

Ridian stood upon The Mire, terror crawling up his spine. He was being watched, though he saw nothing through the thick mist. He could feel it. Then the Gallows Tree appeared, a body hanging from one of the branches by a rope about the neck. With a long creak, the body slowly spun about. Dank hair hid the woman's face. Ridian didn't move, but he was nonetheless drawn closer. Suddenly, the woman's face snapped up. Her eyes were scabby holes—pecked empty by crows—but they glared at him all the same. It was his mother.

"It's your fault!" she screamed. "Your fault!" Maggots crawled from between her gnashing teeth. "Your fault! Your fault! YOUR FAULT!" The rope snapped. She landed in a deep squat—legs splayed like a toad.

Ridian fled, knowing the corpse shambled after him. He ran and ran and ran, until the haggard, rasping breaths of the creature fell away. Then Rayna appeared, standing upon the edge of Trystan's Well. She was blank-faced, medicated. She was going to jump down into that haunted well. He shouted at her to stop, but he had no voice. He tried to run faster, but his legs plunged into thick mud.

Rayna gazed into the Well, about to jump, and Ridian could barely move. But he could still save her. He reached... reached... reached... and tripped. He fell headlong into the Well, tumbling through darkness into darkness, spinning, spinning, spinning...

Finally, he landed in a bright, golden field—and a plough skewered his thigh. Blood gushed from the wound in torrents, enough to fill a lake, an ocean. It flooded the field, causing the crops to wilt and die. Then his blood ran up a tree, covered the leaves, and they began to fall...

A dead field and a dying tree.

A hand grabbed his shoulder. It was Mother, eyes pecked,

mouth full of maggots. "Your fault!" she screamed.

Ridian awoke with a start, heart hammering. Sweaty sheets twisted around him. He sat up, trying to remember where he was. Then he did, and sighed. *Just a dream,* he reassured himself. *Just a—*

A ghostly figure was peering down at him from the windowsill—a wolf, but ablaze with a cold silver fire.

Ridian reeled backwards in alarm and crashed against the bedhead. He blinked and looked again: the windowsill was empty, the room was just as it should be—peaceful, quiet, and empty. The moon shone through the window, right where the glowing silver wolf had been. Ridian laughed at himself. *The moon. Just the moon.* But he didn't feel relieved. He took a few deep breaths, but his heart didn't slow. *Just a nightmare,* he told himself. *A waking nightmare is all. I've had many before.* But it was so real, so clear, and a cruel voice at the back of his mind told him what he didn't want to hear.

It's started, the voice said. *You're beginning to crack.*

Chapter 15

Theodor shook Ridian awake. "Wakey, wakey. Big day today."

Ridian groaned. It was still dark, and his tired bones told him it was early.

Theodor grinned, bright as the midday sun. "Come downstairs. Breakfast is ready."

Breakfast proved appetising: porridge topped with berries, walnuts, and a drizzle of honey. Ridian ate while Theodor fussed about the kitchen. Ollie emerged with an enormous yawn and a rub of the eye. Feya stared vacantly at her bowl, her hair wilder than ever.

After breakfast, they left. Outside, stars still glittered, and owls hooted. It even *smelled* early. Theodor rattled up with the cart, beaming. "First day. Very exciting. You always remember your first day."

Ridian, Feya and Ollie climbed aboard, and they trundled up the hill. Feya and Ollie slumped against the rail and tried to sleep between bumps in the road.

"You excited about your first day, Ridian?" asked Theodor, spinning around in his seat.

"Sure." Truthfully, Ridian was sick with anxiety. He needed to impress Tann—that was paramount. It was his one decent chance of saving Rayna. And he had less than three months. But on the other hand, three months might be too long if he was going crazy. The ghostly spectre he'd seen last night burned before his waking eyes. How long till he truly lost his mind? And what version of insanity would he take? The raving lunatic? The homicidal maniac? The harmless crackpot like old Willem?

"You should be excited," said Theodor. "You'll be introduced to the three disciplines of the Fidician Order: Clerics, Stewards, and Knights. I wonder which discipline you'll lean towards? I hope you become a Steward. We can always do with more good Stewards."

Atop the hill, Ridian was again awestruck. Nestled beneath the mountains, the hospital soared skyward, canopy swaying. Surely, this was the same Living Fort in 'The Tale of the Elder Three,' fashioned by Valaria to protect the United Resistance. Now it served as a mere hospital.

Theodor dropped them by the large double doors of the Living Fort. "Good luck, Ridian. First day. Very exciting." Feya and Ollie yawned their goodbyes, and Theodor rattled away. It looked dark inside the hospital, and Ridian wondered how they would find their way.

A life-sized copper statue stood before the hospital entrance. Somehow, Ridian had missed the rusted green statue the day before. It was a man, slim and messy-haired, playing a lute. A raven perched on the minstrel's shoulder. Fidic, surely, and the wild god, Roki. Welcoming words were carved upon the pedestal beneath Fidic's feet:

Come tired,
Come poor,

Come hungry,
Sick, footsore.

Come needy,
Come afraid,
Come forgotten,
Lost, enslaved.

Beneath and around the pedestal was a ten-foot water basin. Hundreds of circular leaves, the size of large coins, floated atop the waterline. Flicking the leaves aside, Feya and Ollie scooped some water from the basin with cupped hands and slurped.

Ridian wrinkled his nose. "Isn't it stagnant?"

"Nah," said Ollie, wiping his mouth. "You should have some."

"Why?"

"You'll see."

Ridian took a sip of the water and braced himself for the foul aftertaste. Instead, a refreshing sweetness rippled over his tongue. He scooped more and drank more. Was it sugar water? Did they mix honey into it? Or did the floating leaves produce some delightful nectar? Before Ridian could ask, the Living Fort began to glow a soft green. Ridian gasped as it grew steadily brighter. Now the wood was burning with the gentle light of dying green embers. And there was no flame, just a hazy green aura. It was just like the wolf last night, only green. Ridian's heart felt like lead. He was losing his mind. But Ollie and Feya were laughing.

"Don't worry," said Ollie. "You'll get used to it."

"How...?" began Ridian.

"Valaria's work," said Ollie. "She created lots of nifty plants."

Then Feya led the way inside, going slow so Ollie's braced legs could keep up. Ridian gawped up at the Living Fort for a few moments longer, taking it all in: the vast, glowing trunks and the complex network of branches. The leaves, however, were not illuminated. They were like fluttering black bats. Ridian was bemused. This strange, ethereal glow was just like the silver wolf last night. Perhaps the wolf was real. Perhaps Fidicia had glowing silver wolves on the loose. It wasn't a comforting thought.

Ridian followed Feya and Ollie inside the quiet Emergency Wing with its corridors and stairways going hither and thither. Just like Ridian remembered, the walls and ceiling and floor were smooth panels of the seamless, living wood. No joints, no nails, nothing. Just a perfect hall with the occasional trunk serving as a pillar. Only now the surfaces were a dull, glowing green. By this light they found and entered a passageway at the far end of the hall. A creaking, groaning sound thrummed in the walls and beneath Ridian's feet: the sound of old joints stretching, of a forest fighting the wind. Yes, this place was alive alright. Corridors branched off, but they continued straight until the passage ended upon a rock wall with a dark hole—a natural tunnel boring into the mountain. They plunged inside; the temperature plummeted, and all sounds save Ollie's heavy, clanking footfalls died. The tunnel twisted this way and that, until finally, a cavern appeared: about thirty feet wide, seventy feet deep. Stalactites clung to the ceiling, and candles flickered in the smoky gloom. There were statues and tapestries and paintings along all the walls.

At the end of the chamber loomed a seven-foot statue of a raven with its wings spread. Before the statue stood Mother Asarah, clothed in her Clerical black. Brown-robed Novices sat clustered before her.

The real eye-catcher, however, was the giant wooden mural stretching from wall to wall on the right side of the cavern. It glowed with that strange, green glow, carved scenes rippling along its surface.

"We're late," said Feya, and they scurried across the carpeted floor to join the group.

None of the Novices paid them any heed, but Mother Asarah's bright eyes flicked over them. Ridian silently cursed. *So much for making a good impression.* He looked about for Tann, but he was nowhere to be seen.

"As I was saying," said Mother Asarah, her frail voice reverberating throughout the cavern. "Humans have three aspects: body, mind, and soul. The body is what you see before you." She gestured vaguely at herself. "Blood, flesh, and bone. Simple. The mind is more complex—thoughts, emotions, and memories operating on conscious and unconscious levels. But the soul. Ah, the soul is another thing entirely. Both mysterious and profound, it is, quite simply, who you are. Who you truly are. The real you. Not the person you think you are, even in those rare moments when you are honest with yourself. No. The soul is eternal. The soul is what lives on when the body dies…"

As she went on, Ridian's eyes wandered back to the glowing mural. Interestingly enough, many of the carvings he recognised from 'The Tale of the Elder Three': Fidic the Minstrel standing before Kyros on a bridge as fireworks exploded above; Fidic conversing with a raven upon a mountain; Fidic healing the giant Daegan with song. Ridian's favourite image was of Daegan locking swords with Kyros, while Fidic raised his healing hands, and Valaria summoned a hedge around them. The final image was of Fidic slumped against a tree, a sword pinning him through the eye. Daegan and Valaria wept at his feet, while a raven flew skyward.

But the images weren't carved, Ridian realised. Not in a traditional sense. Looking closer, he could see the flawless finish. He could see the root twisting down from a crack in the ceiling to stretch and spread and mould to become the mural itself. This was another living work of Valaria's. Another miracle.

"Ridian?" said Mother Asarah, jolting Ridian back into the moment. She was gesturing for him to join her, and all eyes were upon him.

Feya gave him a nudge, and he shuffled self-consciously to face the group beside Mother Asarah. His cheeks flushed.

"Let us formally welcome Ridian," said Mother Asarah.

The Novices stood, then responded in lazy, bored unison. "May Roki comfort you in your sadness. May he smile at your joy. And may he nourish you when you are weary." The Novices bowed, then left in silence. Feya and Ollie mouthed a 'good luck' before turning to leave. Whatever came next, Ridian was to do it alone.

Mother Asarah smiled, her face a complex of wrinkles. "Would you sit with me?" Ridian nodded, and they sat cross-legged, side by side before the towering stone raven. As the last of the Novices left, an eerie silence filled the chamber. Ridian peeped at Mother Asarah from the corner of his eye. Still, she gazed up at the stone raven.

"This is a special place," said Mother Asarah at last.

"Stonecrow Cavern. It was here that Fidic performed his first miracle, healing his brother's arm. Where Daegan became a Soulcaster. Where Valaria unlocked her true potential, though, perhaps more importantly, this is where she began transcribing Fidic's Sacred Words. Words that guide us, nourish us, and protect us… often from our own folly." Mother Asarah's voice took on a rehearsed air, a recitation. "A Soulcaster lives not for himself. Indeed, a Soulcaster gives all—body, mind, and soul—and in giving, receives…" She turned to look at Ridian. "Do you understand why this is so important? That we instill Fidic's Sacred Words into the hearts of every Soulcaster?"

Ridian nodded slowly, then quickly shook his head.

"Consider what would happen if a Soulcaster was not bound by a moral code. What would happen if a Soulcaster—imbued with such tremendous supernatural power—lived by their own rules? Did their own thing? Did whatever they fancied, when they fancied?"

Ridian hesitated. He recalled Tann killing the soldiers barehanded with apparent ease. He thought of Hector, killing thirteen people to capture Rayna. He considered himself, cracking and going insane, but with the strength of ten men. "They could be dangerous," he said at last.

"Exactly," said Mother Asarah. "That is why we Clerics are an indispensable part of the Fidician Order. Without us imparting Fidic's wisdom, we would devolve into moral degeneracy, and become just like our Kyrosian neighbours, forever fighting amongst ourselves, divided. That is our great task: to preserve and to learn Fidic's Sacred Words. Our second is the training of Soulcasting itself."

Ridian perked up. This was why he was here: for

Soulcasting, not moralising. Mother Asarah gestured at one of the images of Daegan and Valaria on the mural wall. Streaks of light emanated from their eyes as Fidic and Roki watched on.

"It was easy for them," said Mother Asarah. "They learned Soulcasting in a flash, from divine inspiration. It will not be easy for you. You are old, too old, some would say, and ignorant. I do not mean to offend, but it's true. And even if you weren't those things, many still fail. And even if you do succeed, you will be forever changed. Knowing this, are you still committed?" Mother Asarah's kind, hundred-year-old eyes reflected the cold green glow of the mural wall. They searched Ridian, reading him. Even the raven seemed to gaze down at him with its hard, stone eyes.

Ridian nodded.

She gave a sad smile. "You wish to save your sister. That is understandable, virtuous even. But you have much to learn and little time. Becoming a proficient Soulcaster takes years—*years*."

Ridian's heart sank. He didn't have years. He had months. "I have to try," he said.

Mother Asarah bowed her head solemnly. "Very well. Let us begin." She cleared her throat, and Ridian listened with rapt attention. "The goal of Soulcasting is to bond with an animal Familiar—a beautiful thing. But the first fundamental skill of Soulcasting is Splitting—the act of separating soul from body. It involves tremendous willpower and great strength of mind. You remember Splitting during your Awakening, no doubt?"

Ridian nodded. Of course, he did. It was the most bizarre experience of his life, tearing from his body to hover in that strange, dark place.

"The Astral Plane," said Mother Asarah, answering Ridian's unasked question. "That's where you went. A realm where matter is stripped away, leaving only that which is eternal. What the kids call 'going into the Black.'" She chuckled. "Not very decorous, but I can see why."

Ridian smiled back. He could too.

"But Splitting is no small matter," Mother Asarah continued. "Your untrained mind is like a bird flapping about in a cage. Only a clear, focused mind can pick the lock and become free." She pointed to a nearby candle with a gnarled finger. "Meditate on that flame. Think of nothing else. *Concentrate*. And when all distractions perish from the intensity of your focus—when that flame is all that exists— maybe then you will untether your soul."

***

Meditation proved a boring waste of time. Ridian tried and tried, but after what was surely hours alone in the cave—no matter how special it was—his soul remained very much tethered. Mother Asarah had long gone, and the Mural Wall had even stopped glowing; the illuminating qualities of the sweet fountain water had evidently worn off. And where the hell was Tann? The bastard still hadn't bothered to show up.

Eventually, Ridian heard footfalls approaching. *Tann's finally here,* he thought. He straightened his back and stared transfixed at the candle. Lost gods, he was nervous. It was surely going to take a mini-miracle to win Tann over. The feet drew closer.

"Look at you," said Theodor. "First day and already focusing beautifully."

Ridian sighed, relieved and frustrated in equal measures.

Theodor beamed at him, Felix clinging to his shoulder. "On behalf of the Stewards, I've been tasked to show you around the hospital and introduce you to our ministry. But I could come back later if you would prefer to meditate for longer?"

Ridian followed Theodor out. He'd meditated plenty.

Back in the hospital, patients wandered around aimlessly or lay in their beds, while white-robed Stewards hurried about with a keen sense of purpose: trolleying patients, carrying food, hauling linen, communicating with patients... Familiars of all kinds stalked the corridors and perched about the canopy. Much like the Mural Wall, the hospital no longer glowed. Theodor explained that was due to the rising sun.

Theodor was an enthusiastic and thorough guide; starting from the bottom floor and working his way up, he led Ridian down corridors, up natural staircases, along parapets, and in and out of natural tunnels and towers. There were whole wings dedicated to various branches of medicine: Paediatric, Geriatric, Psychiatric, Palliative Care, Acute Care, and more. Views from the higher levels were incredible. Ridian could see the town of Fidicia down in the heart of the valley about the banks of the Raven's River far below, the wide expanse of Valarian Firetrees, and the aptly named Ring Mountains, encircling the entire valley.

Ridian's guess that the hospital had once been the Living Fort—the ancient holdfast of the Elder Three and the United Resistance—proved accurate.

"Fidic was a healer, after all," said Theodor. "So, the Stewards formed in the aftermath of his death to continue his Ministry, and where better than here?"

The Stewards themselves were a colourful lot. Greta, a plump, middle-aged midwife, flirted outrageously with Ridian. Neville, a gangling physician with a severely hooked nose, shooed them away from his sterile surgical room, saying, "You're covered in germs." Esther, a gorgeous blonde, ran rehabilitation exercises on a wide, sunny balcony. "Sunshine, fresh air, and exercise are the best medicine," she said. Adrian scowled before one dark doorway. "No entry," he growled. Ridian wasn't tempted. The room quarantined infectious patients.

Ridian's favourite place was the apothecary tower. Tallest of the tree towers, a natural staircase wound around the inside, boring through the trunk like a corkscrew. Atop this climb, a twisted bundle of branches wove together into a circular room where Stewards stooped over workbenches and tinkered with various instruments, glassware, and paraphernalia. There were scales, funnels, flasks, beakers, and jars of every size and description, containing potions, powders, herbs, and crystals of every colour. It was cluttered, but everything appeared to have a place and purpose, including the Stewards themselves. There was an elderly gentleman by the name of Master Sheema, and a pimply Novice called Remmy. An owl kept them company, sitting in the rafters and swooping to retrieve a vial or instrument when Master Sheema called.

"Of course, Fidic healed people like *that*." Theodor clicked his fingers. "But Valaria was also highly instrumental in the formation of the Stewards. She created new plants that made potions that we use to this day. Fidicia is full of flowers, herbs, and roots—bursting with salubrious qualities—and the pharmaceutical team are always on the cutting edge of discovering new medicines."

Tour finished, Theodor looked gravely upon Ridian. "Fun's over, I'm afraid. Now I've got some bad news."

It was bad. Ridian's first job as a Novice was the collection and cleaning of chamber pots. According to Theodor, waste disposal was a noble role that saved more lives than physicians. The job was simple: pick up the ceramic pots of the sick and dying, carry them in a little wheelbarrow, individually upend them into a cesspit, and then scrub them clean in a nearby stream. There were dozens of chamber pots—*hundreds*—all swimming with urine and soggy excrement. Most demoralising, however, was that by the time he'd completed a lap of the hospital, more dirty pots awaited right where he'd started.

Ridian was more than a little vexed. What did potty disposal have to do with Soulcasting? How was this helping him? And where the hell was Tann? The depravity of the work was offset by the Living Fort, however. On every level there were little nooks and crannies, secret passageways, novel staircases, and hidden tunnels yet to be explored. The design was as beautiful as it was intriguing. The work of a true master in love with her craft, not just a druidess in need of a fortress.

Hours and many pots later, Ridian was replaced by a sour-faced Novice called Bernie.

"Good job, Ridian," said Theodor with zeal as he led Ridian away from the cleaning stream. "First day, very exciting." He handed Ridian a small linen bundle. "I made you a little lunch. Hope it's enough."

Ridian's little lunch consisted of two apples, a cheese wheel, a dozen cherries, and three sandwiches with mustard, ham, and relish. "Who am I sharing this with?" asked Ridian. It was more food than he'd usually eat in a whole day, never mind lunch.

Theodor chuckled. "With you, yourself, and nobody else. Oh, and I wasn't sure if you liked the crusts or not. So, I played it safe and cut them off. But I got worried and thought you might like them after all, so I left them for you." Sure enough, the crusts were stacked in a neat little row. "We'd better walk and eat, I'm afraid. We don't want to keep Sevron waiting. He's rather precious about his time."

Ridian remembered Sevron: the glaring, one-eyed Commander of the Fidician Knights who thought Ridian a nuisance, a liar, and an outsider.

Theodor must have read the concern on Ridian's face. "Don't worry about Sevron. He can be a bit... well, he can be a bit uptight, if not pig-headed, and he has an odd interpretation of Fidician doctrine, and he's rather closed-minded, and he can be a bit obtuse." Theodor marched faster as he spoke. "But at the end of the day, he's bound by his word and Fidician Law to introduce you to the Knights appropriately. He has no say in the matter."

Theodor clearly had some issues with Sevron, and Ridian wondered what they could be.

"Will Tann be there?" asked Ridian.

"Not sure. Haven't seen him."

As Ridian ate, they marched down the street, passing Clerics, Stewards, Knights, and Novices in their respective Black, White, Grey, and Browns. There were regular townsfolk as well. Nobody was fussed by the pair of wolves snapping at each other, or the eagle perched upon the ridge of a smithy, tearing the skin off a rabbit.

Outside the perimeter wall, Theodor led Ridian across the swaying, waist-high meadow grass towards a solitary oak. The tree was expansive, ancient, and gnarled. Thick, twisting branches went hither and thither, and some were so old and so long they sagged all the way to the ground. And there was something else about the ancient tree that Ridian couldn't quite put words to. Something alluring. Something that drew the eye and held it.

Sevron stood by the trunk, tapping his foot, his massive wolf at his side. Both man and wolf glared.

So much for not wasting Sevron's precious time.

"Thank you, Theodor, you may leave," said Sevron, as Theodor and Ridian passed beneath the shade of the tree's creaking, long-stretching boughs.

Theodor didn't move. "I was hoping to stay and—"

"Attend to your duties, Steward, so I can attend to mine," said Sevron curtly.

Felix popped out from Theodor's pocket to hiss. Theodor clenched his jaw, and for the first time, Ridian realised how tall Theodor was. Tall and broad and perhaps just as intimidating as the one-eyed commander.

Sevron looked unfazed, but his Familiar bristled. An almost inaudible growl rolled about in its throat.

"Fine, Commander," Theodor finally said through tight lips. "I look forward to Ridian's full and unabridged report." He placed a strong, affectionate hand upon Ridian's shoulder, nodded, and then left without another word, leaving Ridian alone with Sevron and his massive wolf.

Sevron glowered at Ridian, not masking his disdain. Ridian stared back, chin up, though he withered on the inside. *You must stand up to bullies.* Rayna's words from long ago coming back to him. *Scratch the surface and you'll find a coward.* Ridian was no stranger to bullies, but at least the ones back home feared him on some level, feared the madman he would become. But Sevron was a powerful Soulcaster with nothing to fear from Ridian. Ridian's resolve broke, and he glanced away.

Sevron snorted with contempt at the easy victory. "You stand upon Last Stand Meadow," he said, not taking his iron-hard eye off Ridian. "Where long ago, the United Resistance fought against Kyros the Terrible. You stand before Hero's Tree, where Fidic died. Where Daegan slayed the tyrant king. Where Valaria wove her thorny wall. This place is holy." The ancient tree creaked, and its leaves whispered secrets. Still, Sevron glared. "This is where Fidicia died, and Daegan killed. This is important both historically and symbolically: to wear the Grey, you must be willing to both die and kill in defence of Fidicia, from foes within and without. From those who would attack us by day and from those who would steal its secrets by night." Sevron let the words sink in. *I will kill you if you betray us,* his silence seemed to say, and Ridian believed it. "Are you—a stranger and an outsider—willing to die and kill for Fidicia's sake?"

There was only one answer. "Yes."

Sevron snorted with disgust; he knew Ridian was lying.

He has to initiate me, Ridian realised. *He doesn't want to. But he has to.* The thought gave him confidence. "I am willing," said Ridian with more steel in his voice, forcing himself to gaze levelly into that single angry eye.

Sevron turned to brush his fingers reverently against the gnarled bark of the trunk. "Many believe Fidic's soul passed into this tree so he could forever watch over his beloved people." Sevron's eye flicked back onto Ridian. "Do you believe that?"

Ridian squirmed. Fidic's soul trapped inside? Was Sevron being serious? What did he want to hear? "Um…"

"It doesn't matter if his soul is in this tree or not," said Sevron. "It was not the dead Fidic who drove Kyros' forces out of Fidicia, but the giant Daegan. It was Daegan who defended Fidicia, and we Knights fight in his place…" He sighed with resignation. "And so, fighting you must learn. Come with me." Sevron and his wolf turned and marched away from Hero's Tree and Last Stand Meadow towards the sheer mountain wall. Following a few steps behind, Ridian could almost feel the irritation radiating from Sevron.

As they drew closer, a slim six-foot gap in the mountains appeared—a narrow sliver of a canyon, like the one he'd used to enter Fidicia. Sevron gestured. "Sanctuary Forest lies beyond. There your Varki teacher awaits."

"Varki?"

But Sevron and his wolf were already storming away, having apparently had a gutful of the troublesome outsider. Ridian didn't mind; he was happy to see them go, and he entered the narrow canyon. It was dim and winding. Sheer, slick rock loomed on either side, with only a slice of sky far, far above. He followed it for some time, curiosity mounting.

Varki? Surely some sort of martial art, and about bloody time he learned something useful. Surely, Tann would be on the other side. Tann was his official teacher, after all, and Ridian well remembered his fighting skills upon The

Mire.

The canyon opened onto an expansive forest, though it appeared to be enclosed by a ring of mountains, much like Fidicia itself. A Sanctuary Forest, indeed. Just inside the forest was a clearing, and inside the clearing were a dozen or so kids in brown. They looked perhaps eight years old. They punched and kicked and pivoted in unison to some unheard beat, crying heartily with each strike.

Ridian approached with embarrassed disbelief. Sure, he'd never had formal martial arts training, but he'd been in his fair share of scraps and come out okay. Besides, he was twice the size of these kids. This was a joke. An attempt by that arsehole Sevron to hold him back and humiliate him.

A man in Grey strolled among them. He held his hands behind his back and frowned with displeasure as he shouted terse critiques. "Chin up. Stand straight. On your toes, not your heels...."

Ridian's heart turned to ice. It wasn't Tann but Lukas, the hostile youth who had held a knife to Ridian's throat and whipped him all the way to Fidicia. Lukas spotted Ridian and grinned with predatory glee.

Chapter 16

Lukas waved Ridian over, his manic grin stretching his taut, handsome face. Ridian approached warily, scanning for weapons. Lukas appeared unarmed, but he moved with a feline grace that suggested a deadly athleticism. His wolf was nowhere to be seen.

A boy in formation with the others passed in front of Lukas with a punch, punch, kick. Lukas scanned the boy with a quick down and up, then he grasped the child round the scruff of the neck. The boy cowered as Lukas hissed something in his ear, his face twisting in fury. The other children continued to punch, kick, and pivot in time, their eyes fixed ahead. A couple shot scared glances, and none dared intervene. Eventually, Lukas flung the boy back and smiled at Ridian. It made Ridian shiver.

Lukas gave two brief claps, and the children snapped to attention, silent as stones.

"Class," said Lukas with false cheer. "We have a special visitor, from far, far away. Ridian of Mudwall, would you come join me? Come, come, don't be shy."

Ridian approached, every instinct screaming for him to run.

"That's it," Lukas encouraged. "All the way. Now turn and

face the class."

Ridian obeyed, though he kept his eyes on the young warrior.

Lukas clapped a hand on Ridian's shoulder; Ridian flinched. "Class, Ridian is the latest outsider to join our school and learn our sacred ways." His fingers dug into Ridian with unnecessary pressure, though his smile was bright as sunshine. "He's also the reason I have the immense pleasure of teaching you this term. If it weren't for Ridian, I would be out in the field doing unimportant things like—oh, I don't know, furthering my career and bringing honour to my family. Everyone say, 'Thank you, Ridian.'" He said these last words in a high, sing-song tone.

The children repeated in a long drawling chorus.

Lukas frowned. "Oh, surely you can do better than that."

"Thank you, Ridian," the kids sang in joyless tones.

Lukas let go. Ridian released a breath, unaware he'd been holding it.

"Awfully big for an eight-year-old, isn't he?" Lukas chuckled. "You know the basics, of course. Don't you? Proper footwork? Correct posture? Right breathing?"

Ridian looked down and shook his head.

"You don't?" said Lukas with mock surprise. "Well, what do you know about Varki?"

Ridian's mouth was dry. "Nothing, really."

"What's that? Speak up." Lukas leaned forward and cupped his ear, his eyebrows raised in melodramatic curiosity, though he had clearly heard the first time.

Ridian fought to keep his voice even. "Nothing."

"Oh, of course you don't." Lukas' voice was sickly sweet. "As an outsider, you know nothing about our time-honoured martial tradition, sacred as the ground beneath our feet." Lukas tapped his chin. "Hmmm… How do I get you up to speed?" He then raised a finger with a sudden, bright idea. "I know, a demonstration! Any volunteers?"

There were none. The children stared at their feet, desperate not to catch his eye.

Lukas nodded at a boy. "You. The Mountain."

Immediately, the boy demonstrated an elaborate routine with high-sweeping kicks and impressive aerials. Part dance, part acrobatics, but with an unmistakable martial quality.

"Sloppy," said Lukas, "and keep your guard up or I'll whack you across the ears next time." He turned to Ridian. "Your turn."

Seriously? From a single viewing? A hundred demonstrations wouldn't be enough.

Ridian shook his head. "I can't."

Lukas turned to a girl. "You. River Flowing."

The girl gave a dazzling display, spinning and twirling with balance and poise.

Lukas looked at Ridian, a cruel invitation. "No?" He rounded on another boy. "You. Sunrise."

A boy leapt into another vigorous routine. Ridian missed it, too busy burning with humiliation.

Lukas' eyes glittered. "Well? What about the Sunrise? It's a basic sequence."

Ridian shook his head.

"Come on. Show us *something*."

Anger overtook fear, and the words that escaped Ridian were scolding hot. "I said, I don't know anything. Stop asking."

Lukas' smile soured, and his mask of friendliness fell away, fully revealing the seething hatred beneath. "Fine," he hissed. "A new lesson."

Ridian barely saw it coming; Lukas slapped Ridian's ears simultaneously with a tremendous *boom*. A loud ringing and a searing pain followed. With a cry, Ridian clutched his ears. He was dizzy and wobbly on his feet.

Lukas' voice cut through the high-pitched whine. "Thunderclap," he declared to the class. "It discombobulates, disorientates, and distracts. The three Ds. Hit hard enough, and it will perforate the eardrum." Lukas twirled, quick as a spinning top, and kicked Ridian's legs, causing him to fall hard upon his side.

"The Scythe," Lukas continued. "Not very powerful, but an effective takedown nonetheless." Lukas gripped Ridian's wrist and twisted, forcing Ridian to roll onto his stomach. Ridian felt Lukas' boot press against his back, crushing his chest and face into the dirt. Ridian's arm was then wrenched upwards, and his shoulder screamed in pain.

"The Water Pump is one of my favourites," said Lukas, bright with enthusiasm. "A submission hold rendering one's opponent completely helpless."

Groaning, Ridian tried to wriggle free.

"Stay still," said Lukas playfully, levering Ridian's arm a fraction, making the pain crescendo.

"Okay, okay," said Ridian in panic. If Lukas pushed even a quarter-inch, Ridian's arm would surely snap off at the shoulder.

"Good boy," Lukas cooed, releasing the pressure on Ridian's shoulder by one percent. "From this vantage, you can easily dislocate the shoulder, tear certain ligaments, and even fracture a few small bones. One small twist and…" Ridian heard a *pop* from Lukas, the old finger-in-the-mouth trick one learns as a child. "Off comes the shoulder. From here you could also break fingers, easy as kindling, easy as pie."

Ridian clenched his fist, but Lukas pried open his pinkie with ease, just like he said, and wrenched it backwards. There was a brief flare of pain, but Lukas soon let it go with a chuckle. "That's all for today," he said. "Class dismissed." His grip on Ridian's wrist remained, however. So did the pressure in his shoulder. So did the pain.

Straining, Ridian craned his head to look up. The kids were walking away, guilty-faced but walking all the same. Not a hero among them. Soon, Lukas and Ridian were alone.

Still twisting Ridian's elevated arm, Lukas knelt and hissed in Ridian's ear. His breath still stank of old eggs. "If it weren't for your stupid, slut sister, my brother would still be alive."

"What are you talking—" Agony flared from a slight twist of Ridian's wrist.

"I know you killed him, or at least your Kyrosian friend did."

He's going to do it, thought Ridian with horror. *He's going to break my arm.* "Lukas, I swear, I had—"

"Shut up!" Lukas twisted again, and Ridian cried out. "Your sister crossed the uncrossable Great Waste to meet a band of Kyrosian terrorists. It was orchestrated. Planned. Her actions speak for themselves. And *you...* You were right on their tail, eager to join them." He laughed, a bitter thing. "And we welcome you into our sanctuary, teach you our sacred ways, and share our holy secrets."

Lukas pushed Ridian's face into the dirt with a rough hand. The pressure in Ridian's shoulder mounted, creeping towards breaking point, and he waited for the inevitable *snap*. "Because of you, my wolf has abandoned me. Bonds are supposed to last for life. But the death of my brother has—has changed me, and now my own wolf won't even bond with me." The stink of old eggs was overwhelming. "Don't come back."

***

It took a long time for Ridian to return to the Thunderfells'. He took a slow, wandering path and quickly scurried upstairs while Kess was preoccupied with changing Ella's diaper. Exhausted and sore, he scanned his injuries. There were no marks, no bruises. Nothing to prove Lukas' cruelty. Was that intentional?

He felt defeated. None of his training seemed useful in his quest to become a Knight. Meditation was a waste of time, potty cleaning was pointless, and Lukas had no intention of imparting anything but pain. And Tann? Tann had abandoned him, which was exactly what Ridian deserved.

Theodor's voice rang through the house. "Dinner time!"

Rushing feet thumped from every corner of the house towards the dinner table: Kai's quick strides, Ollie's slow clanking, Feya's deft footfalls.

"Ridian?" called Theodor from downstairs. "It's getting cold…"

"Thanks, but I'm not very hungry," called Ridian.

There was a moment of silence, then muffled voices

and the tinkling of cutlery. Soon, the stairs creaked from Theodor's plodding footfalls, then a little *rat-tat* on Ridian's door.

"Can I come in?" asked Theodor.

"Sure," said Ridian from where he sat on the bed.

Theodor backed into the room carrying a tray of food. "Thought you might prefer eating in bed." Theodor stopped to give Ridian a speculative look-over. "You okay?"

"Yeah." The lie came easy. It even sounded true.

Theodor's mouth went to form a question, but he bit it off and instead laid the tray on the bed. The tray was fully laden: a goblet of mead, grilled trout with a garnish of lemon and dill, roast pumpkin, roast onion, honey-glazed carrots, and a hot loaf with dipping oil. There was also a strange dark bar.

"Chocolate," said Theodor, handing it to Ridian on its small dish. "Special treat all the way from the Horoc Desert. A bit naughty before dinner, but no one need know. Besides, we're celebrating."

"Celebrating what?"

Theodor looked surprised. "Why, your first day, of course."

"Oh." Ridian was stunned. He had no words.

Theodor nodded at the chocolate and gazed expectantly at Ridian. "Go on. Try some."

Feeling awkward, Ridian picked up the strange dark bar and took a bite. It was sweet, creamy, delicious.

Theodor sat on the bed with a sigh, looking serious as he stared at the wall. "First days can be... Well, first days can be downright miserable, to be honest. I remember mine. Homesick, a million miles from home. I remember thinking

I should run away, go home, and give Mum a hug." He gave a little chuckle. "Of course, she would have given me a smacked bottom and an earful, but a smacked bottom and an earful from my mum seemed better than not seeing her at all. I missed her for the longest time… miss her still, truth tell." Theodor turned his kind eyes upon Ridian. "Look, Ridian. I don't really know what you're going through. But I can see you're in a strange world, fighting for a chance to prove yourself and save your sister. You must be under enormous pressure, and I just wanted you to know that I'm here for you if you want to talk—or even if you don't."

To Ridian's horror, a sudden lump formed in his throat. He looked away, bit his lip, and frowned furiously to compose himself. What was happening? What the hell was wrong with him? The chocolate was melting in his fingers, and he took a nibble. Anything to distract himself. "More of this chocolate would help," he managed to say.

Theodor laughed. "Cheeky devil." And like that, the lump in Ridian's throat sank safely back down to where his sadness and anxiety lay permanently lodged in his chest.

"Why don't you come downstairs," said Theodor. "You don't have to talk if you don't want to, and I bet *my* block of chocolate that you'll feel better."

With more chocolate on the line, Ridian followed Theodor downstairs. Everyone was there: Kess was trying to shove spoonfuls of food into a defiant, food-splattered Ella; Felix nibbled cheese; Zeke perched in the rafters; and Feya, Ollie, and Kai cheered and thumped the table as Ridian descended.

There were pats on Ridian's back and earnest words of encouragement from all. Even the timid Felix scampered over to give Ridian's hand an affectionate lick. He thanked them bashfully, and soon enough, banter bounced around the table. Ridian listened along, enjoying his food in silence.

Chapter 17

Ridian's second day started the same as the first. An early wake-up, a rattling cart trip, and then Stonecrow Cavern. After a lesson that largely went over Ridian's head, Mother Asarah dismissed the other Novices, and they sat side-by-side before the seven-foot raven statue. Candles flickered before them, and as Mother Asarah remained quiet and still, Ridian presumed he should meditate upon one—and did. The flame, orange at first glance, proved to be composed of every shade of white, blue, orange, and red. Smoke curled towards the hanging stalactites in intricate, twirling, ever-changing patterns. The wick pulled wax with the slow grace of the moon. A long time passed. The green glowing Mural wall faded, and Ridian learned the meaning of boredom.

"What gives a Soulcaster strength?" said Mother Asarah at last in her weak, crackling voice that broke the eternal quiet.

Ridian had no idea.

Mother Asarah turned to look at him. "Rava."

Rava? Ridian had never heard of it.

"But Rava is not exclusive to Soulcasters. No. Rava is the life force that flows through all living things. In fact, Rava can be thought of as Life itself. Rava keeps us breathing, keeps our hearts beating, helps us grow, helps us heal. A spark of Rava creates life within a mother's womb. Its flow sustains us throughout our life, and when it leaves, we die. Understand?"

"Rava is life," said Ridian cautiously.

"In humans," Mother Asarah continued, "Rava saturates our brains, granting us high intelligence. In predatory animals, Rava preferences the body—the muscles, the bones, the tendons. That is why they tend to be faster, stronger, and hardier than us. Soulcasters, however, are special. We draw Rava from a Familiar and infuse *our* bodies with Rava, making *us* strong. However, as we draw, we also donate, granting our Familiar some level of intelligence." Mother Asarah smiled at Ridian's apparent confusion. "Let me explain. Soulcasting involves the mutual transference of Rava: from Soulcaster to Familiar. The Soulcaster imparts intelligence; the beast donates strength, and so the two complement each other. Understand?"

"I think so," said Ridian, the strange ideas clicking into place. "Rava makes humans smart and animals strong. But Soulcasters can make themselves strong and a Familiar smart."

Mother Asarah nodded, satisfied. "Very good. Now close your eyes and meditate upon the smells in this sacred room."

Ridian groaned internally.

***

Potty cleaning was just as bad as the first day, and, somehow, Lukas was even worse. Though Ridian dreaded it all day, he somehow showed up, determined to stress his innocence.

189

But Lukas didn't listen. He just smiled his nasty smile and proceeded to teach pressure points, called Meridians, that could render extreme pain if struck. Ridian learnt five Meridians that day: the Solar Plexus, both floating ribs, the navel, and the liver. He learnt them well, gasping and twitching on the floor as pain radiated in all-consuming waves. He learned more the next day and more the day after. There were dozens apparently, and Lukas knew them all. Sometimes, the pain lingered for minutes, sometimes hours, and sometimes days. But never any marks. It was strangely comforting; it suggested Lukas was not allowed to mistreat Ridian. If he were, he would have left marks. Lukas was the sort that would, given the chance.

Ridian's fourth day was particularly painful. Lukas demonstrated how all the joints, from head to toe, could be manipulated into awkward angles and pushed to their end range of motion. Lukas always gave Ridian a squirming, flailing attempt to defend himself, relishing Ridian's pathetic efforts.

"See, class," he would say. "See how easily I took control. And if he tries to wriggle away…" Some twist, squeeze, or pull would follow, and Ridian would need to bite his lip to stop from crying out. Sometimes, he still did.

And no Tann. Ridian asked around, but no one had seen him. Maybe Tann was keeping tabs on him from afar? Maybe it was all part of some elaborate test of resolve? Maybe he was giving Ridian a taste of his own medicine? Whatever the reason, Ridian couldn't stop his training, such as it was. It wasn't useful, but what else could he do.

And despite his frustrations, Ridian did learn some things about Soulcasting. He learnt Familiars were exclusively predators. Apparently, prey animals were too skittish temperamentally to enable a bond. He learnt that a Soulcaster rarely had more than one Familiar. "It would be like having more than one wife," said Theodor with a twinkle in his eye, loud enough for Kess to hear. "They would all get jealous, and you'd be left with no Familiar." Ridian also learned that Sanctuary Forest was, indeed, a vast mountain-bound sanctuary where Soulcasters roamed in search of Familiars. Ridian asked Mother Asarah if he should be searching, but she shook her head. "Without the ability to Split, your wanderings would be in vain. Focus on your meditations."

Of Tinker, Basher and Sneak, Ridian learnt nothing. This was the most frustrating thing of all. He asked about them frequently, but people either didn't know or wouldn't say. Kai, being a Knight, had the most information. Apparently the three Kyrosians were being interrogated daily, but had thus far kept their mouths shut. It was vexing in the extreme—they knew what was going on with Rayna—but at least Kai promised to tell Ridian if they spilled the beans.

To his relief, Ridian had no more bizarre nightmares or hallucinations, and his fears of going insane subsided. The silver wolf was just a dream, he decided, and with each passing day, he became more convinced.

Lessons with Mother Asarah, potty cleaning at the hospital, and Varki training with Lukas. Those three tasks filled his days, while dinner with the Thunderfells filled his evenings. The food and company were always superb, and he became accustomed to each of them and the role they played in the family. Theodor was the doting, pampering father. Kess was the necessary disciplinarian, earning her the title of 'Tyrant Queen,' a title she was very fond of. Charismatic and outrageous, Kai got the most attention and the most laughs. However, he was also the prime target of cutting, depreciating jokes—something Feya excelled at. She would wait quietly on the edge of the conversation until the opportune moment and then lash Kai with her stinging wit. Ollie provided ample enthusiasm. Ella made mess, cried, and giggled, to the delight of all.

Ridian contributed little to the conversation, but they seemed to like him anyway. It was weird but nice. Not being treated like a Caveborn freak on the edge of madness was certainly a pleasant change.

One night, however, Ridian piped up at the dinner table, "Who is Hector?"

Everyone went silent, and all eyes turned to Theodor and Kess. Theodor's smile faded, and he became very concerned with his food. It was Kess who answered, though she wiped Ella's mouth with excessive care, not looking at Ridian. "Hector was a Kyrosian General who started the Last Soulcaster War." Spoons scraped along bowls, water was gulped, and the wind whined through a crack in the window. Thankfully, someone changed the subject, then somebody made a joke, and the awkward moment that Ridian didn't understand passed. He didn't ask again.

***

After a week in Fidicia, Ridian had an unexpected encounter in the hospital. He was on the fourth level in Paediatrics, crouching to retrieve a potty from beneath a bed, when a young voice said, "Hey, Ridian."

Ollie was sitting on the bed, red-faced with embarrassment. He had a book in hand and a dozen scattered on the bed. "Sorry."

"Oh, no, that's okay," said Ridian awkwardly. He placed the potty on top of the reeking pile stacked in his wheelbarrow.

"Worst job," said Ollie. "But you'll get other jobs soon enough. Every now and then, they get me to do it, but I'm too slow, and I dropped too many. After a while, they got sick of it and gave me something else to do. Can't even clean poo properly." He smiled at his own joke, but he seemed off, somehow.

Ridian jerked his thumb at the potty pile. "You saying if I drop these, I get to do a different job?" He edged towards the wheelbarrow and made a show of tipping it over.

Ollie grinned. "Careful, they might just give you more practice."

Paediatrics was a long room with beds lining one wall, each with its own window. There were only three other kids. Two were unconscious, and the third writhed on his bed, groaning as he hugged his belly. A Steward fussed over the boy.

"What are you doing here?" asked Ridian. "You okay?"

"Me? Yeah, I'm fine. I've been having these weird spells. That's all."

Ridian felt a familiar sinking sensation. The same feeling he got whenever Rayna's health took a turn. Ollie was even doing the same dismissive, minimising strategy Rayna employed. "What do you mean, weird spells?"

"It's nothing to worry about. I just get a bit dizzy and a bit confused and sometimes I forget where I am and what I'm doing. But it only lasts a few moments. It's not a big deal, but they still make me come in, do a bunch of tests, and try some new disgusting potion. It's so annoying. Nothing ever works and it doesn't exactly help my case with Sevron."

Ridian frowned. "Sevron?"

"Didn't you know? He won't let me learn Varki."

"Why?" But even as Ridian said it, he glanced at Ollie's bandy legs, hidden beneath the blanket.

Ollie saw. "You guessed it," he said, rapping his metal braces with a knuckle. "Apparently, there's no point learning to fight when I can't even walk properly, even though he's been told my legs will *eventually* straighten themselves out. Mum and Dad think Sevron's just excluding me because I'm an outsider like my brother and sisters."

"People think you're an outsider?" asked Ridian. Kai and Feya looked foreign. But Ollie was fair like the rest of the Fidicians he'd seen.

"Well, Kai is part Horocian, the desert people from the south. Feya is part Wrathwoli, the nomadic tribe that roam the Wrathwolds in the north. And I'm part Ottish, the lake-dwelling folk in the west. Thankfully, we were born in Tor, otherwise we might never have been accepted into the Fidician Order, even though we have Torian blood."

"But you're all Soulcasters, right?" Only Soulcasters were accepted into the Fidician order, Ridian knew.

"Yes, but there's one line from Fidic's Sacred Words that people argue over." Ollie gazed upward as he recalled the words. "I think it's, 'A Soulcaster must belong to Tor completely—body, mind, and soul—lest his heart and cloak be turned'. Some think this means only full-blooded Torians belong. Others think being born here is enough. Mum and

Dad think both ideas are stupid. Belonging is more than just birth or blood, Dad always says. If you moved home, your heart would follow." Ollie shook his head. "Anyway, that one line has caused us a lot of trouble. It's why Kai isn't allowed out in the field, though he's a full-fledged Knight. It's why Feya's fighting skills are discounted, and it's why I can't train Varki at all."

That's why Sevron was so reluctant to accept me, thought Ridian. *I'm the biggest outsider of them all.*

"It's also probably why I don't have many friends," Ollie blurted, then fiddled with his book, embarrassed.

Ridian didn't know what to say. The way Ollie said 'many' sounded like 'none' to him. Suddenly, Ollie's books seemed more than just the obvious interest of a boy with weak legs. Perhaps they offered an escape, somewhere to belong.

"Friends are overrated," said Ridian at last. "You don't need friends when you have family."

Ollie narrowed his eyes sceptically. "What makes you say that?"

"Because I don't have any friends either." Ridian was surprised how easily the truth came out.

"Really?" asked Ollie in wonder.

"Really."

"None?"

"None."

Ollie grinned. "So, we're both losers?"

Ridian laughed. "Seems so."

"I'll make you a deal," said Ollie, back to his enthusiastic baseline. "I'll be your friend if you'll be mine."

Ridian made a show of deliberation; he frowned, stroked his chin, and sucked his teeth. "Hmmm… seems like you're getting an awfully good deal. What do I get out of this?"

"Come on. You're just as desperate as I am, admit it."

"Fine," said Ridian, and he shook Ollie's hand. "But you should probably know I have poo on my hands."

Ollie tore his hand away. "Yuck! You're gross."

Ridian trundled his cart away with a grin. "We're both gross."

Chapter 18

The next morning, Ridian was awake and ready before Theodor even crept up the stairs to wake him. He was neither excited nor nervous. It was just routine. This was life now, and if he stopped to think, he just got nervous. So he got up and went.

Sleet lashed them as the cart trundled them up the hill to the Living Fort. Ridian wrapped his cloak tight about his chin, yet the freezing slush still found a way to trickle in. A blue-lipped Ollie shivered; Feya looked miserable; even Theodor was less than his usual ecstatic self. At least Stonecrow Cavern was dry. Nonetheless, Mother Asarah, who appeared to have a dozen layers on, dismissed the class and gave Ridian a brief instruction to meditate on the sound of running water before hurrying off to find a warmer venue.

Shivering, Ridian couldn't even hear the water at first. It was only when everyone else had left, and he strained his ears that he heard the faintest trace of it. Maybe he just imagined it. Either way, it was boring, and he soon amused himself by dripping droplets of hot candle wax onto the stone floor. His little wax tower was over two inches high when a familiar voice startled him. "Using your time productively, I see."

It was Tann, beard trimmed, striped black-and-white hair clean and neat about his shoulders. He'd even filled out a bit. He looked less like a corpse and more like the hardened poacher Ridian remembered. He wore the Grey of a Fidician Knight, and though he smirked, he didn't seem happy to see Ridian.

A tense energy filled the chamber. Ridian knew he should say something. His reasons for abandoning Tann? No, that would just piss Tann off. An apology? *Sorry for leaving you to die?* But that didn't sound very good. Instead, to his horror, he blurted, "Where have you been?"

"Oh, talking raven help me," said Tann, rolling his eyes. "You sound like my old girlfriend. Well, if you must know, I've been visiting old friends—the few I have anyway—trying to convince them to come on a suicide mission with me." He sighed. "There weren't many takers."

"So, you'll take me?" asked Ridian eagerly.

Tann scoffed. "I agreed to train you, not take you."

"You said—"

"I know what I said," said Tann sharply.

Ridian swallowed. Yes, Tann was pissed off alright.

"Look," said Tann with forced calm. "If you become a Knight *and* impress me before spring, basically if you're a prodigy, then maybe." Tann pinched the bridge of his nose. "I really am desperate, aren't I?"

"Thank you. I really appreciate you giving me a chance."

"Don't get me wrong. I'm not being nice. I agreed to train you because I'm interested in killing Hector and foiling his plans. But I don't know his plans. So, if I can uncover whatever magic lies within you, then maybe I can better understand your sister, and if I can understand her, then maybe I can understand Hector's plans. That's what I care about. I'm not doing this for you."

A massive silence swelled between them.

"Either way," said Ridian. "Thanks."

"You won't be thanking me soon. I'm Kyrosian, and our methods are…" Tann smiled, eyes glittering with dark amusement. "Let's just say there's a reason why our hair turns prematurely white." Tann turned and strode away. "Come. Your real training starts now."

Stomach knotted, Ridian followed Tann out of the hospital, out the gates, across the meadow, and down the hill. It was still sleeting, and Tann marched in front with silent determination beneath the bleak sky. Partway down the hill, Tann took a muddy trail that left the road. It wound between Valarian Firetrees and boulders, before climbing upwards again. By now, water had crept into Ridian's shoes, freezing his toes numb.

"Where're we going?" asked Ridian, clambering over a large, waist-high root.

"You'll see," said Tann, and they soon hit the mountain at a secluded point.

Yanala waited for them, alive and well after apparently guiding the enslaved women of Mirecross Castle back to Mudwall. The wolf gazed menacingly at Ridian.

Does the wolf know I left Tann? From the wolf's demeanour, it certainly seemed so.

An unusual structure loomed over Yanala. It looked like a giant stone bridge, stretching east all the way across the valley. The wolf stood beneath the shelter of one stone arch, but there were hundreds supporting the structure.

"What is that?" asked Ridian.

"An aqueduct," said Tann. "Carries water out of Fidicia. Daegan's work. Amazing what a giant and a dedicated team of Soulcasters can accomplish."

Why? There appeared to be no shortage of water.

They marched through the stone arch and up a crumbling, rocky path between mountain bluffs. Yanala bounded ahead, while Tann and Ridian clambered behind. Slick, unsettled stones rocked beneath their feet, and Ridian treaded warily to avoid rolling an ankle. As they climbed, the sound of falling water grew until it became a near-deafening roar.

Finally, they entered a cylindrical place—circular rock walls rose on all sides, save the narrow entrance they'd just entered. Water burst from a hole high up in the rock wall and plunged into the frothing, churning plunge pool before them. A waist-high, man-made stone wall ringed the basin and directed it towards a tunnel. Miniscule water droplets peppered Ridian, and he shivered anew, clinging to his waterlogged cloak though it gave him no warmth.

"Madman's Falls," said Tann over the roar.

Despite the freezing cold, Ridian was thirsty, and he leant over the man-made wall to scoop a handful of water.

Tann snatched Ridian's wrist, his grip vice-like. "Are you stupid? Why do you think it's called Madman's Falls? The water's poisonous. It's the same water that drove Kyros' army insane all those years ago."

"You're hurting me."

Tann let go hesitantly, ready to snatch again if need be. "You can get away with a few drops, a sprinkling. But not a mouthful. The dose makes the poison, as they say. You'd go mad as a flaming rat. Trust me. I've seen what this stuff can do. You'd go bat-shit, toys in the attic, crazy. Crazy and violent. Not a good mix."

Water continued to thunder into the roiling cauldron, along the narrow channel, then into the tunnel. Without the redirection, the water would have spilled down the path they had just taken. The aqueduct made perfect sense now. It carried the poisonous water out of the Fidician Valley.

Ridian raised his hands. "No drinking. Got it."

Tann relaxed. "Okay, let's get down to business. There's no training manual for preternaturally gifted Ardens, so I'm just going to train you as a Soulcaster and see what happens. Remember your Awakening? Remember Splitting from your body?"

Ridian nodded, eager to appear eager.

"Well, that was a fluke," said Tann. "You need to learn to Split at will."

"Through focusing my mind, right?"

Tann snorted. "I respect Mother Asarah, but meditation takes years. I've got a more better way." He gestured at the foaming water. "Jump in and hold your breath."

"In the crazy crackpot water?" asked Ridian.

"Just keep your mouth shut. And yes, I mean that both ways."

Ridian wiped his cold, dripping nose. "But it's freezing."

"That's the other reason why I waited a few days to train you. For winter to properly set in." Tann grinned. "Makes this exercise more worthwhile."

"But what's the point?"

"To teach you."

"Teach me what?"

"Water first, lesson later."

Ridian glared at the man. Was this training or petty revenge? "I'm not going in there."

"Then have a nice life." Tann turned to walk away.

"Wait!" Ridian groaned. "Fine."

Shivering, Ridian undressed down to his small clothes, and flecks of slushy snow landed on his goose-fleshed skin. He removed the Elderflower necklace and placed it atop his clothes. Tann stared at it as if he still couldn't believe it. Then, trembling all over, Ridian sat on the wall and dipped a toe in the water.

"Lost gods and Sun Above!" said Ridian, pulling his foot away. "The water should be frozen solid."

"Something in the poison allows the water to drop below freezing temperature," said Tann with something akin to glee. "Interesting, huh?"

"Most intriguing," said Ridian, seething as he lingered on the wall. *Come on, Ridian. You can do this. Just don't think about it.* Ridian eased a leg into the pool. His body screamed at him, but he willed it deeper, then another leg. *Don't think about it. Don't think about it.* He sank forward, panting furiously, and instantly fell chest deep. Ridian gasped. "Is that enough?"

Tann pointed. "Head under and hold your breath."

Groaning, Ridian counted to three, stalled, counted again, then plunged—

His head exploded with cold, the thunder of Madman's Falls booming in his ears. He tried to distract himself, imagining he was far away, somewhere warm, somewhere dry—but failed. He tried to think of nothing and failed. His lungs were being crushed. They screamed for air. He couldn't take it anymore. He shot up, gasped, and dragged himself over the wall, a quivering mess.

"I told you to hold your breath," said Tann.

"I—I d-d-did." Ridian's teeth were chattering like a shaken bag of walnuts, and his fitful breath came out in a fog.

"Then why did you get up?"

"I ran out of air."

"No, you didn't."

Ridian glared. "I did. And it was too bloody cold."

"No. You just think it was. Your body is *way* stronger than that."

"What's this got to do with Soulcasting?!"

"Everything!" Tann picked up a leaf, threw it in the churning water, and gestured at it. "This is you." The leaf spun about the whirlpools and eddies, before being sucked towards the cascading water and buried in the turbulence. Moments later, it popped up, only to be pulled back towards the falls and dragged down again. "You are weak-willed, tossed about by every frivolous thought and emotion. You shirk effort and avoid pain. Soulcasting requires willpower and a bloody backbone. You have neither. You're softer than a floating, week-old turd."

The words stung. Ridian was wet, shivering, and half-naked, but he still had his pride.

"Soulcasting," said Tann, "involves Splitting your soul from your body. Think about it. When else does your soul leave your body?"

There was only one answer. "When you die."

Tann nodded gravely. "Yes, and believe me, Splitting feels every bit like dying. Every impulse, emotion, and instinct will be binding your soul to your body. Existential fear will tether you. The desire for self-preservation will tether you."

Tann foraged around, found a stick, and threw it in. "Remember: fear is the gate, pain is the key." The stick floated, and for a few moments, it seemed like it would drift towards the falls like the leaf, but it got caught in the current, zoomed along the channel, and passed into the tunnel and out of sight. "To unleash your soul, you must embrace pain and face your deepest fears. To become a Soulcaster, you must be willing to die."

***

Ridian submerged beneath Madman's Falls more than a dozen times that morning. He tried and tried, desperate to develop the willpower Tann said he lacked. But it was never enough. No matter how long he remained immersed beneath the bone-chilling water, Tann kept shaking his head and saying 'Again.'

Eventually, Tann said he could have a break, and by 'break,' he meant backbreaking exercise. There was a steep, thousand-step staircase around the corner and thousands of melon-sized stones lining the dry, unused riverbed. Ridian's task was simple: carry stones to the top. But if he didn't go fast enough, Yanala would bite his backside—not enough to draw blood but stinging as any whip. The exercise burned his arms and legs like Sunfire, and his back ached. "Fear is the Gate. Pain is the Key," was all Tann said whenever Ridian complained.

Finally, when Ridian collapsed, Tann called him to stop. "That's enough for today," he said, lounging upon a patch of grass at the top of the staircase.

Ridian was too tired to respond. He fell upon the grass, indifferent to the gorgeous view. Surely, he'd developed the necessary willpower. Surely, he'd endured enough pain. *Surely*.

"Up you get," said Tann, nudging Ridian's ribs with a toe. "You've finished training for today, but you still have work to do."

"Work?" replied Ridian in horror. "What do you mean?"

"Chamber pots don't clean themselves."

Chapter 19

Ridian was very sore the next day. That didn't stop Tann from pushing him harder, however, and it didn't stop him the day after, either. Tann was unrelenting. Each day was a bit harder and more painful than the previous. Ridian gave the submersions and the exercise his all, and if Tann was impressed, he didn't show it.

"How's training going?" asked Theodor across the table one night.

Hungry, tired, and sore beyond belief, Ridian felt like a battered lump of meat. He pulled a face.

Theodor chuckled. "That bad, huh? Well, Tann is a bit of a—what would you say?"

A sadist? Hard-arse? Ball-breaker?

"Tann's a product of his environment," said Kess delicately. "And Kyrosia is a hard place."

The next afternoon, he finished collecting the chamber pots in record time. The hospital, initially a maze, was yielding its secret passageways and shortcuts, becoming familiar. Hands clean and dry, he dragged his feet to Varki Training, the usual dread sitting in his guts. It was a windy grey afternoon. *At least it's not raining.*

Ridian had expressed his displeasure regarding Lukas

to Tann, but his master had dismissed Ridian's complaints outright. "Fear is the gate, pain is the key," Tann had said irritably. "How many times do I have to tell you? Besides, I hear Lukas is an excellent fighter. Apply yourself and stop whinging."

Partway through the narrow canyon leading to Sanctuary Forest, Ridian saw Ollie and Feya up ahead and ran to catch up. "Where are you guys heading?"

Feya beamed. "Dad just got permission for Ollie to start Varki Training. We only found out an hour ago." She nudged Ollie with an elbow. "He'll be picking fights soon."

Ollie smiled, but he looked a little pale.

Ridian looked at Ollie: the glasses, the awkward posture, the bowed legs held together with metal and leather. Lukas would tear him apart.

Feya must have mistaken Ridian's concern. "He's entitled, same as everybody else," she said sternly, sticking out her chin.

"Of course," said Ridian. "I'm just surprised he wasn't training already."

Feya relaxed. "I know. Sevron's a right prick for holding him back all this time."

Ollie wrung his hands. "He was just being cautious."

"No," said Feya. "He was just being a massive arsehole."

They were the first to arrive at the clearing.

"Fey, you'd better go," said Ollie, removing his glasses self-consciously and hiding them in a pocket. "Before the rest get here."

"But I want to watch and see what you've got." She threw a few pretend jabs at him.

Ollie looked mortified. "Having an older sister babysit

you, no matter how well-intentioned, is social suicide."

Feya scoffed. "Kai said that, didn't he?"

"No. Well, yes, but Fey, please. I stand out as it is."

"Okay, okay," said Feya, backing away. "Good luck, little brother. Proud of you." She left, and Ollie relaxed somewhat. Ridian was also relieved. Being tormented by Lukas in the kids' class was embarrassing enough. He didn't need the added humiliation of Feya watching. As she left, the other kids arrived in twos and threes.

Squinting at the kids he could barely see, Ollie shuffled closer to Ridian. "Can I—um—train with you?"

"Yeh, no problem," said Ridian.

Then Lukas arrived. The children's bright chatter died, and they quickly formed into neat rows. Ollie was slow to form rank, his clanking, shuffling strides ringing out.

Lukas pointed a stern finger at Ollie. "You. Here. Now," he demanded.

As Ollie clanked his way to the front, kids glanced at each other, and some sniggered.

Little brats.

"And who might you be?" asked Lukas. Ridian couldn't see Ollie's face, but his posture gave the impression of a field mouse standing before a tabby cat.

"Oliver Thunderfell, Master Lukas. You—you know me, sir."

"What are you doing here?"

"Um… Master Sevron said I could—"

"Do you have written permission?"

"Um… No."

"Then go get it."

"But—but Master Sevron…"

"If you don't have written permission, you can't stay."

Ollie hesitated, glanced self-consciously behind him, then ran as best as he could through the rows of kids. He wasn't crying, but he was close.

Ridian burned with anger. Before now, Ridian hadn't liked Lukas, but he had understood him. Lukas believed Ridian had colluded in his brother's death, and, instead of justice, received clemency and an honoured position in a sacred rite. From his perspective, of course Lukas tormented Ridian. But now Ridian saw Lukas in a new light. Lukas was a self-righteous, puritanical, elitist arsehole. Anger blazed within Ridian like a fan-flamed furnace.

Lukas smiled his nasty smile. "Let's start with some light sparring. Everybody, pair up." He descended upon Ridian.

Not today, thought Ridian, clenching his fists. *Today, I'm going to wipe that smile right off your stupid, smug face.* Ridian planned it out. He would pretend to cower, then step forward pre-emptively and surprise Lukas with a punch, right in the mouth. He would have to make it up from there. But it would involve Ridian's knuckles pulverising Lukas' pretty face. Lukas was almost within range. Almost… almost…

Lukas kicked Ridian squarely between the legs. Pain exploded, and Ridian collapsed, curling into a ball.

"The groin, of course, is a very vulnerable area," Lukas declared to the class.

Ridian's eyes were shut, but he could imagine the kids' expressions: appalled, fearful, and yet grateful it wasn't them twitching on the ground, hands between their legs.

Lukas tugged Ridian up by the nostrils with a pair of cruel, hooked fingers. "Up you get." Then Ridian felt Lukas' arm close around his throat in an iron chokehold. Blood rushed to his face. He couldn't breathe. He clawed. He kicked. All useless; Lukas had complete control. Ridian tried to relax. Soon—any second now—Lukas would let go. But the grip held fast, and Ridian's vision began to blacken around the edges. The edges constricted, constricted, constricted…

***

"…kay?" Feya was gazing down at him. Her face and hair covered the entire sky.

"Huh?"

"I said, are you okay?"

Ridian sat up, dizzy and disoriented. His groin still radiated pain; he mustn't have blacked out for long. Indeed, Lukas was there, and there was the class. "Yeah, fine."

"What's going on? I came to sneak a peek at Ollie's first lesson, and he runs past crying his eyes out, and then I see you being choked."

Ridian massaged his sore throat. "I've had worse."

"This isn't the first time he's hurt you?"

Ridian laughed grimly, then stopped as a wave of pain hit him.

Feya turned to glare at Lukas. "Sevron will hear of this."

Lukas gave an infuriating shrug. "By all means, tell him."

Feya helped Ridian up. "Come, let's go."

"No," said Ridian, staggering and holding Feya's arm for balance. "I should stay."

"No way. We need to go and make a formal complaint. For you and for Ollie."

"No." Ridian let her arm go. "Complain for Ollie, not for

210

me."

"What? Why?"

"Fear is the gate. Pain is the Key." The words came out automatically, and Feya looked confused. "Never mind," said Ridian. "Tann's orders."

Feya looked shocked. "There's no way Tann would allow this."

"Tann said I have to apply myself with Lukas. Please, don't tell anyone."

"And allow Lukas to get away with hurting you?"

Ridian looked at Lukas, who strolled with an air of nonchalance. "Afraid so."

"And how are you supposed to pass the Trials getting your arse kicked like this?"

"I don't know," Ridian admitted.

Feya chewed her lip and stared into the distance. "I do. You're going to need a proper teacher."

"Who?"

"Me."

***

"Outrageous!" said a fuming Theodor at the dinner table that night. "How dare Lukas exclude Ollie? We've petitioned for months and months. We've done all the right things. And just when we were granted permission—which is just ridiculous to begin with—that impetuous little son of a…"

Kess laid a firm hand on Theodor's arm, though her eyes burned hot as coals.

Grumbling, Theodor grabbed a loaf and tore it in half. Kai made a cough that sounded just like 'prick,' and Feya muttered 'Lick-Ass Lukas' under her breath. Ollie appeared disengaged as he spoon-fed Ella.

"Aren't you angry?" Kai asked Ollie. "We need Sevron's signature and he's buggered off for a few weeks. Maybe even months."

Ollie shrugged, giving no eye contact. "Lukas was just being careful, I guess."

Everyone erupted in outrage.

"It's unacceptable."

"He has no right."

"He'd better be careful."

"Guys," snapped Ollie. "Can we talk about something else?"

Ella began crying, and Ollie bounced her on his knee to calm her, while everyone else exchanged glances.

"Ridian," said Theodor, looking for a conversation starter. "How was Varki for you?"

Ridian didn't look at Feya, and he could feel her not looking at him.

"No one can know that I'm training you," Feya had said earlier that day. "No one. If they find out a Novice is teaching another Novice, we're screwed. The Order takes unauthorised teaching very seriously. Even sparring outside formal practice is forbidden."

Feya went on to explain that Varki was a great secret. Street gangs, highwaymen, common thieves, and other miscreants would all pay a premium to learn the martial art. Therefore, only full-fledged Fidician Knights had the authority to teach it, and even then, only in formal classes.

"No one can know," she kept saying. "Best case scenario, they'd expel us."

"Would they still let me do the Trials?"

Feya just snorted.

Stakes being what they were, Ridian agreed to Feya's clandestine plan.

After dinner, when everyone had gone to bed, Ridian lay awake, waiting for sounds of life to die throughout the house. After about an hour, Ridian heard a twitter outside his window. Sure enough, Feya hid in the shadow of a tree as promised. A minute later, they were climbing the hill. Late as it was, they saw no one. Still, whenever Ridian inadvertently snapped a stick underfoot Feya would shush him furiously with a finger to her lips, and she would check up and down the road. Feya's own feather-light footfalls were utterly silent.

They crested the hill, passed Hero's Tree, and marched through the canyon into Sanctuary Forest. They crossed over the clearing and followed a trail that wound through the forest. A minute later, the ground sank into a wide crater, covered with a thick fog.

"We made it," said Feya, finally relaxing. "We should be safe here."

Ridian agreed, though he thought Feya was a little paranoid. "What is this place?"

"Lover's Hollow. Apparently, couples come down here to canoodle." She smiled at him, then panic flared in her eyes, and she looked away, leaving Ridian to squirm.

They descended through the fog, climbing over fallen tree trunks and skirting towering boulders. Around the rim of the hollow were caverns. It was eerily quiet, save for the occasional hoot of an owl. In a small triangular-shaped clearing, between a boulder and two fallen trees, Feya turned to face Ridian. "I have only one simple rule," she said. "No whinging, whining, or excuses."

"That's three rules."

"And no sass-mouthing," Feya added.

"Four rules. Got it."

Feya raised her eyebrows in warning. "We can go straight back home if you like?"

"No, no. I'm listening. I'm just—you sure you want to stay up late and sneak around to train me? All for my sake?"

Feya smiled. "I've been sneaking up here to train for years. It's no accident I'm the best fighter in the school." She then assumed a stern expression and coughed to clear her throat. "Let's begin. People forget where Varki comes from. It is very old. Developed by a Torian slave who disguised it as dance." She leapt light-footed into the air, twirled, and landed gracefully. "Allowing him to practice and even perform before his Arden masters to avoid suspicion. And though Varki looked like dance, it hid secret martial power." Feya leapt again, repeating the movement, only this time she emphasised the twirling leg—a vicious kick.

"Runaway slaves were outnumbered and often unarmed. Thus, Varki emphasises constant motion. A fight stops when a fighter stops, as they say. Therefore, a slave would slip, slide, dodge, and dart without pause. The hardest target is the moving target. But more than that, the hardest target is the one that misleads, fools, and tricks..." Feya dashed at Ridian and made a dozen strikes with fist and feet, but each was merely a feint, allowing her to slide this way and that.

"And of course, an unarmed slave should remain out

of range, except when *they* decide to strike. And when they strike, strike only once—quickly and decisively. *One strike is better than two*, as they say." Feya kicked out unexpectedly, her foot whooshing past Ridian's nose. She finished her pirouette, slow and controlled, coming to a standstill. "These are the three core principles of Varki." She counted off with a finger. "Constant motion, deception, and decisive attack. Say it with me."

"Constant motion, deception, and decisive attack," they said together.

Ridian was thrilled. He was finally learning something useful, and Feya clearly knew her stuff.

"Look at me," said Feya. "I'm not big, I'm not strong, I'm not even that quick. And if I tried to fight someone bigger or taller or quicker—on their terms—I wouldn't stand a chance. So, I play to my strengths—to my flawless form, my perfect timing, and my deep knowledge of the art. You will have none of these advantages, so your only chance will be strict adherence to these three core principles. Understand? Good, now show me your fighting stance."

Ridian did, shuffling his feet apart and putting his fists up.

Feya looked appalled. "No, no, no. Everything's wrong." She adjusted his posture, nudging him here and there. "You've got the wrong foot forward for a start. Now, bring your feet closer together. Closer. Too close. Perfect. Tread lightly on the balls of your feet. Bend the knees. Now twist. More. Twist at the hips—that's it. Smaller target that way. Hands up, shoulders up, drop the chin."

Feya got Ridian to shuffle forward, backward, and side to side, continuing to fine-tune his stance as he did.

"How's it looking?" asked Ridian.

Feya shook her head. "Horrible, almost beyond redemption. Regardless, let's start." Feya then demonstrated the Stone sequence, the first of *The Four and Forty*, a collection of sequences that contained all the Varki moves. The Stone sequence was a semi-squat, a front kick, a change of direction, a side kick, and then a wide squat—all painfully slow, all with perfect posture. Feya made it look easy, but it wasn't. Legs burning, Ridian lost his balance many times, and every time he sped up or compromised his posture, Feya was quick to correct him.

Some time later, Ridian was sweating despite the chill and grunting through yet another failed sequence.

"Relax," said Feya. *"Breathe."*

"Varki is so awkward."

"No, you're awkward."

Ridian was going to retort when they heard a couple of approaching voices.

Feya's eyes widened in panic. "We need to hide," she whispered. She looked about frantically, saw a cave, and pulled Ridian towards it. They plunged into the cold, inky blackness. It only went a dozen feet deep, but they'd be invisible.

Feya trembled, and Ridian's heart hammered. *Was someone tracking them?* His breath echoed in the cavern, so he held it as best he could. They gazed out the cave entrance, praying the voices would go away, but they only grew louder.

"You're so naughty," said a young woman's voice.

"You love it," said a young man.

"Do not."

"Do too."

The young woman giggled. "Well, maybe a little."

Feya made a quiet sound of disgust. Kai and his girlfriend had also decided to sneak out to Lover's Hollow.

When Kai and Sabrina finally left, Ridian and Feya made their way home through Sanctuary Forest. There was only a sliver of moonlight, and Feya walked slowly to avoid stumbling in the dark. The pace suited Ridian. He could see just fine but he limped along on doubly abused legs—first by Tann's training and now by Feya's. But he was in good spirits. One-on-one Varki training with Feya was his best chance of passing the upcoming trials, and it gave him a modicum of hope.

"I thought Lukas' lessons hurt," he said softly, his breath pluming out in frosty white.

"Poor baby," said Feya good-humouredly.

Ridian chuckled—then froze in horror. Ahead, upon the path, was a blazing silver wolf—glowing with the same cold fire as the moon.

Ridian grabbed Feya's arm. "Look."

Feya looked about bewildered. "What? Where?"

The silver ghost gazed at them, silent and still, bright as a campfire.

Ridian pointed. *"There!"* It was directly ahead, no more than twenty feet away.

Feya squinted ahead. "I don't see anything. And keep your voice down."

She can't see it, thought Ridian with mounting terror. *Why can't she see it?*

The ghost shot away, disappearing into the woods with a streak of silver.

"There's nothing there," said Feya, frowning at Ridian. "You're more paranoid than me."

Silver afterimages lingered in Ridian's vision from where the wolf had been. The same wolf that had appeared on his first night in Fidicia. The one he'd convinced himself was a dream.

"Sorry," said Ridian, forcing a laugh. "I—I thought I saw something." Ridian fought to keep the burning panic contained in his chest. There was no doubting it now. He was seeing things others could not. He was going crazy.

Chapter 20

Ridian slept terribly. He hid under the covers, tossing and turning, and when he finally slept, he soon awoke to fret all over again. It was happening. The Silver-eyed Caveborn freak was finally cracking. Would he hear voices next? Voices that grew louder, more intense, more insistent, more commanding, more persuasive? Or would he just wake up full of murderous cravings? Ridian imagined himself stalking from room to room, covered in blood—Theodor's blood, Ollie's blood, Feya's blood… covered in blood and grinning.

He remained anxious all that next day. Meditation with Mother Asarah was a write-off, training with Tann proved a painful distraction, and he kept getting lost in the hospital. With so many people around, he was forever checking over his shoulder. People were giving him funny looks. Could they see his slipping mask of sanity? Were they even real? Or did he just look strung out? He certainly felt like crap. He was bone tired, and his guts roiled as if full of snakes. He asked a random Steward sweeping a third-floor corridor if any of the local animals maybe, you know, glowed. The old Steward paused his sweeping and said, "Sorry, I don't get the joke. I'm a bit out of touch with youthful humour these days."

Ridian even skipped Lukas' torture session. He couldn't bring himself to do it, choosing to spend the afternoon biting his nails instead. At dinner, he was even quieter than usual. At one point, Theodor asked if he was okay, and when Ridian looked up from his uneaten food to lie and say he was fine, he found everyone staring at him with concern.

"You up for tonight?" whispered Feya as they stacked the dishes. "You look like hell."

"Of course," he said. "Tiredness never killed anyone." *Caveborns do*, said a nasty, unsolicited part of him. Nevertheless, they snuck out, same as the night before.

"Varki was created by a Torian slave called Varkil who escaped into the Wrathwolds as a boy," said Feya, down in Lover's Hollow. "Growing up amongst the Wrathwoli Nomads, he was greatly influenced by their Windchasers—magicians who can capture and harness the Wind, enabling the best of them to fly. That's why Varki has an aerial quality to it." Feya twirled into the air to demonstrate.

"There are people who can control the Wind?" asked Ridian. It seemed unlikely, but then again, if Sungazers could harness fire, and Soulcasters could bond with animals, anything was possible. An owl hooted somewhere in the night, and Ridian spun to look, unnerved.

Feya nodded. "Yes, but there aren't many left. Most of the Windchasers died during the Last Soulcaster War… The war that killed my parents," she added casually.

Ridian locked onto Feya, his attention riveted for the first time that day. Did she just say what he thought she'd said? He thought so, but she'd said it so offhandedly, like it was nothing. What should he say? He tried the most obvious thing. "I'm sorry." He meant it, but it seemed to fall short of what he wanted to convey.

Feya shrugged. "It's okay. It was a long time ago. I was very young when it happened. I can barely remember them, to tell the truth. When I try, their faces—their faces morph into Theodor and Kess." She blew through her nose, amused. "Can you believe that?"

"I never even met my dad," said Ridian before he realised what he'd said. The words just slipped out. He looked at Feya.

Feya looked back. "I'm sorry."

It was Ridian's turn to shrug. "It's not a big deal. Don't even think about him. There's nothing to think about, really. I don't know anything about him. Did he die? Did he abandon us? Was he imprisoned? Did he go crazy?" A bolt of anxiety shot through him as he said the word 'crazy.' He wanted to change the subject and get the attention off himself. "How did you end up with the Thunderfells?"

"After my parents were killed in a Kyrosian attack," said Feya. "Theodor found me on the front lines and took me to a foster home. I hated my foster parents. They were cruel and abusive in a hundred different ways. But Theodor would come visit me as often as he could. He would pop in and give me some little treat—some flowers or a doll or some sweets. But what I loved most was that he just sat with me, talked with me, listened to my prattle. When I was older, after a particularly bad beating, I decided to run away. It was midnight. I had a key. I had supplies. There was nothing stopping me. But I couldn't do it. I couldn't leave. If I did, I would never see Theodor again." Feya blew out a long sigh. "Thankfully, after one battle, he injured his leg and returned to visit me. He saw my bruises and adopted me on the spot."

"Theodor fought in the war?" asked Ridian. "I thought Stewards didn't fight."

"They don't. Theodor was a Knight back in the day. High ranking and everything."

"Really?" asked Ridian. He struggled to imagine the jolly Theodor as a warrior. Then again, he'd seen Theodor with his anger stoked. He'd seemed to grow in stature.

"It's rare," said Feya. "But it happens. After Theodor and Kess lost their son, Theodor abandoned the Grey to wear the White."

"They lost their son?"

Feya nodded. "Died in the war. They don't talk about him very often, and when they do, Theodor tears up and Kess goes quiet. You saw how they were when you asked about Hector the other night."

Ridian was thoughtful. Theodor and Kess lost their son, and instead of getting bitter, they opened their hearts and home to more children—ones not their own. A family bound not by blood, but by… well, Ridian wasn't sure, but it was a family nonetheless.

"Enough chit-chat," said Feya. "Let's get to work."

Ridian continued to practice The Stone sequence. Feya commented and corrected frequently, taking him back to the start with every mistake, and when the moon hung high in the night sky, Ridian had yet to complete the sequence uninterrupted.

"What's wrong?" said Feya, after yet another mistake. "You're even worse than yesterday. You seem distracted."

He was. He couldn't help it. He kept glancing around the

Hollow—checking for anything that shouldn't be there.

"I'm just sore," he lied, sweaty from exertion.

"Have a quick breather. I need to take a leak. No peeking." Feya then dashed out of sight.

Alone in the misty hollow, Ridian was seized by a burst of paranoia and looked about for the hundredth time. It was quiet, not a breath of air, and he didn't see anything—

There it was… Silver light was emerging over the lip of the hollow. It grew brighter and brighter until a blazing wolf appeared. It stopped to gaze down at him, silent and still. The luminous wolf stared and stared and stared… Ridian watched in abject terror as it slunk down into the Hollow, lean muscles rippling under its glowing fur, eyes locked on Ridian.

Ridian's heart pounded in his ears, his stomach plummeted in a sickening free fall. He couldn't move—couldn't even scream. *It's not real, it's not real, it's not real…* The wolf was down in the hollow now. Ridian managed to get his feet moving, stumbling backwards only to slam against a giant boulder. He collapsed into a crouch and covered his eyes with trembling hands. *There's nothing there.* But when Ridian peeped from behind his fingers, the wolf was there alright. There and advancing: twenty feet, fifteen, ten, eight…

"Back to it," cried Feya from around the boulder.

The wolf zipped back up the slope with a streak of silver, disappearing before Feya marched back into the clearing. "No more slacking off," she said, then her face fell when she saw Ridian. "You okay? You look ill."

Ridian made a show of being calm, but he was panting. "Yeah, I just…" Ridian's eyes were inexorably drawn to where the wolf had been, and there in the dirt, something caught his eye—pawprints.

"Do you... see that?" asked Ridian warily, pointing at the prints.

Feya walked closer to peer down at the prints. "Yeah, wolf tracks. So what? There are heaps of wolves around here. You're not scared, are you? Cause you're not going to get very far becoming a Knight if you're scared of wolves."

Ridian wasn't scared; he was relieved. More relieved than he'd ever been.

Hallucinations don't leave tracks.

Chapter 21

The wolf was real—*real*—but what was it? Feya hadn't seen the wolf, though it blazed like silver fire. He tentatively asked Feya about the local wildlife. He hedged, of course. Any unusual nocturnal animals? Ones with shiny coats, perhaps? She had frowned at him and said no. And asking Ollie was a mistake. The boy ripped open a book and bombarded Ridian with a deluge of information—none of it useful. Ridian asked a few Stewards at the hospital, but nobody seemed to know what he was on about.

"You're worse than yesterday," said Feya in Lover's Hollow the following evening.

It was true. Ridian was scanning the Hollow even more than when he had been paranoid, and it made him sloppy.

Feya clicked her fingers in front of his face. "Hey. Concentrate. You're supposed to get better with practice. Not worse."

The wolf will come, or it will not, thought Ridian, and he committed to his practice.

The night wore on, and Ridian made progress, successfully completing the Stone sequence twice without errors.

Finally, Feya yawned. "Call it a night?"

"Nah," said Ridian. "Go on without me. I want to perfect

this sequence."

Looking impressed, Feya bade him goodnight.

Alone, Ridian looked about the Hollow. There were fallen logs, boulders, shallow caverns, and fog, but no glowing wolves. He waited. Nothing. *I might as well practice,* he thought, and returned to the Stone sequence. But despite his practice, his legs tangled, and he fell on his backside. *Good thing Feya didn't see that one.*

He picked himself up, massaged his rump, and—

The silver wolf stood mere feet away. Startled, Ridian cried out and fell on his backside again. Silent and still, the wolf stared, its eyes fixed and unblinking. Breathing heavily, Ridian stared back, his heart pounding. He sat up. Besides the strange silver glow, the wolf looked like any other wolf: spiky coat, lean, pointed ears, wet nose, triangular face. It was on the small side, but it seemed cunning and clever. Those intelligent silver eyes certainly seemed to be reading him.

It's just a wolf, Ridian told himself. *Just a wolf. A wolf that I need.* If he was going to become a Knight, he needed to have a Familiar. Why not get a headstart and bond with one now?

Ridian got to his feet. "Hey, boy. I'm—I'm Ridian."

The wolf cocked its head at him, curious, moving for the first time.

Ridian retrieved a sausage he'd hidden in his coat pocket. "Hungry?" He flung it towards the wolf. The sausage rolled to a stop. The wolf crept towards it, sniffed, nudged it with its nose, and then snatched it up, chewing noisily. Sausage devoured, the wolf licked its lips and looked expectantly at Ridian, clearly wanting more.

"You can smell it, can't you?" Ridian dropped into a crouch, pulled another sausage out, and dangled it. "Come on," he coaxed. "Come get it."

The wolf made one cautious step, then stared, bracing for a retreat. When nothing happened, it took another step and stared again.

"Come on," said Ridian, stretching his arm out as far as it would go.

The wolf snuck further, almost within reach, extended its neck, snatched the sausage, and dashed a dozen paces away. When it finished, Ridian extended an open palm, the same way he had whenever he had met a friendly-looking stray back in Mudwall. The wolf approached with less caution than before and sniffed Ridian's hand. Ridian flinched as the wolf's rough tongue licked his fingers. It tickled, and the wolf's breath stank. Yes, this wolf was real, alright.

It ran a dozen feet and stopped, tail wagging. It seemed to be waiting for something—waiting for Ridian.

"Want me to come?" asked Ridian.

The wolf began to whine impatiently.

"Okay, I'm coming," said Ridian, and he followed tentatively, but when he got close, the wolf sped another dozen feet and stopped to whimper, same as before. Curiosity piqued, Ridian followed the wolf out of Lover's Hollow. Deep into the forest they went, the wolf shining like a silver lantern. Whenever Ridian fell behind and lost sight of the wolf, the canine would lope back and wait for Ridian to catch up. *Where is this crazy dog taking me?* Soon they began to climb. Up and up they went, and at times, Ridian needed to scramble on all fours to find purchase. Finally, the wolf slipped through a bush and disappeared into a narrow tunnel, concealed behind the shrubbery. If not for the wolf's brilliant coat, the tiny entrance—a little less than a yard wide and a yard high—would have been invisible. Ridian waited, not sure what to do, but the wolf scurried out and whimpered.

"You want me to go in there?" said Ridian. "I can't. It's too small."

Still, the wolf whined.

"I can't," said Ridian. "It's tiny."

The wolf snatched his trousers and tugged him forward, growling—just like a dog with a bone.

"Okay, okay," said Ridian, laughing at the absurdity of it all. "I'll try."

Satisfied, the wolf let go and disappeared into the dark hole. Shaking his head, Ridian wriggled inside, worming painfully on elbows and knees. A dozen feet in, the air became thick and hard to breathe. Were the walls narrowing? What if he got stuck? But before he could panic and think of backing out, Ridian saw the wolf standing a few feet away in a larger opening. Ridian crawled on and slid into the larger cavern. When he looked up, he gazed in astonishment. He was now in a larger tunnel crossing the one he'd just left. It was about twelve feet wide and eight feet high, with a subterranean river running through the middle. But what made Ridian's jaw drop was the glowing silver orbs. Hundreds—*thousands*—of silver spheres lined the walls, ceiling, and floor. They were the size of small plums, and shone with a cold silver fire. They shone like the wolf. They shone with the soft, silky light of the moon.

The wolf upended one with its nose, ate the stem, but left the cap.

Mushrooms, Ridian realised. Then a memory surfaced: of the Fell Caves as a toddler. Of Mother singing. Of another glowing mushroom. Of men coming and taking him away… Ridian tried to push the memory away, for he knew what came next. Another memory: clear, sharp, and searing—

Of a dead field and a dying tree.

Ridian pressed his palms into his eyes, but he couldn't push the images away. Not this time. They played out like real life, like he was there, now. Rayna writhing amid the dead field. Mother gazing upon the dying tree. His own small, childish leg gushing blood. He didn't want to see what came next. He couldn't remember what it was, but he knew it was the worst thing that had ever happened to him. He tugged his hair. The pain helped. He pulled harder— he might have been shouting, it was hard to tell—and the memory began to fade.

Ridian was back in the cave with the strange wolf. He was crying, unsure why. How can you understand a memory you can't remember? The blazing wolf nuzzled him, and without thinking, Ridian clung to the wolf's neck. He pressed his tear-streaked face into its fur, though it stank of wet dog, and eventually, his sobbing slowed and stopped.

Ridian pulled away from the strange glowing wolf to wipe his nose with the back of his hand. "Alright, blubber time's over." He laughed. "I got snot on you." Indeed, a streak of snot marred the wolf's glowing neck. Then Ridian leant back against the tunnel wall and gave the wolf a speculative look-over. "So, what am I going to call you?"

But he knew the wolf's name. It was Silver.

Chapter 22

In bed later that night, Ridian examined the mushroom he'd plucked from the cave wall between his finger and thumb. The mushroom cap glowed like a little moon, but its gills and stem were an ordinary, dull grey. Questions and convictions tumbled around in his head. He'd seen a similar mushroom as a toddler in the Fell Caves. Mother couldn't see it. But he could. Much like Feya couldn't see the silver wolf, yet he could. Why? How could his silver-flecked, Caveborn eyes see what others could not? Answers—he would find them tomorrow.

Tomorrow came, and Ridian climbed the winding staircase boring through the apothecary tower to the highest accessible part of the hospital, the apothecary itself. The little room swayed disconcertingly, hundreds of feet above ground. It smelled strongly of chemicals, while herbs of every description were in various states of being boiled, dried, steeped, or steamed. Jars were everywhere. As Ridian entered, elderly Master Sheema was pouring a beaker of steaming green liquid into a series of vials with care. A funnel prevented any spillage. "Hello, Ridian," he said, his eyes never leaving his work. "Always a pleasure."

Ridian bowed. "Likewise, Master Sheema."

Young Remmy, pimples proliferating across both cheeks, placed a crucible into a furnace with a blackened pair of tongs. He then squeezed a wheezing bellows to fan the flame. Given they were in a giant tree, it was a relief to see overhanging sandbags with emergency drawstrings above the furnace. That explained why they were in the highest tower, Ridian supposed. Fire burns up, not down, after all.

"Wormwood, Remmy," said Master Sheema.

"Wormwood!" said Remmy. Oh, shoot. I forgot." And he pulled the crucible from the furnace in quite a fluster.

"Remmy," chided Master Sheema ever so softly. "Plan...?"

"I know, I know," said Remmy, removing his mittens to search for something on a shelf full of jars. "Plan, proceed, perfect. It won't overbrew, promise."

"Very well," said Master Sheema serenely. "Remember..."

"...Test and retest. I know, Master Sheema, I know."

"Good lad."

An owl fluttered across the room and landed on Master Sheema's shoulder. It unfurled its clasped talon to reveal a glass dropper.

"Thank you, Argyll," said Master Sheema, taking the dropper, then his eyes left his work for the briefest of moments to flicker over Ridian. They returned swiftly to his steady fingers, the dropper already sucking and squeezing liquid. "You have a question, Ridian?"

Ridian swallowed. "I do."

Master Sheema did not pause from his duties, but his voice was kind. "It's good to be curious."

Ridian pulled the glowing mushroom from his pocket. In the sunlight, it appeared to be nothing more than an ordinary grey mushroom.

Ridian was still formulating his question when Master Sheema said in an alarmed voice, "Don't move." He then glided across the room, smacked the mushroom from Ridian's palm, and guided Ridian forcefully towards the sink. "Don't touch anything. I'll turn the tap." He did, and, gripping Ridian's wrists, he held Ridian's hands under the water. "Have you licked your fingers or bitten your nails?"

"No," said Ridian. "I don't think so. Why? What's wrong?"

"Just keep washing," said Master Sheema, totally unlike his usual serene self. "Remmy. *Quickfix*. Now." Remmy ran to a cabinet and rifled through bottles, tinkling and tipping them in his haste.

"What's going—"

"Sit," said Master Sheema. "Sit and I will answer all your questions."

Ridian obeyed.

"Do you feel odd or strange in any way?" said Master Sheema, examining Ridian very closely.

"I feel tired, I guess," Ridian answered.

Master Sheema seemed to file the information away in his mind.

"Please, what's wrong?"

"That mushroom is the *Boletus Furosis*," said Master Sheema. "It contains secondary metabolites with psychoactive properties, which, if ingested in sufficient quantities, can precipitate a psychotic episode of indeterminate length and intensity. Symptoms may include hallucinations, delusions, amnesia, rage, and, in most cases, the uncontrollable desire to consume living human flesh."

Ridian shook his head. "What?"

Remmy scurried over and handed a vial to Master Sheema.

"Loony Shrooms," he said. "They make you bat-shit crazy."

"And dangerous," added Master Sheema, handing the vial to Ridian. "This is the antidote. Please drink it."

The mushroom lay innocently on the floor.

"Ridian, *please*," said Master Sheema, shaking the vial. He looked terrified.

Ridian uncorked the vial and drank the heady tonic in one swig. "Ugh! Disgusting."

Master Sheema sagged onto a bench, drew a long sigh, and took off his glasses to wipe them on his tunic. "So, Ridian. You came to ask a question?"

"Shoot," said Remmy, dashing to his crucible. "Ohhh, no… I think it's overbrewed."

Ridian's stomach churned as the antidote settled. "Question? Oh, yeah. I—um—found that mushroom and I just wanted to know what it was." Given the circumstances, Ridian felt his question sounded very lame.

"Remmy? Would you care to answer young Ridian's question?"

Surrounded by steam, Remmy's pimpled face shone with sweat. "Yes, Master Sheema. Let's see… the *Boletus Furosis*. Native to Fidicia. It excretes toxins from its gills. Let me think, what else? It only grows in dark, wet areas and only on certain mineral-rich surfaces. Was created by Valaria to poison the Kyrosian Army…"

It suddenly made sense. "Loony Shrooms are what poison Madman's Falls," said Ridian.

Remmy nodded. "It's considered five times more potent than rabies."

"And the dose-response?" asked Master Sheema.

Remmy hesitated, frowning at the ceiling as he retrieved

the information. "A moderate dose is required for acute symptom manifestation. However, even small doses over a prolonged period can precipitate psychosis, catatonia, hysteria, and other psychiatric conditions." He looked at Master Sheema, hoping for positive recognition.

The elderly master nodded his solemn approval. "Very good."

Ridian was thinking very hard, his heart fluttering like the wingbeat of a startled bird. Looney Shrooms grew in the Fell Caves Prison back home. People went into those caves and came out crazy. It wasn't darkness that instilled insanity. That was just Sol propaganda. It was these mushrooms. The Asylum back home was full of people who had been poisoned. His mother included.

"Is there a cure?" asked Ridian.

Remmy fired off an answer. "Quickfix. The stem is the primary ingredient. You just had some."

There was a cure. The fact made him dizzy. Maybe—just maybe—this Quickfix could save his mother. It seemed too good to be true. But what about Ridian? He was born in the caves but hadn't gone crazy. Then an answer came to him in a flash: his mother had drunk the poisoned water running through their prison, and Ridian had drunk her milk. She had filtered out the harmful toxins, but trace elements had still found their way into his developing eyes, sprinkling them with silver flecks—helping him see what others could not.

But what about Trystan Caddock? He'd drunk his mother's milk, developed silver-flecked eyes, and then cracked years later. Why? Then it came to him. *It grows in dark, wet areas and only on certain mineral-rich surfaces,*

Remmy had said.

Trystan Caddock had been digging a well: dark, wet, and lined with mineral-rich stones. Ridian could imagine the tragedy all too easily: Trystan digging away, deeper and darker, until, one day, he sees something… something glowing in the depths.

Ridian was a Caveborn, but he wasn't crazy.

***

That night, at dinner, Ridian met Sabrina Crawford—Kai's 'special friend.' Ridian was especially introspective and happy for someone else to be the centre of attention.

"Sabrina," said Kess. "Kai tells us you're pursuing the path of a Steward?"

Sabrina was lost in Kai's eyes and didn't respond. Spellbound, Kai stared back at the strawberry-blonde. They'd barely even touched their food. Feya and Ollie clasped their hands, battered their eyelids at each other, and sighed dramatically. Kai and Sabrina remained oblivious to their teasing.

"Ah, Sabrina?" said Kess.

Sabrina broke from her trance. "Sorry," she said with surprise. "Did someone ask a question?"

"You're becoming a Steward?" Kess prompted.

"That's the plan," Sabrina answered eagerly. "For years I thought I wanted to become a Knight, but the more I thought about it, I realised my heart belonged elsewhere. That it belonged with the sick, the poor, and the needy."

"Explains why you're dating Kai," said Feya, to a chorus of laughter, including Sabrina, who consoled a wounded Kai by hugging his arm.

"Ollie," said Kess. "It's rude to read when we have guests."

Ollie peeled his eyes away from a book, hidden beneath the table.

"Treasure hunting again?" asked Theodor knowingly, eyes twinkling.

"What treasure?" said Sabrina.

"This." Ollie flipped his book out and pointed to a picture of a leaf-shaped lute.

Kai rolled his eyes. "Not this again—you're obsessed."

Ollie turned up his nose. "Fidic's Lute is a national treasure of incalculable worth, thank you very much. It's worth obsessing about."

"It doesn't exist," said Kai with the lofty superiority afforded to older brothers.

"Of course it exists," said Ollie, outraged.

Feya puffed up, wagged a knowing finger, and assumed a stuffy air. "Indeed, Fidic's Lute is one of the most well-recorded artefacts in all of Torian history."

"Shut up, Fey," said Ollie. "I don't sound like that."

"Ollie," said Kess. "We don't say 'shut up' in this family. And Feya, stop goading your brother."

"I believe Fidic's Lute exists," said Sabrina, giving Kai a defiant, flirtatious look.

Outnumbered, Kai raised his hands in surrender. "Okay, okay, okay. Fidic's Lute existed a long time ago. Of course, that's true. My point is that it's been lost for centuries. People have been searching forever and found nothing."

Ollie flicked through a few pages of his book and then read aloud, "'It is widely believed that Valaria stowed Fidic's fabled Lute in one of the many caves in the Fidician Valley.

There are over two hundred known cave systems in the Fidician region alone, though experts agree there would be dozens, and perhaps hundreds yet undiscovered.'" Ollie whipped off his glasses and stowed them in his pocket. "They find new caves all the time. This one time—"

"Yeah, yeah, yeah," said Kai. "We've all heard about the little ditch you found."

"I think it's marvellous you take an interest in history, Ollie," said Theodor. "Fidic's Lute would be quite a find. But! The real treasure is what's hidden *inside* the Lute."

Everyone rolled their eyes this time. All except Ollie, who leaned forward, and Sabrina, who showed genuine interest.

"Not this again," said Feya. "You're more obsessed than Ollie."

"Perhaps," said Theodor. "But Ridian and Sabrina haven't heard me talk about Fidic's Final Words, have you?" He looked between Sabrina and Ridian questioningly, though he knew the answer.

Sabrina and Ridian shook their heads.

"There you go, then." Theodor settled into his seat and assumed a storytelling air, ignoring the looks of 'here we go again' being passed around the table. "It's widely known that Valaria wrote all Fidic's sermons down. However!" Theodor raised his eyebrows and spread his hands, inviting intrigue. "It is believed that Fidic had one final sermon, one he planned on giving after his fatal battle with Kyros. It is believed this last sermon would reveal the deepest mystery of Soulcasting, that this final lesson was more important than all the other lessons that came before… But of course, he died, and his secret with him… But it is believed that a copy of his sermon was stowed away within the hollow of his Lute." He gazed at Ollie who was relishing the well-known details of the familiar story. "Waiting to be discovered."

The fire crackled in the silence.

"*Please*," said an incredulous Kai. "Fidic's Final Words is a bedtime story. It's not even in one of Ollie's silly books."

"Hey!"

"*Kai*," warned Kess. "Be nice."

"A thousand apologies, Mother. But all I'll say is this: you'd have as much luck finding Daegan's long-lost sword in the backyard as you would finding Fidic's Lute."

"I've seen Daegan's Sword," said Ridian, without thinking.

The table stopped and stared.

"You've seen Daegan's Sword?" asked an awestruck Ollie.

"You're so gullible, Ollie," said Kai. "Ridian's just joking." He looked at Ridian, suddenly uncertain. "You are joking, right?"

Ridian felt like a pinned display moth, exposed under a bright light. He couldn't leave it there; he needed to say something. And the longer he remained silent, the more they stared, and before he knew it, words were spilling out. "Well, I'm pretty sure it was Daegan's Sword. It was hanging up at Mirecross Castle—the one out on The Mire—the Great Waste, I mean. The sword was certainly big enough. It was eight, maybe nine feet long. And it had a black-stone pommel, same as the painting of The Elder Three in the hospital. A black stone just like this." He pulled out the Elderflower Necklace from beneath his tunic.

Eyebrows raised. Jaws dropped. They couldn't have been more shocked if Ridian laid an egg right there on the table.

Ollie spoke in a reverent whisper. "Is—is that...?" He

fumbled in his pocket for his second pair of glasses, swapped them with the pair on his face, then leaned across the table. "Is that Valaria's pendant? How did you find it? Where did you find it? Are you a treasure hunter?" Ollie seemed to be the only one who could talk. The rest looked too stunned. "Wait, is it real?"

They all looked at Theodor, who nodded. "It's real."

"You didn't tell them about—about me?" Ridian asked Theodor. Judging by the way Kess blinked in astonishment, Theodor hadn't even told her.

"It wasn't my place," said Theodor simply. "Besides, in our family, people share if and when they are ready, not before."

Ollie bounced in his seat. "Tell us where you found it."

"You have to tell us now," said Kai.

"Yeah, forget the family rules," said Feya. "Spill the beans."

"Guys," said Theodor. "Stop badgering Ridian into sharing."

But Ridian was surprised to find he wanted to share, and so he shared: being an Arden, life in Mudwall, living with Rayna, the Sol Oppression, Rayna's disappearance, finding Tann, crossing The Mire, meeting Locke, seeing the massacre. He shared it all, his story unspooling readily and easily as if he'd planned on sharing it all along. Everyone listened with rapt attention, and only when Ridian had finished did they ask questions. There were many, and Ridian answered freely, late into the night. Of Caveborns, Ridian made no mention. Not for fear of judgment, but because it didn't matter. Not any more.

Chapter 23

As midwinter approached, the days grew colder and darker, with occasional thin snowfalls. Despite the cold, Ridian and Feya continued their secret Varki practice late into the chilly evenings, breath billowing, fingers swollen and numb. And when Feya left, Silver would appear. Ridian would follow the wolf around, play with it, and feed it snacks. One time, Silver returned the favour, dumping a dead rabbit at Ridian's feet; another time, a large rat, and another, a slobbering mouthful of Looney Shroom stems. Ridian felt like he was getting to know the wolf quite well. How it liked being scratched under the chin. How it wagged its tail, as all dogs do, when happy. How it liked to play tug-o-war. How it liked playing chase but refused to play fetch—it was a wolf, not a dog, after all. And Ridian felt like the wolf was getting to know him. It seemed to sense Ridian's mood. It would play if Ridian felt lively, explore if Ridian was curious, or sit in Ridian's lap and stare at the stars if Ridian was tired.

Ridian was constantly trying to bond with the wolf— whatever that meant. All in secret, of course. Bonding before graduation was expressly forbidden. A bonded Soulcaster was a nearly unstoppable force, and the Fidician Order could not afford to have renegade Soulcasters outside of their control nor unknown Familiars stealing, murdering, and committing all manner of crimes on their Soulcaster's behalf. It was a matter of security, and the Fidicians took it very seriously. Consequently, Bonding was restricted to full-fledged members of the Fidician Order. Still, Ridian needed whatever advantages he could take, and he didn't care if he cheated or broke the law, providing he didn't get caught, of course.

However, Splitting—that elusive yet fundamental skill of Soulcasting—escaped him. Meditation did not seem to help, despite his modest improvements in concentration. Over time, Mother Asarah had Ridian focus on a range of different things: the faint, never-ending sigh of an underground spring, the once-a-minute drip of some unseen water, the near-silence of a burning candle. Even his thoughts. "Watch your thoughts as if from a distance," Mother Asarah had said. "Watch them as you would a flock of birds. Do they swoop past? Circle around? Hover? It does not matter. They will come. They will go. Just watch."

And despite the rapid advance of winter—the frost, the sleet, and the occasional snow—Ridian willingly surrendered to the bone-deep chill of Madman's Falls. *It's just pain,* he told himself. *Just pain. It will come. It will go.* He found acceptance was the key. If he accepted the pain, rather than fought it, he could control himself and the urge to resurface. Submersions were lasting longer, and Ridian began carrying larger stones up the hill at a faster pace. And though Ridian and Tann had settled into a habit of saying as little as possible, Ridian thought he saw a growing, begrudging respect from Tann.

Thankfully, his work within the hospital diversified

beyond potty cleaning: patient transfer, surgery assistant, elevator operator, note taker, assistant cook, dish cleaner, orderly, and supply gatherer. He learned a lot and surprised himself—and others—when he gave Master Sheema advice on treating his own headache one day.

"You might find Feverfew a tad better than Milk Thistle for migraines," Ridian said off-handedly to the elderly Master. "Especially if you crush some ginger and a pinch of peppermint with it."

To his credit, Master Sheema prepared and drank the infusion as suggested and was delighted with the results. Since then, the elderly Master occasionally called upon Ridian for an opinion, and Ridian found he often had an answer.

"How do you know so much about herbal medicine?" Master Sheema kept asking.

Ridian would shrug and say, "Just something my sister taught me."

Even Lukas' lessons were getting easier. Similar to Madman's Falls, Ridian was learning to accept the pain and detach from it, imagining himself stepping away and observing the pain from a distance. Whatever he did, it worked. Lukas would do his worst, and Ridian would smile, knowing it drove Lukas mad. Of course, it spurred Lukas to greater cruelty, but still, it was worth it to irritate the prick.

Feya and Ridian trained every night without fail. Feya was an excellent teacher, with the right balance of push, patience, and encouragement, and Ridian progressed quickly. He could see the difference as well. He'd never been soft—life in Mudwall didn't permit that—but now a lean, wolfish figure stared at him from the mirror. Muscles rippled when he flexed, and with his newfound strength, each successive sequence of The Four and Forty was easier to learn than the previous. He also learnt some basic submission holds and how to escape them. Most exciting, however, was when Feya sparred with him.

"Twenty percent," she would say, and they would fight, Ridian giving one hundred percent effort, Feya twenty. Initially, Ridian still lost. But as he improved, he started to land a strike or two, and Feya's percentages crept higher.

Perhaps the biggest change in Ridian's day-to-day, however, was the time he spent with the Thunderfells. Ridian was no longer the passive listener. Questions from the family abounded, and he answered every one of them. However, the family seemed especially interested in Arden history and were perplexed by Ridian's lack of knowledge.

"You don't know anything?" Ollie had asked.

Ridian shook his head. "Not really. The Sol erased everything. They believe in the 'homogeneity of belief' and, therefore, enforce their 'One Story Policy'. For peaceful unification, apparently, only Sol dogma, history, and culture can survive."

Ridian also learnt much about the family. Kai had been in a street gang as a boy, surviving on the streets of Lindon, Tor's biggest city, far to the east. Feya had topped her class in Varki since arriving as a young girl. Ollie was three years ahead in his knowledge of medicine. And Ella's favourite colour was green.

Days blurred, and the Soulcaster Trials crept closer: four weeks, three weeks, two weeks to go. Snow turned to sleet, sleet to rain, and then grey skies turned blue. And as spring approached, Ridian became increasingly anxious, and he wasn't alone.

"Feya, eat something, please," Kess said one night. "You're getting too thin."

"I'm not hungry," said Feya, mindlessly twirling her fork.

"Worried about the Trials?" asked Theodor.

Feya shrugged.

"Don't be ridiculous," said Kai. "You're the best fighter in the school. Ridian, however…"

Ridian laughed at the playful jab. "Remind me, Kai. How many times did you fail the trials? Was it three or four times?"

"It was twice, and you know it," said Kai, and the family chuckled.

But Feya didn't laugh. She just stared at her fork.

"You'll be fine," said Theodor, putting a hand on hers. "You've been kicking butt since—"

"Varki's not the problem," she said, clinking her fork down. "It's Splitting. You know I've never done it. Not once. Not in all these years." She looked up self-consciously.

"I've told you a thousand times," said Theodor. "Your time will come. I know it."

Feya sank further into her chair, unwilling to be comforted.

"Have you tried freezing water and backbreaking exercises with a sadistic Kyrosian?" asked Ridian.

Feya gave a reluctant smile. "Guess not."

A week from the Trials and the first day of spring, pilgrims from all over Tor began pouring into Fidicia. The Trials, it turned out, were not merely a Soulcaster examination, but a cultural event—a festival. Tents and market stalls popped up all over Last Stand Meadow, and on one cold evening, Ridian, the Thunderfells, and Sabrina strolled among the maze of boutiques. Merchants and artisans sold all manner of goods, from wineglasses to whistles and from paintings to pots. Grocers sold berries, bacon, broccoli, and more. Puppet shows delighted kids and adults alike, and kites flew, only to crash into stalls and unsuspecting heads. Bards played and sang from atop barrels, while Familiars prowled upon the trampled grass, perched atop tents, and occasionally swooped to snatch up unattended treats. One hawk snatched a lamb shank right out of a man's hand.

The family were having a blast. Ollie pointed at the sword display. Feya tried on ridiculous hats. Ella gazed at the coloured lamps. Kai and Sabrina held hands, aglow in young love, while Kess tried to persuade a reluctant Theodor to buy a new rug. Ridian, however, found it hard to join in the festivities; he was running out of time. The Trials were in a matter of days, he'd only learned sixteen sequences from The Four and Forty, and Splitting still confounded him. Sometimes he thought he felt close during his morning meditations. Sometimes he felt close beneath Madman's Falls. Sometimes he felt close when he was with Silver. But close wasn't enough. If he couldn't Split, he couldn't bond, and if he couldn't bond, Tann wouldn't take him to save Rayna. It was that simple.

Only the Wrathwoli Windchaser show captivated Ridian's preoccupied mind.

"Quick," said Feya, tugging Ridian through the jostling crowd to get to the front as the Wrathwoli musicians began playing on a makeshift stage. The flutist, lutist, guitarists, and drummer were less polished than traditional Fidician bards, but they appeared to be having the time of their lives, drinking and laughing as they played. They were a scruffy lot, clad in crude leather jackets, trousers, and fur parkas. And they were all small of stature, wild-haired, and had black, monolid eyes just like Feya.

An old Wrathwoli man pushed through a curtain at the back of a wagon and hobbled onto the stage supported by a cane. He plucked an imaginary flower, sniffed, sneezed, and—to Ridian's astonishment—flew ten feet into the air. He hovered for all of three seconds, wind blowing wildly from his palms and bare feet, before landing lightly. There had been no ropes, no harness, nothing. He'd flown. Ridian's mouth dropped open, and Feya, who looked ecstatic, laughed at his bewilderment.

The old performer, who was actually a young man with make-up, continued with various gags. One involved trying to catch his hat, which hovered inexplicably out of reach. He made desperate swipes with his cane, trying to hook them, but each time, the hat fluttered out of reach. He then made a loud flatulent noise, launched into the air, coat-tails fluttering, and snatched the hat once and for all. The crowd was beside themselves with laughter. It was unbelievable. He was controlling the wind, harnessing magic—extraordinary magic—and he was using it for fart jokes.

A juggler came next, juggling six balls which never touched his hands. Then the twirling dancing girls—a pair of long-legged, full-breasted beauties, clothed in little more than strips of silk and bangles. Theodor made a show of adjusting his glasses, earning him a playful slap from Kess, and Sabrina clung to Kai and checked his line of sight. Feya just rolled her eyes. The dancing pair leapt in time with the music. Each time they jumped, they got a little higher. The music quickened; the girls rose, spiralling around each other into the night sky. Soon, they were soaring above the crowd and blasting them with great gusts of wind from their palms and bare feet. Hats toppled off heads, tents billowed, stands tumbled over. The music died, the wind died, and the dancers fell. People screamed as they plummeted to the ground until a last-minute puff of wind, and they landed soft as a kiss. The crowd went wild: whooping, clapping, and tossing coins as all the performers bowed.

Ridian cheered with the rest. "That was amazing," he said, turning to Feya. But her face had dropped. Ridian followed her gaze. Theodor was striding towards Sevron, fists clenched, determined. Felix bristled on his shoulder. Sevron sauntered through the crowd, a gorgeous brunette on his muscular arm, his wolf prowling at his side.

"Oh no," said Feya. "Dad's going to make a scene."

"Welcome back, Sevron," said Theodor through his teeth, his voice somehow carrying above the clamour of the crowd. "Did you know you would be gone for a couple of months when you gave my son *verbal* permission to train?"

Sevron's wolf growled, people turned to stare, and the rest of the Thunderfells looked mortified. Sevron grumbled something and went to walk on, but Theodor stepped in front of him. "No, it can't wait, Commander. I want you to sign this. *Now.*" Theodor pulled a scroll and pen from his pocket and thrust it at Sevron.

It had gone very quiet, and Ridian could feel the awkwardness radiating from Feya.

"This is unbecoming, Steward," said Sevron with distaste.

"You tricked an eight-year-old boy. *That's* unbecoming."

Sevron's partner frowned up at him, while Sevron glanced uncomfortably at the nosey crowd. People looked away, pretending not to listen, but their eyes darted back. Finally, Sevron snatched the scroll and pen from Theodor's hands and scrawled a furious signature. "Fine. But I take no responsibility for the injuries he will likely sustain." He shoved the scroll and pen roughly back at Theodor. "And if it were up to me, I would have all your little misfits expelled from the Order."

"Sevy," said Sevron's partner in a reprimanding tone.

"No," said Sevron. "Let me speak my mind. I'm sick of our noble tradition being tainted by his little inbreds."

Theodor seemed to swell. But before he did anything, Sevron's partner slapped Sevron smartly across the face.

"Don't you dare say another word," she warned, pointing a finger. "Don't you dare." Then she disappeared into the gawking crowd, some of whom beamed with apparent glee at the drama.

Sevron felt his cheek in stunned humiliation before a cold fury filled his eye. He shouldered Theodor out of the way and barged through the crowd, straight toward Ridian. To Ridian's surprise, as Sevron blustered past, he stopped momentarily in front of Ridian. "You will never be a Knight," Sevron whispered, not looking at Ridian. "I swear it." Then he stormed off, and everyone turned to the person next to them to gossip like mad.

***

Later that night, the family sprawled about the lounge. It

had been a sombre ride home, and Theodor was working hard to raise everyone's spirits. "I asked Kess out every week for four weeks," said Theodor brightly. "I was the most desperate, lovesick fool in all Fidicia. And each week she said no and broke my heart."

Kai, Ollie, and Feya sat staring at the wall, not listening to the evidently well-worn story. Felix slept, curled before the fireplace. Zeke perched in the rafters.

"Well, clearly, I was too good for him," said Kess, picking up the story. "But on the fifth week, when Theodor didn't ask me out, I realised I actually liked the desperate, lovesick fool."

"And that's when she started chasing me," said Theodor, winking at Ollie. "Advanced tactics, my boy, advanced tactics." When Ollie didn't smile, Theodor frowned. "Okay, who died?"

Feya scoffed.

"Don't leave it there," said Theodor. "Spill the beans. What's wrong?"

"I don't know," said Feya. "Maybe the fact that everyone hates us."

"Everyone doesn't—"

"I'm going to bed," said Feya, and she pounded up the stairs. Ridian stared after her; he'd never seen her this agitated.

Theodor went to call after her, but Kess laid a hand on his arm. "Give her space. You know she's stressed about the Trials."

Indeed, Ridian had heard Feya fret about Splitting on numerous occasions in recent days. How it was impossible, and she'd never get the hang of it.

Theodor threw up his hands. "What did I do wrong? Tonight's a good night. Ollie finally gets to start Varki. We should be celebrating."

"Honey," said Kess, "read the room."

Theodor looked around. Kai had his arms crossed, and Ollie didn't meet Theodor's eye. Feeling awkward, Ridian gave a commiserating smile, and Theodor appeared grateful.

"It was pretty embarrassing," said Kai finally.

"You saying I shouldn't have confronted Sevron?" asked Theodor.

"No, it's just—Ollie, are you okay?" said Kai with sudden alarm.

Ridian looked at Ollie, and his heart froze.

Ollie was rigid as a plank of wood, his unblinking eyes locked on the ceiling, and then he began to shudder and twitch.

Theodor leapt from his seat to kneel before the boy. "Ollie? You with us?"

Not appearing to register anything, Ollie continued to tremble and stare at nothing. He didn't even blink.

"Wake up, Ollie!" said Kess with growing panic. "Wake up!"

Then, as quickly as it came, it went. Ollie blinked in groggy confusion. "What? What's happened?" he slurred, going limp.

"It's okay," said Theodor calmly, stroking Ollie's shoulders. "We lost you for a second. That's all."

"Sorry…"

"No, don't apologise," said Theodor. "It's not your fault."

Everyone was on their feet, even Felix, and Zeke fluttered

onto Kai's shoulder to gaze at the young boy. Ollie's eyelids drooped and his head lolled as if struggling to stay awake.

"What the hell's wrong with him?" asked Kai.

"Nothing," said Theodor dismissively. "He just needs rest." Then he scooped Ollie up in his arms and whisked him upstairs, Felix scampering after them.

"Mum, what's wrong with Ollie?" demanded Kai, clearly dissatisfied with Theodor's answer.

Kess stared up at the stairs, a hand covering her mouth. After a moment, Kess looked at Kai with surprise and flashed a smile. "Oh, don't worry. Nothing a good sleep can't fix." Then she, too, trotted upstairs, leaving Kai and Ridian to look at each other with concern.

Chapter 24

Ridian's nerves were fried the next day. Not only was he woefully underprepared for the Soulcaster Trials in two days, but Ollie's episode still unsettled him. He didn't buy Theodor and Kess' dismissive attitude. Every instinct told him Ollie was seriously ill. His worry peaked as he accompanied Ollie to Varki training. Though the boy appeared healthy and neither of them mentioned his episode, he was withdrawn as he clanked toward Sanctuary Forest.

He has every reason to be nervous, thought Ridian. What had Sevron said? 'I take no responsibility for the injuries he will likely sustain.' Ridian didn't like the sound of that. He knew how cruel Lukas could be.

The kids stared as Ollie handed his signed permission slip to Lukas.

"Stand in line and keep up," Lukas said curtly, not even looking as he snatched the note and shoved it into a pocket.

Hobbling into line, Ollie did his best to blend in.

"Let's start with some sparring," said Lukas. "Pair up."

Ridian and Ollie went to pair up.

"Oh no," said Lukas, pointing at Ridian. "You're with me."

Ollie looked about self-consciously. "Master Lukas, um—

everybody is already paired up."

"Don't worry," said Lukas. "Once I'm finished with Ridian, I'll spend some time with you."

Then, before Ridian was ready, Lukas jabbed him in the stomach. Winded, Ridian felt Lukas' strong hands twist his arm behind his back. *Here we go again...* Ridian closed his eyes and tried to detach from it all. It was harder today. Anxiety for Ollie stopped him from drifting away. But he took a breath, accepted the pain, and was just about to visualise stepping out of his body when –

"Master Lukas! What are you doing?"

It was Ollie. Ridian peeped an eye open to see the boy standing before them with a look of outrage. The sight and sound of the boy sent Ridian crashing back to reality. He felt the pain now—all of it. Lukas had Ridian's wrist twisted high up his back in a hammerlock, and it felt like a nail was scraping the inside of his shoulder joint. Ridian groaned; he couldn't help it.

"Stop! You're hurting him!" Ollie cried.

"If I stop with him, I start with you," said Lukas. "So shut your mouth."

Ollie looked among his peers for support. He found none. He was alone.

"It's okay, Ollie," Ridian managed to say between gasps. "It's okay. Just leave it."

But Ollie didn't leave it. He reached out and grabbed Lukas' arm. "Please, sir. Let him g—"

Lukas palmed Ollie hard in the chest, sending him flying, but Ridian didn't see him skid across the ground. He untwisted from Lukas' grasp—just as Feya had taught him— and swung his elbow into Lukas' face. Lukas' head snapped to the side, and his eyes seemed to spin in their sockets. Ollie was a groaning, crumpled heap. Blood leaked from one nostril, and one of his lenses had shattered in the shape of a star. Lukas swayed, disoriented, and then his bleary eyes found Ridian, and his face went white with fury. All this time, Lukas had shown self-control. All his punishments had been tempered, restrained. Now, an unthinking rage clearly possessed the young master. There would be no holding back this time. He would break Ridian... *easy as kindling, easy as pie.*

Lukas launched at Ridian and kicked a savage roundhouse that might have decapitated Ridian had he not spun away using the first three moves of The Windy Weathervane. He could almost hear Feya's words, *the hardest target is the moving target.*

So consumed by fury, Lukas didn't even register surprise at Ridian's deft evasion. He simply hurled after him, closing the distance. Again, Feya's words *...the one that misleads, fools, and tricks.* Ridian threw a fake jab. It made Lukas blink, and in that split second, Ridian slid away, using the wide sweeping steps of The River Flowing. *The fight stops when the fighter stops.*

Lukas came on, seeking to grasp, to pin. Ridian couldn't let that happen. Lukas would snap him into pieces. Ridian kept moving, half-learned sequences blurring together. He dodged, darted, slipped. A few blows found a mark but were glancing. Lukas managed to grip Ridian's collar, but Ridian pulled away, tearing his tunic down the neckline. Only a few seconds had passed, but Lukas' pale face was red. His rage drove him to attack recklessly, to drop his guard, to make mistakes. Mistakes a sober Lukas would never make. *And when they strike, strike only once—quickly and decisively.* Ridian needed to capitalise on Lukas' anger before his calculated precision returned. So, amid the storm of blows, Ridian waited. Soon, Lukas would come within reach and make some fatal error. Still, Ridian waited, even as he darted away like a startled cat.

Then Ridian saw his opportunity. Lukas was winding up for a thunderous right hook—and *there!* The left hand sagged, exposing the jaw.

Now! Ridian struck with his own right hook. He put everything behind it. It screamed like an arrow, like lightning, like—

Lukas flicked Ridian's punch aside, and his own right hook smashed into Ridian's face with the force of a horse kick. Ridian reeled backwards, a metallic taste in his mouth. Through the dizziness, Ridian saw Lukas sweep his back foot into his head, kicking the world sideways and sending him crashing to the ground.

Ridian lay panting in the dirt. Everything whirled. Dots danced before his eyes. Lukas' feet approached, crunching in the dirt. One foot swung back, then thudded into Ridian's side. Pain exploded in Ridian's guts. He couldn't breathe. Another kick, harder this time. Ridian tried to accept the pain and step outside of himself like he always did. If Lukas was going to beat him to a pulp, he didn't want to be around to feel it.

"GET OFF HIM!"

Ridian peeped an eye to see Theodor hurtling towards them like a javelin. His arms and legs fluttered in a Soulcaster blur. He swooped down upon Lukas and struck him three times in the gut in quick succession. Ridian couldn't see them, they happened so fast, but he could hear them. Lukas crumpled, clutching his stomach. Theodor was nearly unrecognisable. Veins bulged along his neck, and he looked enormous as he stood panting over Lukas. Where had the friendly Steward gone? For the first time, Ridian saw, fully revealed, the decorated soldier, the veteran, the leader of men.

The kids in the class stared with a mixture of astonishment, horror, and, to Ridian's delight, satisfaction. Lukas had had this coming.

Theodor pressed his boot heel into Lukas' groin, pinning him to the ground. Lukas squirmed and released a shrieking, high-pitched squeal.

"How dare you?" said Theodor, his voice like iron. "If you ever touch one of my children again, I will break my sacred vow to Roki himself to do no harm. I will abuse my knowledge of the human body to ensure your injuries never heal, that you become a cripple, and remain forever in pain."

"Please," whimpered Lukas, gasping.

Ridian heard Ollie's clanking braces. He limped to his father's side and grabbed Theodor's sleeve. "Dad, let him go. He's not worth it."

Theodor remained glaring at Lukas. "When you attack my kids, you attack me. And I defend myself. Understand?"

"Yes!" cried Lukas. "I understand."

Theodor finally stepped off Lukas' nether region with a look of disgust. "Come on boys, let's go home."

***

"Did Dad really stomp on Lukas' balls?" asked Kai for the

fifth time that night, shaking his head and grinning as he set the table.

Ollie nodded from the couch, beaming.

"I'm surprised he had a pair," said Feya, not looking up from the story she was reading Ella.

"I'm not sure, but he might have pissed himself as well," said Ollie, though everyone knew it was an embellishment.

Kess' voice found them from a bedroom. "*Ollie*—language."

"She has ears like a bat," Feya whispered. She looked at Ollie, hungry for more details. "Did he though?"

Ollie considered. "You know, I'm pretty sure he did."

Kess popped her head out. "Enough gossip. You know your dad is in trouble."

"He'll be fine," said Kai. "He only attacked Lukas to defend a Novice, and he didn't use excessive force or inflict any undue damage. Well, at least physically. Lukas' reputation, however…"

Ridian was only half-listening.

When you attack my kids, you attack me. That's what Theodor had said. *My kids.*

What did Theodor mean by that? Did he just mean Ollie and the others, or was Ridian included? Probably not. But embarrassing as it was to admit—even to himself—Ridian wanted Theodor to include him as one of his own. But beneath the embarrassment lay a deep sadness. He rarely thought of his own father. The man was a near non-entity. But when he did, he wondered how different his life might have been. Perhaps his mother wouldn't have lost her mind. Perhaps he and Rayna wouldn't have been born in a prison. Perhaps they would have all lived happily together. Perhaps not on The Edge. Perhaps, perhaps, perhaps…

When you attack my kids, you attack me. What had Theodor meant? Ridian couldn't help but wonder.

258

Chapter 25

The next morning, Stonecrow Cavern buzzed with pilgrims, mumbling prayers. It was terribly distracting, so Ridian left his meditations early. He made his way through the Living Fort, which was bustling despite the early hour. Beyond the wall, Last Stand Meadow gleamed with shimmering dew. The lack of frost would make his submersions beneath Madman's Falls easier, but for Ridian, easier didn't mean better. *Fear is the Gate, pain is the key,* after all. Less suffering meant less progress. And the Soulcaster trials were tomorrow. *Tomorrow.* It was a depressing thought. Even if he miraculously won all three fights, without Splitting, he couldn't bond—and without that bond, Tann wouldn't take him to kill Hector and save Rayna.

Tann and Yanala were already at Madman's Falls, arguing with a soaked, blue-lipped Knight. "I can't leave, alright," shouted the Knight above the roaring water. "Just take no for an answer." The man shivered beneath his water-clogged cloak, his nose a strawberry red.

"Come on," said Tann. "I've got one more lesson before the Trials. Your presence will be a distraction."

"You think I enjoy standing out here freezing my arse off? I'm a Fidician Knight, for Fidic's sake. I didn't sign up for this. But there's always some idiot this time of year who goes for a swim to impress a girl or drinks the water on a dare."

"At this time of day? Come on. One hour. Give me one hour."

"Sevron has ordered a guard around the clock. It's my neck if I leave."

"I'm a Fidician Knight too, you know. Yanala and I can stand guard."

Yanala stretched out and yawned.

The Knight's red nose dripped. He sniffed and looked about, clearly tempted.

"One hour," said Tann. "Enough time to get a hot breakfast and be back before anybody knows."

The Knight's resolve broke. "One hour. And don't let anyone else pass." Then the Knight squelched past Ridian without a glance, eager for his hot breakfast.

"You're early," said Tann, turning around. "Good. We can get started."

Ridian entered the tall ring of towering stone, and shivered from the gentle fall of water, drifting down like snowflakes. He looked at the churning water and lost heart. "What's the point," he said. "All bloody winter, I've been tormenting myself, and it hasn't worked."

Tann raised an eyebrow. "You giving up?"

"No, it's just… I've heard the passes into Kyrosia will be open in a matter of days. Would you take me if—"

"If you're not bonded with a Familiar, you can't come," said Tann. "We'll be infiltrating a cult of Soulcasters. It will be very dangerous, and if you're unable to harness a Soulcaster's power, you'll be easy pickings. Worse still, you would compromise the whole mission." Tann sighed. "You've done well, Ridian. You have. You've shown more grit than most. You should be proud of yourself." Tann nodded at the roaring falls. "Come. Yanala's got a good feeling about today."

Ridian undressed and climbed over the low wall containing the water. He was goose-fleshed, and his whole body shivered, but he'd been through worse. He was about to step into the water when he hesitated. "Tann?" he said. "I'm... I'm sorry."

Tann frowned. "For what?"

"For leaving you to die. It was a pretty crappy thing to do. And, well, I'm sorry."

Tann looked away awkwardly and scratched the back of his neck. "Oh, that's—that's fine. It's nothing. You'd just lost your sister. No hard feelings. Besides, seeing you suffer all these months has softened my heart." He grinned.

Ridian grinned back, even as he shivered. "Sick bastard."

Tann laughed, and the sound made Ridian feel a little lighter. He hadn't even realised how much he longed for Tann's forgiveness. Not just to manipulate the man into helping him, but because... well, he wasn't sure why. But it still felt good.

"Alright, mate," said Tann. "You know what to do."

"Be willing to die? Some nonsense like that?"

Tann winked and made a clicking sound with his mouth. "That's right. Fear is the gate."

"Pain is the key," said Ridian, teeth chattering, breath steaming, every instinct telling him to stay out of the water. He took a long breath, embraced the coming pain, and slid into the skin-burning, chest-pounding, skull-crushing water. It boomed in his ears as his head went under, and the urge to resurface was immense. *It's just pain*, he told himself. But he couldn't quite detach today, and he went to shoot up—

But strong hands clamped onto his shoulders and held him under. Panic exploded through Ridian as he looked up: Tann's face was rippling and undulating above the surface of the water. Tann was drowning him. Ridian thrashed, squirmed, and clawed at Tann's hands. All useless. Tann was impossibly strong. It was like pushing against a mountain. *I'm going to die.* Then, through the panic, a realisation struck Ridian. *Tann's not trying to kill me; he's pushing me. But he can only take me so far.* Ridian stopped fighting. As he did, Tann let go, and to Ridian's surprise, he didn't immediately shoot to the surface. His lungs screamed for air, but he let them scream.

Pain is the key.

Then, through the crescendo of pain, something strange happened. A horizon of sheer Nothing opened up before him. Ridian couldn't see it, but it was there. It was the Nothing after Death. It yawned open to receive him, and black terror swelled. Ridian almost fled, and he knew that if he had not endured countless hours of suffering in recent months with Tann—and with Lukas, strangely enough—he could not have withstood it. He just needed to step forward into it, into the Nothing. If he did, he would Split and become a Soulcaster. He knew he would. He knew he could. But abject terror tethered him. How could he possibly step forward into it? It was all he could do to stand there, upon the edge of that endless, dark plane.

Then he remembered Rayna. He remembered stepping

onto The Mire, into certain death. He'd done this before, he realised. He could do it again.

Terror swelled. He embraced it. Just like the cold-crushing pain. If he could embrace that, he could embrace this. He pushed forward, against the fear. He pushed, pushed, *PUSHED*—

And shot away from his body like an arrow into The Black. Into the Astral Plane. He couldn't see. He couldn't hear. He couldn't feel. But he could sense things—living things. There was Tann, Yanala, and his own body below. Rivulets of dazzling light ran through their translucent forms. It trickled through their veins, nerves, arteries… The colours were strange and unearthly. Colours he'd never seen with his physical eyes. He went closer; he could do that. A quivering ball of light emanated from Tann's head, like a tiny sun. It was the source of all the trickling rivulets of light.

Tann's soul, Ridian knew with certainty and awe.

He looked at Yanala. Her soul sat in her chest and fed her body Rava. Yes, Rava. Ridian knew the strange light to be Rava. Life itself, as Mother Asarah had said. He just knew it.

A silky river of light connected Ridian's floating mind to his body. He knew that connection kept his body alive, and if it disappeared, he would die. He needed to go back. Already, the cord was thinning. Soon, the connection would be lost. He shot back along that cord of light, quick as a whip, and opened his eyes.

He was lying on the ground, staring up at Tann and Yanala, who stooped over him.

Tann shoved a vial in Ridian's face. "Drink this," he

commanded, and before Ridian could do anything, the vial was poured down his throat. It had the pungent taste of Quickfix, and Ridian gagged.

"So?" asked Tann. "Did it work?"

"You drowned me, not knowing if it was going to work?"

"Did it though?"

Ridian grinned.

"I knew it," cried Tann, jumping to his feet, shaking his fists in triumph. Yanala danced in a circle, then lifted her snout to howl.

"Think you could do it again?" asked Tann.

Ridian searched within himself, and, to his surprise, he could feel his soul, sitting in his skull, deep within his brain. "You know what? I do."

Chapter 26

With the Soulcaster Trials starting tomorrow, Ridian, Kai, and Feya practiced and discussed Varki tactics late into the night. Feya seemed determined to bite her nails to their roots, and though Ollie was allowed to stay up, he'd long fallen asleep, sprawled on the couch.

Ridian could Split. He didn't tell the family. Telling Feya he had achieved in a few months what she had strived for years to accomplish would just make her more nervous, not to mention resentful. He didn't want to deal with that now. He needed to focus on Varki.

Kai stopped Ridian midway through the Tumbling Boulder sequence. "You know," he said sincerely, "to give that jerk Lukas Lick-Ass some credit, he's taught you pretty well. You're actually not that bad."

When they finally went to bed, Ridian tossed and turned, thinking of the day to come. The Varki Tournament: all Novices could enter, though only the older ones dared. They wouldn't be sparring tomorrow. No, they would be fighting for a place among the Fidician Knights, and apparently, nobody pulled their punches. Ridian would have to face three randomly selected opponents and beat two of them. Would they be bigger? Maybe. Stronger?

Probably. More skilled? Definitely. All he had was sheer desperation.

When Ridian woke early, he knew he'd get no more sleep. So, he dressed and went downstairs. Feya was already there, haggard-looking, rifling through the kitchen, looking for something to eat. *Her nails must have finally run out*, thought Ridian.

Theodor emerged soon after, fresh as hot bread. "My little champions!" he said, arms wide to embrace them. "Big day! *Big day!* Let's make you something to eat."

Theodor fussed over them all morning until it was time to go. The whole family were dressed for the occasion: Theodor in his pristine Whites; Kess and Ella in their best; Kai looking dashing in his Grey; while Ridian, Kai, and Ollie wore freshly cleaned Browns.

"You two won't be needing those for long," said Theodor to Ridian and Feya with a smile.

The road to the Living Fort was busy with pilgrims: singing, chanting, banging drums, blowing whistles, and almost dancing uphill. Apparently, today was an exciting day for everyone involved. Everyone except Ridian and Feya. Nerves fluttered in Ridian's stomach, and Feya looked sick. Ridian kept trying to catch her eye, to reassure her—or perhaps himself—but she stared fixedly into the distance, cross-armed and sullen. The cart rattled on, and Ridian's dread grew.

They had left Felix and Zeke at home. When Ridian asked why, Kai replied, "All Familiars are forbidden at the Trials. Stops people cheating."

"Aren't Familiars illegal before initiation anyways?" asked Ridian.

Kai shrugged. "Cheating and law-breaking are close relatives. Those tempted by one are often tempted by the other."

Near the top of the hill, the road became more congested, and they decided to park the cart at the side of the road and walk. The sun was glorious, birds sang, and strangers clapped Ridian and Feya on the back and wished them luck. None of it made Ridian feel any better. Soon enough, they crossed Last Stand Meadow and entered the bailey. All the shops were closed. Everybody, it seemed, was heading to the Trials. Soon, the glorious Lion's Den rose before them, and they followed the crowd through an arched tunnel leading to the amphitheatre.

Halfway through, before it spilled onto the sandy arena, Feya pulled Ridian aside. "This way," she said, pulling him towards a side door.

Two Knights stood guard, flanked by a pair of wolves, but allowed Ridian and Feya in with a nod. Ridian looked back in time to see the Thunderfells waving them off eagerly and wishing them good luck. The passageway was narrow and dark, and the bustling noise of the crowd became more muffled with every step. Down the passageway was a gloomy room full of Brown-robed Novices. A single skylight allowed a vertical shaft of dull light to partly illuminate their nervous faces. Some sat on the benches that framed the room. Most were hunched over and holding their heads. Others paced and rolled their shoulders, warming up. Others stuck out their chins and shot hard glances that said, *I'm not afraid of you.*

Ridian felt sick; soon he would be fighting one of them—no, three of them—and they all seemed so menacing. Even the smaller ones were tendon-lean and dangerous-looking. He felt as if he were sitting in a wolf's lair. The room was full of tense silence, which deepened as everyone turned to stare at the newcomers. Their faces fell as they saw Feya. *Please, not her,* their expressions declared. But as they looked at Ridian, their eyes filled with something akin to hunger. Some of the Novices murmured to each other and sniggered. Ridian was clearly an easy win.

Ridian forced himself to stand tall as he followed Feya to an empty bench.

"Good luck," said Feya to a girl nearby.

"Good luck," the girl replied, but neither of them meant it. They might have been friends outside of this room, but not now. Now, they were opponents.

Feya sidled up close to Ridian. Their knees touched, and her wild hair tickled his shoulder. "Everyone knows you're new," Feya whispered. "And they all know you've been training with the little kids. But they don't know you've been training with me. They will underestimate you."

Ridian hoped so. It was the only advantage he had.

Minutes rolled by, and more Novices entered to receive the same speculative look-over from their peers. They waited, listening to the noise of the crowd swell, until Nawar, the young Knight who had arrested Ridian, entered. He stood solemn and expressionless in the doorway. "Come," he commanded, and they followed him down another corridor. The light grew, and before Ridian knew it, he was standing in dazzling sunlight to thunderous applause.

Squinting, Ridian saw hundreds—*thousands*—of people cheering from the rising stands. Shoulder to shoulder, row upon row, and tier upon tier—Ridian had never seen so many people in one spot. And they were all here to see him get his arse kicked.

Ridian and the rest of the initiates walked to the centre of the arena. Sand crunched unheard beneath their feet. For the longest time, he saw no one he recognised, until Feya nudged him and nodded up at the Thunderfells, who sat waving near the front row. Ridian returned a tiny wave, making the family bounce in their seats with excitement.

Beneath a shaded dais sat Mother Asarah, Prince Bevrik, and Commander Sevron. Mother Asarah rested her spotted hands on her cane and smiled, Prince Bevrik kept readjusting the crown that slid down his ears, and Sevron scowled at them with his single angry eye. Did the eye linger on Ridian? Knights surrounded the dais, ready and alert. They gripped sword handles and loosened the blades in their sheaths. They were even flanked by Familiars that weren't supposed to be present.

They're twitchy, thought Ridian. It reminded him of Mudwall soldiers whenever they caught wind of rebellion.

"What's up with them?" Ridian asked Feya.

"There's been a jailbreak. Runaway psychopaths make them jumpy. But they'll find them. Always do."

Ridian agreed; he couldn't imagine convicts getting far when Fidicia was full of Soulcasters and their Familiars. *Speaking of psychopaths.* Lukas was nowhere to be seen. Rumour had it that he'd been sentenced to guard duty at Madman's Falls as punishment for his 'unmasterly' transgression. Ridian hoped so. He imagined a sulking Lukas red-nosed and shivering, and it cheered him up.

And there was Tann, standing at the farthest and highest

row. It was strange seeing him here. When not training Ridian, Tann seemed to disappear, and given the dirty looks people were giving him, Ridian could see why.

The crowd continued to roar until Sevron stood and held up a hand, and, like magic, he received a quick, expectant silence, tense as a bowstring. "Who dares Trial for the Fidician Order?" boomed Sevron with his arms wide to the audience.

"We do!" shouted Ridian and the other Initiates.

Sevron's eye settled on them. Silence reigned. "Who dares think themselves worthy to become a Knight in the line of Daegan the Lion?"

"We do!" Ridian and the initiates declared again.

"Who dares prove their prowess at Varki, the sacred combat of our people?"

"We do!"

"Then let the names be drawn!"

The crowd roared into life as a Knight carried a bowl towards Sevron. The crowd hushed as Sevron dipped his hand into the bowl and drew out two strips of paper. He read them, then bellowed, "Dannion Mathews and Cassandra Beston!"

At these names, a hooked-nosed boy and a muscular girl among the Initiates bowed.

Sevron pulled more slips, called the names, and the pairs were matched. Feya was paired with a mousy brown-haired girl, who looked devastated.

Finally—

"Ridian of Mudwall and Jacob Althrow!"

Ridian bowed, feeling the weight of many eyes upon him. He peeped around, looking for his opponent, for this Jacob Althrow. None of the Initiates returned his gaze until a hulking, thick-set boy grinned at him with perverse delight. *You're no match for me,* the boy seemed to say with a dismissive shake of his head. Ridian agreed. Taller, broader, and far more muscular, Jacob Althrow was a living bloody weapon.

Other names were called, but Ridian didn't hear. He felt like he was freefalling. He'd worked his arse off the last few months, hell-bent, focused, grasping at even the smallest semblance of hope. Now that his opponent stood sneering before him, it felt like he was losing Rayna all over again.

With names called, Sevron took a seat while Nawar led Ridian and the other Initiates to open seating in the front row. All except Dannion Mathews and Cassandra Beston, who remained in the arena. Jacob Althrow never took his eyes off Ridian. He grinned like a wolf circling its prey. Ridian pretended not to see.

"Feya," said Ridian. "Is that Jacob Althrow—"

"As terrifying as he looks?" said Feya. "You want the truth?"

Ridian nodded, not sure that he did.

Feya scrutinised the brute with a professional eye. "He's the best fighter in the school. I've got better form, but he's far superior in terms of sheer power. Pretty rotten luck."

Ridian frowned at Sevron. *Rotten luck indeed.*

"And he's not just strong," Feya continued. "He's fast. Usually, guys his size are a bit slow, but he's…" Feya saw something in Ridian's face and changed tack. "But his ego's bigger than he is, really. Ego's a weakness. Besides, you have two other fights. Oh look, the family's waving."

They were. Waving and beaming, desperate to convey

their pride. Ridian didn't know why, but seeing the family's unabashed love for her made him a little sad—and jealous. Lost gods, he was pathetic sometimes.

Nawar approached the two fighters, and the noise of the crowd dimmed. He said something, then signalled to a nearby Knight, who flipped a sand timer and struck a bell. The crowd erupted into cheers as Dannion and Cassandra began their fight. And what a fight it was. They spun and struck and blocked and weaved a furious dance. Ridian caught snatches of Varki sequences, but mostly, he saw a bemusing flow of movement. Fist, elbow, knee, foot—all were used to strike and block and strike again. He turned to Feya with what must have been dismay clear on his face.

"You'll be fine," said Feya, with hollow encouragement.

Soon enough, the sand timer ran out, the bell rang, and the fighters sprang away from each other. Gasping for breath, Dannion took a swig of water, while Cassandra paced the arena. Their break was short-lived, however. A smaller sand timer ran out, and the bell heralded another furious round.

After the third round, the fight was over. Dannion and Cassandra were heaving and slick with sweat. Nawar consulted with Sevron, and after a moment of secret discourse, Sevron exclaimed, "Dannion Mathews, three points; Cassandra Beston, seven!"

Cassandra raised her muscular arms in victory to the cheering crowd, while Dannion dropped his head and slunk away. The following fights were just as impressive, with each pair seeming a near-perfect match. All except Feya and her partner. Feya slid around her opponent with calm assurance, controlling the flow. She wasn't faster, Ridian saw. No, her real strength came from moving only as far as needed, when needed. The girl would strike, and Feya would dodge a mere inch, or take a small quarter-step back, no movement wasted. She seemed able to predict the girl's every move, sending a tight jab whenever the girl came into range. Consequently, Feya appeared fresh and relaxed in the third round, while her overworked opponent panted from exertion. Finally, the girl made the smallest of mistakes and was instantly punished. She lost balance—only for a second—and Feya launched a swivelling back kick into the girl's head, knocking her nearly senseless. The bell rang early to declare Feya's victory. *When you strike, strike only once.* Feya offered a hand to the stunned girl, and they walked back to the seats, one supported by the other.

"Nice work," said Ridian. "You made that look so easy."

Feya shrugged as she plonked herself down, but for some reason, she looked troubled.

As fights came and went, Ridian's anxiety grew, until at last, Sevron's voice echoed through the arena. "Ridian of Mudwall and Jacob Althrow!"

Time slowed and the chanting seemed to dwindle to a faint and distant roar. Vaguely, he heard Feya say, 'Get up.' Then, somehow, he was shuffling onto the arena and into the white circle painted in the sand that marked the ring. His legs seemed to move of their own accord. And there was Jacob—the weapon—Althrow: grinning, grinning, grinning, muscles rippling. He was a perfect specimen, and the smug bastard knew it. His eyes never left Ridian's. Ridian struggled to hold his gaze, but glanced away after a few seconds—only for a moment, but it was enough. Jacob's face lit up with glee. *I've already broken you,* that smile said.

You're already done.

Nawar strolled towards them, emotionless as always. "Fights start and stop when you hear the bell. Any strikes outside of that will be penalised. If you leave the ring, you will be penalised. The rounds go for two minutes. The fight ends after three rounds or if an opponent goes limp or calls for a stop. Understood?"

Ridian and Jacob nodded, and Nawar marched away, leaving Ridian and Jacob alone.

"You'll be screaming for that bell in less than five seconds," said Jacob. "I'm going to smear the ground with your soft, newbie arse. Five seconds, you'll see."

It was all Ridian could do to stand his ground. What had Feya said? *They don't know you've been training with me. They will underestimate you.* And Jacob had a big ego. How could Ridian exploit that? And like that, an idea revealed itself. Ridian allowed all the fear he felt to manifest itself on his face, then he assumed his old stance— the wrong foot forward, legs too far apart, torso too square. He held himself stiff, flat-footed, hands low. Everything was wrong. The crowd mumbled and laughed amongst themselves. Jacob chuckled. *This is too easy,* his smug grin said.

He's buying it, thought Ridian, and he did his best to hold the now unfamiliar posture. He glanced at Feya. Her eyes danced with delighted knowing. The bell rang, and the world shrank to a mere ten paces as Jacob shot toward him. As planned, Ridian did the obvious thing: a clumsy back step, the reflexive retreat of a scared, soft-arse newbie. Only it wasn't. Ridian planted the foot, sank into his now familiar combat stance, and jabbed out a stretching front foot. The kick passed Jacob's unsuspecting guard and struck his face.

Jacob stumbled backward, wiped his lip, and stared at the blood on his fingertips, confused.

The crowd roared. It was easily the quickest point of the day, and Jacob flushed with embarrassment and anger. He looked at Ridian, seeing him as if for the first time.

Ridian bounced on his toes. "That's five seconds."

All swagger gone, Jacob advanced, and though his eyes blazed, he didn't lose his composure. He was cautious now, sending out tentative jabs and exploratory kicks, never once giving Ridian an opening. Ridian would not land another hit, that he knew. Jacob was quicker, stronger, more skilled, and had better instincts. So Ridian ran. Side-step after side-step, pirouette after pirouette, he protected himself and his one precious point. Over the whole ring, he scampered—away, away, away.

The bell rang, calling the first round to an end. Jacob roared in frustration, and the crowd returned to Ridian's attention with a blast of noise. People cheered, happy to support the underdog. It was exhilarating. The Thunderfells were beside themselves, and even Tann looked impressed.

Ridian ran to his seat, where Feya whooped and cheered, and took a swig from his waterskin. The water was warm, but he didn't care. He was thirsty, and it did the job. By this time, Kai had worked his way down to the Initiate seating. "Holy Fidic's Fiddle, Ridian! I didn't know you could fight this well. You're doing awesome."

Feya wore a wry smile. "Lick-Ass taught you well, didn't he?"

"Remind me to thank him, will you?" said Ridian.

"Nifty trick," said Kai. "Pretending to suck, then bam!" He gave the air a tidy uppercut. "Right in the kisser."

Feya frowned, suddenly serious. "Ridian, listen. You're doing well, but don't let him grab you. If he does, it's over."

Ridian nodded. "The fight stops when the fighter stops." Then he ran back to the ring where Jacob waited for him.

The bell rang, and Jacob hurtled forward. He didn't even flinch at Ridian's fake jab, but grasped the outthrust wrist. Ridian tried to pull away but failed, and a second later, he found himself on his knees, pain smarting through his locked elbow. Reflexively, Ridian slipped into his detached state of mind. He would be damned before he gave in. Jacob would have to snap his arm. But the bell rang, announcing Ridian's loss. The second round had only lasted five seconds.

***

Ridian sat with his chin resting on his palm. He didn't watch the fights, he didn't talk, he didn't listen to Feya prattle on about how he'd done well and how he shouldn't be discouraged. Ridian had duped Jacob and gotten a single point. *Whoop-de-doo.*

The bell rang a handful of times; fights came and went. Ridian knew he should be analysing the fights and studying his prospective opponent's strengths and weaknesses. But what was the point? Ridian was no match for these guys. They'd trained their entire lives for this. It was over. He was finished.

Sevron drew the names for round two. The first pair was… "Ridian of Mudwall and Feya Thunderfell!"

You've got to be kidding. Heart sinking, Ridian looked at Feya. She looked stricken. She didn't want this—an easy win at Ridian's expense. That was something, at least. She stood and walked into the arena. Ridian followed, numb. He stole a glance at the Thunderfells. They didn't look happy either. That was also something. *At least Feya will have her spot in the Fidician Order.*

Within the ring, they faced each other. Feya couldn't meet his eye. Was it guilt?

The bell rang, and, as the crowd roared, Feya met his eye and mouthed, "Fifty per cent."

Fifty percent?

She launched at him, but not as fast as she might have. She threw a few punches, quick as viper bites, but they lacked real sting, and Ridian swatted them aside. She sent a twirling kick, beautiful but obvious—Ridian saw it coming and lunged backwards, out of the way. *She's giving me the fight,* Ridian realised with astonishment as he countered with his own low kick.

Feya blocked with a raised shin. "Sixty percent," she hissed, mouth barely moving. "We need to make it look good, or they'll think it's rigged." She struck out, faster, harder. Ridian dodged, but it was a close thing.

"Seventy."

It was on. Seventy percent was the highest intensity they had sparred at, and Ridian often lost.

"Eighty."

Ridian scampered back, overwhelmed by the onslaught. Her strikes were like whip cracks. How was he supposed to win at eighty percent?

"Moon and Riverstone, ninety percent," she said, then, amid her flurry of kicks and punches, she began performing the Moon sequence. Ridian understood immediately. Feya would perform the Moon sequence, then transition into Riverstone—the two sequences she always warned never to do back-to-back.

"They're both good sequences," she had said. "But when you transition between them, there is a moment where you leave yourself totally exposed."

Ridian remembered that moment, even as he blundered away from Feya, who was a torrent of seamless, effortless, furious motion.

Feya was close to the end of the Moon sequence now. Crouching low, Feya switched feet and shot a low, sweeping roundhouse kick.

Now! Ridian jumped over the whooshing leg, and, as Feya twirled, her face rotated out of sight. As it came back around, Ridian met her spinning cheek with his fist. Not hard. At the last moment, he took the sting out of it. Still, it stopped her in her tracks, and she crumpled to the ground. As she lay dazed, Ridian was only vaguely aware of the ringing bell.

✳✳✳

"Why?" was all Ridian could ask when they were back in their seats. Feya, it turned out, wasn't as hurt as she made out. She even winked at him when he helped her up.

"You needed a win," Feya replied as she massaged her jaw. "Besides, I'll win the next one."

The win had been handed to him, but it still counted. Maybe he could squeeze another win from his next opponent? Maybe they'd be injured? Maybe they'd be tired? He wasn't tired. He'd only fought one full round and two brief ones. He was fresh and injury-free, while most of the other fighters appeared to have fully exerted themselves over numerous rounds. Hope rekindled, Ridian's legs bounced with anxious excitement as he examined the remaining fights very closely. Who was fast? Who was slow? Who was strong? Who favoured their right leg? Their left? What was their primary style? Defensive? Offensive? Responsive? Opportunistic? He watched them all and took note.

When the round two fights ended, Mother Asarah stood, stooping over her cane. She looked around and smiled, and that was enough to hush the crowd. "Just as Fidic told a riddle for Kyros," she said, her thin voice carrying over the stands. "I, too, shall tell a riddle for you." She cleared her throat, and the crowd fell into an even deeper, more expectant silence.

> "Bones of stone, skin of wood,
> Dry blood understood.
> Cut me, I sharpen,
> Hold me, I darken."

There was a delighted murmur when Mother Asarah finished. You could feel the collective intellectual strain. "Say it again," someone cried, and she obliged. Then someone shouted, "An axe!" Another said, "Hammer!" But Mother Asarah just shook her head and smiled, all pleased with herself. After a few seconds of silence, tense as a bowstring, an excited voice squealed, "Pencil! It's a pencil!"

It was Ollie. He was on his toes, his index finger stretched into the air as far as it would go.

Mother Asarah croaked a laugh. "A pencil, indeed. Well

done." Then the crowd clapped and cheered and slapped their foreheads as if they couldn't believe they didn't get it straight away.

"Ollie won!" cried Feya, slapping Ridian's arm. "Can you believe it! He won!"

Beaming, Ollie grinned in his seat, cheeks red as apples, while Theodor and Kess grabbed him by the shoulders and throttled him in their excitement. *Good for you, Ollie,* thought Ridian, finding himself cheering just as loud as Feya. *Good for you.*

Mother Asarah raised a hand, and silence slowly returned. "For your Fidic-quick wit, you and a friend shall enjoy a seat of honour at our cherished fireworks."

More applause, but a bored-looking Sevron stepped forward, plucked paper strips from the bowl, and began calling names. Finally, he boomed, "Ridian of Mudwall and Dain Trembel."

Ridian looked about for this Dain and found a wiry boy stealing a glance at him.

"What's the go with Dain?" asked Ridian.

Feya's eyes were wide with excitement. "Dain's an amazing fighter—but Ridian—his heart's not in it. He hates the idea of becoming a Knight. He wants to become a Steward. He's only going through the motions to appease his father. You can do it, Ridian. You can beat him, I'm sure of it. He wants to lose."

Ridian's legs were really bouncing now. This was more than he could have hoped for. "Are you sure? He wasn't just playing mind games with you?"

"Mind games?" Feya laughed. "Trust me. Dain's not the mind-game type."

There were two fights before Ridian's. All the while, Feya whispered instructions. "Remember, he's still a better fighter than you, and known to have a temper. If you hit him too hard or hit him in the face, he may change his mind and thump you back. We don't want that. All you need to do is land some soft torso shots and dance away. Remember, he has his pride. He just wants to lose with some dignity. He's already won a fight, and you beat me, so there's no shame in losing to you now. Just don't hit him in the face."

It was time. Ridian took a last-minute swig of his warm water before entering the ring. Dain seemed to drag himself, and Ridian almost felt sorry for him: a skilled fighter who needed to lose to a newbie to live the life he wanted. Facing each other, Dain made a show of bouncing on the balls of his feet, but it was lacklustre, and his guard was low and lazy. And he wasn't scanning for weaknesses the way Ridian was. Feya was right, he wanted to lose. Adrenaline coursed through Ridian. He might actually beat this guy—a step closer to joining the Fidician Order; a step closer to saving Rayna.

The bell rang, and they circled each other, sending out a tentative jab here and a half-hearted kick there. Seconds passed with little action. Dain wasn't committing, and neither was Ridian. They just kept sliding around the arena, waiting for the other to do something. Someone in the crowd booed, and others joined in. They did not appreciate the gutless display. Dain glanced at the crowd, and his face seemed to harden. He darted forward and popped a few smart punches. Ridian blocked the jabs but caught a right cross, which glanced off his temple. The crowd applauded, and Dain's frown relaxed. Feya was right: Dain wanted to lose, but he still had his pride. Ridian needed to up the ante. He needed to look impressive, or else Dain might choose to beat him after all, his own future be damned.

Ridian committed to an assault: jab, jab, front-kick, switch, jab, hook. His guard was sloppy, he knew, but he trusted Dain not to counter. To Ridian's delight, he landed a turning kick into Dain's side. A soft blow—probably why Dain let it through—but the crowd still loved it, showing their appreciation with whoops and cheers. The bell rang, and Ridian ran to his seat, elated.

"Great work!" said Feya. "Keep the intensity up. Just don't hit his face."

Ridian looked up at Tann, who pulled a face that said, 'Not bad.' Coming from Tann, it was a compliment like no other. Grinning, Ridian took a swig from his water skin and got a shock as the water passed his lips—it was freezing. In fact, the skin itself was beaded with cold condensation.

Is this mine? thought Ridian. It looked the same, and it lay right where he'd left it, but it was ice cold. *Never mind.* Nawar was signalling for round two, and Ridian jogged back to face Dain.

I've got this, thought Ridian, and he glimpsed over Dain's shoulder at Feya, upright and eager, and behind her—

Was Lukas.

A bolt of anxiety shot through Ridian. The hated teacher hid beneath a deep hood, and the expression of perverse joy on that wretched face turned Ridian's stomach. Lukas grabbed the cold waterskin Ridian had just drunk from and disappeared.

Dain's fist slammed into his Ridian's face. He'd missed the bell. Ridian stumbled backwards and shook his head clear, tasting blood. *Focus, Ridian.* Dain wasn't going to prostrate himself and give him the win. But Ridian still glanced back to find Lukas—the man had vanished, and that disturbed him even more.

The round was a shambles. Ridian did little but parry and run, and he even lost a point from his foot sliding outside the ring.

"What are you doing?" Feya admonished after the bell.

Ridian scanned the stands full of smiling, laughing faces—parents, children, friends, family. All innocent. All mirthful. He couldn't see Lukas anywhere. "Lukas," said Ridian. "He was here."

"So?"

"He took my waterskin."

Feya flung a waterskin at him. "Take mine."

"No! He took mine and—"

Feya slapped him smartly across the face. "Ridian. Wake up. Think of your sister."

Stunned, Ridian stared at her. "You're right," he said, rubbing his cheek. "Thanks. I needed that."

Feya pushed him onto the arena. "There's more where that came from. Now, get a hit and back off. Get a hit, back off."

Ridian ran back into the ring, but as he did, he suddenly felt very weird. His legs wobbled, his hands shook, and what's more, the crowd sounded strange: low, warped, and stretched—as if time were slowing down. Indeed, Dain was moving with glacial slowness. Time was slowing down. But not his heart—oh, lost gods—not his heart. It hammered along like the hooves of a dozen galloping horses. Blood pounded in his ears.

Dain turned to face him, but Dain was no longer there. It was *Rayna*.

Ridian was too stunned to speak, to move. Rayna just stood there, smiling at him, with a curious smile he didn't recognise, her head cocked in amusement. Then her smile grew and grew and grew until it was a giant, leering grin. It stretched wider, wider still—too wide. Her lips began to tear down the middle. Ridian cried out in horror, and she laughed, a terrifying laugh of many voices, her mouth snapping open and closed, open and closed. With each laugh, her lips kept tearing—towards the nose and down her chin. Then she grabbed the torn flaps and gave a sharp tug, tearing the skin of her face down the middle. From neck to forehead, her skin was split, and she began peeling it away like a sticky, sinewy mask. Shivering with twisted satisfaction, she laughed that legion laugh. She tugged again and again, until, to Ridian's horror, the skin of her whole body was shed. And beneath the flayed skin lay a nightmare of blood and bone—a demon that twitched and drooled and gnashed its jaws.

Ridian screamed and ran, tripping over in his panic. It would chase him, he knew, and he would feel the piercing claws and the sinking teeth. He glanced back. The demon was gone. The stadium was gone.

Just a dead field and a dying tree.

Mother stood, gazing over the hill, waiting. What was she waiting for? Then the demon came into view, cresting the hill. Then another appeared, then another, then another…

"WITCH!" the demons shouted in voices like rending iron, and they dashed down the hill to devour Ridian's mother. But Ridian was shaking with an unspeakable rage. He would

rip them apart. He would crush their bones. *He* would devour *them*.

Then everything went black, and he remembered no more.

Chapter 27

Ridian awoke to the taste of vomit. He lay in a strange bed in a dark room. The image of Rayna tearing the skin from her face flashed across his mind with startling clarity. He went to sit up but couldn't. Leather straps bound him from his forehead to his ankles. He strained: the bedframe rattled, the leather creaked, but he couldn't move an inch. He couldn't even cry out; something clogged his mouth. Suddenly, a man loomed over him, and Ridian released a muffled scream of fear. The man adjusted his glasses and peered down at Ridian. It was Theodor, but as he'd never seen him. He was haggard and worn, his eyes sunken and black-rimmed. "Ridian? Is that you?" His voice was tremulous and strained.

Ridian glared at him. *Who else?*

Theodor must have seen something in Ridian's eyes, for the tension melted from his face. "It is you! Thank goodness. You've been out for almost eight hours. How are you feeling?"

Ridian mumbled.

"Oh, your mouthguard," said Theodor, and he removed a wad of cotton, drenched in strings of saliva from Ridian's mouth. Theodor wiped Ridian's chin dry with a hanky.

"Where am I?" croaked Ridian. His throat felt strained from shouting.

Theodor shushed him, the same gentle shush he used to calm little Ella. "It's okay, Ridian. It's okay. You're in the hospital. You're safe."

Ridian looked about. The small windowless room was padded. "The psychiatric wing?" His heart quickened. "Why am I bound up like this?"

"The straps were to keep you safe. The mouth guard was to stop you from… from biting." Theodor began unbuckling the leather straps, starting with the one across Ridian's forehead. "We've been so worried about you. The family has not left your side. The only reason they aren't still here is because visiting hours are over, and the bloody higher-ups forced them out. I only managed to stay by pulling a few strings."

Ridian couldn't think straight. "What the hell happened?"

"You were poisoned." Theodor took a long, shuddering breath. "But you're okay now. That's the main thing." He smiled, and just like that, he was something of his old self again.

Ridian was astonished by the depth of Theodor's emotion. "Poisoned?"

"*Boletus Furosis*," said Theodor with a long sigh. "It's a local mushroom. It—"

"Looney Shrooms," Ridian cut in. "They poison Madman's Falls. They make you bat-shit crazy." Ridian laughed dryly, remembering Remmy's apt description, then stopped with sudden realization. "Did I hurt anyone?"

Theodor undid the buckle about Ridian's chest, then shot his hands skyward in an emphatic gesture. "Thank Roki, no!

You attacked the dais, of all places. They thought you were trying to assassinate the Prince! I almost died. Everyone's been on such high alert because of those escaped convicts. But thankfully, Nawar knocked you out quick-smart before any damage was done."

Ridian's wrists were now free, and he rubbed a lump on his head gingerly. "How was I poisoned?"

Well-concealed anger broiled in Theodor's eyes, and Ridian caught a glimpse of the old war veteran. "Turns out, some resented your presence at the Trials. I heard rumours, of course, but shrugged them off. Who could be so prejudiced? So pig-headed? So puritanical? But when they pitted you against Jacob, then Feya, then Dain—the three best fighters in the school!" Theodor huffed. "Coincidence? I think not."

Theodor fumbled with the last strap about Ridian's ankle. It slid off and clanked against the bed leg. Ridian stretched and rubbed his tender wrists. Sevron's bitter words from the fair came back to him: *You will never be a Knight. I swear it.*

"Sevron rigged the ballot?" asked Ridian, sitting up.

"Seems so," said Theodor. "Impossible to prove, though. But rigging a ballot is one thing. To poison a student..." He shook his head in utter disbelief. "Who could do such a thing?"

Ridian remembered the ice-cold waterskin, and Lukas grinning beneath his hood. "Lukas," he said with mounting fury. "Lukas poisoned me." He clenched his fists, and for a moment he was so frustrated that he almost punched the wall.

Theodor took off his glasses and wiped them on his shirt.

"Um—Ridian, there's something I've been meaning to talk to you about. Kess and I have reached a decision—one we don't take lightly—and well, we've been waiting for the right time, and the right time hasn't presented itself, so now will have to do…" He was prattling on, and he wasn't meeting Ridian's eye. For some reason, he was embarrassed. "You've probably gathered that we take family very seriously. It's the most important thing, really, and well, you've been staying with us for some time now, and—well, how do I say this?"

Oh, I know what's happening, thought Ridian with a horrible sinking feeling. *He wants me out of his home.* He didn't want to hear this—not now. Not after everything. But, then again, it was only a matter of time. "It's okay, Theodor," said Ridian, in a cold, flat voice. "I get it. I'll leave as soon as the Trials are over."

"Leave?" Theodor looked aghast. "No, you misunderstand me. We don't want you to leave. We want you to stay." He took a breath, a man summoning courage. "We want you to join the family."

Ridian was dumbstruck. Theodor was actually wringing his hands, scared Ridian would say no.

"I know you have your own family," said Theodor. "Your sister and mother. We don't want to take that from you. But if you wanted to stay, and not just as a guest, we'd love to have you."

Ridian's head whirled. *Family?* They wanted him to be family. The prospect scared him, and he had no idea why. "Theodor. I—I don't know what to say…" Then a nasty, hot, prickly feeling filled his chest. *Why is Theodor asking me now?* "Wait. When do I get a re-trial? When do I fight Dain again?"

Theodor just blinked.

"Theodor? Answer me."

"The Varki Tournament is over," said Theodor carefully. "I'm sorry, but there won't be any re-trials until next year."

"What?"

"I'm sorry, but—"

"But I was poisoned."

"I know."

"I was *poisoned*."

"I know."

"But that's not fair!"

"I kn–"

"Don't tell me you *know*!" Ridian jumped to his feet. The blood in his veins felt hot as boiling acid. "You have no idea what I've been through! No idea!" *Why am I shouting at Theodor?* He didn't know why, so he stormed towards the door. "I'm going to talk to Mother Asarah. She'll listen to me."

"We've already implored the Council, but Sevron was adamant. He said—"

"I DON'T GIVE A SHIT WHAT SEVRON SAYS! I'm getting out of here." He grabbed the door handle. It rattled, but would not budge. He thumped his fists against the padded door. "Let me out! Let me out!"

"Ridian, please…" Theodor approached cautiously, hands raised and open.

Ridian whirled on him. "Just give me the keys and piss off!"

Theodor flinched as if wounded. He stared at the ground, heartbroken, and Ridian felt a sharp stab in his own chest. Silence filled the small, padded room. The only sound was

Ridian's heart, thumping away in his ears. He could still fix this, he knew. He just needed to say sorry. That's all he needed to do. But he couldn't do it.

"The door's open," said Theodor as if speaking to his shoes. "It opens anti-clockwise."

Ridian opened the door and fled.

Chapter 28

Ridian stormed out of the Living Fort and into Last Stand Meadow, which was a bustling carnival: bards played, youths danced around fires, couples strolled, children chased each other, drunks staggered, families feasted. Everybody looked so happy. And why not? The Trials were over. It was time to celebrate. Ridian ploughed through it all—the smiling, the laughing—and entered Sanctuary Forest, leaving the frivolities behind. Through the forest and up he climbed, until at last, he crawled into his secret tunnel, aglow with Loony-Shrooms.

He wandered the tunnel for a long time, following the subterranean stream until it came to an abrupt end at the top of Madman's Falls. He peered out of that cavernous entrance and into the starlit night, listening to the roar below. His mind indulged in vengeful fantasies for a long time, but his anger eventually spluttered out. Getting back at Lukas or Sevron wouldn't help him. He considered begging Sevron to give him a re-trial, but he knew it was hopeless. Sevron had intentionally paired Ridian with the three best fighters in the school. He'd sworn Ridian would never become a Knight, and now he'd made good on that vow. And as the anger settled, he thought of Theodor. The man had shown him every kindness, and right when he welcomed Ridian into his family—when he asked him to become a son—Ridian had told him to piss off. *So much for that.* They weren't family. They weren't blood. Nothing held them together but Theodor's goodwill—and Ridian had ruined it.

He thought of Rayna. Could he follow Tann's squad as they hunted Hector down? Of course not. Stalking a skilled team of assassins was like chasing a pack of wolves. No. Ridian had run out of options. He'd failed, dooming Rayna to whatever fate Hector had in store.

Flashes of Ridian's Loony Shroom induced psychosis flickered: the skin-tearing demon, Mother, a dead field and a dying tree… His heart lurched. Why did that image scare him so much? He let his fingers dip into the freezing current and visualised the image floating away over the falls to drown beneath the pounding, never-ending torrent.

Meanwhile, he waited for Silver. Sure enough, the wolf finally plonked onto his lap, and Ridian stroked the glowing fur. They sat for a long time, gazing out of the tunnel, watching the glittering moonlit specks of water vapour drift up from Madman's Falls beneath them. Eventually, Silver padded a dozen feet away and turned to look at him; he wanted Ridian to follow.

"Not now, Silver."

The wolf dashed back and tugged on his sleeve with a whine.

Ridian knew better than to say no; Silver was way too stubborn. So, Ridian followed the lantern-like wolf through the mushroom-lit tunnel, deep into the mountain, the weight of the world beating down upon him. Silver finally stopped. Mushrooms glowed on the ceiling, the walls, and even reflected on the inky black water. But there was a patch of darkness to the left. Evidently, another tunnel without Looney Shrooms. The wolf padded inside, casting his silver glow about, banishing the darkness. It was a cavern, no more than twenty feet deep, though it widened considerably as it approached the far wall.

The far wall… Astonished, Ridian recognised it immediately. How could he not? He'd spent countless hours meditating before it in Stonecrow Cavern. It was made of wood, not stone—the very Mural Wall upon which Fidic's life had been portrayed, magically carved by his sister, Valaria. Only this was the other side and it was smooth as marble. And there was something near the base—a chest. It drew the eye. It drew Ridian. He knelt before the chest and wiped the thick dust from the lid. It was featureless and unadorned. "What's this?" he asked the stagnant air, though Silver just blinked at him. Ridian then flicked the latch and pried open the lid…

It was empty, save for a single object wrapped within. Holding his breath, Ridian picked it up—it was light—and unwrapped it. It was a lute.

No, Ridian realised with stunning certainty. *Fidic's Lute.*

Leaf-shaped and wrought from a single piece of sweet-smelling wood, the Lute spoke of Valarian magic. From the intricate head to the subtle frets, to the decorative grille covering—it was the spitting image of the one he'd seen in the painting of the Elder Three. It was so beautiful, so delicate, so cunningly made. It spoke of love and of genius, the perfect present from a gifted sister to her triplet brother. It just needed strings. Astonished, Ridian gazed at the history, the myth, and the magic in his hands. Remembering what Theodor had said lay within, he carefully pulled off the grille covering. Sure enough, within the circular sound hole lay a tiny notebook. Ridian looked at Silver, as if to ask for permission, then plucked it out with trembling fingers. It smelled of wood oil, leather, and of secrets. He knew the significance of this find, and not just for the ever-enthusiastic Ollie.

Then gently, as if the Lute were a sleeping newborn, Ridian laid the Lute aside and, under the silky light of Silver's coat, flicked through the fragile, crackling pages. They were streaked with tight, precise handwriting and sketches of naked women—languid and enticing. Each page contained a little poem (or perhaps a lyric) and a nude woman. One poem ran thus:

Annabelle, oh, Annabelle,
The time I spend dreaming,
I cannot tell.
The dreams I dream,
For dream I must,
Are the closest thing to heaven,
When I choose to live in hell.
My dearest Annabelle.

About halfway through the notebook, the frivolous poems and sketches stopped, and strangely, it was the lack of nudity that caught Ridian's eye. Terse journal entries followed:

Tidings are grim.
They say the Living City has fallen.

They speak of a massacre.
They say Arden blood floods the streets.
They say the upstart Kyros is King.
What of my sister?
I am sick with worry.

The passage rang a bell in Ridian's mind. Was this 'The Tale of the Elder Three' as told by Fidic? After Kyros had bested Daegan, outwitted Fidic, and climbed Valaria's Living Wall? After Kyros had marched upon the Living City of Terillion with an army of freed slaves and wild animals, the likes of which the world had never seen? Ridian read on.

A woman passed us on the road.
Her feet bled, but she didn't notice.
Her eyes were vacant.
She was like a sleepwalker.
We tried to wake her.
She just kept walking.

More refugees today.
All in shock.
All sleepwalking.
Nobody can wake them.

I played my music.
I played of home, of family, of friends.
It stirred them, woke them.
Their eyes cleared, and they wept.

The refugees won't stop talking now.

I can hardly stand it.
Blood. Death. Despair.
They call Terillion the Dead City.
My fears for Valaria are unbearable.
I can't sleep.

Ash falls from a black sky.
The distant flames are mountain tall.
The Living City is burning.
Burning. Burning. Burning.
The world must be ending.

I'm scared.

The strangest thing happened today.
We were attacked.
I panicked and... Split from my body.
No words can better explain it.
I left my body and went into a black place.
I thought I was dead.
But no. I returned to my body...
And killed the soldiers barehanded.
All twelve. It was easy.
My strength was terrible.
I tremble to think of it.
I, an Arden, possess Torian magic?
How is this possible?

I have bonded with a raven.
We are One.
How else can it be said?

I call him Roki.
He comprehends much.
I think I can get him to speak.

Ridian frowned. These last few passages differed from The Tale of the Elder Three. Roki was a god, not just some ordinary raven. Ridian shrugged; stories change with the telling. Maybe Fidic would uncover Roki's apparent divinity later.

Daegan and Valaria are safe!
They are mute with grief.
Still, I am grateful.

Another strange happenstance.
A miracle.
I healed Daegan's arm.
I don't know how.
It just happened.
I heard an ethereal music,
a Song, as the Arden druids say,
and my brother was whole.
What is happening to me?

I healed again!
A man's smashed and rotten leg.
Blood and pus vanished before my eyes.
Takes its toll though.
I'm exhausted.

I healed again!

A woman's fatal burn.
She's scarred from head to heel.
But still, she's alive.

Daegan shared a family secret today.
Father broke the Interbreeding laws.
We are half-blood bastards.
Half-Arden, half-Torian.
Not sure how Father covered it up.
But he did.
Otherwise, we would be dead.

Been thinking.
Daegan, Valaria, and I are gifted.
Daegan, a Giant.
Valaria, a Maker.
And I, a Healer.
How?
The mingling of Arden and Torian blood?
Surely.
Kyros is the only other half-blood I know.
And his gift is terrible.

More refugees.
Both Arden and Torian.
Kyros hunts them.
Gone mad, they say.

Everyone looks to me.
To lead. To save them.
I tell them no, but they won't listen.

I'm a bard, a storyteller, a scoundrel.
I can't help them.

Been thinking.
Perhaps I should become their saviour.
Perhaps I should heed this divine calling.
Pretend anyway.
It would give them hope. Unite them.
A reason to fight beyond mere survival.
I just need a good story...

I've got one.
Roki shall be our god.
My own made-up god.
(May the true gods forgive me).
And I, his human hand.
The hand to unite Arden and Tor.
What a terrible, necessary lie.

As he read, Ridian's stomach slowly sank. What was he reading? Theodor had said Fidic's Journal contained sermons—not blasphemies—and yet, Fidic had lied about Roki's divinity. Fidic was a liar, a charlatan. The implications for Fidicia were tremendous. Ridian flicked to the last page that still contained writing.

I pray no one reads this.
If they do, it means I am dead.
It means we were slaughtered.
And yet, I want people to know.
They say, lies crave the light.

I believe it.
Why else do I write these dangerous secrets?

Valaria is my only confidant.
She has sworn that if I die,
she will make me a martyr.
A hero, dying for his people.
She promised to immortalise The Lie.

Head reeling, Ridian cradled the Lute and Journal in his arms and began the long walk home. Fidic was a liar. A good man, perhaps, but still a liar. He had never been chosen by the wild god Roki upon that mountaintop. Roki was a bird. An ordinary bird—a *Familiar*. Still, Ollie would want to see Fidic's Lute, and Theodor the journal, regardless of what it said.

As Ridian crawled on his belly through the tiny tunnel towards the outside, he began thinking of the Mural Wall in a new light. It was not just a homage to Fidic, it was a barrier between the world and this dangerous little journal. Ridian could imagine it all. Fidic's body being laid to rest at Hero's Tree. Valaria going to throw his Journal into a furnace, but unable to go through with it. He imagined her taking the Journal, the Lute, and the chest into this cave and crafting the Mural Wall, sealing away her brother's secrets.

Ridian scrambled out of the tiny tunnel and stared down at Sanctuary Forest. For some reason, his legs wouldn't take him down. He was too busy thinking. The entire belief system of Fidicia was predicated upon a lie. Fidic's journal undermined everything Fidicia was built upon. If the Fidician religion fell apart, their entire society would fall apart. How would the Thunderfells treat Ridian, the bearer of bad news, the unwanted herald? Reject him? Surely. Ridian remembered his last meeting with Theodor. Their relationship was already strained enough. Besides, without Fidic's ethos of welcoming the sick, the poor, and the needy, any last string holding Ridian to the Thunderfells would be severed.

Ridian peered around to check that he was alone. He was. Just him and Silver upon a lonely mountainside. Then he shoved the Journal and Lute deep into the secret tunnel, and left. The Lie was too big to share. Too dangerous. No one needed to know.

Chapter 29

Ridian blustered through Sanctuary Forest, Silver alongside him, until they stood upon the lip of Lovers' Hollow. Silver never followed beyond this point, and as Ridian nodded a farewell, Silver slunk away. He tried to ignore Fidic's Lie burning inside him. If he didn't think about it, it would go away. He would forget all about it. But deep down, he knew secrets didn't work like that. Secrets were like seeds. If you buried them, they grew...

Ridian had almost passed through the narrow canyon that led back to Last Stand Meadow when he was startled by a deafening *BANG*, loud as a thunderclap. He sprinted the rest of the canyon, just in time for another *CRACK*, and the sky above Last Stand Meadow blossomed in a spray of crackling red fire. A whizzing, shooting sound, then another deafening explosion of sparkling blue lit the sky. Fireworks. Of course, there were Fireworks. Fidic—The Liar—had tried using fireworks upon Riddler's Bridge to scare off Kyros. *Another homage to the charlatan.*

Spectators screamed with delight and oohed and aahed. All Fidicia, it appeared, stood upon Last Stand Meadow, peering skyward expectantly. Sure enough, a sizzling projectile exploded into crackling green rain. Another burst into purple. Another orange. Each explosion rumbled in Ridian's chest. Afterimages danced before his eyes, and the settling smoke smelled of sulphur.

Between the crackling fireworks and the ringing in his ears, Ridian caught a voice: "It's time." It was a clear voice—distinct and articulate. Where had he heard that voice before? Ridian looked: a few feet away stood two men, hooded, backs turned. One was a great bull of a man, the other was a tall spindling creature.

The bull whispered as if gravel were in his throat. "You sure?"

The spindling man nodded. "It's now or never. Farewell, Brother."

"Farewell."

They grasped each other's forearms in an emphatic goodbye. As they did, the tall man's long, pointed nose jutted out beyond his hood.

The memory fell like a hammer: Tinker's long, pointed nose protruding past the prison bars. Ridian was stunned. Tinker? Basher? What were they doing here? They were supposed to be under lock and key. But of course—Feya and Theodor had mentioned escaped prisoners. Only Ridian had never imagined the prisoners to be these two. But what of the third? The nasally voiced Sneak?

Ridian didn't have time to think. Tinker and Basher had parted ways and were weaving through the crowd. He deliberated for a moment, feet pinned to the ground, heart galloping. Who to follow? He decided on Tinker, the trio's apparent leader. It was easy. The spindling man was head and shoulders above the rest, and he slid through the crowd slowly, cautiously. Not wanting to give himself away, Ridian kept twelve or so paces behind. Once, Tinker looked over his shoulder, and Ridian froze and looked up at the sky with a big stupid grin, hoping to blend in with the crowd. A firework exploded, and he breathed out an exaggerated, 'Wow,' praying Tinker didn't recognise him.

When Ridian looked down again, Tinker was slinking through the crowd with slow deliberation. Focused on the fireworks, no one paid any heed to the tall stranger, wading patiently through the throng. Ridian looked for Basher, but the brute had disappeared amongst the crowd.

What did Tinker mean, 'It's now or never?' What were they planning? Ridian looked ahead. A brilliant yellow firework crackled overhead and illuminated Hero's Tree. Knights and their Familiars surrounded it in a protective ring. Still, Tinker beelined towards them. Why would Tinker—a known fugitive—advance? In fact, why would he and Basher come anywhere near here? It seemed the last place for fugitives to be. A purple firework crackled and fizzed overhead, and Ridian saw Prince Bevrik almost bouncing with excitement on his throne beneath Hero's Tree. He beamed skyward as leaf-shaped shadows danced across his young, purple-lit face. Tinker slid through the crowd towards the boy like a snake in the grass. The Knights standing guard looked distracted, oblivious to the quiet menace. The firework fizzled out, casting everything into darkness, and Ridian knew with terrible certainty what Tinker and Basher were up to.

What should Ridian do? Alert the guards? That would get Tinker and Basher killed. But if Ridian did nothing, Tinker and Basher would attack and die anyway. Either way, they would be dead, and Ridian would be left without answers.

Answers he desperately wanted.Tinker was close now, a handful of feet from the guard line. What should he do?

A booming firework washed Hero's Tree in blue. Prince Bevrik clapped giddily. Sevron sat on Prince Bevrik's left; Mother Asarah, his right. And upon Mother Asarah's lap—

Was Ollie.

He bobbed on her old knee, amazement blazing across his face. Feya stood alongside, her dark eyes reflecting the blue fire. They both looked so happy, so enthralled. It was the perfect picture, the perfect moment. Then the light died, and Ridian felt a chill scuttle up his spine, knowing Tinker wove his way towards them. There was no more deliberation; Ridian crashed through the crowd. "He's an Assa–"

A booming firework blew his words to pieces.

"An As–" Another firework cut him off. Then another, then another, then another… The sky erupted in earnest, all dazzling colour and *noise*. One firework after another, building to an apparent climax.

"Assassin! He's an assassin!" Ridian screamed, shoulder-ing his way through the crowd. But nobody heard him. The spectacle of thunder and colour made it impossible. Finally, the last firework fizzled out, but still, nobody could hear Ridian because the air was thick with smoke, applause, and *screams…*

Confusion swelled, people bolted, and panic spreading like wildfire. But not Tinker. He stood before the guards, still as a windless tree, patient as spring, the only tranquil thing in the whole world. Then, through the screaming crowd, Ridian spotted a bull of a man wielding a long, massive, makeshift club—a large stone lashed to a timber shaft. Who else but Basher? The club must have weighed sixty pounds, yet when he swung the club, he did so effortlessly, as if it were a ribbon. It whooshed in a sightless arc, impossibly fast—the strike of a Soulcaster. The blow sent a guard flying dozens of feet to land in a mangled, contorted mess.

Ridian couldn't believe his eyes. The blow was too quick; the guard flew too far. And yet, another blurred movement of Basher's club sent a guard hurtling. Even for a Soulcaster, Basher's strength was astonishing. Knights and their Familiars shot towards Basher, causing gaps to form in their ranks. The ring of guards constricted, and the gaps closed. Still, Tinker waited.

Prince Bevrik, Mother Asarah, Ollie, and Feya had retreated to the trunk of Hero's Tree, panic etched upon their faces. Sevron stood protectively in front of them, sword drawn, his eye burning. Feya unsheathed Prince Bevrik's sword and went to join Sevron, but Mother Asarah snatched Feya's wrist and shook her head with profound reproach. Feya obeyed and stayed put.

A shriek drew Ridian's gaze back to the fighting. Basher was surrounded, but even as Ridian watched, a guard pinwheeled in the air from a near-invisible blow and struck the ground, a mashed corpse. Basher twirled his club in wild arcs, in full control, and the Knights with their swords couldn't get close. One did, and the whispering club snapped his legs like dry kindling. The guard screamed, and Basher pressed towards Hero's Tree, towards Prince Bevrik, Ollie and Feya. More guards left the protective ring to intercept the formidable foe, and only then did Tinker begin walking towards Hero's Tree.

Basher's the diversion, Ridian realised, and he dashed forward and screamed, shredding his vocal cords. "HE'S AN ASSASSIN! AN ASSASSIN!"

Tinker spun around and fixed his narrow-set eyes upon Ridian. The force of the glare stopped Ridian in his tracks, making him all too aware of the meagre ten paces between them. But Ridian had done his job. He'd caught a Knight's attention, and the man and two other Knights marched warily towards Tinker, their wolves bristling behind them. Ridian felt relief wash over him. Tinker no longer had the element of surprise. Ollie and Feya would be safe.

Twirling, Tinker flicked his robe aside and drew a sword, as long and thin as he was, and darted at the guards, streaking through the night like a bird in flight.

So quick, thought Ridian with bewilderment. Did Soulcasters move that fast?

The middle guard, the one who'd heard Ridian, was caught unawares and received six inches of blade in the eye. His comrades stepped back in alarm. Tinker drew circles in the air with his needle-like sword, and though his back was turned, Ridian could sense him smiling.

A guard struck with his own sword. Tinker parried and jabbed in one fluid motion, a tiny flick of the wrist, quick as a blink. Ridian thought Tinker had missed, but the Knight was pulling a near-comical expression of surprise as blood began pouring from his Adam's apple. And before he even fell to his knees, Tinker descended upon the startled third guard, jabbing, jabbing, jabbing. Tinker was so fast. He lunged, a twitching dart, and his blade slid into the Knight's shoulder. The guard cried out, then abruptly stopped as Tinker skewered his open mouth.

Hearing cries, Ridian turned to see Basher step over a mangled body and advance.

Sevron's eye flicked in alarm between Basher and Tinker—his Knights were falling like wheat before reapers. "Protect the Prince!" he bellowed.

The guards obeyed as best they could. But it wasn't enough. Even now, Tinker and Basher were cleaving their way through. One with a twirling ball of stone, the other with a slither of iron. Sevron joined the fray, terrifying in his composure. Yet, even he barely contended with the deadly duo. A streak of grey followed another streak of grey. It was Tann and Yanala, falling alongside Sevron and his Knights. Sevron glared at Tann, and Ridian thought he was about to strike him down, but Tann jerked away to swing at Basher. The swipe clanged harmlessly off the stone head of the club. Tann then spun out of range and aimed a blow at Tinker. The spindling Kyrosian deflected Tann's sword that screamed towards him, their blades sliding off each other with a raking *hiss*. Tinker then countered with a swishing of his sword. Tann blocked and countered with a powerful strike that would have cleaved Tinker's head from his shoulders, but Tinker doubled backwards with a frenetic jerk, and the sword whistled past his neck.

A Knight tried to stab the man in the back, but the dextrous Tinker twisted nimbly and skewered the man in the chest. Then Tinker—a terrifying blur—turned back to jab again and again with his darting, twitching blade. He was too much, and he forced Tann and the others back towards Hero's Tree. Meanwhile, Mother Asarah tottered forward to stand guard. Ridian watched, rooted to the spot. *Why don't they run?* Then he saw Ollie's bowed legs and knew why. Then he saw something that made his stomach drop—

From the tip of Hero's Tree, a tiny man was climbing down deftly. He slid down the trunk and leapt from branch to branch. *Sneak*, Ridian realised with a cold terror. Prince Bevrik, Ollie, and Feya were all huddled at the Tree's base, oblivious. Sevron and his Knights were all busy fighting for their lives. It was up to Ridian to do something. But that would put his life in jeopardy. And if he died, who would save Rayna? Nobody. Intervening was clearly a very bad idea, but as Sneak slunk down towards Feya and Ollie, Ridian realised he had to do something. Feya and Ollie, meant something to him. They mattered. He cared for them. Then, without thinking, without knowing what he would do, Ridian pelted forward, crying, "Feya!"

Feya's eyes, shining with fear, met Ridian's.

Ridian pointed frantically up at the shrimpy man, skulking down the tree. "Look out!"

Feya looked behind, then turned back, confused.

Ridian dashed past a gap between two guards. One tried to stop him, but received a brief slither of iron from Tinker and fell.

Sneak was halfway down now, a shadow among shadows.

"Look out!" Ridian screamed again, but again, Feya failed to see.

A basket of littered apples emerged out of the darkness ahead. Instinctively, Ridian snatched one up, wind stinging his eyes as he sprinted. Sneak slipped further down and squatted upon a low-lying branch. He was right above them, ready to pounce. A knife gleamed.

Ridian zoomed past Mother Asarah, got within range, and pitched the apple as hard as he could. The apple hurtled into the night and vanished. He prayed, and for two terrible seconds, he waited. Sneak was on his toes, on the very verge of leaping down, when the apple smacked into his face. The assassin cried out, dropped his knife, and then pinwheeled his arms as he toppled backwards. He fell and landed hard on his back, splayed before Feya and the two terrified boys who dashed around the far side of the tree.

Feya flew at the winded and wheezing Sneak before he could draw himself up. She slashed at the assassin with Prince Bevrik's shortsword, but Sneak, who stood little more than five-foot, rolled away, quick as a ferret, and pulled another knife from his sleeve. Hissing, he launched at Feya like a feral cat. Feya slashed, and Sneak dodged with a frenetic twitching motion that was almost too quick to register. Feya slashed again, and the near-midget slid under the blade and sliced a shallow cut across Feya's thigh. She gasped and used—Ridian couldn't believe he noticed—River Flowing to retreat a safe distance towards the boys.

But she was limping and she was scared, and the sight of her pain and fear filled Ridian with a mindless, unspeakable fury. She would die if Ridian did nothing. And that thought terrified him more than words could express. Then, many things happened at once.

A wolf's howl cut through the night and reverberated in Ridian's mind. At the same time, Ridian felt something—a presence—shoot towards him. It was Silver, Ridian knew, streaking towards him and calling him. Calling him *out*.

As Silver called, Ridian's mind *pushed* against the bonds of his body. He felt the certainty of Death and the eternal Nothing—just beyond the confines of his skull. He also felt a profound urge to retreat within himself. But he knew

Silver was out there in that Nothing. He knew he wouldn't be alone. And knowing that gave him the courage to *push*—

And his mind burst free, hurtling into The Black. Already, the urge to return was nearly overwhelming. But Ollie needed him, Feya needed him. He loved them, he realised, even as he zoomed towards Silver, even as he collided with the wolf's dazzling, luminescent soul—

In a flash, Ridian's soul was laid bare. Silver could see him, all of him: the parts Ridian liked, the parts he hated, even the parts Ridian did not know. And the terror of the exposure was almost as great as the fear of dying itself. The wolf saw him—all of him—and Ridian knew the wolf had the power to reject him and fling him back out into the terrible Nothing that lay between them. But the wolf accepted him, and they became One.

A surge of energy unleashed from Silver and hurtled Ridian back to his body like a slingshot. In that brief black moment without sight, smell, taste, or touch—Ridian could sense the ethereal lights all around—the Souls of Feya, Sneak, Mother Asarah, Ollie, and Prince Bevrik. But the greatest light of all was Hero's Tree. Trickling rivulets of light illuminated every branch, twig, and leaf. Even the roots glowed as they burrowed beneath the unseen ground, searching for water. Perhaps Fidic's soul did lie inside?

Then, the world returned in a flash. Only a second had passed. Ridian was just in time to see Feya thrown backwards from a kick in the chest from Sneak. But before Sneak could do more, Ridian snatched up the knife the assassin had dropped, falling from the tree, and shot towards him with reckless fury. He closed the gap like a bolt from a crossbow, distinctly aware of the new link between himself and Silver. He could feel it. The wolf was some distance away and closing fast. And he could certainly feel the supernatural energy—the Rava—flowing between them. It made Ridian feel so light, so strong, and so in control. And Sneak seemed to have slowed. A few seconds before, the little man zipped around, almost impossible to keep track of. Now, he was merely quick.

Ridian lunged. Sneak twisted, barely dodging the blade. Ridian closed the distance and sliced, missing the neck but nicking the shoulder. Sneak stabbed. Ridian parried, but Sneak seemed to have expected this. He spun in a full circle, utilising the momentum Ridian had offered with the parry, and the back of his hand smacked across Ridian's head.

Ridian's teeth rattled. The world spun. Pain exploded through his skull and down his spine. Rava from Silver did not protect Ridian from pain, it seemed. And there was Sneak, already lurching towards him. Ridian went to dodge, but he seemed to have momentarily lost control of his legs. Sneak stabbed at him, and Ridian knew the blade would plunge into his guts, sure as sunrise. Ridian braced himself for the impact, the hilt-deep penetration, vaguely aware of Sneak's face puckered up in rage. The knife was shooting towards him, a mere handspan away, when something flashed between them like silent, silver lightning. Sneak screamed and pulled his hand away, or what was left of it: a few half fingers bubbling up blood.

Silver skidded to a halt, snapping his jaws at Sneak, his glowing fur bristling. Ridian could sense Silver coiling for another pounce—somehow he knew the wolf's intent— when a sword suddenly sprouted from Sneak's chest. The little man looked down at the unexpected blade, puzzled.

The blade slid away, Sneak fell to his knees, and it was Feya who held the sword. She frowned with a grim determination, a determination to keep her horror at bay.

Silver finished the job. The wolf leapt onto Sneak, mauling him to the ground with terrible ferocity, churning the screaming face into pulp with his snapping teeth. Sneak's shrieks were sickening, and only stopped once Silver latched onto his neck and tore out a large chunk with a violent jerk. The wolf then bounded towards Ridian, tail wagging. It licked Ridian's hand with a blood-smeared tongue and looked up as if to ask, *Who's a good boy?*

"Good boy," said Ridian, though he wasn't sure if he said it aloud. Either way, he knew Silver had heard. The wolf leapt around in a circle and nuzzled Ridian with a bloody snout. Sneak lay still, his mangled face unrecognisable. Feya still held the Prince's sword aloft, seemingly frozen in place.

"Feya? You okay?" Ridian asked.

Feya blinked at him in surprise, then her eyes widened in alarm. "Look out!" And she tossed the sword to Ridian.

Ridian caught the handle as it whooshed through the air and whipped around.

Tinker had broken through the Guards and was rushing towards them, quick as a hare, and Ridian drew another surge of Rava from Silver. Somehow, he knew how. Then Ridian, who had never held a sword, slipped into his Varki stance and was pleasantly surprised to find the sword complemented the posture. It was almost as if he'd been practising with it all along. But Tinker wasn't interested in Ridian; he was darting towards Prince Bevrik.

And Feya stood in his way.

Ridian drew a surge of Rava from Silver and cut Tinker

off with a tremendous burst of speed. He then struck at Tinker, who parried with a casual flick. Desperate, wild, and with no semblance of Varki training, Ridian swung the sword in a powerful horizontal arc. In response, Tinker took the smallest step back, whipped his sword like a chef whipping eggs, and flung Ridian's sword from his hands. Unbalanced, Ridian's legs twisted, and he fell. Tinker would have skewered him, easy as a pork sausage, but Silver bit the man's calf, allowing Ridian a chance to roll away. Tinker cried out and would have stabbed Silver, but Ridian ordered the wolf back with a blaring telepathic burst. The wolf heard and obeyed, missing the darting blade by a whisker. Tinker then looked back at the Prince and hobbled towards the boy. He was much slower now. Whatever magic fuelled him appeared to be running out.

Seeing the Kyrosian shamble towards them, Prince Bevrik and Ollie began to scramble desperately up the tree. Prince Bevrik managed to hook a leg on a low-hanging branch and swing himself up, but Ollie lacked the mobility. He tried jumping but fell short. Nothing stood in Tinker's way. Nothing stopped him from—

To Ridian's astonishment, Mother Asarah leapt nimbly after the towering man, spry as a deer. She twirled with the grace of a falling leaf and smacked Tinker across the mouth with her cane, spraying blood. The ancient woman did not relent. Strike upon strike, her cane cracked against Tinker's sword, occasionally swatting his forearm, shoulder, or elbow. Tinker could barely contend with her. His magical strength was definitely fading.

One of Mother Asarah's strikes snapped Tinker's slender sword, and the deadly tip tinkled to the ground. Spin, spin,

spin—Mother Asarah spun and struck, spun and struck in a furious onslaught, forcing Tinker to stagger backwards. Ridian got to his feet and dashed forward, summoning Silver as he went. Maybe he could stab the bastard in the back when he wasn't looking. Cowardly, yes, but he didn't care. Ridian was halfway there when—mid-spin—Mother Asarah froze, Tinker's half-sword lodged in her chest.

"No!" Feya cried.

Tinker slid the half-blade out with a jerk, and Mother Asarah crumpled to the ground. Then a large shadow hurtled through the dark and bore down on Tinker with terrifying speed. The shadow swiped its giant paw, sending Tinker crashing into Hero's Tree. Tinker slid down, senseless.

Mother Asarah's bear stood up on its hind legs—a towering eight feet—and growled, strings of saliva flying. Ridian backed away. Huffing, the bear dropped on all fours and hovered over the old woman protectively, swinging its giant head from side to side, scanning for danger. Mother Asarah pointed a trembling finger at Basher, and, after a moment's hesitation, the bear loped towards the man obediently.

Feya and Ollie rushed to kneel by Mother Asarah's side. Feya pressed down on Mother Asarah's wounded chest, blood seeping through her fingers. "Help!" she screamed into the night. "We need help!" Ollie just stood there and cried. But nobody seemed to hear. Everybody was focused on Basher, who seemed to be slowing as Tinker had, winding down like a mechanical toy. Soulcasters were finding gaps in the terrible swinging club and slicing the man up.

Silver barked in alarm. Ridian turned: Tinker, bloodied

and mangled, staggered to his feet and began climbing Hero's Tree after the terrified Prince. If Tinker killed the Prince, the man would never see the light of day. Ridian would get no answers. He needed Tinker alive.

Ridian was there in a Rava-fuelled flash. In the nick of time, he reached up, grabbed the slender ankle, and yanked the man down with astonishing force. Tinker tumbled and landed awkwardly on an ankle that snapped audibly beneath him. Grunting in pain, Tinker lurched to his feet, eyes bulging. He lunged at Ridian, hobbling on his twisted ankle, shambling like a demented scarecrow. Ridian raised his sword but –

Tinker hurtled into Hero's Tree again—only this time, there was no bear. A sudden, tremendous gale had swept him off his feet, pinning him against the trunk. Leaves rustled furiously, his hair flung back, and his clothes billowed as he strained against the raging wind.

Ridian turned to see Feya, feet planted, frowning in concentration, her palms aimed at Tinker. A powerful wind blasted from her hands, slamming into the man. Mother Asarah's blood, smeared across her skin, was stripped away—whipping up her fingers and trailing down her wrists. She was a Windchaser.

There was a cry of "Save the Prince!" from someone, and Feya dropped her hands as if she'd been caught doing something naughty. The moment she did, the windstorm ended.

Tinker tried to stand. But Silver pounced and sank his jaws into the man's forearm. Ridian pounced as well, twisting the other wrist and locking the shoulder. Tinker tried to wrestle free, but knew from many painful lessons with Lukas how to hold someone still. He turned the arm with the ease of a doorknob, and the shoulder popped from its socket, easy as a cork from a bottle.

Tinker screamed, spraying blood and shards of broken teeth, his arm dangling useless in Ridian's hands. Ridian had complete control. And that's how Commander Sevron, Nawar, Tann, and all the other Soulcasters found them: Tinker spread-eagled between Ridian and Silver, with a body full of broken bones and a face full of shattered teeth. They gazed in astonishment. Ridian—a mere Novice—had crippled the man who had cut their elite troop into pieces. All without a scratch. Sevron's eye shone with something like fear. *Perhaps he is a secret weapon,* that eye seemed to say. Of course, none of them had seen the man's failing strength, Mother Asarah's strikes, the bear's vicious swipe, or Feya's Windchaser magic. Not even Prince Bevrik. He'd been scampering up the tree, and Ollie had been crying at Mother Asarah's side.

Ridian found Feya's frightened eyes. He went to say something, but she glared at him with sudden panic and shook her head sternly. *She doesn't want people to know she's a Windchaser.* Ridian wondered why.

Knights took hold of Tinker, relieving Ridian and Silver. A couple dashed to help Prince Bevrik. Some tended to the screaming wounded, others to the quiet dead. Feya hugged Ollie as he buried his face in her chest. Silver blazed bright as a campfire at Ridian's side. Ridian still trembled with supernatural strength, and Silver gazed up at him with intelligent eyes, full of knowing. Instinctively, Ridian cut the flow of Rava between them. His body felt instantly heavier, and Silver's eyes emptied of intelligence and filled with dim, animal stupidity. Ridian was also suddenly exhausted, and his temples throbbed. Soulcasting was evidently very draining.

People gathered around Mother Asarah's body, faces pale. Her bear lumbered through the crowd, sniffing her ancient face, then let out a long, heart-wrenching bellow—and Ridian knew she was gone. Surprisingly, a pang of grief clenched in his own chest, and he had to take a deep breath to keep the lump from rising to his throat.

Once back on the ground, Prince Bevrik surprised Ridian by marching towards him. "You saved my life," he said solemnly, sniffing away tears. "Such a deed should not go unrewarded." He turned to Sevron. "Your sword."

"Pardon me, my Prince?" asked Sevron.

"Your sword." Prince Bevrik held out his hand.

Sevron frowned "Prince Bevrik, this is most unusual."

"*Commander!*" Bevrik glared with severe reproachfulness that was all the more intense given his grief.

Sevron shot a hostile one-eyed glare at Ridian, drew his sword, and then offered the handle. The boy took the long, too-heavy sword and ordered Ridian to kneel. Astonished, Ridian obeyed.

"Do you swear to serve Fidicia and protect it from all its enemies?" said Prince Bevrik.

"Yes," said Ridian.

"Very well." The young Prince lay the flat of the sword clumsily on each of Ridian's shoulders. "Then I, Prince Bevrik, dub thee a Knight of the Fidician Order."

Chapter 30

I'm a Knight! I did it! Silver wagged his tail and bounced in a circle, apparently sharing Ridian's elation. In fact, he *did* share it. Euphoria coursed through them both. Ridian could feel it.

Prince Bevrik handed the sword back to Sevron and returned to the mourners crowding around Mother Asarah. Sevron was visibly disgusted by Ridian's grinning face and turned his back on him. Ridian felt ashamed, and his smile died. Sevron was right: there was too much death and injury for Ridian to be grinning. Besides, Ridian would never have another lesson with Mother Asarah. It didn't seem real, but it was true.

Ridian looked at Silver. The wolf looked self-conscious and scared: ears low, tail tucked, darting eyes. He looked ready to slink away and disappear into the night. *It's okay,* Ridian said within himself. *I'll look after you.* And he sent a wave of—of what? Reassurance? Courage? Hope? Regardless, it worked. The ears raised, the tail untucked, and Silver stopped cringing. They didn't just share emotions, Ridian could manipulate Silver's. Could Silver influence his?

Tinker knelt nearby, arms bound behind his back, ankles

tethered to his wrists. Four Soulcasters guarded him. Sevron also loomed over Tinker, lip curled, his eye full of murder. Tinker smiled up at Sevron with what remained of his shattered teeth.

"Commander Sevron," said Tann, coming to stand beside the man.

"What do you want?" asked Sevron, still glaring down at Tinker's grinning face.

"Let me question the Kyrosian. Your boys have tried for months without success. Give me one hour."

Sevron turned to look at him. He still didn't like Tann, but a begrudging trust had settled in the commander's eye. "What makes you think you can make him talk?"

"Talk? I'll make him sing Fiddler's Riddle in soprano."

Sevron was not unimpressed.

"Look," said Tann, regrouping. "I'm not bound by Fidician law like you. I can do things the council would deem… unsavoury."

Still, Sevron glared.

Tann straightened and matched the stare. "I'll get the bloody job done."

"Fine. I need to clean this mess up anyway. You have one hour, no more, and my men stay with him." Then Sevron stormed away.

"Tann, Tann, Tann," said Tinker, shaking his head and smiling. "You're one sneaky son of a bitch, you know that?"

Tann knelt on one knee, eye to eye with the lanky Kyrosian. They both shared the same white-streaked hair. "Hello, Tink," he said pleasantly. "Thought I was dead, didn't you? Well, my getaway was rather slick."

Tinker spat blood into Tann's face. "Traitor."

Yanala might have mauled Tinker there and then, but Tann waved her back. "That wasn't very nice. Now I'll have to get nasty."

Tinker scoffed. "I won't tell you anything. I'm not a squeaking rat like you."

Tann looked grim. "We'll see. Take him to the surgery room." The Knights holding Tinker obeyed, hauling Tinker roughly away in the direction of the Living Fort.

"Let me come," said Ridian.

Tann opened his mouth to protest, but then he looked down at Silver thoughtfully. "Since when?"

"Since five minutes ago."

"He's a bit small."

"You can't just say you're impressed, can you?"

Tann snorted. "Impressed is a stretch. Surprised, more like." Then he turned to catch up to Tinker and his guards.

Ridian smiled; Tann was impressed, and he didn't stop Ridian from following. Ridian glanced back at Feya and Ollie, but they were lost in the crowd. Ahead, Tinker sagged in the Knight's arms, so different to the lightning-quick swordsman from before.

"How will we find Tinker's Familiar?" asked Ridian, glancing around, waiting for a slender, Tinker-like wolf to burst from some shadow.

"He doesn't have one," said Tann. "He's a soul snatcher."

"A what?"

"A soul snatcher… someone who murders their own Familiar to trap the animal's soul within them." He shook his head. "Unspeakable."

Ridian looked at Silver. *How could anyone do such a thing? It would be like killing your brother.* "Why?" asked Ridian with baffled horror. "How?"

"How? Well, as a Familiar dies, their soul is, for a brief moment, unprotected, allowing a Soulcaster to snatch it up and store it within themselves. And why? An unfettered soul is a lasting and potent source of Rava. You saw how powerful they became." Tann looked disgusted. "Those leeches."

Five minutes later, Ridian, Tann, Tinker, four Soulcasters, and six Familiars entered the hospital, which glowed a blazing green once Ridian drank some of the sweet fountain water near the entrance. They wound through various corridors and up a few staircases until they entered the surgery room. Powerful disinfectant smothered a nasty cocktail of smells. In the middle of the room was an empty operating table, while a side table held a series of slender knives, scissors, and a bone saw... Shuddering, Ridian had grisly visions of surgeons slicing through pus-filled flesh, then grating through bone. Ridian looked at Tinker, then back at the bone saw, and felt sick.

Ridian then felt a growing claustrophobia from Silver—their connection was so palpable—and again, Ridian emboldened the wolf. It was hard to say how. But the wolf calmed down, while Ridian's anxiety peaked. Did manipulating Silver's emotions alter his own? It appeared so. In order to stave off the wolf's anxiety, he needed to feed his own. The fear didn't disappear, it just went from one vessel to another.

At the sight of the table and the surgical tools, blood drained from Tinker's face. He closed his eyes. "Pain will set me free. Pain will set me free. Pain will set me free..." He repeated the mantra over and over, his voice growing with fervour with each repetition.

The guards threw Tinker upon the bed and strapped him to it while he blared his inane prayer. "Pain will set me free! Pain will set me free!"

Once fully restrained, Tann loomed over Tinker and gazed into the bleeding, pinched face. "I want to know three things, Tinker. Where is Hector? What are his plans? And how many men does he have?"

Tinker was breathing hard, eyes clamped shut. "Pain will set me free. Pain will set me free. Pain will set me free..."

Tann turned towards the door. "Let's give him time to decide just how free he wants to be." They filed out and closed the door, leaving Tinker to his incessant prayer.

Outside, Tann wrote one of the Knights a note. "Ask Master Sheema to cook this up." The man took the note and sped off.

"Alright," said Tann to them all. "Let me tell you the plan."

He did, and it was the most ridiculous plan Ridian had ever heard.

✳✳✳

A while later, the Knight returned and handed Tann a small vial.

"Everyone know their part?" Tann asked.

They all nodded, then walked into the operating room, leaving their Familiars outside.

"Pain will set me free. Pain will set me free..." Tinker's face was trancelike. Foam caked the corners of his mouth, and the conviction in his voice was absolute.

Tann and the Knights wasted no time. They pinched

Tinker's long nose, pulled back his head, and forced the green contents of the vial down his throat. Straining against his bindings, Tinker choked, spluttered, swallowed.

"The potion you ingested will enhance your senses a hundredfold," said Tann to Tinker. "The dim light in this room will blind you, our voices will deafen you. Perfume will be like acid in your nose. A cool metal spoon will feel like ice. A warm mug like fire. And pain… ah, any pain you feel will be the most brilliant, exquisite experience of your life. A paper cut will be like an amputation. A punch will be like a hammer. And though the pain will be enormous, you won't pass out. I've added a potent stimulant to ensure you stay very much awake. You listening to me?"

"Pain will set me free. Pain will set me free…" Besides one wet burp, Tinker's mantra had been unrelenting. However, with each passing phrase, his voice began to slur—just as Tann said it would.

They waited, and only once Tinker's voice really began to drawl did Tann commence his plan, drawing his sword with a dramatic flourish. "Surprise attack!" he declared like an actor, overplaying his part of noble hero, and he struck a Knight slowly and deliberately with the flat of his sword. It didn't cut the man, it wouldn't have even hurt, yet the man fell in an exaggerated paroxysm of pain.

"Don't worry, Tink," said Tann with verve, turning his sword on another. "Your deliverance is at hand!"

The Knight drew her sword in defence, and together, she and Tann engaged in a parody of swordplay, like children banging sticks. Indeed, their blades rang out in a predictable rhythm: *cling, clang, cling, clang.* Then Tann stabbed. It went between the woman's arm and torso, a clear miss. But she groaned as if skewered and slumped to her knees. Another Soulcaster received a tap from the flat of Tann's sword, wailed, and keeled over. Ridian received a slice across the belly. It didn't even cut his shirt, but nonetheless, he fell with a cry and lay still.

Within moments, Tann was the only one standing. Tann dashed to Tinker's side and began unfastening the man from the bed. Drooling and slack-faced, Tinker wore the perplexed expression of a drunkard. His bleary eyes roamed the room, struggling to focus. He didn't seem to see the shallow breathing of those pretending to be dead.

"Tann," said Tinker, as if waking from a deep sleep, "why did you kill your own men?"

"Tinker is a fanatic," Tann had said thirty minutes earlier. "He will never betray Hector, and torturing him would just send him into the Black. That's where the potion comes in: part sedative, part analgesic, part hallucinogenic. He'll feel calm, a little groggy, and see and hear things that aren't necessarily there. That's the potion's best quality. It makes people highly suggestible. The only catch is he'll be asleep within minutes, and we can't re-dose him for another few days without killing the bastard."

"Why did I kill my own men?" said Tann, making a show of unclasping the buckle over Tinker's chest. "Well, because they're *not* my men. I'm here to rescue you."

Tinker's eyes drooped, on the verge of sleep, then opened with a start. "But why?"

"Isn't it obvious? I'm undercover. I was going to murder Commander Sevron, take his place on the Free Council of Fidicia, and manipulate the Fidicians from the inside. Just as Hector ordered."

Tinker narrowed his bleary eyes. "Why blow your cover?"

"Because Hector values you too much. You're too important to him."

"Hector thinks I'm important?"

"Of course! You're one of his favourites."

Tinker's groggy face lit up with child-like pleasure, like an orphan finally finding his parents after tireless years of searching. Tears filled his eyes. "One of his favourites... I never knew. Well, if I'm important to him, I'd better get back to him."

"Excellent idea," said Tann, still making a show of releasing Tinker's chest buckle. "I know a secret way out of Fidicia. But where do we find Hector?"

Tinker didn't even hesitate. "Hector's on Sky Island."

"Sky Island?" said Tann with poorly masked surprise, breaking character for a moment, while two of the Knights opened their eyes to look at each other in open alarm. This was big news, though it meant nothing to Ridian.

"Yes," said Tinker. "And with our Soulcaster army we can finally—"

"What's that? An army you say?" Tann voice was just the slightest bit strained.

Surely Tinker will see the deception, thought Ridian. For an undercover agent, Tann was a dreadful actor.

Tinker smiled, his shards of teeth slick with blood. "Yes, a Soulcaster army." Torso finally free, Tinker sat up and began clumsily unstrapping his legs with his good, not-dislocated arm.

"You were saying?" asked Tann. "With our Soulcaster army we can finally...? Finally what?"

Drunk beyond belief, Tinker tapped the side of his nose

conspiratorially. "I misjudged you Tann. You're not so bad. You're a good fella. A real top chap. A real…" Tinker slumped forward, unconscious.

Tann dropped his façade in an instant and whirled around to bark orders. "You three—throw him in the dungeons. You—inform Commander Sevron of what he said. And you…" He looked at Ridian.

Ridian saw him deliberating, clearly torn. "I'm ready," said Ridian eagerly. "I'm a Soulcaster and a Fidician Knight, just like you asked. My Familiar is just outside that door, and I'm willing to die for this mission. Besides, you're desperate."

Tann sighed and spoke to the ceiling. "I'm going to regret this, aren't I?" Then he fixed his eyes upon Ridian. "Get back into your old Mudwall clothes and meet me by the north Gate in two hours. Don't be late, or I'll have to kill Hector without you."

Chapter 31

Ridian was stunned. He was going north with Tann to kill Hector and rescue Rayna. Silver poked his head through the doorway. They blinked at each other. Ridian snapped out of it, and together, they sprinted home.

Home. That's what he called it, he realised, as he approached the Thunderfells'. Panting, he wrenched open the door and was surprised to find the whole family looking up from the lounge with puffy, tear-streaked faces. They were huddled around Feya and Ollie, comforting them. Of course, they were. Feya and Ollie had almost been murdered, and Mother Asarah…

"Ridian!" cried Ollie, who was hugging a pillow.

Ridian glanced at Feya, then quickly looked away. Something about the way she looked at him made his stomach lurch, though he didn't understand why. Was it the secret between them? Her being a Windchaser?

Theodor stood. Ridian had thought the man looked heartbroken when he'd told him to piss off a few hours ago. Now he looked shattered, more like Theodor's husk than Theodor himself. Guilt and fear weighed heavily upon Ridian. He'd pushed Theodor away; now it was his turn to reject Ridian. Silver sidled up to Ridian, and Ridian felt himself fortified against the rejection to come—for the polite request to come back later, to give the family space. Ridian didn't blame Theodor; the family had been through a lot tonight.

Theodor took a step, then another, and then he dashed across the room and engulfed Ridian in a massive, bone-breaking embrace. "Thank you, thank you, thank you," was all he could mumble between sobs.

Confused, Ridian stood awkwardly, unsure what to do within Theodor's arms. Then it clicked. Theodor was thanking Ridian for saving Ollie and Feya. Relief swelled through Ridian. He thawed and hugged Theodor back. His first hug in—lost gods, how long? He didn't care about the thanks. He was just relieved to be forgiven. Then again, had Theodor even held a grudge in the first place?

The rest of the family swooped in. Hugging, thanking, and clapping Ridian on the back. They marvelled at Silver, who hid between Ridian's legs, and they congratulated Ridian in earnest on becoming a Knight. And they weren't just happy for him—they were proud. And their pride in him led to a stunning realisation: he was family. He could see it in the way Ollie looked up and admired him. In Kai's gushing compliments. In the warmth of Kess' embrace. In Ella's outstretched arms. In Feya's dark eyes…

Ridian still couldn't hold her gaze. It sent his insides tumbling. Truth be told, the family's extravagant affections were too much for Ridian to handle, though a deep part of him yearned for their love.

Love? Yes, love. But it would have to wait. He imagined the Firetree outside his bedroom window and shared it— there was no other way to explain it—with Silver. *Meet me there,* he thought, and the wolf dashed out the door.

"Sorry," said Ridian, to the group at large. "I need to sleep. Been a big day."

They all nodded in weary agreement and let him go. Halfway up the stairs, Ridian stopped to look back at them. He might never see them again, he realised, and he tried to burn the image into his memory. The sight was nothing special. Just the family dispersing, getting ready for bed. He peeled himself away and hurried into his room. In no time at all, Ridian changed back into his old Mudwall clothes, packed a few essentials into a sack, and climbed out the window and down the tree where, sure enough, Silver waited.

Ridian's feet had barely landed when a voice said, "Where are you off to?" It was Feya, leaning against the wall, lurking in the shadows, just as she had that first night. Only Ridian saw her clearly now. She wasn't borderline pretty as he'd previously thought. She was beautiful. Her too-thin face, snaggle tooth, big hair... All her apparent imperfections culminated in a unique beauty that was all her own. He wouldn't change a thing. Ridian's mouth opened and closed like that of a stranded fish, and his guts started doing somersaults again. "Tann's taking me to kill Hector," he managed to say. "I—I have to go."

Feya stepped forward, hands raised. "It's okay. I'm not going to talk you out of going. But I still need to talk sense into you. No, don't roll your eyes. You might think you're some fancy-pants Soulcaster now, but you're still green as caterpillar poo, you still have no idea what you're doing, and you still suck at Varki."

"Thanks for the confidence booster."

"I'm serious, Ridian. Overconfidence will get you killed. You're not dealing with Lukas, who wasn't allowed to hurt you, or me sparring at seventy percent. You saw those Kyrosians tonight. Their mates will unzip your guts like *that*." She clicked her fingers. "Listen to me. If you get into trouble, don't play hero, don't save the day, just run. And stick close to Tann. Okay?"

Silver padded forward, causing Feya to gasp and clutch at her chest in surprise. "Holy Fidic's Fiddle, your wolf scared the hell out of me. Has he been there the whole time? He's like a shadow."

A shadow? The wolf blazed like a lantern, casting a warm silver light over Feya.

"Just promise me you'll run, okay?" said Feya. "You're too much of a soft arse to survive in the wild."

Ridian laughed.

"Don't laugh. Promise me."

"Okay, I promise."

Silence grew between them. He didn't want to say goodbye. That was why he had wanted to slip away in the first place. But also, he had to know. "You're a Windchaser. Why keep it secret?"

Feya sighed deeply, then checked over both her shoulders to ensure they were alone. "My life was a miserable nightmare before I came here. One foster home after another. Nobody wanting me. Then *they* found me and actually wanted me. Not just for monetary compensation, not just to indulge some sense of moral duty. They actually wanted me." Feya hugged her elbows and bit her lip. She was holding something back.

"You can tell me," said Ridian. "I'll be dead soon, so I won't be able to tell anyone."

"That's not funny," said Feya, then she groaned in frustration. "They think I'm a Soulcaster. That's why I'm here. This is a home for Soulcaster orphans and foundlings. If they knew I was a Windchaser, they'd realise I'm not a Soulcaster and that I don't belong."

"That's stupid," said Ridian. "Theodor and Kess wouldn't care."

Feya shook her head. "You don't get it. I've been lying to them for years. I've been lying to them since we first met. My entire relationship with them is based on a big fat lie." Feya's dark eyes were shining with ethereal silver light—a light invisible to her.

She's so beautiful. How had he not seen it before? "They'll understand," said Ridian.

"Will they?" Feya shook her head. "I can't risk it. I just can't…" Then she pointed to something over Ridian's shoulder. "What's that?"

Ridian turned to look. As he did, he felt Feya brand his cheek with a burning kiss. He caught a brief glimpse of her wild hair and a whiff of her scent—leaves, grass, and wildflowers—before a blast of wind knocked him back. Coughing from knocked-up dust, he found his feet. Feya had disappeared, but Ridian was just in time to see the curtain of her second-story bedroom being drawn closed.

Chapter 32

Ridian vaulted the garden wall and dashed into the night. Silver streaked ahead, trailing wisps of light. Ridian's mind roiled, his heart leapt. *She kissed me! She kissed me!* On the cheek, but still. He'd never been kissed before. Was she falling for him? Was he falling for her? Maybe. It felt like it. He felt drunk with excitement. And he already missed her. It was pathetic but true. He shook his head clear. *Focus*, he told himself. *Focus on Rayna.* Romance was the last thing he needed right now. One girl on his mind was more than enough.

Down the hill they sped, then along the northbound road, passing quiet homes huddled along Raven's River. After thirty or so minutes of jogging, the path began to climb. Up it went, switching back and forth. As he began to tire, Ridian drew Rava from Silver. It was instinctual, almost automatic, and it allowed him to continue on tirelessly. However, the higher he climbed and the more he drew, Ridian felt a growing mental drag. His brain began to feel drained, even as his body was nourished. It became hard to think. Several times, he lost concentration and stumbled. Not from any physical weariness—indeed, his body thrummed with vitality—but from a loss of mental clarity.

Silver, on the other hand, was panting furiously, and sweat foamed along his flank. The poor wolf was hurtling towards exhaustion. They were leeching each other dry. Ridian sucked physical strength even as he bled intellectual vigour. If they didn't pace themselves, they would both soon pass out. Somehow, he knew Silver agreed.

With a mental flick, Ridian cut the link between them and was shocked into a slow, lurching jog as acid filled his legs and his side twisted into a painful knot. He slowed to a march, and slowly—very slowly—his head began to clear. After some time, he reopened the link and allowed the tiniest trickle of Rava to flow between them. The pain eased, and he marched a little faster. Silver paced alongside him as they climbed towards the stars.

At last, at the top of the trail, high above the Fidician Valley, a large tunnel appeared—the only apparent way forward. This high up, a vestige of winter still remained. There were shallow pools of cracked ice, and here and there lay retreating clumps of snow.

Tann, Yanala, and two others stood before the tunnel, breathing plumes of icy air. One was a woman, tall and wiry, a bow slung across her shoulder. An enormous scar raked across one side of her face, erasing an ear and a large patch of hair. Ridian shuddered to think how she'd done it. Her eyes were the first to flick over and detect Ridian. They narrowed as Ridian approached. The other was a stocky man with enormous sideburns and enough weapons to fill an armoury: an assortment of knives, dual hatchets, a tiny crossbow, a slingshot, and even a blowgun were tucked into the leather holsters crisscrossing his body. He gave the weaponless Ridian a condescending up-and-down look.

"This kid's your guy?" said the man, scratching his sideburns. "He looks like a liability to me."

The woman frowned in agreement, stretching her tight scar.

Offended, Ridian stood a little taller as he strode towards them.

"Guys, trust me," said Tann, a longsword strapped to his back. "Ridian will do fine. Have I ever made a bad call?"

"Yes," said the man.

The woman crossed her arms and nodded. "Many times."

"Look, I know he doesn't look like much…" Tann looked at Ridian, and truth be told, seemed a little underwhelmed himself.

"*But?*" coaxed the man.

"But what?" said Tann.

"You said, 'He doesn't look like much'…but? We're missing the 'but'."

"There is no 'but'. I'm just saying he doesn't look like much."

The scar-faced woman groaned and slung a sack across her shoulder. "We're losing dark. The kid stays."

"Hector has his sister," said Tann. "She might still be alive."

Tann's words seemed to have a strong effect on the pair. They still weren't impressed by Ridian, but their frowns eased, and their shoulders relaxed.

"Sorry for being a bastard," said the man, readjusting the leather holsters across his chest. "I'm Mal. Welcome to the Doomed."

Ridian shook Mal's hand and tried not to wince from the crushing, stone-like grip. Ridian then offered his hand to the lady, but she didn't take it.

"I'm not here to make friends," she said curtly. Then with a spark of flint, she lit a torch and marched into the tunnel.

Mal chuckled. "Don't take it personally. Ari's a hard woman to win over, but she'll keep you alive. That's worth more than a handshake."

Ridian did a double-take: a lynx had appeared from nowhere. It slunk alongside Mal into the tunnel with soundless, padded feet, its whiskers nearly identical to Mal's outrageous sideburns.

"The Doomed?" Ridian asked Tann, once Ari and Mal had passed out of sight.

"Killing Hector is a suicide mission. You okay with that?"

Ridian shrugged, though hot fear rose in his chest. "Sure. You?"

Tann gazed at the twinkling lights of Fidicia far below with a hint of sadness. "Love requires sacrifice." Then he, too, entered the silky blackness of the tunnel.

***

A long stretch, a few twists and turns, and the tunnel ended. Outside, a tall, semi-circular wall kept out the north and everyone beyond. A rough street of a few huts led to the gate-house. The simple fortress rang with commotion. Soldiers bustled: patrolling the ramparts, fortifying battlements, erecting stalls, fletching arrows, hammering swords, and packing provisions. Wolves prowled, gnawed bones, and started fights. A nervous air coursed through the place.

A young Knight dashed up to Tann. "Preparations are underway, sir," he said breathlessly. "Triple the guard, triple the supplies, triple the vigilance. Precisely as ordered." He stood straight as a pencil, awaiting some acknowledgment.

"Um… excellent work," said Tann, and the boy nodded and returned to his duties.

Mal frowned after him. "Awfully eager, isn't he?"

"Never seen war," said Tann dryly.

"Or death," added Mal.

"Aye, or death."

Walking down the crude street, they passed an old man pedalling a grindstone and scraping a sword across the spinning wheel in a fluster. Similarly, a fletcher was binding arrowheads as if the quantity, not quality, mattered, while a pair of smiths worked in a rush. One pumped the bellows, the other hammered away. Both panted and glistened with sweat.

Tann turned to Ridian. "Come with me." And they left Ari, Mal, and their Familiars to enter a hut. Lining the walls were weapons of every description: swords, spears, bows, arrows, axes, hammers. Every size. Every shape. Ridian was awed and overwhelmed. There were too many to choose from. Then his eyes fell upon one sword. But not just any sword. The blade gleamed sleek and deadly in the moonlight. The hilt was black as death. The pommel was a snarling wolf's head. *This is the one*, he knew. It seemed to call to him, to sing. As he reached for it, Tann slapped a ten-inch scabbard into his hands.

"There you go," he said.

"A knife?" said Ridian, outraged.

"A dagger," Tann corrected. "There is a difference."

"You want me to go on a suicide mission with just that?"

"Don't worry, it'll do a fine job cutting up dinner."

Ridian was not impressed.

"Listen," said Tann. "Each of us has a role to play. Ari's our Scout—our eyes and ears. Mal's our Stalker—he'll exact sudden, unexpected death. And I'm the Tracker—I can find anyone, anywhere."

Ridian rolled his eyes at the old brag. "Then what am I?"

"You're our Runner, in case we need to send a message back."

Ridian bristled. "I'm not coming back empty-handed."

Tann's face flashed with sudden anger. "Listen here, Ridian. You're lucky to be coming at all. I might have vouched for you before, but you probably are a liability, just like Mal said. So, if you do not intend to obey my orders—immediately and without argument—then you can stay right here." With that, he stormed away.

Ridian sighed, attached the dagger sheath to his belt, and followed. Ari and Mal waited for them beneath the gatehouse. Mal's lynx curled between his legs, while an eagle perched on Ari's leather-protected forearm. Ari stroked the severe-looking bird with great affection.

"A tawny owl has been staring at the gates," said Ari, her eagle nibbling her scar-torn ear.

"A spy?" asked Tann.

Ari nodded.

"Can you take it out?"

"Do Mal's farts smell?" Ari remained deadpan, but Tann and Mal grinned. Ari then pecked a kiss on her eagle's sharp beak. "Remind Tann what you can do," she whispered, and with a powerful beat of its wings, the eagle soared into the night. Ari closed her eyes, her face scrunched in concentration.

Tann heaved the crossbeam from the gate and opened the

great doors a fraction. "Get ready," he said, and they waited in silence, then somewhere beyond the gate, a bird—perhaps an owl—screamed. Ari's face twitched as if caught in a vivid dream, while the owl's shrieks tore through the night. It screamed a loud crescendo and then fell into silence.

Ari opened her eyes and smiled, a disturbing thing. "His Companion won't get far."

Tann turned to glare at Ridian. "Obey my orders. Under-stood?"

Ridian nodded, and their small party slipped through the gate and pelted downhill towards a mountain pass perhaps a quarter-mile wide. Trees covered the pass and crept up the flanking mountains until they became sheer and naked. *The Wrathwolds*, Ridian knew, the great mountain range separating Fidicia from Kyrosia. The others shot ahead with Soulcaster speed. Already exhausted, Ridian drew Rava, and they were soon all slicing through the forest, trees and bracken whipping past.

"This way," cried Ari, and she led them off the road to crash through the undergrowth: they leapt over icy trickling creeks, hurdled fallen trees dusted with snow, and skirted house-sized boulders that must have slipped off the mountainside a millennia ago. Soon enough, a man appeared, swinging his sword wildly in the air. Unseen by the man, Tann, Mal, and Ari surrounded him, quiet as shadows. With a clumsy step, Ridian snapped a stick underfoot, and the man whirled to face him, eyes bulging. His face was streaked with a couple of nasty gashes, and though young, his jet-black hair was streaked with thick lines of premature white: a Kyrosian.

"Fidician scum," he spat venomously. Then, quick as a

whip, he changed sword hands, pulled a knife from his belt, flipped it so he held the blade, and then raised it, ready to throw at the stunned Ridian. At that moment, a winged shadow swooped from nowhere and tore a red streak across the man's cheek. The man had barely flinched when Ari shot from her hiding spot and leapt upon him. Her knees barrelled into his chest, smashing him into the ground, and the tremendous impact sent the man's knife and sword skittering. Ari whipped out her own knife and looked as if she would bury it in the man's face.

"Stop," said Tann sharply. "He might have information."

Reluctantly, Ari resheathed her knife and clambered off the man.

"Er… Tann," said Mal, scratching his sideburns. "He's dead."

"What?" said Tann.

Mal pointed. "His ribs have punctured his lungs or I'm a Wrathwoli princess."

Even as Mal said it, the man released a final gurgling breath and remained still.

Ari shrugged and gave a wry smile. "Whoopsie."

Tann rubbed his temples and sighed. "Ari, you can't just kill every lunatic with a knife."

"But he was going to kill our young liability," she said, looking doe-eyed at Ridian, full of fake motherly care. Her eagle landed on her shoulder and glowered at Ridian.

"Just promise me you'll be more careful next time," said Tann. "Prisoners talk. Corpses don't."

"Promise," said Ari, then plucked something from the man's mouth—a bloody tooth. She pulled a purse from her belt, undid the drawstring, and dropped the tooth in with a faint tinkle. Gloating, she rattled the pouch at Mal.

"Show-off," said Mal. "How many now?"

"Not enough." Scars stretched as Ari grinned. "But still more than you."

Curious, the wolves and Mal's lynx loped up to sniff the dead man.

"Let this poor sod teach you a lesson," said Tann to Ridian. "If your Familiar dies, you're screwed."

All things considered, it was a very effective lesson.

***

Ridian, his new companions, and their Familiars tore through the Wrathwolds at a cracking pace: up ridges, down valleys, and around bends in the mountains. They kept well clear of the established pathways, remaining deep in the forest—clinging to animal tracks high up the slopes. And though secrecy was paramount, they covered many miles. They ripped past trees, sending leaves aflutter, and leapt over half-frozen streams, tinkling with freshly melted snow. The night wore on, and Ridian's exhaustion made him strangely introspective. A lot had happened since he awoke from his poison-induced coma a handful of hours earlier: Fidic's Lute and Journal, Mother Asarah's assassination, bonding with Silver, Feya's kiss… It all churned around in his mind, even as his body tormented him.

"Wait," hissed Ari, and the party skidded to a stop. Ridian's hands were numb with cold, and his nose ran with snot. His lungs, however, burned hot as he rasped for air. Ari stood still, shoulder's heaving, eyes closed. Tann and Mal looked at her expectantly as they caught their breath. After a moment,

Ari opened her eyes and pointed. "There are four men and four wolves at a campsite a mile ahead. A man and a wolf keep watch. The rest are asleep."

Ridian's heart quickened. "Soulcasters?" he asked.

They all frowned at him, and he decided to keep his mouth shut.

"Kyrosians?" asked Mal.

Ari nodded.

"How do you know?" asked Tann.

"They're as ugly as you are," said Ari.

"Can we slip past?" asked Tann, ignoring the quip.

Ari shook her head. "The pass narrows at an elevated chokepoint. There's no way around it. It's the perfect lookout."

"Let's get a closer look," said Tann.

From that moment on—and to Ridian's great relief—they went slowly, stealing through the forest as if breaking into a house. Every time Ridian's footfalls made a crunch or snap, he received vicious glares from his silent counterparts. A mile or so later, Ari pointed up a tree, and they all climbed up. The lynx joined them, leaping deftly from branch to branch, while Silver and Yanala waited below. Ari's eagle was already there, perched upon the topmost branch. An able climber, Ridian peered from a lofty branch, creaking above the forest canopy. Ari was right. Ahead, the pass narrowed as it rose, until it reached a narrow gap between two mountains. The gap itself was all stone, bare as a baby's backside, totally exposed. Of wolf or man, Ridian saw nothing.

They waited. Stars twinkled overhead. The tree swayed from a breeze that cut through Ridian's clothes. Had he ever been this cold or this tired? Finally, Ridian saw a man coming over the rise: first his head, then his torso, then the rest of him came into view as he walked towards them, framed within the gap at the end of the rise. The man fiddled with his belt, then urinated off a ledge, a pipe clenched between his teeth. The pipe glowed from an intake of breath, washing his scruffy face in dim light. A moment later, the light faded, and smoke curled from his lips. He then took a seat on a nearby rock. A wolf sauntered into view and sat by his side.

"Tann?" whispered Mal, sitting upon a nearby branch. "Is there another way?"

"There are many ways to Sky Island," said Tann. "But most are obvious and well-guarded. This is as good as we're going to get. Any ideas?"

"They might not be Hector's," said Mal. "They could be harmless travellers."

Tann snorted a laugh. "Four harmless Kyrosian Soulcasters. Unlikely."

"Besides, posting a lookout is suspicious," said Ari. "I say we sneak up to the tree line. I take the first guy out with my bow, and you guys rush in and take care of the rest."

"Nay," said Tann. "The moment your shot lands, the Familiar will raise the alarm. And if even one of them escapes and warns Hector, our mission is over. They will triple their guard and then hunt *us*. No. Everything hinges on surprise. We either sneak past or kill them all quickly. But then again, they might be harmless Kyrosian travellers. We can't just kill someone because he took a piss and can't sleep." Tann held his chin thoughtfully. "What if I pose as one of Hector's men and see how he responds? I look the part, don't I?"

"You are ugly enough," Mal agreed.

"What if they don't buy it?" said Ari. "They'll raise the alarm, and there goes our secrecy."

Tann considered this. "You could wait with bow drawn, and Mal could sneak his cat up and take down the wolf quickly if need be?"

Mal sucked his teeth, considering. "It's pretty bare terrain. Would be a hard thing to sneak up without being spotted. It's the perfect lookout, like Ari said." He wet his finger, then held it aloft. "And if the wind changes direction, they'll smell us for sure, and the jig will be up."

"It's risky," said Tann. "But with Yanala by my side, it'll be four against two. That's good enough for me. Let's get as close as we can." They all went to climb down, but Tann stopped Ridian. "No," he said. "Not you. You're too noisy. You'll trip over and get us all killed. Stay here."

Ridian didn't argue, and within moments, he was alone. But not alone. Silver illuminated the base of the tree and stared up at him. Ridian closed his eyes. When he focused, the link between them was quite palpable. He could *feel* the wolf's presence. In his mind, he imagined their bond—the link between them—like a ribbon of glowing moonlight. It was a bizarre image, but it was what he saw. Then, with a mental nudge, he spurred Silver to stalk after Tann and the others. As the wolf obeyed, he felt the supernatural thread between them grow taut, as if under strain. *The further Silver goes, the harder it is to sense him.* Ridian opened his eyes to peer after his wolf, but Silver's glow was lost beneath the shivering leaves of the canopy.

Ridian closed his eyes and reached within himself. Deeper

and deeper he went, like a bucket down a well, until finally, he found his centre—his soul, safe and sound within. Steeling himself, he *pushed* against his soul. Fear swelled as he felt the sensation of dying, of slipping away into the Nothing. Only now there was that link, that slither of moonlight connecting him to Silver, and his fear wasn't as strong. Dying wasn't so bad when you weren't alone, it seemed.

He *pushed* harder, and his soul suddenly tore free. It hurtled through the Black, along that ribbon of moonlight like a bolt of lightning, until he slammed into the wolf, and, in a flash, he was looking through the wolf's eyes...

Ridian could see clearer, sharper, crisper—the moon and stars burned brightly above. And his field of vision had widened, allowing him to see more without needing to turn his head or even move his eyes. Ridian—through Silver—gazed at Tann and the others. They were crouching behind the last of the trees, oblivious to Silver's presence. Beyond lay the bare pathway, rising towards the Kyrosian lookout. There was the man, smoking beside his wolf, and the acrid smell of tobacco filled Silver's nose. All smells, in fact, were a hundred times amplified: the rich decay of rotting wood, sodden moss, fermenting leaves, frozen sap, squirrel dung, and the cold, crisp smell of melting snow. Another sniff brought other scents: the blood congealing on Ari's new tooth, Tann's greasy hair, Mal's body odour. Yanala reeked of wet dog, while Mal's lynx smelt clean, though with a tang of fish—perhaps its last meal? Weak and strong, near and far, Ridian could smell it all.

Minutes passed. Nobody stirred. Just the Kyrosian, puffing away on his pipe and humming a lazy tune. Finally, his wolf yawned and laid its head on the man's lap. With painstaking care, Ari nocked an arrow into her bowstring and gave Mal a nod. Mal nodded in return, closed his eyes, then his lynx darted from his side out onto the bare pathway. It went a dozen feet, then lay flat on its belly, barely a ripple. If Ridian hadn't been watching it, he would have seen nothing, perhaps just a stone. Neither the Kyrosian nor his wolf seemed to notice. The man puffed his pipe, the wolf slept soundly in his lap.

The lynx dashed against the nearby mountain wall and seemed to melt into it. It was difficult to see, even when Ridian knew it was there. But Ridian could still smell the elusive cat's clean fur and tang of fish. Another dash, another stop. Now the lynx crept, stretched and low, little more than a shadow. With a long in-breath, the Kyrosian's pipe glowed, illuminating his weary face. He scratched his stubbled cheek absently. Closer and closer the lynx crept. Twenty feet from the man. Fifteen. Twelve… Ari edged around the tree, bow at the ready. Tann had just pointed at his chest, then up the path when suddenly, the lynx shot off the path to shrink behind a stone. Tann froze, and Ari spun back behind the tree, mouthing a silent curse. A moment later, the Kyrosian wolf looked up, ears cocked, and the man pulled the pipe from his mouth—alert.

Seconds ticked by. The man and wolf gazed down in their direction—terribly suspicious. Ridian could almost hear Tann, Mal, and Ari's galloping pulses. He could certainly feel Silver's heart hammering away within his lean ribcage. *What happened?* Then Ridian realised: the smell of tobacco had vanished. The wind had faltered and was fitfully changing direction. The Kyrosian stood up, his fingers curling around the handle of his sword. Then wind blew down from the rise, and the acrid smell of tobacco filled Silvethen sher's nose.

Tann was gesturing frantically to Ari. *I'm going to go. No! Don't stop me. I'm doing this.* Then he and Yanala stepped out of the tree line and boldly approached the Kyrosian, their feet crunching on the path. Ari aimed her bow at the Kyrosian and pulled the bowstring to her chin. Mal's eyes were scrunched shut in concentration.

"Hail, brother!" Tann declared.

The Kyrosian leapt back in surprise and dropped his pipe. But before he could cry out, Tann shouted again. "Does the blood of the Father live?"

The Kyrosian frowned down at Tann, his wolf bristling at his side, taut as a drum.

"Does the blood of the Father live?" Tann called again.

"Indeed, the half-blood lives," the man said warily.

"Be his name Hector?"

"Indeed, his name be Hector!" Exchange done, the Kyrosian visibly relaxed, taking his hand off his sword.

"You scared the hell out of me," said Tann with a jovial tone, not breaking his stride.

"Me?" said the Kyrosian with amusement. "You scared the hell out of me! Almost shat meself."

Tann chuckled.

"You alone?" asked the Kyrosian.

"Aye."

"What are you doing out here?"

"Relaying a message."

"At this hour?"

"Afraid so. Drew a mighty short straw."

"I'll say. Thought I had it bad, standing watch on the arse-end of nowhere."

"Could be worse. Could be mining in the far north, freezing your bollocks off just so you can give half your pay to our dear southern neighbours."

"Ha! You mean two-thirds!"

"Not if you have a knack for hiding semi-precious stones up semi-precious holes."

The Kyrosian laughed and picked up his fallen pipe. "So, you're a northy. Won't hold that against you. Any man's pecker would freeze off up there. No shame in it."

"How very kind, my western friend. Then I won't hold your mother-loving against you, either." And they both laughed.

Tann passed the lynx, crouching behind a stone a mere few feet away. Ari trembled with the strain of holding her drawn bow; the arrow nock quivered against her scarred cheek.

"Say," said Tann, striding ever forward. "Could I trouble you for some leaf? I ran out of chewy and could use a hit."

"Sure. I've only got a small pipe's worth, and it's the crap we get from those lazy easterlings." He rummaged in his pocket.

"Many thanks," said Tann, quickening his pace slightly, only a dozen strides away.

Ridian was wondering what Tann was going to do, when the wind turned hard and fast, blowing through Silver's legs and up the hill with a strong, sudden gust. The Kyrosian wolf sniffed the air with sudden interest, and the next moment, the Kyrosian man's eyes widened in alarm. "Guys! Wake up! There's—"

Ari's bow twanged, the arrow disappeared and then reappeared in the man's throat, making his mouth gape open in an 'o' of surprise. Simultaneously, Yanala and the lynx dashed at the Kyrosian wolf, trading furious swipes and bites. Growls echoed through the valley.

Swearing, Ari and Mal pelted forward. Some pack instinct urged Silver to follow, and the wolf shot up the rise, pebbles flying behind its paws. Beyond the Kyrosian with the arrow in his neck, three more Kyrosians—two men and a woman— charged around a bend with the speed of galloping horses, their swords drawn, their wolves sprinting behind them. Tann drew his own sword calmly from the sheath on his back. A second later, a Kyrosian slashed at Tann with tremendous force. Tann parried—a quick, delicate stroke— then swiped his longsword in a monstrous diagonal arc. The Kyrosian blinked, stupefied, then split in half, from his shoulder to the opposite hip.

Ari stopped to draw her bow and fired at the shrieking woman. The feathered arrow sprouted from the screaming mouth, and the woman sprinted another ten feet before she toppled over, dead. Mal cocked a tiny crossbow and shot the first wolf through the throat. The last Kyrosian skidded to a stop, eyes shining with fear, then fled back down the canyon.

"He's getting away," cried Tann.

With Tann, Ari, and Mal all having stopped momentarily in combat, Silver found himself closest to the retreating man. Possessed by some hunting instinct, Silver sped after him, hurtling past the two stray Kyrosian wolves bereft of their Soulcaster Companions. The canyon approached, and then the stone walls whipped past as Ridian spurred his wolf on, knowing if the man got away, the mission was over. Together—through the wolf's eyes—Ridian and Silver caught glimpses of their runaway prey. With every glimpse, the man got closer. They were gaining. Then they skidded around a corner and found the man lying face down, his wolf nowhere to be seen. Cautiously, Silver crept up to the body. There was no breath, no discernible heartbeat, and the trousers were soaked in piss. He was dead. Silver sniffed and recoiled from a noxious smell: the pus of a certain poisonous toad, Silver knew. The image of a black-backed toad Ridian had never seen nor heard of flashed through his mind. Ridian marvelled: his wolf had just taught him something. Looking closer, Silver saw a feathered dart poking from the man's backside. Mal, with all his lethal accessories, must have fired it.

The sound of dashing feet made Silver turn. The two Kyrosian wolves were flying around the corner. Growling, hackles raised, Silver braced for the attack. But the wolves zipped past, reeking of fear.

Silver trotted back to find Tann rummaging through the Kyrosian camp. He frowned directly at Silver. "Let me be more specific. If I say stay, that includes your wolf. Got it?"

With a mental nudge from Ridian, Silver nodded his head.

Tann walked around the corner and peered down into the forest. "And if you're still in that tree, get your ass up here."

Silver looked out: down in the valley, floating above the dark canopy, was a cold silver flame, sitting atop a young man's head. Astonished, Ridian realised he was looking at himself, his hair glowing like the moon, shining just like Silver. Then, letting go, Ridian slid from the wolf's body and back to his own.

Chapter 33

Ridian awoke upon a cold stone slab, with the wind roaring outside their little cave. It had been a cruel couple of days, speed-hiking all night, then sleeping through the day. They'd covered countless miles, and Ridian felt every weary step. Mal snored nearby, his lynx sitting serenely beside him; Ari fiddled with an arrow, while Tann and Yanala huddled beneath a blanket near the entrance and gazed at the howling tempest outside.

Ridian sat up and rubbed the sleep from his eyes as Silver nuzzled into him, seeking warmth. A grey midmorning light fell into the cave, and in that light, Silver's coat was soot black, without a trace of his usual ethereal glow. *This is what everyone else sees. A mangy, malnourished wolf.* Indeed, without a glowing aura, Silver looked rather shabby.

With a stretch and a yawn, Ridian went to join Tann by the entrance. The sloped ceiling was low, forcing Ridian to stoop in places as he shuffled forward. Tann didn't acknowledge Ridian as he came to stand beside him. He just stared, transfixed, at the gale, and what a gale it was: trees were bending and twisting and thrashing from the most vicious wind Ridian had ever seen. It was a wonder the trees weren't being uprooted and flung away.

Finally, Tann looked up at Ridian, almost surprised to see him. "Scary, huh?"

Ridian drew his flapping coat tight. "I'll say. Never seen such crazy wind before."

"Well, this place is famous for crazy winds." Tann pointed past the wind-whipped trees at a flat-topped mountain with sheer, vertical walls—wider than it was tall. "That's Sky Island—an island plateau—the very heart of the Wrathwolds. Sacred Land, the Wrathwoli would say. Where The Great Winds converge and forever battle for dominion. Legend goes that it was from Sky Island that Toomi, the Forgotten One, leapt and never fell."

Ridian remained silent, an invitation to tell the story Tann was teasing.

Staring at the raging wind, Tann began. "Lomon, the Wrathwoli Elder, had five sons: tall, strong, and fearless. All except Toomi, the youngest, who was deemed too small and weak by all. Nevertheless, as the time to pick an heir approached, each of Lomon's sons attempted to win their father's blessing. The eldest travelled to the frozen north and returned with flint and steel to warm the tribe in the Winters to come. The second son crossed the blistering Raaki desert in the distant south and established a lucrative trade with the Sunburnt people, bringing back a chest of gold. The third son traversed the great inland sea to the west and learnt the mysteries of agriculture so the tribe would never know hunger. The fourth son climbed the monolithic mountains to the east and tamed a giant Eagle to watch over and warn the tribe of oncoming enemies. While Toomi, the youngest, who was deemed to small and too weak, stayed within the safety of the tribe."

The wind roared louder for a moment, forcing Tann to pause his story. Leaves flapped wildly upon flailing branches, before settling as the wind eased. "When the time came," Tann continued, "the four elder sons knelt before their father to present their gifts: of fire, of gold, of grain, and an eagle's protection. Lomon was at a loss. To whom should he bestow his blessing? It was then that Toomi cried from the top of Sky Island. 'Father, it is I, Toomi, the Forgotten One. I present my gift.' And he flung himself from the precipice. People screamed, and his father cried out in grief, but little Toomi never fell. Indeed, he swooped over them and flew around the mountain three times before hovering before his awestruck Father. 'While my brothers left for the four corners of the Earth, I, Toomi, the Forgotten One, stayed. Not because I am small and weak, as people say, but because I listened to the ever-changing Wind. Every time I left, the Wind called me home. The further I strayed, the stronger the call. *Come home,* the Wind cried. *Come home.* I did, and the Wind carried me. But the gift of flight is not the gift I offer. For you, my father, I give something even more precious.' Then Toomi landed gently beside a woman and three young children. 'My gift is my children, who carry your blood. My gift is their laughter. My gift is their joy. My gift is their sorrow when you pass, and the promise that you will be remembered.' Seeing his wisdom, Lomon gave Toomi, the First Windchaser, his blessing."

Story told, Tann stared into the distance, at the empty grey sky. Ridian let the silence stretch out. He sensed a terrible sadness within Tann and knew the man had more to say. Finally, after a howling burst of wind, Tann spoke. "Windchasers used to live here. Lots of them. On windy days like today, you would see dozens flying about, riding the War Winds, worshipping whatever wind prevailed." Tann's hair flailed about his face, but he didn't blink. He was lost in some memory. In fact, he didn't seem to be talking to Ridian at all. "I remember my daughter flying for the first time."

Ridian's eyes widened in surprise. *Daughter?* Behind him, Ari fiddled with her fletching, and Mal no longer snored, though he ostensibly remained asleep.

"She was so scared," said Tann. "But not nearly as scared as I was." Tann laughed, though his eyes might have filled with tears. *"I don't wanna jump, I don't wanna...* Oh, West Wind, she must have said that a hundred times that day. I would have given in—I did give in, but her mother was so strong." Tann smiled and grimaced as if the memory both pained and pleased him. Then he spoke in a high falsetto, overlaid with a thick Wrathwoli accent. *"Tanny. She's my daughter. She's a Windchaser. And I don't care how old she is. She jumps, or I push her off. Either way, she flies."* Tann kept staring at the empty sky. "She did jump in the end." Tann spoke as if he still couldn't believe it, even after all these years later. "She screamed her head off, and I almost died. But when I saw her glide..." Tann cocked his head slowly, as if to track his daughter's flight in his mind's eye. "She flew and flew and flew. I could have watched her for hours, days even, and not been bored. Of course, her mother rubbed it in. Gods, her mother drove me crazy."

Ridian thought of Feya: the burning kiss and the burst of wind as she flew back up to her second-story bedroom. He was about to ask what had happened to Tann's wife and daughter, but stopped. Something tragic, obviously. Tann spoke about them in the past tense. They were gone. In all likelihood, they had been killed in the Wrathwoli genocide—a genocide caused by Hector.

"How many Windchasers are left?" asked Ridian.

Tann looked at him as if noticing him for the first time. "Hard to say. The few that survived The Windless Storm rarely visit their blood-soaked home. They consider Sky Island a graveyard now, and no wonder. Plus, they're skittish. They take one look at an outsider and zip away. Hard to keep track of people that can fly."

"She's coming back," said Ari.

"Great," said Tann with verve, snapping abruptly from his rare moment of vulnerability. "What did she see?"

As it turned out, Mal was awake; he sat upright, staring at Ari keenly, eager for the report.

"Give me a second," said Ari, closing her eyes. "It's so darn windy. She's distracted. It makes it harder to—"

Ari screamed, making them all jump.

Tann was by Ari's side in a flash. "What? What do you see?"

Ari's scar-streaked face was a rictus of horror, eyes open but blind. She shook her head. "No, no, no…"

"What do you see?" Tann shouted.

"They're killing her!" she wailed.

Ridian's blood turned to ice. Even the wolves and the lynx cowered.

"What the hell's going on?" cried Mal.

Ari's unseeing eyes were bulging. "She can't get away. There's too many of them. She's dying."

"Do not bring her back here," said Tann sternly. He grabbed her by the collar and shook her. "You hear me?

Do not bring her back here!"

Ari's face scrunched up in pain, then she collapsed into a ball on the floor. "She's gone," she cried. "Gone, gone, gone... I'm alone. I'm all alone." Ari hugged herself and sobbed on the stone floor. Ridian's heart was slamming against his ribs. Tann and Mal exchanged a disturbed look, neither of them knowing what to do. Eventually, Tann laid a hand on Ari's shuddering shoulder, and she flung it away. Tann tried again, and this time, she let it stay.

"Please," said Tann carefully. "I'm sorry, but what did you see?"

Ari fought to regain control of herself. She took a shuddering breath and spoke in bursts. "There are hundreds... maybe thousands... and as many wolves and cats and—and..."

"Birds of prey," said Mal grimly, and Ari sobbed anew.

Tann looked pale. "An army of Soulcasters?"

Ari nodded.

Tann shook his head, stunned. "How? How is this possible? I know Tinker said so, but hundreds? Thousands? The Kyrosians are bound by law to declare their Soulcasters. A few might slip through, but not that many." He frowned, lost in furious thought, before whirling on Ridian with sudden resolve. "Run back to Fidicia with all haste. Warn Sevron. Tell him another Soulcaster war is nigh."

"I can't just leave," said Ridian.

"Go!" shouted Tann. "There's no time to lose."

"What about my sister?"

Tann drew his sword with a harsh hissing sound and pointed it at Ridian, an inch from his chest. "Go, or I'll kill you myself." His nostrils were flaring like a maddened bull.

Ridian recoiled against the wall, disturbed by Tann's fury. But Tann sighed, calming himself, then re-sheathed his sword. "Your sister's not the only one in peril. If we kill Hector, perhaps we can stop this war. But if we fail—and we probably will—untold thousands will die. Fidicia must be warned."

Ridian and Tann glared at each other. Nobody spoke. Even Ari had composed herself, sobered by Tann's stark words. Tann was right. Rayna's life wasn't the only one at stake. War would endanger the Thunderfells. Feya, Ollie, Kai, Theodor, Ella, Kess… Fidicia needed to be warned.

Ridian nodded. "I'll go."

"Very good," said Tann. "Run as fast as you can, and do not stop."

Ridian looked at them all—at Tann, Mal, and Ari— perhaps for the last time, some dark part of him thought. Then he shot out into the storm. The wind was even more ferocious than it looked. It howled in his ears, snapped his coat wildly, and blew him off track. Trees flexed to near breaking point, then shot back like slingshots as the wind momentarily eased. Pebbles rolled along the ground, while sticks and leaves tore through the air. Shielding his eyes, Ridian squinted in the direction he needed to go: a twisting downhill path that took him away from Sky Island. He took it, and Silver followed, and they were soon out of sight of the little cavern. He couldn't believe it. All this way just to turn around and—

"Ridian," called a high-pitched voice, half drowned in the roaring wind.

Surprised, Ridian looked about, but saw nobody.

"Ridian," the voice called again. It was close and so high-pitched it barely sounded human.

Neck prickling with fear, Ridian looked all around. Still nothing. Then something zipped across his vision: a finch. The tiny, wind-buffeted bird flapped furiously against the gale and managed to steady itself momentarily before Ridian.

"Ridian," it trilled. "I'm a friend. I can help you find Rayna."

Ridian recognised the bird. The last time he'd seen it was back at Mudwall, in the rye field, the night he'd lost Rayna.

It was Chirpy.

Chapter 34

Ridian was gobsmacked. *Chirpy? Talking? Talking about Rayna?* Thoughts raced and tripped over each other in his mind, rendering him mute. A twig whipped his cheek, snapping him out of it.

"You can talk?" said Ridian, first with disbelief, then with indignation. "Since when?"

The tiny bird fluttered about, unable to hover in the violent wind. "Not long," it chirped. "It took me a long time to learn how to work the bird's vocal cords."

The bird's vocal cords? Chirpy was a Familiar. But Ridian was told only predators could become Familiars, that prey animals were too timid to bond with a Companion. Nevertheless, someone was pulling the bird's strings.

"Who am I speaking to?" demanded Ridian. Anyone could be staring at him from within those beady little eyes.

"A friend."

"Friends don't hide their name."

"You will know soon enough."

"What kind of answer is that?"

"The only one you will get for now."

Ridian clenched his teeth. *The little smart arse.* How long had the bird been following him anyway? Since Mudwall?

Surely not. And what was this bird—and the Soulcaster within—doing in Mudwall? What was it doing now?

"So, you know where Rayna is, do you?" Ridian asked suspiciously.

"Yes. She's with Hector. We need to hurry."

"Why must we hurry?"

But the finch had already zipped away in the direction of Sky Island.

Competing thoughts collided in Ridian's head. Fidicia needed warning. Rayna needed saving. Was this a trap? Providence? Was Chirpy a friend? Foe? Was Ridian crazy to follow? Was he crazy not to? Chirpy was getting further away, flitting from one thrashing tree to the next, struggling to fly straight in the ferocious crosswind.

Ridian looked at Silver; Silver blinked back and seemed to say, *Where you go, I follow.* That was all Ridian needed. He ran after Chirpy, quelling the guilt curdling in his gut. He would warn Fidicia as soon as possible, but he couldn't pass up an opportunity like this. Rayna came first, after all. That was why he was here, a thousand miles from Mudwall. Rayna was a captive, and who knew what kind of torment she was suffering, what weird experiments these Kyrosian freaks were doing to manifest their 'secret weapon'? No, he had to save her. It was his duty as her brother, and he would die trying if he had to.

Ridian and Silver caught up to Chirpy, and together they fought through the wind. They dashed from tree to tree, enjoying the brief windbreak each trunk offered. Ridian kept asking the bird questions, but Chirpy kept shooting ahead. Time passed in this manner for a couple of long, gruelling hours: Chirpy leading the way, Ridian and Silver following, until they came to the base of Sky Island. The sheer escarpment loomed over them, a wall of smooth, unclimbable rock. They followed its base for half a mile before halting at a narrow crack splitting the cold, windswept stone. Chirpy flitted a dozen feet up the slender fissure—barely a yard wide—before perching on a lone branch jutting from the rock. "Climb up," he said.

Ridian scanned the crack with wind-stung eyes. He had to crane his neck—the wall went up and up and on and on. *You've got to be joking,* he thought, stepping inside the tiny fissure and feeling about with his hands. There was the odd handhold and foothold, sure, but it was hardly a flight of stairs—and it was certainly impossible for Silver.

"My wolf can't climb this," said Ridian. "Is there another way?"

"This way is secret and quick," said Chirpy. "All other ways are long and guarded."

Ridian did not like this one bit. Separating from Silver when he might be walking into a trap? Chirpy—or rather, whoever controlled Chirpy—was asking too much.

"I'm not going anywhere without my wolf."

"Suit yourself," said Chirpy, then he shrugged his tiny shoulders and flew away.

"Wait!" cried Ridian, and the bird returned.

Was it tapping its tiny, clawed toes with impatience? Ridian groaned. "Sorry, Silver. I have to go."

Silver cocked his head and frowned in confusion.

"Just wait for me, okay?"

With a whimper, the wolf sagged, ears drooping. Silver knew Ridian was leaving. And it wasn't just hard for the wolf. A pain lodged in Ridian's chest, compelling him to stay.

Surely, this is the stupidest idea ever, a part of him cautioned. But his sense of duty overwhelmed him. He couldn't give up now. He'd heard firsthand from Tinker that Hector was on Sky Island. And here he was, at its base. Taking a steadying breath, Ridian sent a wave of reassurance towards Silver. But the wolf slumped onto his hind legs, dejected. *At least he's stopped whimpering.*

"I'll be back soon. I promise." Then Ridian peeled himself away from the wolf, for the first time since their bond was forged, and began the climb. Silver whined up at him, but Ridian ignored it. If he had to leave, he had to leave. No point in torturing them both.

Ten long minutes later, Ridian made the mistake of looking down: Silver was a tiny, black speck, and the ground seemed to zoom away. Trembling, forearms burning, Ridian clung to the wall, unable to move. Fear paralysed him.

Chirpy fluttered above him. "There's a foothold near your left knee and a handhold just above your right hand. Just pop the leg, stick your toe, and push. You can do this."

Ridian tried to breathe. *I can do this. I can do this.* And somehow, Ridian popped his leg, stuck his toe, and pushed. The climb wasn't just high, it was difficult, and despite his guilt at leaving Silver, he drew Rava liberally from his wolf to fuel the ascent. Without it, he wouldn't have made it half this far.

At long last—perhaps an hour or perhaps a hundred—Ridian heaved himself over the ridge. Relieved beyond what words could express, he lay panting on his back, staring up at the grey sky, thanking whatever gods watched over reckless idiots. Eventually, however, he caught his breath and sat up. The view was a true wonder. The forest below swayed in a frenzy, while all around, snow-capped mountains rose like the spine of some massive stone dragon.

"This way," said Chirpy.

Ridian turned. The land that had looked flat from down below was actually undulating, and at the centre was a small, squat mountain. Chirpy beelined towards it. Ridian followed, prickling with fear. If this was a trap, it was a bloody good one. He was all alone, and his link with Silver was becoming more and more tenuous with each step. Still, Ridian marched on, and the mountain drew near. With the howling wind, there was no need to keep quiet, and the wind-tortured trees provided ample protection from unwanted eyes. They climbed a foothill, and at its crest, Ridian's guts gave a sickening lurch. Below, in a wind-protected dell, tents flapped in a clearing, billy cans hung over fire pits, and clothes hung on makeshift lines. *Hector's camp?* Ridian dropped to his stomach, palms tingling. Hector and his men would consider him an intruder, a spy, an assassin. They would surely kill him, or worse.

Chirpy fluttered onto his shoulder, tiny claws digging. "The campsite's empty."

It was true. Pigs grunted from pens, goats bleated on the end of chains, and roaming chickens clucked. But no people—or predators, for that matter.

"Where is everyone?" asked Ridian.

"They gather to hear Hector at the mountain," said Chirpy. "Rayna will be there."

Ridian's heart slammed against his ribcage. "Is she locked up? Guarded? And how do we get off this Sky Island? We can't climb back down, surely." Ridian suddenly realised his full predicament. He was trapped up here with only a shifty bird guiding him towards a dangerous cult leader. Why hadn't he thought of how they would escape? He reached for Silver's presence—but their bond was barely a thread.

"No, no, no," Chirpy tweeted merrily. "Rayna's fine. And don't worry. You'll be able to leave whenever you want." Then Chirpy fluttered ahead.

"Don't worry," muttered Ridian, following the bird along a dark track overhung with twisted, tortured-looking trees. As he did, he recalled everything he knew about this Hector—an alleged descendant of Kyros the Terrible, the general who led the massacre of the Wrathwoli, started the Last Soulcaster War, united the Kyrosian gangs, and went to extraordinary lengths to kidnap Rayna, believing her to be a secret weapon. Ridian wondered how useful this information would be. Not much, he concluded. Hector was a powerful warrior and an influential leader, and Ridian felt like a duckling walking into a fox's lair.

Soon, voices emerged through the wood ahead. Many voices. *Hundreds.* The gathering was close. Rayna was close. Many dozens of birds circled overhead, and Ridian's blood curdled at the memory of Ari screaming, *"They're killing her!"* And then, Ridian began to see men, women, and children, as well as lurking wolves and great prowling cats. Ridian could barely breathe as he pulled his hood far over his head, just like he always did in Mudwall. But somehow, he kept walking. *Blend in,* he told himself. *Hide among the crowd. They won't see. They won't...*

"The Mother's Embrace," said Chirpy, and Ridian understood why. The crowd was nestled between two foothills at the base of the mountain that wrapped around in giant curving arcs, like great arms, almost touching. They provided a wide space within, protected from the savage wind.

Ridian kept his head down and kept walking, eyes peeled for any trace of Rayna. As he passed within reach of the mother's arms, the wind died, and the noise of the crowd rose. They talked excitedly and stared at the mountain in great expectation. But not the mountain per se, at a natural rock platform that jutted ten feet from the ground like a lofty altar at the end of an open-air cathedral. Upon the altar burned a bonfire.

Chirpy landed on Ridian's shoulder. "Get as close as possible. You'll see Rayna soon."

Ridian scanned for any suspicious behaviour, of anyone catching strange glances at him. He saw nothing, yet felt a profound unease. He searched for Silver's presence, but his link with the wolf had well and truly vanished. Ridian recalled stepping onto The Mire, into certain death. If he could do that, he could do this. He entered the chattering crowd and gently pushed through the congregation, sliding past people, wolves, and great cats. People gave way without issue, and except for one white tiger that turned to growl at him, nobody seemed to care about some teenager making his slow way forward. He edged closer—twenty paces from the altar—and stopped. The dense crowd smelled of old leather, sweat, and wet dog. The collective body heat was intense. Birds of prey wheeled and screeched overhead. Long seconds passed. Ridian scanned the crowd: most heads were prematurely streaked with white, and many of the faces were leathered and lined. Not old necessarily, just weather-beaten faces hardened by hard lives. And between the missing teeth, scars, and wiry muscles, everybody looked tough as nails.

"It's time," said Chirpy in Ridian's ear.

Sure enough, a man emerged from a cavern behind the altar.

"Hector!" somebody shouted in jubilation, and the crowd lurched forward in a crush, eager to get close. Ridian was surprised to find himself strangely elated to see this Hector—the man who had caused him so much heartache.

The man who emerged leaned heavily upon two walking sticks, each step awkward and shaky. The crowd hushed and breathed as one, leaving a heavy silence and the clattering of the man's footfalls. *Clack. Clack. Clack. Clack.*

Wooden legs, Ridian realised with surprise, and with his walking sticks, the man was an awkward, trembling quadruped. But Ridian could easily see he had once been formidable. He was broad and barrel-chested, with beefy arms and a thick, muscular neck. Now, however, he grimaced in pain with each short, shuffling step. A living ruin.

The tragic figure looked upon the crowd with sorrowful eyes. A wolf and a snow leopard loped up and stood by his side. An eagle fluttered down upon his bowed shoulder. A fox curled between his wooden legs. And a majestic stag stood behind the man and completed the picture.

"My children," said the man, who was surely Hector, his voice thick with emotion. Nobody breathed. All eyes were riveted to the broken man. "You all know the story," Hector continued. "Kyros broke our chains, became King, and was betrayed... And we who remained faithful were banished to a frozen wasteland to know hunger, pain, and death. Generations have passed, yet the betrayal still feels like yesterday."

Heads nodded in profound agreement. Tears rolled down cheeks. Hector's words were like food to the starving, and nobody spoke lest they spoil the meal.

"Kyros' blood flows through my veins," said Hector. "But we are all his Children. We are all orphans bereft of our rightful inheritance. Freedom. Peace. A home to call our own. Is this too much to ask?"

"No!" some cried out.

Then Hector's voice fell upon them like a hammer. "Who is responsible for our suffering?"

"FIDICIA!" roared the crowd as one.

"Who betrayed us?"

"FIDICIA!"

"Who cast us into Exile?"

"FIDICIA!"

The crowd could no longer restrain themselves. They wailed and cursed and cried, overwhelmed with grief and outrage..

Hector nodded approvingly, then he raised a hand and received swift silence. "But they are right to fear us. Every day, our numbers grow." He gestured with his walking stick, and a young boy and a woman walked up the rocky staircase towards him. Atop the altar, the boy stood shyly before Hector, who laid a meaty hand upon the boy's shoulder. "Have courage, my son, and remember, pain will set you free."

Pain will set you free? Tinker's mantra upon the surgeon's table. Then five men climbed the staircase, rope in hand. The boy spotted them, lost his nerve, and hid behind the woman's dress. The men tried to pry him away, but the boy clung tight to the woman's leg. There was a smattering of laughter, and the woman, presumably his mother, gave an embarrassed smile and pried the boy's fingers away. Once loose, the men swooped in and tied rope around each of the boy's wrists.

Someone from the crowd shouted, "Pain will set you free!"

Then someone else. "Pain will set you free!"

Then the whole crowd took up the chant. "PAIN WILL SET YOU FREE!"

Ridian dreaded what might happen next.

The boy whimpered as the four men pulled the ropes, spreading the helpless boy's arms wide before the congregation. The crowd's passion escalated. Some closed their eyes in ecstasy. Some laughed at the sky. Others sobbed into their hands.

"PAIN WILL SET YOU FREE!" the crowd cried in unison. "PAIN WILL SET YOU FREE!"

"Mum! Please! Don't let them hurt me!" the boy screamed, and, to Ridian's horror, the mother cried, "Pain will set you free!"

Hector approached the boy with his slow, four-legged walk. He brushed the boy's fringe from his panicked eyes and said something to him. The boy's panting slowed, and soon he was blinking away tears and frowning, jaw set, determination etched into his young face. "Pain will set me free!" he cried again and again, his confidence appearing to increase with each refrain.

One of the men pulled an iron rod from the sweltering bonfire and approached the boy.

The boy screwed his eyes shut. "Pain will set me free! Pain will set me free! Pain will—"

The man pressed the red-hot tip against the inside of the boy's forearm. The boy screamed, and although he thrashed in earnest, the men held him fast.

"PAIN WILL SET YOU FREE!" roared the crowd, drowning out the screaming boy and the sizzling arm.

His mother stood by, hands clasped, tears running into her smiling mouth. Ridian felt sick, but was unable to look away. The torturer removed the iron rod, leaving a waxy white streak of burnt flesh, and then he cauterised another strip with a hiss. More screams and more writhing followed. Then the boy's eyes rolled back in their sockets. At this, the crowd took an excited, expectant intake of breath. The boy's eyes flicked back, and the veins along his arms and neck stood on end. Corded muscles flexed. And he screamed, not in fear, not in pain—in fury. Then, eyes wide and nostrils flaring, he jerked the ropes with tremendous strength, pulling all four of his torturers forward. One stumbled, and the boy pounced on him like a rabid dog. But before he could do any damage, ropes were pulled, and the boy was yanked off his feet. He was up in a flash, and the burly men struggled to keep the tiny boy restrained. Every ferocious twist of the boy pitched them forward, and for a moment, it seemed the boy would break loose. Then, another man threw a noose about the boy's neck and tugged. This did the trick. The men dug their heels, and the boy keeled backward, grunting and writhing, barely overcome by the collective strength of five men. The crowd whooped and cheered until, finally, the boy sagged, utterly spent. Immediately, the men undid the knots about the boy's wrists, and his mother fawned over him, beaming, proud as punch. Beaded with sweat, the boy looked up and smiled as if this were the happiest moment of his life. Perhaps it was. He'd just survived his Awakening. Was this how Hector was raising his Soulcaster army? With torture? It was certainly more effective than meditation and even cold-water submersions. Perhaps Tann *had* been rather soft with him after all.

Ridian looked up at Hector, and his blood turned to ice—

Hector was looking straight at him. Not at the crowd. Not in his direction. At *him*. Ridian withered under Hector's gaze. Hector *knew*. Ridian couldn't seem to move.

Something fluttered above Ridian's head and screeched in a high voice. "This is the one!" It was Chirpy—betraying him. Of course it was. All eyes locked on him. Ridian made a dash, hoping to break away. But the crowd braced themselves and pushed him back. Ridian lunged again, but the human wall held. Whirling this way and that, Ridian saw dozens of jeering faces, red with raucous laughter. Ridian closed his eyes and searched for Silver. He felt nothing. He was alone. He fumbled for the knife at his belt. But the moment he did, iron-like hands came out of nowhere and lifted him above their heads and carried him. Panic washed over him as they bounced him above the crowd and up the stairs, and before Ridian knew it, they'd placed him before Hector and a thousand pairs of eyes.

Hector examined him with an inscrutable expression. The eagle perched on his shoulder screeched at Ridian, while Hector's wolf, his snow leopard, and his fox circled Ridian and sniffed him. The stag looked on with indifference. Chirpy fluttered onto Hector's other shoulder and ruffled his feathers. *Chirpy is Hector.* But the revelation barely registered. He was trembling too much, his heart was hammering too hard.

People began walking off the altar to join the crowd below, leaving Ridian alone with the cult leader. "What are you going to do to me?" Ridian croaked, his mouth paper dry.

Hector took a few wobbling steps towards him on his peg legs and smiled, a glittering, friendly smile. "Nothing," he said sincerely. "I just want to know you."

Ridian was baffled. "What do you mean?" he asked, mind all in a muddle. "Why?"

"Because he's family," said an unmistakable voice from the tunnel beyond the bonfire.

It can't be... But it was.

Rayna was grinning at him like it was her birthday, her hair braided and strewn with flowers, her sun-kissed cheeks glowing. She sped around the bonfire and flung herself into Ridian's arms, laughing with delight. The crowd cheered, and Hector smiled, tears of joy twinkling in his eyes.

Chapter 35

Ridian couldn't move. He couldn't speak. He couldn't even hug Rayna back. He'd been convinced he would never see her again. Had for months. He just couldn't bring himself to admit it. And yet here she was. Then something finally clicked in his mind, and he hugged her back.

"You're breaking my ribs," said Rayna with muffled laughter.

Ridian finally let go, and became all too aware of the staring crowd.

"Sorry for the theatrics," said Hector to Ridian. "I feared if I told you who I was or if I led you through the main entrance, you would think it was some trap and wouldn't come."

Ridian just stared at him.

"You two catch up out the back," said Hector. "I'll be with you soon."

"I can't believe you didn't tell me he was coming," said Rayna, slapping Hector on the arm playfully.

Hector chuckled. "I do like surprises."

Rayna shook her head. "You're impossible." Then she whisked Ridian away, up a trail that led over one of the bald arms of the Mother's Embrace. Soon enough, they crested the foothill and passed out of sight of the congregation. From this vantage, Ridian could see scattered campsites nestled within little dells, and the edges of Sky Island plummeting downward on all visible sides. It was indeed an island in the sky—a perfect fortress. Thankfully, there was no wind on this side of the mountain, allowing them to speak with ease.

Rayna frowned at him, though Ridian knew she was delighted. "What the hell are you doing here? I told you to stay home."

"I'm—I'm rescuing you," he managed to say, though it somehow sounded very lame.

"What?"

Ridian checked over his shoulder to ensure they were alone. "I'm here to rescue you," he whispered.

"Rescue me?" said Rayna, not keeping her voice down. "But I want to be here."

"What?"

"I said, I want to be here. I'm happy."

"So you're... you're okay?"

Rayna laughed. "Yes."

"You're fine?"

"Yes."

"They haven't—they haven't touched you, have they?"

"What? No! Oh, Ridian, you've been here two minutes, and you're already fussing like an old hen."

Months' worth of pent-up anxiety transformed into anger in a flash. "Well, if you're fine, what the hell are you doing here?"

Rayna's smile faded. "Didn't you read my note?"

"Yeah, I read your stupid note. *Sorry to leave without a*

goodbye," Ridian quoted in a bitter, sing-song tone. *"I'm fine. Promise. Not sure when back. Please don't follow, and please don't fuss."* He glared at her, ears burning. "What kind of a note is that?"

Rayna's smile had well and truly gone. "Didn't you read the back?"

"What back?"

"The back! The back of the note. Did you read the back?" She kept flipping her hand.

"No, what…?" Ridian deflated as realisation dawned. Rayna had written on both sides of the paper. He was such an idiot.

Rayna puffed up as if she'd sucked up all his frustration. "You didn't read both sides? You didn't check. That's such a—such a *you* thing to do."

"What's that supposed to mean? And don't answer," he added quickly. "It's pretty bloody rich to blame me."

"Well, I hadn't signed off, had I?"

"Hadn't signed off." Ridian's voice dripped with sarcasm. "Well, my mistake then. A thousand apologies." He bowed extravagantly.

"Why are you so angry?"

"Because I thought you'd been kidnapped!" he shouted, scolding hot anger spilling from his mouth. "I thought you were a hostage. I thought you were a *slave.*" He laughed bitterly. "And after all these months, I find you with flowers in your hair, having parties with a bunch of new friends. I've been worried out of my mind. I've been worried sick. How could you just leave me like that?" Ridian turned away from her, hating how pathetic he sounded.

"You have no idea why I left, do you?" she said quietly.

Ridian shook his head miserably. "No."

"Well, I'd better tell you then." She scratched her scalp. "Hm, where to start?"

"The beginning, and tell me everything."

"Okay, let's start with the tricky part. Remember the Moonflowers?"

"Yeah, they bloomed a month early."

Then Rayna grasped a nearby shrub that clung to a crack in the mountain, and closed her eyes purposefully. To Ridian's astonishment, the leaves of the shrub began to shrivel up—crinkling and curling as if a season-long drought had swept through in a matter of seconds. Rayna then stretched out her other hand as if divining for water, and upon the ground, directly beneath her downturned palm, a tiny green something began to grow. It crept along the dirt, then slithered slowly up the wall, sprouting new shoots with the speed of slow-running honey. By the time Ridian caught his breath, the vine was seven feet tall with a dozen white flowers blossoming like little yawns. When Rayna finally opened her eyes, the vine was ten feet tall and covered with flowers, while the hardy shrub—leaves, branches, stem and all—was stone dead.

"Wow," breathed Ridian. "You're a druidess, like an Arden of old, like Valaria."

"Yes," said Rayna excitedly, but also deeply surprised. "Exactly. I can serve as a link between plants. I can channel life between them. Starve one, nourish the other. That's why things always grew around me, like our home. That's why weeds died. But it all happened without me knowing. And I was doing it wrong. I was giving *my* life away. That's why I kept getting sick. I was getting sucked dry. Life itself was leaking out of me. And the night of Sunfall—with the Moonflowers—I gave too much. That's what caused the seizure. Only when I woke up, I found myself in a dead patch of rye, which I'd instinctively killed to revive myself. That, of course, is when Chirpy started talking to me. I probably need to explain Chirpy, don't I?"

"Well, I know Chirpy is Hector's Familiar," said Ridian.

Rayna's surprise grew. She went to ask a question, but Ridian cut her off. "But I don't know why Hector's been spying on us. And I still don't know why you left."

At that moment, Chirpy flittered in from nowhere to perch on Rayna's shoulder. "She left because the Sungazers were going to burn her alive," cheeped the bird.

Rayna nodded emphatically. "That's why I left so quickly, without a proper goodbye. Hector warned me I was being hunted, and I didn't want to tell you in the note because I knew you'd stress out, like always. Of course, I thought I'd gone nuts. Chirpy talking is straight out of some old Mudwall superstition. I can just imagine it, a Faery taking the shape of a talking bird to lure a maiden into The Mire. Ha! But then Chirpy told me I had magic… lost Arden magic. He told me I had the ability to hear the Song of Silent Growing. That I could transfer life from plant to plant. I told Chirpy he was a hallucination and he should piss off. But he told me to listen to the field, and sure enough, I could hear—well, something. I sound crazy, don't I?"

Ridian looked between the dead shrub and the new flourishing vine. "Well, if you're crazy, so am I."

Chirpy ruffled his feathers, drawing Ridian's attention. "So, Chirpy said you were being hunted, did he? Why?" He narrowed his eyes at the bird.

Rayna laughed dryly. "Well, it turns out General Selkyrie didn't like her emotions being tampered with." She shot Chirpy a mock-accusing look.

"Manipulating emotions is a delicate art," chirped the bird. "It's hard to get right."

"Wait, what are you saying?" said Ridian.

"Hector can influence the emotions of other people," said Rayna. "That's *his* magic. And he fiddled with General Selkyrie's. That's why she let us go. Only his manipulation was as subtle as a slap in the face. So, when her head cleared…"

"She wanted to burn the witch who bewitched her," said Chirpy.

"Right…" said Ridian. This was a lot to take in. Rayna had druidess magic, and Hector could manipulate emotions. Ridian decided to go with it for now. In the last few months, he'd seen a Sungazer wield fire, entered the Astral plane, gazed through Silver's eyes, been infused with Rava, seen Feya blow wind from her palms, and now Rayna could kill and grow plants with her mind. Why not emotional manipulation? He could influence Silver's emotions, after all, and Silver could influence his.

"So, I rushed home," continued Rayna. "Packed my things, wrote the note—on both sides, I might add—and followed Chirpy into The Mire. Thankfully, Hector sucked out my fear, otherwise I don't think I could have done it." Rayna's smile faded. "It was the hardest thing I ever did, you know, leaving you like that, not knowing when I'd see you again."

She meant every word, and with that, the last of Ridian's anger melted away.

Chirpy bobbed on her shoulder. "Tell him what happened

next."

"Then," said Rayna, with sudden excitement. "I found a secret way across The Mire. A hidden road made of—"

"Roots," Ridian interrupted, "all woven together, stretching for miles and miles, straight as an arrow."

"Okay," demanded Rayna. "Your turn. I'm not telling you any more until you spill the beans. How on earth did you get here? And how do you know so much?"

"Not until you explain why *he*—" Ridian jabbed a finger at Chirpy. "– is helping us."

"I made a promise to your dad," said a deep voice behind Ridian.

Ridian turned to see Hector hobbling around the corner on his wooden legs and walking sticks. A gentle wind tousled his white-and-black streaked hair.

What did Hector mean, *their dad*? The bastard had vanished before they were even born. Ridian looked at Rayna, who gave a wistful smile.

"You knew our father?" Ridian asked warily.

Hector nodded gravely. "He was my twin brother."

Twin brother?

Rayna stood beside Hector and clung onto his thick arm affectionately. "That's what I wrote on the other side of the note: *I've found our uncle. He'll look after me. We'll come back for you.*" Rayna spoke with such sincerity, and Hector gazed with such genuine affection that Ridian knew it was true.

Uncle? This changed everything. Up until now, Ridian and Rayna had been alone. No father. Catatonic mother. No extended family. No other siblings. It was just them. They were alone. *Uncle…*

Hector smiled. "Follow me, and I will tell you everything."

Chapter 36

A short walk around the mountain later, Ridian, Rayna, and Hector entered a shallow cave with a rickety door. Within lay a room of sorts, its rock walls leaning inward, making a triangular space. There was a shabby mattress, a wonky chair, and a small desk. Groaning, Hector fell into the chair, propped his walking sticks against the wall, and kicked out his wooden legs with a sigh. Rayna sat cross-legged on the mattress, beaming at each of them.

"You'll want to sit," said Hector, gesturing to the space next to Rayna. "It's a long story that starts centuries ago, with a man called Kyros the Great." Hector chuckled good-humouredly. "Now, I know what you're thinking. What does some ancient, long-dead king have to do with me?" He looked frankly at Ridian. "In short, *everything*."

Ridian doubted it, but he would indulge the man. Besides, didn't Hector claim to be Kyros' descendant? If that were true, it would also mean…

"I also know what you've probably been told," said Hector. "The Tale of the Elder Three, of Kyros the Great but not yet the Terrible, of how he rose to power only to become a mad, black-hearted tyrant." Hector shook his head. "History is written by the victors, and they give it their own self-serving spin. Let me tell you the true story. Kyros the Great, whom the Fidicians *call* the Terrible, was the most remarkable man to have walked the earth—but he was born of scandal. His mother was a prominent Arden druidess; his father a Torian slave. Now, this was more than just a scandal. Breeding between the two peoples was expressly forbidden. But Kyros' noble Arden grandparents had privilege and power. They made Kyros' father disappear—whether with gold in his pocket or a noose around his neck, history is undecided—and they hid their daughter until she gave birth to two squalling infants… a boy and a girl. *Twins.*"

Hector arched his eyebrows meaningfully; twins were evidently important to the story. "Kyros' mother refused to give her children up. 'They are my blood,' she said. 'And I will shed mine before parting with them.' Her parents relented, and so Kyros and his twin sister, Lyra, were raised as Ardens. And as they grew, none were the wiser. They proved themselves excellent students, gifted orators, and became influential in the Arden courts, rising to prominence among the elite. But eventually they learned the inescapable, inconvenient truth: they were half-bloods; half-Arden, half-Torian. This revelation changed everything for them. The Torians were no longer mere cattle, but brothers and sisters, and they began petitioning for their freedom. Though opposition was fierce, they made allies, and their following grew. At the height of their influence, they led the Wheat War, barricading grain reserves during one fell winter. After months of heated negotiations, the Last King Kidian granted Torians the right to rest on the seventh day, a small but symbolic victory: for the first time, freedom was in sight." Hector shifted to get comfy, and the chair creaked beneath him.

"But the twins were divided. Lyra insisted that while revolutionary fervour was at its zenith, they should storm the palace. Kyros disagreed: violence would sow seeds of future violence. 'History will forget the diplomacy and remember the blood,' he said. 'The manner in which we win matters.' However, while the twins deliberated, the Last King Kidian ordered an unprovoked attack, slaughtering hundreds of Torians, including Lyra herself, butchering her before Kyros' very eyes. During the attack, Kyros had his soul Awakened and was thus able to fight his way through the bloodbath and escape into the wild, where he lived like a beast for years, grief-stricken. It was during his exile that he realised that tyranny could only be overcome by force, and so he trained with single-minded determination, pushing his body and mind harder than any before, and explored his Soulcaster potential. And it was he who first learned how to Split and bond with a Familiar. Believing other Torians had the same ability, he formalised his Soulcasting theories.. The significance of this cannot be understated. Prior to Kyros, an Awakening was a one-off event in the life of a Torian, never repeated. Now, Soulcasting could be learnt, mastered, and weaponised. If Kyros' story had ended there, he would still be considered great. But he was indefatigable. Fuelled by righteous anger, he disseminated his findings across the country in secret. He sparred with slaves in the fields and held underground meetings. Word spread. Slaves ran from their masters to join him, and soon he had the makings of an army. And all the while, Kyros pushed his own magical capacity. He was more than just a Soulcaster, he realised. He could do something nobody else could…"

Hector leaned forward and enticed them with a long pause. "He could draw Rava from other Soulcasters and their Familiars. He could redirect the Rava flowing between Soulcasters and their Familiars into himself, granting him tremendous strength. Thus, the greater his Soulcaster army, the stronger he became. And, as the stories tell, with an army of slaves and wild beasts the likes of which the world had never seen, Kyros the Great marched upon the Living City of Terillion. He defeated the giant Daegan, outsmarted Fidic upon Riddler's Bridge, and climbed Valaria's great living wall. Kyros smashed our chains and became the First Free King of Tor." Hector's face darkened. "And while he delivered us from the yoke of tyranny and gave us the gift of Soulcasting, his enemies conspired against him. They spread lies, poisoned his reputation, spun stories of cruelty, of genocide, of a King gone mad. Foremost among the conspirators were Daegan, Fidic, and Valaria." Hector almost spat the names. "The Gifted Three lured Kyros into their mountain home under false pretences. 'Peace,' they said. 'Peace…'"

Hector gazed at the stone wall, expressionless. "They killed him," he said at last, matter of factly, though anger seethed beneath his calm exterior. "Killed the greatest man of his generation and drove his faithful followers into a frozen wilderness to starve, suffer, and die—all under the pretence of peace." Hector's frown lines ran deep, and his shoulders sagged under the weight of generations of Kyrosian suffering.

This was a big diversion from 'The Tale of the Elder Three.' In that story, Kyros was portrayed as a paranoid and murderous tyrant. He was the mass murderer who hunted innocent people, and attacked the noble and heroic Elder Three and their United Resistance. Hector's account, by contrast, painted Kyros as the betrayed hero and the Elder Three as usurping villains. Some instinct told Ridian it wasn't true. Then again, Fidic had lied about other things…

"But we have not been without hope," Hector continued. "Kyros had a daughter. And though she was ordinary, her twin children were not."

Again, the mention of twins…

Hector could see Ridian catching on. "Identical boys, Ewan and Kayden, and like their grandfather, they could wield new and unprecedented magic. While Kyros drew Rava from the bonds of others, these boys could draw from plants—much like Arden druids." Hector nodded at Rayna. "Only they drew the Rava into themselves and made themselves strong. But they were too young, too foolhardy, and too full of the false immortality of youth. Ewan died from a stray arrow and Kayden from an infected wound." Hector sighed. "History has repeated itself many times. Twins from the mighty bloodline of Kyros are born with fantastic magical abilities, they try to reclaim our home, and fail. Your father and I were the last to try."

Ridian then asked a question he'd been wondering his whole life. "What was our father's name?"

"Priorities, Hector, really," Hector admonished himself. "Forgive me, I do get carried away with history. Your father's name was Norian. Though everyone called him Nori. You actually look an awful lot like him." Hector smiled fondly at Ridian. "And he would have loved you both very much. He certainly loved and looked after me. Though truthfully, he was an absolute rascal. He was forever getting in trouble: pinching apples from neighbors' orchards, starting fights, chasing girls… Not a bad kid, just fearless, and too caring by half. The apples would be for Gran, the fights were to protect me from bullies, and the girls… well, perhaps the girls were just for him." Hector winked.

Rayna laughed, and Ridian found himself grinning.

"Nori was a scallywag," said Hector, "but he believed wholeheartedly in our destiny. 'We are the blood of the Father…' he would always say. 'History is counting on us.' So, he pushed us to train hard, even as kids. Initially, my emotional Manipulation was pretty crude. I was clumsy and inconsistent. But with countless hours of practice with my brother, I mastered its subtleties. It all revolved, once again, with the transference of Rava. I'd channel a touch of Rava into Nori's mind, just a drop, exactly where it needed to go, and he would feel pity, or shame, or sadness, or courage, or whatever I wanted. I then learnt to draw Rava out and suppress emotions. That was a big discovery. That opened the door for bonding with prey animals and, indeed, multiple bonds. I could neutralize the panic of a skittish stag or cowardly rabbit and forge the connection. And I could remove the jealousy of all my other Familiars to maintain a bond with them all. Eventually, your father's mind became so accustomed to my presence that it no longer repelled me, and we achieved the impossible: a human-to-human bond."

Ridian's eyebrows lifted at that.

"It was incredible," said Hector. "He would hike far out into the mountains, sling his soul out to me, and share the view. He would sing many miles away, and I would hear the tune. Distance was no obstacle to our telepathic communication, which was lucky because your father was ever on the move. He was tireless, and that's not an exaggeration. That was *his* magic. He could subsist exclusively upon Rava, needing neither sleep nor food. He could draw Rava straight from plants and work tirelessly, all day and all night, for months. No rest. No snacks. Nothing. He only ate to be social and pretended to sleep so he could sneak out. Norian Nightwalker…" Hector chuckled. "That's what he called himself, anyway. We made a good team, Nori and I, and when our time came, we reclaimed the northern Wrathwolds for Kyrosia, won a dozen skirmishes, and even pushed the Fidicians back into Fidicia itself. We were at its very gates. We were *this* close." Hector made a gap between his thumb and forefinger before releasing a long sigh. "Or so we thought. We were young and foolish and fell for the oldest trick in the book: we underestimated our enemy. We stretched ourselves too thin, too far from home. The Fidicians sprung from their secret caves and surrounded us." Hector sighed, even heavier than before, and his eyes glazed over, seeing nothing except maybe the distant past. "Many died that day, the rest were captured… That was a dark time. I lost the war, my liberty, and my legs in one day. I lay in bed for months, terribly depressed, unable to say a single word. I even lost my ability to manipulate emotions. Imagine that: unable to soothe the pain of others because I was too full of my own despair."

"It was the ever-restless Nori who organised a mass breakout, while I slept the days away. I'll never forget it: one minute, I was lying in bed, miserable; the next, I was running through the fog, shivering upon the edge of a desolate wasteland. Wolves were howling. Men were shouting. All unseen through in the fog. *The bastards have me cornered,* Nori said in my head. *I'm sorry, but I can't go back. I'm going to take my chances out here.* I was confused. Out where? Then I realized where he was: on the edge of the Great Waste. My brother was going to try crossing Daegan's country, which we both knew to be certain death. And though I hadn't spoken in months, I shouted then: *don't go, please, don't go!*"

"*A life of captivity is no life at all,* he said. *Not for us. Not for the children of Kyros.* Then the fog and the cold vanished, and I was alone in my warm bed once more. And though my grief was great, I strapped on my wooden legs and stood upon them for the first time. With my brother gone, history was counting on me and me alone. And so, I manipulated us out of captivity. A little emotional push here, a little pull there. I manipulated the right people in just the right way, and eventually, they let us go. Of course, they took our best lands and taxed us to breaking point, which led to the starvation of thousands." Hector's words became bitter. "And they thought they were being so magnanimous. What a joke." Hector lapsed into a brooding, introspective silence, frowning at the wall like it was responsible for all his life's woes.

"Uncle?" said Rayna.

Hector shook his head, snapping back to the present. "Anyway, three years later, the impossible happened: there I was, sitting on the privy, doing my business, when everything disappeared, and I was looking through your father's eyes once more. He was in a cave with a thick, greasy door. Water dripped somewhere in the darkness, and it stank of urine and feces. He was in prison."

Ridian frowned at Rayna: *the Fell Caves?*

Rayna frowned back: *just listen.*

"I then heard your father's voice in my head," Hector continued. *"Brother?* he asked in a shaky voice, and I could tell he'd been crying. *Yes, it's me,* I said. *Where are you?* But he just hugged his knees and cried, his arms and legs all skin and bone. *This is just a dream,* he wailed, *shaking back and forth. Just another dream. I'll wake up, and you'll be gone.* He was sobbing now. I could taste his tears as they ran into his mouth. *No, it's not a dream,* I said. *It's me. It's really me. I'm here. Talk to me. Where are you? Let me help you.* To say I was disturbed is to say almost nothing. This sobbing mess was nothing like my brother. He'd clearly lost his mind."

Looney Shrooms, thought Ridian. What had Remmy said about them? *…Even small doses over a period of time can precipitate schizophrenia, catatonia, hysteria, and other psychiatric conditions.*

Hector looked on the verge of tears. "I used my powers and sucked out his confusion, fear, and despair. I drew all that I could, though he was countless miles away. Drew it all, though the emotional storm it stirred up in me was more than I could bear. At last, however, he calmed himself and told me his story: how he'd wandered the Great Waste and staggered upon the ruins of Mirecross Castle; how he found the lost Ardens; how he found and fell in love with your mother." Hector smiled, but it was very sad. "How they started a life together, how they were expecting a child. Only they were imprisoned for witchcraft while she was still with child. *Take care of my wife and child,* he pleaded. *Take care of them.* I promised I would. I promised over and over. And then the connection between us was broken, and I was back on the privy… And no matter how hard I tried, I couldn't reconnect with him. It was too far for me. And I couldn't go bodily, not without legs. I tried sending my wolf, but no matter how hard I trained, my wolf would eventually pass from range, and I would lose my connection with it. So, I took to experimentation. I jumped my soul from my wolf to my cat, and to my surprise, I found I could go farther, extend my reach, using my Familiar as a kind of astral steppingstone. What followed was years of practice, springboarding from wolf to cat, to stag, to fox, to eagle, and then finally to my finch. Once I'd mastered it, I was able to travel, in a sense, all the way to the new land of the Ardens.

"Sadly, however, by the time I got there, Nori had passed away." Hector scratched absently at his knee, where the straps of his wooden leg pinched the skin. He didn't make eye contact for a long moment, but when he did, he smiled. "I found your mother, though: alive and well with two beautiful kids. Twins, would you believe? Total troublemakers. You were a delight to watch, and I checked in on you as often as I could. However, it wasn't long before disaster struck. One day, I came to check on you, and you were gone. It was years before I found you again. *Years.* And even then, I wasn't sure how to help. I feel terrible about it. I made a promise to my brother to look after you. And what did I do to help you? Nothing. I am truly, truly sorry. I should have been there for you." Hector bowed his head and stared at the floor.

Rayna lay a reassuring hand on Hector's knee.

"No," Ridian found himself saying. "You did everything you could. It's a miracle you found us at all."

Hector gave a reluctant smile.

"Tell Ridian about twin half-bloods," said Rayna impatiently. "You can't prattle on about Kyros and not tell him about *us*."

"I think I've talked enough," said Hector with dry amusement. "You tell him, and we'll see how well you remember your lessons."

"You're just being lazy," said Rayna playfully, narrowing her eyes at him. Then she bit down on her lip and frowned up at the ceiling as if the memory was written upon the stone. "Hmm..."

"Don't look at me," said Hector. "You're on your own."

"Call yourself a teacher," said Rayna scathingly.

"I know about Rava," said Ridian eagerly. "If that helps?"

Rayna's raised her eyebrows. "Really?"

"Yeah, it's the life force in all living things. And I know the fundamentals of Soulcasting. But I don't know much about Arden Druidism." He frowned, thinking. "In Druidism, Rava is transferred between plants?" he offered. Then, remembering Rayna's words from earlier, he added, "Starve one, nourish the other."

Rayna beamed. "Quick learner."

Ridian examined his fingernails haughtily. "Well, in the womb, one twin usually hogs all the best nutrients. We can't both be smart, can we?"

Rayna whacked his arm. "Shut up."

Ridian and Hector shared a laugh.

"Okay, smart arse," said Rayna, starting at him levelly, "tell me this: what if a Soulcaster like our Father and a Druidess like our mother had a child? What if the races mixed? Something that has barely happened in all history."

Ridian pondered this. Kyros and his line had mixed blood, and they had extraordinary powers. Was it possible for other half-bloods—such as Ridian and Rayna—to have such powers? Perhaps they were secret weapons, after all? *Secret weapon…* Ridian's suspicion towards Hector flamed anew *…She is the linchpin of all of Hector's plans*, Tann had declared to the Council. *A secret weapon.* Ridian hardened his heart against Hector. He might be their uncle, but he was also a cult leader. How was he planning on using her—or himself, for that matter?

Rayna mistook his silence as bafflement. "Well, the offspring of a Druid and a Soulcaster could end up being a druid, or a Soulcaster, or even just your everyday, garden-variety human. But *twins…*" Rayna wagged an all-knowing finger. "Mixed-blood twins, such as you and me, are different. But you would know all about that, all-knowing, all-powerful, nutrient-sucking one…"

"Just get on with it," said Ridian.

Rayna gave a smug grin. "Well, while Soulcasters *trade* Rava with their Familiar, and Druids *transfer* Rava from plant to plant, mixed-raced twins blend both abilities. With us, Rava can be manipulated in strange and unique ways." Rayna turned to Hector. "Okay, lazy bones, break's over. Give us some examples."

Hector considered. "Well, I've mentioned myself—I use Rava to manipulate the neural mechanisms underpinning emotions. Your father used Rava for sustenance. But then there's Edgar Wolf-Rider, for example. He could draw Rava from himself and stimulate his Familiar's growth. In the end, he was a shrimpy five-foot-nothing, but he rode a colossal twelve-foot wolf into battle. His twin sister Katalia Longsword, by contrast, drew Rava from her terribly withered wolf and turned *herself* into a giant. Much like Daegan, though he drew from plants, having more of a Druidic persuasion."

"Wait," said Ridian. "So, the Elder Three...?"

Hector nodded. "Were mixed-race triplets. Yes. Their gifts were a product of their mixed blood. Their story of Roki granting them powers is blathering nonsense."

More lies from the charlatan Fidic, thought Ridian.

"So, what about you?" Ridian asked Rayna, knowing her ability had started all the drama of the previous few months. "What's your special, unique gift?"

"Me? Well, I can sort of bond with plants and donate my own Rava to them..." Rayna grunted a laugh. "Not supremely useful. If I give too much, I have a seizure, as you well know."

Ridian nodded slowly. It made sense, given everything he knew, but it hardly sounded like a secret weapon. "And...?"

"'What about me?'" said Hector, vocalizing the rest of Ridian's question. "'What's my yet undiscovered magic?'" He leaned forward. "Want to find out?"

Chapter 37

"Of course, I want to know what kind of magic I have," said Ridian, though strangely, a scared part of him didn't want to know. Why would he be scared? "Presuming I do have some kind of new fantastical magic."

"Oh, you certainly have some sort of new gift," said Hector cheerily. "A twin descendant of both Kyros *and* Valaria, how could you not?"

A descendant of Kyros and Valaria? Ridian still doubted the Valaria part, even with the Elderflower hanging around his neck. Now Kyros as well?

"I know," said Rayna, smiling at Ridian's stunned expression. "What are the chances? We're probably Kyros' great-great-great-great-great-something-grandkids. Not that it did us any good. Don't remember growing up in a palace, do you?"

"No," said Ridian solemnly, and he thought of giving her the Elderflower necklace there and then as a pleasant surprise. *No, I'll find a more appropriate time.*

"The blood of The Father and the blood of the Flower," said Hector, shaking his head as if he still couldn't believe it. "Truly remarkable."

"Say that's all true," said Ridian. "Why haven't I shown

signs of… well, anything?"

"The mind is a powerful thing," said Hector. "It can block thoughts, emotions, memories…" He shrugged. "Even magic."

"Why would it block magic?" asked Ridian.

Hector's twinkling eyes grew sad. "Magic can be suppressed for a few reasons, but the foremost reason… is trauma."

The image of a dead field and a dying tree flickered across Ridian's vision, and his heart gave a little jolt. He took a calming breath. What the hell was with that dream, anyway?

Hector didn't seem to notice. "Magic is intimately bound with one's psyche, and traumatic events—if left unresolved—can cause something of a festering wound. And if the wound never heals, the magic remains dormant. It is therefore crucial to heal the wound, though of course, healing can be very painful."

Ridian didn't like this conversation. The dead field and the dying tree kept flickering before him, sending his insides roiling. He wanted to change the conversation—now.

"Imagine a boil," Hector continued as a teacher might, seemingly oblivious of Ridian's distress. "You must lance it and squeeze out every last painful drop of pus before it can heal. Rayna's seizures, for example, caused a kind of magical phobia, stunting her magical ability. That's why it remained so subtle for so long. But she contended with her fears, faced them head on, and now she is making leaps and bounds towards her full magical potential." He grinned proudly at Rayna, but she was busy examining Ridian, a curious, concerned frown creasing her brow.

Ridian knew where this conversation was going. Hector

wanted Ridian to talk about stuff he didn't want to talk about. He wanted to bring up things better left alone. Any moment now, Hector would start asking nosey questions, just like the good old doctors at the Asylum: *have you been hearing voices? Seen things others can't? Any thoughts of harming yourself? Thoughts of harming others? Any violent dreams?* So on and so forth. Question after probing question. Well, Ridian wasn't going to give him the chance.

"Pain set Rayna free, did it?" asked Ridian brightly, though blood pounded in his ears. "Just like that boy you tortured?"

Hector's smile faltered. "Well, yes… pain can transform us all."

"That's your justification, is it?" Still, Ridian smiled, though it was strained.

Hector glanced at Rayna awkwardly. "The boy volunteered."

"The boy tried to pull out."

"Ridian," said Rayna disapprovingly. "Don't be rude."

"It's okay, Rayna," said Hector calmly. "Ridian, I know how it must have seemed. But it's our way. Look…" Hector rolled back his sleeve, exposing a heavily scarred forearm with waxy burn marks streaked all along it. "I would never ask anyone to do anything I would not be prepared to do myself."

"Like massacre the Wrathwoli," said Ridian.

"Enough!" snapped Rayna, glaring at him, while Hector clutched his armrests and stared at the floor. The silence stretched on and on.

Finally, Hector drew a long breath, and spoke in a lifeless voice. "Before that dreadful massacre, I tried to form a treaty with the Wrathwoli. I tried to convince them of our united interests… But they broke the rules of engagement and held me hostage. My followers marshalled to rescue me, and by some freak chance, the Sacred Winds abandoned the Wrathwoli, creating the first windless day in…" Hector snorted with mirthless amusement. *"Forever.* And without the wind to draw upon, the Windchasers were defenceless. Of course, I punished the leaders responsible for the slaughter severely, but the damage was done. The Wrathwoli were dead, and we'd started another Soulcaster War. I was devastated. I wanted to create bridges between us, the Wrathwoli, and Fidicia. I wanted peace. But instead, we had another horrific war. A war in which I lost my legs, my brother, years of my life, and countless lives…"

Another horrible silence filled the room. Hector had retreated deep into himself, gazing intensely at nothing. Rayna folded her arms and glared at Ridian.

Ridian swallowed. "Hector, I'm—"

A knock at the door, and a young man entered: clean-shaven, features sharp as a sword. He glanced briefly at Rayna, and though it was quick, Ridian could recognize that lusty stare anywhere. He'd seen it a thousand times in Mudwall.

"Draven, not now," said Hector irritably.

Draven gave an elaborate bow, his thick curls flopping forward. "My apologies, Hector, but I'm afraid it's of the utmost importance." A grey wolf slipped between his legs to glare at them.

Hector pinched the bridge of his nose and sighed. "Never a moment's peace. Very well." He waved Draven over, and the man whispered imperceptibly into his ear. Hector looked up with concern. "Thank you, Draven. I will be there presently."

Draven and his wolf slipped away, though not before flinging a seedy smile at Rayna.

"I'm afraid I have business to attend to," said Hector, gathering his walking sticks and heaving himself up with effort. He hobbled to the door, then turned. "I know I've made mistakes, Ridian, but I'm not a monster." Then he shuffled out of sight.

"Nice work," said Rayna flatly.

"I didn't—I just..." Ridian deflated. "His story is very different from the one I've heard, is all."

"Surprise, surprise. Hector's enemies, the people who have treated Kyrosia unfairly for centuries, have painted an unfair, unjust, unflattering picture of him. He's fighting for freedom, peace, and independence, while Fidicia creates scandals and incites violence. Bunch of bloody warmongers."

"That's ridiculous," said Ridian, but even as he did, he pictured the glowering, one-eyed Sevron shouting, *I say we go to war!*

"Ridian, open your eyes. You've been lied to. Fidicia has an immense financial incentive to demonize Hector. Kyrosia pays ludicrous tributes to Fidicia, crippling their economy and driving the people into abject poverty. All Hector wants is peace. Reconciliation. A fair go. Fidicia just wants to plunder an already plundered country."

Ridian had nothing to say. *All Hector wants is peace.* How could he argue with that?

Rayna raised two placating hands. "No more politics, okay? I'm really happy to see you. Let's just be friends. Okay?"

"Friends?" said Ridian gravely. "You're asking an awful lot. How about acquaintances? I could probably handle that. We could talk of the weather and such."

Rayna smiled. "Deal. Let's go to my place, and you can catch me up." Then linking arms, Rayna led Ridian down into a nearby wind-protected dell, full of shoddy, makeshift little homes. As they approached, a gang of knee-scraped kids ran up and surrounded them.

"Play, Rayna, play," they begged, tugging at her dress.

"Later," said Rayna, chuckling. "I'm showing my brother around."

"You have a brother?" said one dirty-faced boy with delight. Then another pawed Ridian with a grubby hand and shouted, "Tag! You're it!" When the stunned Ridian didn't move, the whole lot tagged and pushed and jostled him with shouts of 'tag, you're it'.

Rayna just pointed and laughed.

"Oi! Buzz off, you lot," said a severe-looking woman, and the kids scattered—but not before she'd shot out a wiry hand and snatched one by the collar. She then flicked him onto his back. "This one's juicy," she said appreciatively. "Still, never hurts to tenderize the meat." Then she tickled the boy, and the kid giggled and squirmed hysterically. When she finally let go, the boy shot away, red-faced and grinning. "Now rack off before I pickle your fingers and put them in a stew," she cried after him. Then she smoothed her dress and turned to Rayna with a smile. "Those little tramps will be the death of me."

"Abi," said Rayna. "Come meet my brother, Ridian."

"Your brother?" Abi's eyebrows arched in surprise. "A real pleasure, Ridian. A real pleasure. Rayna's told me all about ya." She wiped her hands frantically on her apron before giving Ridian's hand a spirited shake.

"Your knee playing up again?" asked Rayna. "You're limping."

"Oh, it's nothing," said the woman with a dismissive wave.

Rayna gave the woman an accusatory stare. "Abi?"

"It's fine, it's fine."

Rayna held her stare.

Abi lifted her chin defiantly. "My dickey knees are the least of your problems."

"You're incorrigible, you know that?" said Rayna. "Let me whip something up for you. It'll be ready in thirty minutes." Then, despite Abi's protests, Rayna led Ridian down the crude street towards—

Ridian stopped midstride to gawp. "Wait, is that…?"

"Yep," declared Rayna with pride. "Guess who made it?" She didn't even wait for Ridian to respond. She pointed both thumbs at herself and nodded. "That's right. Yours truly."

Ridian was speechless. Before them was the strangest tree Ridian had ever seen. The lower portion of the trunk was absurdly bulbous—much too big—with an arched door, a series of circular windows, and a cylindrical chimney. It was a cabin—a *living* cabin. Above the domed roof, a normal looking trunk continued like any other tree, branches and leaves searching for the sun. It was Arden magic alright, and despite its modest size, it could have been made by Valaria herself.

"It took me a whole month to make," said Rayna. "And it's still not perfect, mind you. The door's dodgy and the floor's a bit uneven and…"

"Would you shut up?" said Ridian. "It's amazing. I can't believe you made that."

"You think so?" Rayna was positively glowing.

"You kidding? Look at it." Ridian then grabbed the miraculous doorknob and pulled. The door squeaked a bit and jammed a little, but Ridian barely noticed in his excitement. Inside was a cozy little nook that was oddly familiar. "It's the same as our place back home," he said with a laugh. "Table, chairs, bedrooms, everything."

"I know. Not very original, am I?"

"The kitchen certainly looks the same," said Ridian, pointing to the numerous herbs, vials, pots, and pans littering the place. "So, it's not me who makes all the mess, after all."

"Shut up," said Rayna with a laugh, then she set to work: she stoked the fire, put a pot to boil, then began cutting and crushing herbs hanging from the ceiling.

Ridian smiled. *Just like home.*

Rayna wiped her brow. "So, how did you get here? Tell me everything."

Ridian opened his mouth, having no idea where to start, when an old man knocked on the door, removed his hat deferentially, and asked Rayna for something to help his bowels move. When Rayna introduced him, the man smiled a broad, yellow-toothed smile, and clapped Ridian on the shoulder. "A nephew of Hector's and a brother of Rayna's is a son of mine," he said heartily.

And he wasn't the only one. There was already a line outside. A pregnant woman, asking for something to quell morning sickness, kissed Ridian twice on each cheek. One man, who wanted a fresh poultice for a festering elbow wound, rushed back with his wife and six children to introduce them all. Another man on crutches gave a long-winded, highly confusing explanation of how they were distantly, distantly related. One young girl turned bright red and fled after she heard who Ridian was. Rayna looked on and laughed.

Before long, a whole motley assortment of Kyrosians came knocking. Some asked for some sort of herbal remedy on a pretence, while the rest unabashedly wanted to greet Hector's long-lost nephew. And as they came through to shake his hand and kiss his cheek, Ridian pondered Rayna's words. *Kyrosia pays ludicrous tributes to Fidicia, crippling their economy and driving the people into abject poverty.* Indeed, most of the Kyrosians who passed through the door looked half-starved. And though they looked tough as nails, they seemed decent enough—an interconnected community of families and friends, working together to scratch out a living.

All Hector wants is peace, Rayna had said. *Reconciliation. A fair go. Fidicia just wants to plunder an already plundered country.* Her words troubled Ridian. They absolved Hector and incriminated Fidicia.

"I need to pee," said Ridian, after the last person had finally left.

Rayna didn't look up from the poultice she was mashing. "Behind the herb garden."

Outside, the herb garden proved twice as big and ten times as lush as the one back in Mudwall.

"Looks great," said Ridian.

"Wait 'til you see the crops I'm growing on the other side of the mountain," Rayna replied through the window.

Ridian entered the wood beyond the garden. Checking he was out of sight, he relieved himself with a long sigh. He closed his eyes, satisfied. He'd found Rayna. She was safe. And what's more, he'd found an uncle—family he didn't know he had. He still had some misgivings about Hector, especially about the killing on the edge of The Mire and the assassination of Mother Asarah. But regardless, for the first time in a long time, there was nothing to worry about. Everything was—

Then, with the force of a horse-kick to the head, Ridian remembered: Tann, Mal, and Ari were coming to kill Hector.

Chapter 38

Ridian stopped peeing mid-stream. How had he forgotten? How? *How*? What should he do? He couldn't let them kill Hector now that he was his uncle. But sounding the alarm would set a trap for Tann, Mal, and Ari. They would be captured, maybe tortured, maybe killed. Either way, someone would get hurt.

Without stopping to shake, Ridian shot back to Rayna's cottage. He had to warn Hector. He had to. He was family. He was blood. Ridian would just have to protect Tann as best he could if he was captured. He tried to reach Silver with his mind; maybe his wolf was with Tann. But no. Silver's presence was beyond perception.

Ridian burst through the door of Rayna's cottage. "Where's Hector?"

Rayna looked up in alarm, hands covered in green goo. "I don't know. Why? What's wrong?"

"People are trying to kill him."

"What?!"

But Ridian was already shooting down the street and rounding on a woman who happened to be walking past. "Where can I find Hector?"

The woman had no idea, so Ridian dashed up to a man

who was hanging his washing on a makeshift clothesline. "Hector's in trouble. I need to warn him. Where would he be?"

"Hector's in danger?" asked the man, dropping a wet, tattered-looking shirt.

Ridian recognised the man as the father of six but couldn't recall his name. "Assassins," said Ridian.

The man took only a moment to process the information before he wrenched open the door to his shabby home and shouted, "Everybody, shut up! Hector's in danger. Derren, raise the alarm. Dan, check the northern lookout. Tarna, the southern lookout. Jon, look after the young'uns." He turned to Ridian. "Follow me. He's most likely in his room."

"Ridian, what's going on?" cried Rayna, running towards them.

"Assassins are after Hector."

Her eyes widened, and her mouth opened to form a question. But the man was already dashing away, forcing Ridian to leave Rayna's question unanswered.

Hector's stone room up on the mountain was empty. Breathless, the man swore, then called to a fellow Kyrosian who happened to be nearby. "Where's Hector? He's in trouble."

"Top of Mount Toomi," the man replied, and the father of six dashed along the trail, back to the altar where the boy had been tortured. They whisked past the now low-burning bonfire and into the tunnel beyond. Almost immediately, it turned a sharp right and climbed up a stone staircase. Beams of narrow sunlight slanted in at regular intervals, illuminating the tunnel. Panting hard, they leapt up the stairs, three and four at a time, turned at a landing and climbed some more. It was hard work, and the father of six began to slow. "Head straight up," he panted, giving Ridian space to pass. "You can't get lost."

Ridian overtook him, and as he zipped through the beams of light, Ridian had a growing sense of terrible certainty. He was too late. Right now, Tann and his lethal mates were preying upon his crippled uncle, springing their trap. Ridian turned a corner to face fierce, dazzling daylight. After a moment of blindness, his eyes adjusted to a spectacular view. He stood on a rocky platform that curved around the mountain on both sides. A handful of steps forward and Ridian would plummet to his death, down into the Mother's Arms below, while beyond, the rest of Sky Island baked in a cloudless, late afternoon sun. The wind howled as it whipped the mountainside.

He was not alone. A gang of perhaps twelve men and as many wolves huddled to his right. Ridian had only a moment to take everything in before a growl made him whirl around. A Snow Leopard leapt deftly from an overhanging jut and crept towards him. Ridian started to back away, but a pack of snarling wolves shot from the huddled gang of men and surrounded him. The snapping, snarling wolves closed in, forcing him towards the edge. Trapped between the wild beasts and a yawning precipice, Ridian's guts cinched tight like a drawstring purse.

A whistle from the gang cut through the wind, and the pack dispersed, pacified. The snow leopard slunk forward and, to Ridian's profound discomfort, coiled about his legs in a slow, luxurious embrace. It unfurled and then sauntered away. Hector's Leopard, Ridian now remembered.

"Sorry," tweeted a high voice that could only be Chirpy.

Then the finch fluttered into view and nestled into the crook of Ridian's elbow to escape the gale. "We had a bit of a security scare. Everyone's a bit touchy."

Ridian looked at the gang, and his stomach dropped—

kneeling at their centre were Tann and Mal, wrists bound, faces bloodied, swollen, and darkening with bruises. Tann's eyes were thin slits between swollen cheeks. They locked onto Ridian and flashed with panic. "Ridian! Get the hell out of—"

One of the men, the sharp-featured Draven, sunk a fist into Tann's stomach, pitching him forward with a wheezing gasp. A woman then punched the side of Tann's face with sickening force. Blood sprayed from Tann's mouth, and as the gang began kicking him in earnest, the image seemed to zoom away as if Ridian were falling down a long, long corridor.

"No!" he heard himself cry, though it sounded far off. "Please! Stop!" Seemingly of their own accord, his feet took him forward, but he was pushed back by a mean-faced man whose limbs were implacable as iron bars. A Soulcaster, no doubt. Still, the pummelling continued, with Tann's body crumpling under the impact. Mal looked on, grim as death, his bloody nose making a crimson goatee.

"Stop!" said Ridian, straining against the mean-faced man. "You're killing him!"

"Enough," said Hector, and the beating stopped, leaving Tann to twitch on the ground. "I know you think you know these men," said Hector to Ridian. "But they are not what they seem."

Draven fixed Ridian with hard, unforgiving eyes. "You know these pieces of filth?" His hand found the hilt of his sword. Other hands did the same.

Ridian's mouth opened and closed as he looked from one unfriendly face to another, searching for the right words that never came.

"My nephew is blameless," said Hector placatingly. "He was just rushing to warn me. Weren't you, Ridian?"

Ridian nodded slowly.

Hector's gang were not satisfied; they glared at Ridian with open suspicion.

Tann was pulled to his knees. He was limp but conscious, his face the soft pulp of rotting fruit. He gave a little cough, and blood trickled down his chin. He looked between Hector and Ridian—back and forth—squinting in confusion. But his confusion gave way to horror and dismay as he took Ridian in. *You betrayed us,* his expression declared. *You betrayed us.*

Ridian couldn't hold his gaze. He looked down, away, anywhere but into Tann's tortured face.

"All we want is freedom," said Hector to Tann and Mal. "Is that too much to ask? We're sick of fighting. We're sick of war. At the end of the day, for better or worse, Fidicians and Kyrosians are brothers. We share the same ancestry. The same Soulcasting gift. Why can't history be history? Why can't we tell a new story? One of forgiveness? Of reconciliation? Why can't we give peace a chance?"

"Peace?" said Tann incredulously. "Forgiveness?" He chuckled darkly. "Talk to the Wrathwoli of peace. Ask their bones for forgiveness. You could ask now if you like. We're on a mass graveyard, after all."

Draven went to strike Tann, but Hector shook his head, and the man lowered his fist.

"The Wrathwoli genocide was a terrible tragedy," said Hector gravely. "I regret that day bitterly. But we have made reparations with the Wrathwoli. We are allies now. Their Elders recognize our plight and have donated this land to aid us."

"You don't have to explain yourself to these cockroaches," said Draven, though Ridian sensed Hector was speaking more for his benefit than Tann's.

"The Wrathwoli Elders gave you Sky Island?" said Tann, as if it were the most absurd thing he'd ever heard. "They gave you their Sacred Land, saturated with their blood. Blood *you* shed." He turned to Mal and scoffed. "You buying this malarky?"

Mal just stared into the distance, and to Ridian, he seemed to be summoning the strength to face his death with as much dignity as he could muster.

"Maybe I'm being cynical," said Tann. "Maybe Hector does want peace, but just has a funny way of showing it. All those dead Fidicians upon the Great Waste were just an accident. And those assassins who killed Mother Asarah were just misunderstood."

Ridian recalled the crow-ravished bodies, rotting in the sun upon the edge of The Mire, and Mother Asarah's bear sniffing the ancient woman's dead face. If Hector wanted peace, why had he killed those Fidicians? And why had he sent Tinker, Basher, and Sneak to assassinate Mother Asarah?

Hector sighed with frustration. "Those three fanatics disobeyed my explicit orders. I can't be blamed for the renegade actions of a few extremists. I could have disciplined them myself, you know, but I disavowed them and allowed them to be captured so the Fidicians could have their own justice. It's not my fault the Fidicians allowed them to escape and cause havoc."

Tinker, Basher, and Sneak had been operating of their own accord, then—not Hector's. That seemed fair enough. How could Ridian blame Hector for the actions of other men?

Tann's face scrunched up in contempt. "Hector, I know you. You're a blackhearted, bloodthirsty brute. You won't be happy till you've burnt Fidicia to the ground and pissed on its ashes. You're a spiteful, cruel, unforgiving creature, whose notion of peace is the screams of your enemies' children."

A dozen swords began to unsheathe.

"No," Hector commanded, and the swords slid back with reluctance. "Traitors deserve a traitor's end. Take them."

Men began hauling Tann and Mal away.

Panic coursed through Ridian. "What are you going to do to them?"

Hector didn't meet Ridian's gaze. "Kyrosian Law states that traitors receive neither food, nor water, nor a proper burial. Once dead, their bodies are left in the wild for the animals to devour." Even as he spoke, Tann and Mal disappeared around the corner of the rocky platform. Ridian got a last glimpse of Tann's swollen face, grimacing in pain. Ridian needed to say something. To do something. He couldn't just let Tann die.

"I know this is probably hard for you to hear," said Hector. "But they weren't just planning on killing me... your sister was also a target."

"No," said Ridian, shaking his head. "Tann has beef with

you. He would never…"

Hector spoke with perfect assurance. "Ridian, think, and you'll realise it's true."

Ridian thought it through. It was hard, but he managed it. Tann believed Hector was responsible for the death of his wife and daughter. Tann had then committed his whole life to destroying Hector—his work and his legacy, even to the point of killing his own countrymen. Why not kill some random girl who was part of his plans? Hector's *secret weapon.*

Ridian felt unreality wash over him again. This couldn't be happening. This couldn't be real. "Death, though?" was all he managed to say. "Can't they be imprisoned or something?" It was a weak argument, no argument really. Besides, his voice was flat and uninspired.

"Ridian, what else can I do?"

"Stick to the plan," said Rayna.

Ridian turned: she was red-faced, panting, and the wind had blown all the flowers from her hair. She marched forward, hands balled into fists, her apron stained green. "They kill us. We kill them. On and on it goes, forever and a day. You talk a lot about peace, but at the first opportunity, you beat those men black and blue and sentence them to death. Explain that to me."

Ridian looked at Rayna in amazement. At that moment, she wasn't just his sister: she was an Arden Druidess, Valaria's Heir, a wielder of secret magic.

Hector's men looked at each other uncomfortably, and Hector pushed down upon his walking sticks to stand upright. "I can't allow traitors to go unpunished."

"You can if it's part of your plan. Like I said: *stick to it.*"

What plan? Whatever it was, it seemed to offer Tann hope. Even if Tann had been planning on killing Rayna. The deceitful bastard.

Hector shook his head, though his resolve appeared to be wavering.

"It's better than torturing two men to death," said Rayna. "In fact, sending them back unharmed would demonstrate your commitment."

Hector's men were casting alarmed glances at each other. Draven stepped forward. "Kyrosian Law states…"

"I know Kyrosian Law!" said Hector, turning on the man with a burst of frustration. His pride hurt, Draven clenched his jaw and stared at the ground.

Hector turned back to Rayna with forced calm. "It's too soon."

"Wait?" said Ridian. "What plan?"

"Uncle," said Rayna. "It's time. Stop being such a chicken."

Hector and Rayna glared at each other, a silent battle raging between them. The wind howled, tousling hair and flapping cloaks. Hector broke eye contact first. "Everyone, leave," he ordered. "Ridian and Rayna, stay."

Without a word of protest, though with visible reluctance, Hector's gang trundled away. All the wolves but one followed. The snow leopard meandered back. A stag walked into view. A fox scurried out from a pile of rocks. An eagle landed on a nearby rock. And Chirpy fluttered up to Hector and burrowed into his collar, seeking protection from the wind. Hector's Familiars had gathered about their Companion. Hector waited till his men and their Familiars were out of earshot. Even then, and with the wailing wind, Hector spoke in hushed tones. "The plan was to enter Fidicia under a white flag," he said. "To broach peace, to treaty. Rayna was to accompany me, and extract Fidic's Ring from Hero's Tree."

"Fidic's Ring?" asked Ridian, recalling the black Fellstone ring Fidic wore in the painting of the Elder Three as he plucked his lute. "What are you talking about?"

"Fidic's Ring lies within Hero's Tree," said Rayna, matter-of-factly. "Keep up."

"So what?" said Ridian.

"The Fidicians are a deeply religious, deeply nostalgic people," said Hector. "Finding the relic and offering it in good faith would go a long way towards reconciliation."

Ridian pondered this and thought it might be true. "Okay," he said cautiously. "But how do you even know it's there?" It seemed unlikely that Hector knew its location when generations of Fidicians did not.

"When I was a captive in Fidicia," said Hector. "I was allowed to go for walks. Well, as much of a walk as you can on these things anyway." He rapped a wooden leg with a walking stick with a *clack*. "One day, I found myself at Hero's Tree—the very place Fidic died. I was sitting against the trunk when I saw a bird and tried to bond with it. But..." Hector looked around to ensure they were alone. "Instead of bonding with the bird, I somehow bonded with the tree itself."

Ridian frowned. "Like Rayna?"

"I'm nowhere near as capable as her," said Hector. "I don't have enough Arden in me, I reckon. Anyway, the strangest part isn't that I bonded with the tree, it's who I found *inside* the Tree." Hector let the silence stretch out, an invitation for Ridian to answer.

Ridian blinked at him.

"Fidic," Hector said finally.

"Fidic?"

Hector nodded. "Yes, Fidic. The Elder Bard. Father of Fidicia. The lying weasel who killed Kyros."

Ridian glanced at Rayna; she nodded, confirming she'd heard this story before—and believed it.

"Don't look at me like I'm crazy," said Hector. "You've heard the tale, surely. Fidic died with a sword through his eye, pinned to a tree, and though his mortal body perished, his immortal soul passed into the tree itself, and from that day forward, he has watched over his people from generation to generation."

Ridian had heard the tale. But he understood it symbolically, not literally, a tradition probably started by grief-stricken followers and perpetuated by sentimental idiots.

"Told you he wouldn't believe me," said Hector to Rayna.

"Come on, little brother," said Rayna impatiently. "All the ridiculous stuff you've seen recently, and you can't entertain the idea? Not even to help save your mates' lives?"

Ridian thought back to when he'd last seen Hero's Tree—the night of Fiddler's Fireworks. The night he awoke from being poisoned. The night Theodor asked him to join the family. The night he found Fidic's Journal. The night Tinker, Basher, and Sneak assassinated Mother Asarah. The night he bonded with Silver. The night Feya unleashed Windchaser magic. The night she kissed him...

Big night, he thought, then he remembered seeing Hero's Tree for a brief moment whilst hurtling through the Astral Plane. It was all lit up with little rivulets of light, through root, trunk, branch, and stem. Ridian felt light-headed.

Perhaps Fidic was alive. Alive but just rattling around in that tree. Sounded like a pretty boring way to spend a few centuries.

"What did Fidic say?" Ridian managed, feeling like he was indulging a lunatic's delusion.

"Much and more," said Hector. "He confessed many lies to me and shared the story I shared with you: the *true* story of Kyros' end. He told me how Valaria had implanted his ring within the Tree. At the time, I didn't care. Why should the Fidicians get their precious treasure? I was young and bitter then. But now I understand how we can leverage it to establish peace between our peoples."

"And that's where I come in," said Rayna, stepping forward. "I can coax the Ring out without cutting their Sacred tree down."

Hector shook his head. "It's something of a gamble. They might not let us near the tree. And even if they do, it might not be enough. They might just pocket the Ring and lock us up."

Ideas were colliding in Ridian's mind. He was pulling things apart, putting them back together, and, then, in a flash, the perfect plan emerged like an epiphany.

"What would you say," said Ridian, "if I could get Rayna into Fidicia with minimal risk?"

"Go on," said Hector sceptically.

Ridian spoke rapidly, eager to share his idea. "The two you just saw, I was their runner. My job was to relay information. They're probably expecting me back. And everybody knows I'm searching for my sister. So, if I brought Rayna back, nobody would think that odd. They may have questions, but we could think of a plausible story."

"Still, Fidic's Ring may not be enough," said Hector.

Ridian shook his head and laughed; he still hadn't told the best bit. "What if we could get more than just Fidic's Ring? What if we could get his Lute *and* his Journal? A Journal that tells the truth of Fidicia's origins in his own hand?"

Hector's eyes were riveted to Ridian. "You found his Journal?"

"Yes."

"And it contradicts the Fidician historical narrative?"

"Yes."

The wind whistled along the mountain wall as Hector stared into the distance, a storm of thought raging behind his glazed eyes. Finally, he spoke. "Fidic's Ring and his Lute could both do much. But if we could get his Journal…"

"It would be worth the risk," said Rayna. "Wouldn't it?"

Hector looked at her, then nodded reluctantly.

"Great," said Rayna. "So you'll let those two live?"

"No."

Rayna groaned and Ridian's heart sank.

"You don't understand," said Hector. "Kyrosians have a heightened sense of justice. They're very legalistic. And if I—their leader—did not adhere to Kyrosian Law, it would be seen as an act of treason. You saw how twitchy my men got. If I reduced or even forestalled their punishment, they would surely usurp me, and that would be the end of our hard-won unity. You don't realise how tenuously I hold all the Kyrosian tribes and factions together. Without me at the helm, they would be at each other's throats."

"There's got to be something you can do," pleaded Rayna.

"I'm bound by Kyrosian Law," said Hector. "There's nothing—wait… Kyrosian Law states that prisoners of war can be released as part of profitable negotiations."

"Which means?" asked Rayna.

"Which means we could exchange them as part of a peace treaty. Only…"

"Only what?"

"Emancipation is sanctioned only after a formal agreement is achieved," he muttered to himself.

"Which means?"

"Which means," Hector continued, his patience waning, "we only have three or so days to obtain three long-lost relics and negotiate peace with a nation with whom we have had near ceaseless war for centuries."

"Why only three days?" asked Ridian.

"Because even Soulcasters die of thirst."

Chapter 39

As twilight fell and the first stars appeared, Ridian and Rayna trotted two horses out of the Mother's Arms. Hector remained behind—his body, anyway. His wolf, snow leopard, fox, and stag loped and trotted alongside Ridian and Rayna, while his eagle and finch flew overhead, each Familiar taking turns bearing his soul. They couldn't take anybody else; another Kyrosian would compromise their whole operation, they'd decided. And Ridian could tell by the way Hector kept shooting anxious glances at Rayna, whom he clearly cared about, that the operation was risky enough. *Will I ever see her again?* his eyes seemed to say as he waved goodbye to them.

Thankfully, the horses were exceptionally well-trained. The slightest nudge or pull of the reins and the beasts would comply. This was just as well; Ridian and Rayna had negligible experience on horseback, and they couldn't waste time on unruly steeds. Not with Tann dying of thirst.

Ridian shook his head in disbelief. *Tann was going to kill Rayna.* After everything, travelling and training together, Tann had planned on killing her the whole time. Ridian felt betrayed. But still, he didn't want Tann to die, even if the prick deserved it.

"This way," tweeted Chirpy, fluttering down a path between wind-twisted trees.

Ridian kicked the horse's flank and almost toppled backwards as it burst into a canter, but he managed to stay on with a firm grip on the reins and by squeezing the horse's sides with his thighs. Falling into the horse's rhythm, he checked over his shoulder. Rayna remained in the saddle, but she wore a near-comical expression of fear as she thundered along. On they went, along a well-worn path, surrounded by Hector's Familiars, until a small fort presented itself upon the very edge of Sky Island. Chirpy flittered into the gatehouse, and a moment later, Ridian heard the grinding of chains and the cranking of metal as the portcullis groaned upward.

Chirpy flew back. "Careful. It's very steep."

It was. Beyond the gate, a narrow path zig-zagged down the near-vertical precipice. Rayna whistled as she peered down. Toppling off their horse meant plummeting off a cliff, and to make matters worse, the wind was horrific, and the darkness was deepening. Afraid, Ridian closed his eyes and searched for Silver. Nothing. Not even an inkling. Disappointed, he nudged his horses forward. Finally, after a long, anxious descent and a few hours along a moonlit trail, they made a rough camp in a wind-protected wood. After a cold meal, they sat shivering beneath their blankets, staring at the stars, and sharing stories. There was so much to catch up on. Rayna spoke of life on Sky Island, getting to know Hector, learning from him, growing in magic, and helping the local families. Ridian shared about his journey to and time in Fidicia. They talked late into the night, but eventually, they committed to sleep. Rayna fell asleep within minutes, but Ridian remained restless. There was a lot at stake: Tann's life, peace between nations, the prosperity of the Kyrosians, a historical reckoning for Fidicia, and, to Ridian's surprise, his uncle's favour. Already, he cared what Hector thought of him and wanted to please him.

*****

Chirpy woke them at dawn, and after a rushed breakfast of cold leftovers, they were kicking their horses into a gallop. Sky Island disappeared, hills and valleys came and went, and the path kept coming. They took a different trail to Tann's furtive one, taking the Wrathwoli equivalent of a highway, which allowed the horses to thunder along. Time passed in a long, painful, effortful blur, and the strain on the beasts became apparent. Their coats foamed with heavy sweat, and they began to stumble and trip. And it wasn't just the horses. Ridian's tunic was soaked, his legs burned, and his backside ached. When he stopped to think of it, his whole body hurt.

They rested at a stream to devour some squished bread. In their haste, the horses snorted as they drank, steam curling from their burning coats. Hector's four-legged Familiars also drank and panted with similar vigour.

"We should get going," said Chirpy, after too short a time. "But walk the horses for a bit to warm them back up."

And that's how they spent the day: walking, riding, resting, walking, riding, resting. They rode more than walked, and walked more than rested, and by dusk, they had covered a tremendous distance. One by one, Hector's Familiars fell behind. First the snow leopard, then the stag, then the wolf, then the fox, then the eagle. They were living stepping-stones, Hector had said, enabling him to jump from one to another and remain in an active bond over great distances. In fact, they'd come so far that Ridian began recognizing some of the terrain—Fidicia was close. And thank goodness—Ridian was exhausted. Blisters ran up and down the insides of his legs, and he felt that if he fell off, he wouldn't be able to get back up. But more than that, worry had re-entered Ridian's mind. Would the Fidicians accept Ridian's return without Tann, Mal, or Ari? And with a stranger? He had felt confident when he'd pitched the idea. Now, he wasn't so sure.

Night had fallen when Ridian pulled his panting horse to a stop. "The north Gate is a mile or so away," he said to an exhausted Rayna as she pulled in alongside. "We should leave the horses. They invite too many questions."

Rayna gave a weary nod of resignation and dismounted.

Stiff and bow-legged, they walked their horses towards a small stream. The poor beasts were nearly broken. They drank as if it were an effort, and it took them a long time to finish. Ridian and Rayna then removed all the horse tack, and with their new freedom, the horses munched on the sparse, yellowish grass, jutting between stones on the side of the road.

"That's no good," said Rayna, tut-tutting. "Poor things are starving." She clutched an overhanging branch and closed her eyes. A moment later, grass erupted from the rocky ground beneath her other downturned palm. Long, lush, and vibrant green, the grass grew with the speed of a nice, slow stretch. Simultaneously, leaves on the overhanging branch crinkled and died, and the bark dried and peeled off, the way it does on old dead, firewood. The horses trotted over and chomped away appreciatively.

"Is that hard?" said Ridian.

"Yes and no," said Rayna, plonking down on a stone, looking even more exhausted. "Yes, because some of my own Rava is lost in the exchange. It can't be helped. There's always a cost. But also no, because… Well, because I've been doing it forever. Even if I didn't realise I was doing it." She cocked her head at him. "I wonder what ability you have?"

Ridian had been wondering the same thing. What unique fusion of Soulcasting and Druidism would he possess? Could he turn himself into a giant like Daegan? A healer like Fidic? A druid prodigy like Valaria? Could he draw from other Soulcaster bonds like Kyros? Manipulate emotions like Hector? Subsist on plant Rava like his father? Bond with plants like Rayna?

Leg-sore, they left the horses and ate as they walked up the rise towards the north Gate.

"What's Fidicia like?" asked Rayna, around a mouthful of apple.

"Prettier than Mudwall," said Ridian with a lazy laugh. "Not that that's hard." He tore a chunk from a loaf of bread and chewed it with effort.

"No, I mean the people?"

"There are some arseholes, same as everywhere, I guess." *Sevron and Lukas certainly fit the bill.* "But I've actually met some really nice people…" Ridian paused, wondering how to describe the Thunderfells. He'd already talked about them, but how could he convey what they really meant to him?

"How can you call the Fidicians 'nice'?" said Rayna, before

he could formulate the right words. "After all they've done to the Kyrosians?"

Ridian swallowed and shook his head. "It's not like that. Most Fidicians think they are the good guys. They think Fidic was a saint and Kyros a genocidal maniac. That's why Fidic's Journal is so important. If we can expose Fidic's lies, then—then…"

Ridian stalled. He had his doubts. Would the Fidicians cast aside centuries of ill-will and bloodshed for a few old trinkets and a dusty journal? Would they believe it was really Fidic's? Would they even care?

"If we expose Fidic's lies," said Chirpy, fluttering in from the night, "then all Fidicia's history books will need to be re-written. All their precepts and inherent assumptions about themselves will be thrown into question. They'll doubt the existence of their god and the validity of their religion. Fidicia won't know itself. It'll lose that which unifies them. Different factions will fight for a cohesive sense of identity. They'll tear themselves apart in a cultural revolution. And in the midst of that chaos—if we play our cards carefully—an opportunity for peace may present itself."

"Will they listen to us, though?" said Ridian with growing alarm. He hadn't thought Fidic's Journal would cause that much trouble, and it disturbed him. He wanted peace, sure, but not a complete overthrow of Fidician way of life. "Rayna's a stranger, and they barely know me, never mind trust me."

"The blood of The Father and the blood of the Flower," said Chirpy emphatically. "Who better to unite the two people?"

The descendants of both Kyros and Valaria… Ridian was still stunned by the revelation. If it was true, then they belonged to both sides. Perhaps Hector was right. Perhaps they could serve as a bridge and bring about a lasting peace. Perhaps they could save Tann—even if Ridian was still pissed off at him.

"Hey Rayna," said Ridian. "I've been looking for the right time to give you this, and well, now's as good a time as any." He dove into his pocket and pulled out the Elderflower Necklace.

Rayna squinted at it, then her face lit up as she recognized it. "Is that…? It *is!*" She flung her arms around Ridian's neck and gave him a brief, choking hug before grabbing the necklace and holding it against her heart. "I thought I'd lost it."

Ridian smiled. Her joy was as predictable as it was satisfying. "I found it in the dead rye the night you disappeared."

Rayna slapped her forehead. "Of course… and you kept it safe all this time." She placed it carefully over her head and around her neck.

Ridian shrugged. "No big deal."

"It's a very big deal!"

"Shhhh," said Chirpy. "The northern Gate's just up ahead."

Sure enough, atop the rise and blocking the only way into Fidicia was the northern gate, and the gravity of their mission stole upon them.

Ridian's heart galloped as they drew close. "Let me do the talking," he said.

Rayna nodded, and Chirpy's head twitched up and down, almost too quick to see.

When they got within fifty yards, a voice called from the

guard tower. "Halt and declare thyself!" said the young voice, full of self-importance. It took a moment to find the owner above the guardhouse—a frowning youth with a long nose to look down.

"It's Ridian. I was part of the company who left—"

"I know who you are and when you left and with whom," said the guard haughtily. "Where is Master Tannerion and his two other companions?"

Other guards appeared upon the battlement, leaning through the crenellations.

"They remain in the field," said Ridian.

"Why?"

Ridian swallowed. *Less is more*, he decided. "My report is for Commander Sevron's ears only." Ridian prayed Sevron was not present. He'd rather have all three of Fidic's relics in hand before facing that man again.

"The Commander's ears only, you say?" The guard hid none of his disdain. "Very well. Who's the girl, then?"

"My sister."

"And why does she wish to enter Fidicia?"

"Like I said," said Ridian through his teeth. "My report is for Commander Sevron. Not you." There was a brief silence, and in it, Ridian thought he could sense the man's wounded pride. "Besides, I can vouch for her."

"Oh, you can, can you?" said the guard. "What a relief. Tell her to come closer for us to see. Or is she for the commander's eyes only, as well?"

Sniggers floated down from the battlements. Rayna glanced tentatively at Ridian, before nodding and walking forward into the light.

"Well, well, well... now we can *all* vouch for her," said the youth.

Ridian's ears burned. He was exhausted and had little patience for this uppity little twat. "I demand you let us through immediately."

The guard waved a dismissive hand. "Alright, alright, you may pass. But your sister will have to be detained."

"Why?" asked Ridian.

"All outsiders must be processed."

"How long's that going take?"

"How long is a piece of string?" said the guard. "Perhaps a day or two."

"We can't wait that long," said Ridian, outraged.

"Then she can stay outside. Orders are orders, I'm afraid," said the man with false commiseration.

Rayna turned with a helpless shrug as if to ask, 'What now?'

Chirpy tweeted in Ridian's ear. "Say he was ordered to let you and anyone with you pass without interference."

"What?" hissed Ridian, peering at the bird on his shoulder from the corner of his eye.

"Just lie, and I'll make him believe it." Then Chirpy fluttered up and into the night.

"Well," said the guard. "Are you coming through or not?"

"Um," said Ridian. Then Chirpy's intent became clear, and the lie came easily enough. "Excuse me, but aren't you forgetting Sevron's orders?"

The guard scoffed. "No."

"No? What about the order to let me and anyone with me pass? *Without* hassle," Ridian added.

"What are you...?" But the guard's condescending frown melted as doubt stole over his features. He shot anxious, sideways glances at his companions. "I don't remember being given any such orders," he said carefully.

"Well, you were given them all the same."

The guard licked his lips. "I—ah...?" He turned to the guard on his left. "Do you remember—"

"Just do your bloody job and open the gate!" Ridian glared at the man. "Or would you prefer I tell Sevron you disobeyed his explicit orders?"

The guard was obviously thinking very hard: obey an order he remembered, or disobey one he supposedly forgot. Ridian decided to give him a way out, to make his decision easier.

"You might consider me an outsider," said Ridian. "But I'm still a Fidician Knight. And as such, I can chaperone my sister."

"You take full responsibility for her?" the guard asked for all to hear.

"I do."

"Open the gate!"

The gate opened, and they passed through. The place was busy with the comings and goings of soldiers, Soulcasters, and their Familiars, and so Ridian and Rayna were largely ignored. Nonetheless, they tried to remain inconspicuous as they beelined towards the mountain tunnel that would take them into Fidicia. Ridian grabbed a torch hanging on the mountainside, lit it, and led the way inside. Only when they were halfway through the tunnel, and all sounds from the outside world had died, did Rayna whisper, "That was a risky bluff, Ridian."

Ridian smiled. "Not at all. Hector, which emotion did you manipulate? Uncertainty? Doubt?"

Perched on Rayna's shoulder, Chirpy tweeted a sweet melody as if he were nothing more than an innocent little bird, and they laughed a quick, nervous laugh together.

Through the tunnel, the expansive Fidician valley lay before them. Stars glittered in an ink-black sky, spectacular mountains encircled the valley, and tiny household lights twinkled far below along the edge of Raven's River.

"Beautiful," said Rayna, stopping to admire the view, as Ridian extinguished their torch and set it in the mount on the mountain wall. "Shame it's full of arseholes." She smiled, clearly goading him.

"Let's not delay," said Chirpy impatiently. "We've got three relics to find and near-impossible negotiations to follow."

"But you can manipulate people," said Rayna. "Can't you just—"

"Let's just get moving," interrupted Chirpy. "I'll take Rayna to Hero's Tree to recover Fidic's Ring. Ridian, you get the Lute and Journal."

"Split up?" asked Ridian, not liking the sound of it.

"Yes. It'll be quicker that way."

"Not if Rayna gets stopped and questioned. I just told the entire northern Gate I would chaperone her."

Rayna nodded. "Yeah, I think it would be best if we stuck together."

Chirpy hesitated for a long moment, then shrugged tiny bird-wing shoulders. "As you wish."

As they made their way down the twisting path, they crossed the occasional person or two, but nobody seemed to care. People had their own errands, and nobody looked twice. Well, young men and old looked twice at Rayna—but that was normal. Eventually, they found the path to the

Living Fort. They were already exhausted, so the hill was slow going.

Chirpy encouraged them in earnest. "You're doing well," the bird tweeted. "Almost there. Almost there." After some time, they came across the Thunderfells' house. Light shone around the edges of the doorframe and poured out the windows, illuminating the jumble of shoes around the doormat, and the weeds flourishing in the sorely neglected garden. *What would the family be doing right now? Eating dinner? Reading? Chatting?* The sight of the place made Ridian feel strangely sad. It felt like home, and indeed, he'd been invited into the family, but now… well, now he was the blood of Kyros, their ancient enemy. He was the nephew of Hector, their current enemy. Would he still be welcome? Would it still be home? Without saying a word, he continued up the hill.

Finally, the towers of the Living Fort came into view, and Ridian shot expectant glances at Rayna, waiting for her to comprehend the miracle. Rayna was so intent upon putting one sore foot in front of the other that it was only when the magnificent swaying castle loomed in its entirety before them that she stopped to peer up. Her eyes widened, and then her mouth.

Ridian chuckled. "Amazing, huh?"

"Is—is that…?"

"Alive? Yep. Valaria's work."

Rayna was so enthralled that Chirpy had to tug her sleeve to get her moving. Even then, she kept stealing glances all the way across Last Stand Meadow towards the lonely Hero's Tree. Ridian remembered the first time he'd seen the ancient tree; it drew his eye and held it. And now it was the site of Mother Asarah's murder. But the tree was no stranger to death. The famous Last Stand between Kyros and the Elder Three had been fought beneath its canopy. It had seen Kyros' army turn crazy and devour itself. It had witnessed Kyros himself being cut in two, and watched indifferently as Fidic bled out, pinned by one of Kyros' twin swords.

Ridian, Rayna, and Chirpy drew close. There was nobody in sight. And thank goodness. Ridian was suddenly very sceptical about their plan. Even if Fidic's Ring was inside, could Rayna really pull it out? Growing grass was one thing, but finding and extracting a ring from a centuries-old tree was another. Even if they did, would the Ring, the Lute, and the Journal be enough? Ridian shook his head clear as they passed beneath the long and creaking branches. *We're here now. Best get on with it.*

Finally, they stood before the ancient trunk. Seconds passed, their breath pluming in the cold air, and Rayna did nothing.

"What are you waiting for?" said Chirpy impatiently, bobbing on a low-hanging branch.

"Oh, nothing," said Rayna with a start, and she extended her hand slowly towards the trunk. But her fingers were a mere inch away when she jerked them back. She looked up guiltily at Chirpy. "Sorry, it's just…"

Chirpy flitted onto her partly outstretched hand. "Don't be nervous. You've done this a thousand times. Remember the old mantra: cast thy soul, empty thyself, and bond."

Rayna closed her eyes and sighed. "'Cast thy soul, empty thyself, and bond.' She stretched her hand out again, then pulled back again, as if the tree were hot. "What's wrong with me? Why am I so nervous?"

It was only then that Ridian realised he was also nervous—very nervous. His stomach fluttered, his fists were clenched, and he could barely breathe. Why was he scared?

"You can do this," said Chirpy soothingly.

"I know, it's just… *spooky*. Fidic's inside. I feel like a grave robber taking his Ring. What if he talks to me? What if he's angry?"

That's why Ridian was scared. Fidic's ghost was haunting the tree. Suddenly, this didn't feel like a good idea.

Chirpy laughed a strained, tittering laugh. "Don't be silly. You're not here to converse with the dead. Simply cast thy soul…"

"…empty thyself and bond. Yeah, I know." Rayna stood upright and set her jaw. "Alright, Rayna," she muttered. "Stop messing around. You can do this." She reached out.

"Wait," said Ridian breathlessly.

"Why? What's wrong?" asked Rayna, seemingly relieved at the delay.

"I—I don't know." How could Ridian express his mindless, mounting dread? All he could think about was how Fidic might be in there, and how, if he was, then he'd been trapped for centuries—*centuries*. What would that have been like? Could he see, hear, taste, smell, touch? Was it just endless blindness? Was it torture?

"Are you wetting yourself as well?" said Rayna with a nervous laugh.

"No, it's just… It's just…." Ridian's mind was suddenly a fuzzy blur. He couldn't think straight. Thoughts collided and ricocheted off each other. What was happening? What was he talking about? He couldn't remember…

"Rayna," said Chirpy forcefully. *"DO IT. NOW!"* The little bird's trill voice was somehow strong and commanding and broached no argument. "CAST THY SOUL. EMPTY THYSELF. AND BOND." The finch's words were an incantation, heavy as tombstones.

Rayna's eyes were wide and swimming with moonlight as she gazed at the little bird perched on her knuckle. Her hand trembled. She was petrified. Not of the tree, not of what she needed to do—of Chirpy. Slowly, she stretched out a trembling hand, touched the bark of the tree, and—

Screamed. A long, terrible, blood-curdling scream. She hurled herself to the ground with bone-breaking force, thrashing wildly. Her fists pounded the ground, her heels carved streaks in the dirt. And all the while, she screamed as if she were on fire.

"Rayna!" said Ridian, darting to her side, his foggy mind suddenly clear. Still Rayna thrashed. "You're okay, Rayna. You're okay. You're having a seizure, but it will pass. It will pass." He managed to grab one of Rayna's flailing wrists and pin it.

Suddenly, Rayna stopped screaming and levelled bloodshot eyes at Ridian. *"Unhand me,"* she hissed. Her face was a twisted mask of fury, and her voice was utterly unrecognizable. Ridian's grip slackened, stunned as he was by her sheer, venomous hatred.

"I said, unhand me!" Then, quick as a snake, she wrenched her arm free, slid Ridian's knife from its sheath, and buried it in his stomach.

Ridian looked down at the knife handle sticking from his belly. It didn't make any sense. It was almost amusing. The handle was poking out of him, which meant six inches of cold, sharp steel were inside him. Indeed, blood was spilling out, and yet there was no pain. Nothing. He only had a moment to consider all this before Rayna kicked him in the chest, sending him skidding violently along the dirt. Dots danced before Ridian's eyes. The world spun. And pain entered the world. It lanced bright and brilliant through his stomach, but it was nothing compared to the horror filling his chest.

Rayna lurched to her feet and wheeled about—howling and snarling like a wild animal, blinking and squinting as if bewildered by everything about her.

Chirpy hovered at a safe distance. "My Lord, can you hear me?"

Rayna tugged her hair and groaned.

"My Lord, can you hear me?" said Chirpy again, more insistent.

Still no answer.

"My Lord, Kyros?"

Rayna locked wild, paranoid eyes onto the finch, panting heavily as cogs turned deep in those tortured eyes. *"My name... You said my name. Please, say it again. I'd almost forgotten."*

"Kyros," said Chirpy. "You are Kyros the Great, whom your enemies call the Terrible."

Chapter 40

Kyros heaved great lungfuls of air. *"And who are you, Finch? How can you speak thus?"*

"I am Hector, your descendant," said Chirpy. "Conversing through my Familiar."

"Hector," said Kyros slowly, as if struggling to remember. *"Ah yes, I know you. How could I not? You came to me in the eternal dark. My only reprieve in—in..."* Kyros groaned and buried his face in his hands—for they no longer belonged to Rayna. *"How long has it been? How long have I been trapped in that accursed Tree, deprived of all but my own wretched thoughts?"*

"My Lord. It has been quite some time..."

"HOW LONG?!"

"Three hundred and seventy-three years."

Kyros looked stricken, then his face split into a grin, eyes gleaming with deranged amusement. *"Ha! Is that all! A few trifling centuries? I had expected many millennia to have passed. I thought the mountains would have crumbled to dust. For the sun to have died, and for the end of the world to have been a distant, distant memory."*

Pain spasmed through Ridian's guts from the knife lodged in his stomach, and he released a whimper.

Kyros rounded on him. *"And who are you? You who manhandled me?"*

"My nephew," said Chirpy. "And brother of your host."

"Host?" Kyros frowned at the Finch, then down at his hands. He stared at them in profound confusion, turning them over. *"What is this?"*

"You—you inhabit a new vessel," said Chirpy. "It was a necessary sacrifice for your resurrection."

Kyros felt his chest and stomach. *"Some simpering wench?"* he spat. *"Some prudish little maiden?"* He laughed—sharp and joyless. *"And I thought my degradation was already complete."*

"She was the only one who possessed the necessary magic," said Chirpy defensively. "A half-blood who could bond with fauna. She was the only one. If I could have established the necessary link, I would have offered my own body. Such as it is."

But Kyros wasn't listening. He was staring past Ridian towards the Living Fort. *"And who are they?"*

"Fidicians!" Chirpy shrieked. "Foes! Fly, my Lord! Fly!"

"Fidicians?" said Kyros, as if the word were new.

Ridian looked behind him: striding through the grass was a cohort of grey-clad Knights and their wolves. Sevron took the lead, his single eye glittering with cold fury. "There they are," he cried.

There was a blur of movement as the party sped through the night with the impossible speed of Soulcasters, and within moments, they surrounded Kyros, Ridian, and the Tree.

"Ridian, explain yourself," demanded Sevron. "You were supposed to…" The large commander trailed off as his eye found the hilt sticking from Ridian's belly. The eye then zipped around, scanning the area, before settling on the slim, blonde girl.

"Arrest her," Sevron demanded, his giant wolf bristling at his side.

Two Knights stepped forward. "Kneel!" said one of them.

Kyros threw his head back and let out a joyless, unnerving laugh. *"Kneel? Before a pack of pathetic, quibbling minstrels?"* Kyros snorted. *"I think not."*

"Arrest her," Sevron barked.

The two foremost Knights darted forward. They reached out to snatch Kyros' wrists, but Kyros slid away like a river around a stone. The Knights tried to grasp him again, but he moved with the effortless beauty of a dancer, like a leaf in the wind, like a bird in flight. Then he smiled with dark amusement and snatched the hilt of each Knight's Sword. He spun a beautiful pirouette, unsheathing the blades as he twirled. The Knights stood frozen as Kyros came to an elegant stop, dual blades dripping. Nobody moved for a few heartbeats, then the Knights' severed torsos slipped off their legs and tumbled to the ground. Kyros had cleaved them in two in the blink of an eye.

Sevron and his Knights gasped at the hewn remains and drew their own swords. Their wolves growled.

"Kill the bitch!" said Sevron.

"No!" cried Ridian.

But nobody heard, nor cared. They were already streaking through the night with Soulcaster speed. Then suddenly, all the Knights stopped mid-stride, stumbling to a halt. They glanced between each other and their Familiars with bewilderment and horror. Ridian knew why. They'd lost their supernatural strength. Kyros was stealing the Rava flowing between them and their Familiars. They were no longer Soulcasters, but mere mortals.

Kyros then moved so fast that he virtually disappeared. Men screamed. Wolves whimpered. And the Knights fell like leaves in a hailstorm. A few moments later, all the Knights lay hacked and strewn, their wolves disembowelled. Only Sevron remained standing, his wolf scampering away, abandoning him.

The blood splattered Kyros threw his swords into the ground—the blades sinking deep into the earth—and un-armed, he advanced unconcernedly towards Sevron.

Sevron's sword trembled in his grip. "Who—who are you? What do you want?"

"Vengeance." Then, quick as a whip, Kyros struck Sevron in the face. With a scream, Sevron reeled backwards and clutched his face, blood pouring through his fingers.

Kyros held something between his thumb and forefinger. He examined it with interest. It was an eyeball, the optic nerve dripping as it hung limp. *"For your willful blindness to the truth."* Then he squeezed the eyeball until it popped, making it ooze with a gooey fluid. *"Hector?"* said Kyros, flinging the crushed eyeball away to look for the bird, leaving the blind and moaning Sevron to stumble about.

Chirpy flitted before him. "Yes, my Lord?"

"Have the plans changed since we spoke?"

"No."

"Then let us hasten." Kyros looked down at Ridian. *"What of your nephew?"*

"I'm afraid the wound is—is mortal. Besides, he…"

"Didn't know his sister would be possessed tonight. The betrayal is writ plain on his face." Kyros lay a gentle, blood-

covered hand on Ridian's shoulder. *"What is your name, son?"* His kind voice sounded just like Rayna's, which made it even more horrific.

Ridian's mouth opened, but nothing came out. Warm blood was soaking his tunic and pants. He felt faint.

"His name is Ridian," said Chirpy.

Kyros offered an expression of deep commiseration. *"Ridian, I offer you my deepest regret. You are part of my bloodline, and family is everything. Everything."* He placed a hand over his heart. *"You will not be forgotten."* Then Kyros strode away, even as Sevron cursed and stumbled about.

A second later, Chirpy landed on the ground before Ridian. "Ridian… I'm sorry. You were never meant to get hurt."

"Rayna…what happened to her?" Ridian's voice was weak.

Chirpy stared at his tiny shuffling feet. "She lives within the tree."

Ridian moaned, not from the blade in his stomach, but from despair.

"Ridian, I'm sorry. Rayna was a beautiful, beautiful girl, but this had to be done."

"How could you? She's your niece."

"All Kyrosia is my family, and your sister's sacrifice will benefit them for generations." Then Chirpy fluttered into the night and out of Ridian's life.

Chapter 41

Ridian shivered in his blood-soaked clothes. It didn't matter. He hardly felt it. In fact, he didn't feel much at all. He was on the verge of slipping into a long, blissful sleep. Some part of him knew Rava was leaking out of him, and he would soon be dead. But strangely, he didn't seem to mind.

Sevron had long since stumbled away, and at the Living Fort, bells tolled in alarm. It didn't matter. Soon, Ridian wouldn't hear them. Soon, he would stop shivering, stop bleeding, and feel blessed nothing. He could rest, just like the dead Knights that lay about him. He wouldn't have to think, he wouldn't have to feel. Death would carry him gently away.

Silver. The wolf's presence pulsed loud and clear within Ridian. The sense grew stronger. Whether through the northern Gate or some secret tunnel, Silver had broken into Fidicia and was running towards him. Unbidden, Rava began pouring into Ridian. It gave him strength, but the cold and the pain came back in a flash, waking him from his stupor.

"No," he groaned. He wanted to slip away, not die in agony. But Rava flowed all the same as a silver streak flew across the meadow towards him and pressed a wet, snuffling nose against his face. Something about the smell of wet dog and that cold, snotty nose made it all real again. Hector betraying him. Rayna's possession by Kyros. Her body trapped within Hero's Tree. Him dying.

Tears came. How could they not? His stupid wolf had brought it all back. But he clung to the wolf all the same. The wolf's eyes were glowing silver orbs. They radiated sorrow, and Ridian felt comforted. He wasn't dying alone. He had Silver, and that was something. He looked across the Meadow at the Living Fort, swaying in the night, and remembered the Thunderfells: Theodor, Kess, Ella, Kai, Ollie, and Feya… he wished they were here too. A breeze blew the leaves of Hero's Tree into a flutter, sending the boughs creaking and the trunk groaning. A lump formed in Ridian's throat. It wasn't just a tree; it was a prison. Rayna was in there, and he wished with all his heart that he could say sorry, that he could say goodbye. Then a thought struck him, a crazy, insane thought: perhaps he could. Hector had conversed with the trapped Kyros, after all. That, at least, must have been true.

With incredible force of will, Ridian struggled to his knees, relying solely on Rava. He fingered the knife hilt and winced. The slightest touch set his insides smarting. He took a big breath and, without thinking about it, slid the blade out with a roaring curse. It stung like crazy as blood gushed out. But the pain dimmed somewhat, and with many a grunt and groan, he crawled over and around the littered bodies, until, at last, he was within reach of Hero's Tree. Then, without knowing exactly what he was doing, he stretched out his hand and touched the trunk. *Cast thy soul, empty thyself, and bond…*

***

All was still. All was black. All was silent.

Still. Black. Silent.

And there was no time.

Just Ridian's mind, observing the endless, empty nothing.

Am I dead? No. I'm in the Tree.

Still, he floated.

Where's Rayna?

He couldn't look for her; there was nothing to see. He couldn't call; he had no voice.

Hector did it, he knew. *He talked with Kyros.*

Ridian called Rayna's name into the never-ending black, and his cry seemed to echo through all of existence.

Almost immediately, Rayna answered. "Ridian?" Her voice was perfectly clear, as if she were right next to him, though some part of Ridian knew it wasn't her voice but her mind.

"Rayna!"

She materialised before him, coalescing from nothing, from motes of gathering colour. But she was too young. She was only a child, and she was crying. In fact, she looked exactly how Ridian remembered her when she was three years old. Three years old and afraid of the dark. Ridian was puzzled. This was a strange place indeed, shere where their minds could speak. This wasn't Rayna, Ridian realized, but her projection. Or perhaps it was Ridian's projection of her—how he imagined her. Either way, it was as weird as it was heartbreaking to see the little girl crying into her hands.

Then, without meaning to, Ridian materialized as well.

He was much taller than Rayna, so he knelt to be eye-to-eye with her. "Don't worry," he said, knowing his words were empty. "It'll be okay." He went to dry her tear-streaked cheek, but his hand passed through her like mist, and her face lost its shape like swirling smoke. Ridian pulled back and Rayna's dispersed face reformed.

"It won't be okay," said Rayna, wiping her cheek with a tiny knuckle. "I'll be trapped here forever." Her lip quivered as she sucked in a shuddering breath. "And Kyros… He's—He's inside me."

Seeing her like this was too much.

"Then take my body," said Ridian. He knew she would die within minutes in his own bleeding body, but it was surely better than being stuck here for all time.

Rayna glared at him—a petulant child, protruding lip and all. "You serious? You think I would put you here in my stead? Besides, I can't. You're only partially bonded with this tree. A piece of you remains in your body. Look." She pointed at the silver ribbon of light that jutted from Ridian's chest and vanished into the distance. "Hector did this," she said, suddenly growing in age and stature. She grew and grew until she was ten feet tall. "Hector…" Her voice was harsh as the grinding of stones, and she became wreathed in flame, eyes burning like bellow-blown coals. "He manipulated me. He betrayed me. He lied." Rayna was like a force of nature—beautiful and terrifying.

Ridian cowered. "Why did he do this?"

The fire about Ryan snuffed out, and she shrank in size again, becoming even younger than before: a trembling toddler, hugging herself and sucking her thumb. "Kyros," she whimpered. "I—I got a glimpse into his mind as he tore past me and took possession of my body. Ridian, Hector has no idea what he's unleashed. Kyros is a monster. He's all seething hatred and revenge. He's insane. All he's dreamed of for centuries is revenge. You must stop him."

Ridian shook his head. "I can't..."

"You must. *This* is what Kyros wants." Rayna dissolved as if turned to dust, and then the endless black around Ridian filled with a storm of swirling colour as shapes swiftly took form. Suddenly, Ridian was surrounded by horror: men, women, and children were being nailed to the walls of the Living Fort. Now they were being whipped, burned, cut, mutilated, stretched, drowned... There were strange machines with cogs and cranks and rattling chains. Screams filled the air. Everything was pain, but not death. No. Everyone was kept very much alive. Kyros was there, laughing in perverse delight, ensuring the pain lasted as long as possible. Ridian tried to look away, but the images were everywhere. He tried shutting his eyes, but he had no eyelids to close. He saw everything. He missed nothing. The images were being transferred from Rayna's mind to Ridian's. There was no looking away.

"Please..." begged Ridian. "Stop."

The nightmare ended, and Rayna—seventeen again—gazed at him. "You must stop this," she said firmly. "You *must.*"

"I—I can't... I'm dying. Kyros stabbed me." Ridian had shrunk now. He was terribly small. His hands were the soft, chubby hands of an infant.

Rayna leant down, scooped him up, and cradled him, and for a moment, she appeared as their mother, full of concern, the way she'd been before—

The memory came to Ridian from nowhere. But not nowhere—from the deepest part of him—and to his horror, the memory materialised upon the black landscape around them. He tried to stop it but couldn't. The memory was bursting from his subconscious, and in this strange place, his mind was powerless to push it away.

He was a little boy, chasing Rayna through a golden field that towered above their heads. Wheat stalks whipped past as he chased her around a plough.

"Careful," said Mother. "Plough's dangerous."

They streaked through the field and into their mother's arms. She kissed them, and they squealed with delight. She let them go, and again, he chased his sister around the plough.

"Not near the plough," said Mother, but they didn't listen. "I said, not near the plough. It's—" But she never finished her sentence. As Ridian leapt over the plough, he tripped headlong. A rusty spike sank into his thigh, and he screamed.

In a flash, his mother was there, her expression exactly like Rayna's had been a moment earlier. "You're okay, Ridian. You're okay." She tried to pull the spike out. He fought her, but she was too strong, and she yanked the shard out. Ridian screamed again. There was so much blood. Then little Rayna fell to the ground. She twisted and thrashed, flattening the wheat about her as her mouth foamed.

Then Big Rayna entered the memory to stand over her younger self. "I remember this," she said in earnest. "But I thought it was a dream. Wait… can you hear that?"

"No," said Ridian, his panic rising, but he could. He could hear that ancient call, that gentle chorus—The Song of Silent

Growing.

It was calling to him. It hadn't called in years. Not since this moment, but he recognised it all the same—this song without sound. The melody rose louder, pulsing and swelling around him. It grew and grew until his head resonated with it. *The field*, Ridian realised. *The field was singing.* But more than that: it was urging, compelling, imploring… it wanted to be summoned. Somehow, he knew. Then little Ridian beckoned (somehow knowing how) and the music responded. It washed over and around him like a gentle whirlwind and filled him –

And the field began to die.

Little Ridian channelled the Song towards his bleeding leg and watched in astonishment as the wound stitched itself closed with little strands of darting flesh. Now it was pulling itself closed—*healing*—right before his eyes. Now there was nothing but a jagged scar through the rip in his shorts.

Then he looked up to see an image that would haunt him for the rest of his life: a dead field and a dying tree, its leaves dissolving into ash as they fell.

"Ridian," said big Rayna with wonder and delight. "You're a healer. You can heal yourself."

Ridian ignored her. He needed the memory to end. He knew something bad was coming. The image of the dead field and the dying tree was a psychic gate—blocking whatever came next. But he couldn't stop the memory. It kept unspooling from his mind like a runaway ball of string.

Angry voices drifted over the shallow hill towards them.

"Oh gods," said Mother. "They're coming." Then she pulled little Ridian along by the hand and carried the unconscious Rayna ragdoll across the dead field and into the chicken pen beside their cottage home. Outraged chickens squawked in protest and fled as Mother slumped the senseless Rayna against the wall of the pen.

"Ridian, listen to me," said Mother. "Men are coming. Bad men. I need to talk to them, but no matter what happens, you must stay hidden, okay?"

Ridian clung to her. "No, don't go."

Mother hugged him so tight it was hard to breathe, then she let him go. "I must."

"No, don't go," Ridian wailed again, reaching out.

But Mother shook him firmly by the shoulders. "No. Listen to me." She squeezed his small shoulders till they hurt."You need to look after your sister. Okay? She needs you. Look after her." Her eyes welled, and that scared him more than anything.

Trembling, Ridian glanced at the senseless Rayna. "I'll look after her, Mummy."

"Good boy." Then Mother gave him a brief hug, kissed the unconscious Rayna's head, and shut the door as she left. Shards of light beamed through gaps in the wooden walls, and Ridian peered after her. She crossed their front yard, then stood, staring over the hill. She smoothed her dress and waited, never once looking back at Ridian.

Eventually, men appeared, cresting the hill with pitchfork, hoe, and scythe in hand.

A man with a leather like face pointed. "There she is! There's the witch that killed my crop." Then he and the small gang stormed up to her.

Standing tall, Mother said something Ridian couldn't hear.

"A fire?" blurted the leather-faced man, outraged. "Bullshit! I saw the crop shrivel before my eyes. Cursed it, you did." He leaned in, his ugly face nearly touching Mother's. "Always suspected you for a witch. Now I'm certain."

Ridian pressed his cheek against the rough wood to see clearly, his breath heavy, his heart hammering in his tiny ribcage. The pen reeked, but he didn't register it.

Mother said something indiscernible again, and the man slapped her across the cheek. "Liar!" he spat.

Mother's head whipped to the side, but her feet did not move. She stood upright, chin up, and spat in the man's eye.

The man's leather face puckered up in disgust and he wiped it with a knuckle. "Bitch!" he cried, then he lunged upon her and wrestled her to the ground. Mother fought back and managed to rake her nails across his weather-beaten brow.

"Help me," cried the man, scrunching an injured eye shut. "She's feral."

Nobody moved. They wrung their tools and shot sideways glances at each other.

"Help me!" the man cried again.

The gang shifted their feet.

"Help me teach this slut-sorceress a lesson or you're all fired!"

That did it. One man jumped in, then another, and then the whole mob pinned Mother down. They clustered around, obscuring Ridian's vision, and all Ridian saw was a brief strip of the man's leather face—nostrils flared, eyes bulging—before the memory dashed to pieces like waves upon a rock.

Ridian collapsed under the unbearable weight of the truth.

His mother—*their* mother—had sacrificed herself and been hurt in ways Ridian had never imagined. Somehow, he'd forgotten, but somehow he'd always known. He doubled over as sobs wracked his incorporeal body.

A dead field and a dying tree… That's why the image terrified him. It held back this awful, awful reality.

Rayna's face was a rictus of grief and shock. "Why didn't you tell me?" As she said it, blood poured from her chest, right where her heart would be. All that was missing was a knife.

"I—I…" stammered Ridian.

Anger flashed across Rayna's eyes and a sudden storm began to rage about her. "How could they do such a thing? How could anyone…" As she became lost for words, lightning flashed, thunder boomed, and hurricane like winds tore about her. She glared at Ridian. "Why didn't you tell me?" she demanded. Her voice was more powerful than a thunderclap, it shook the ground and threatened to break Ridian apart.

"I didn't know!" said Ridian. "I—I…" And being unable to withstand the sight of Rayna's fury, he fell away. Down, down, down he fell, falling faster and faster, until the storm surrounding Rayna was far away.. At last, he landed in a small, dark cave—the same cave he was born in—the last place he truly felt safe.

"I'm sorry, I'm sorry, I'm sorry," muttered Ridian, hiding his face in his tiny, toddler-like hands.

Far away, the tempest about Rayna crackled and rumbled on.

"I didn't know," said Ridian. "I—I must have pushed it away." He gasped, chest heaving, the words strangling him.

The dark clouds about Rayna swirled into a hurricane, with her suspended in the middle—the eye of the storm. "What am doing?" she said, her whisper somehow carrying over the howling wind. "What am I saying?" There was the last weak rumble of thunder, and the storm dissipated. She descended, slow as an autumn sunset. "I'm sorry," she said at last, meaning it. "I'm not angry at you. Not really. But, why didn't you tell me?"

"I don't know," whispered Ridian, pressed up against the cavern wall. "Even if I did remember, how could I tell you that…" He buried his face in his hands again.

"Ridian," said Rayna, tenderly. "Look at me."

Composing himself, Ridian looked up: a giant eye at stared down at him from the end of a long tunnel, but not a tunnel, a well—Trystan's Well. "Ridian, don't hide," said Rayna. Her giant eye blinked and kept staring. There was no hiding.

Ridian curled himself into a ball.

"Please," said Rayna. "Come out."

Ridian looked again. He lay upon the palm of a giant hand, big as a paddock. It was Rayna's, and her face was also immense. It filled half the sky and shone with a faint, gentle radiance. She fixed her wet colossal eyes upon him. They were so big and so full of sadness. But there was no trace of anger. "Ridian, talk to me."

Words refused to form. What could he say?

"This is a lot to take in," she said. "It's going to take me a while to figure out, and a long time to get over. But I guess it explains… well, it explains why mother is the way she is… Ridian?"

Ridian remained silent.

"Ridian, please. That was a really messed up thing to happen. Yes, it must have hurt mother, but it definitely hurt you."

"Well, it's my fault," said Ridian. The words sprang out of him like a rabbit from a snare.

"What?"

"It's all my fault," replied Ridian with careful unwavering conviction. "It's all my fault she was attacked. It my fault she was taken away. She lost her mind because of me."

"Ridian, that's crazy."

Ridian ignored her.

"You shouldn't blame yourself," said Rayna. "You did nothing wrong."

Ridian scoffed. "Obviously, not. Look what happened." Though, in the back of his mind, there was a faint, flickering doubt. *Perhaps it wasn't his fault?* No. It was—it had to be.

"So, you're to blame," said Rayna. "It's all your fault, is it?"

Ridian shrugged, but the seed of doubt was growing, and fast. Already, its roots were burrowing through him and taking hold.

"Yeah?" said Rayna. "Then tell me, what exactly did you do wrong? Trip over playing tag?"

Despite himself, Ridian released a shallow laugh.

Rayna began to shrink. "You realise how dumb and unfair it is to blame your four-year-old self for—well, anything, don't you?"

Reluctantly, Ridian did. He was a child. A small boy. How could he possibly be held responsible? No. Like Rayna said, he just tripped over and… *healed* himself. That's what he did. He healed himself.

Rayna was shrinking rapidly now: her palm was now

the size of a dinner table, her face the size of a barn door. "Ridian, you're being stupid, and you know it."

They stood opposite each other now, both the same size, seventeen again. Rayna hadn't shrunk, Ridian realised: he had grown.

"You're right," said Ridian. "I *am* being stupid."

"Of course, I'm right," said Rayna with a glittering laugh. "I'm older, remember? Older and infinitely wiser."

But the memory flooded back to surround them. There was his mother's pain, and his failure to protect her.

Rayna gripped Ridian's hands. "Look at me. *Look at me!*"

Ridian tore his eyes away and stared into Rayna's tear filled-eyes.

"This wasn't your fault," she said, her fingers becoming root-like tendrils that wrapped around Ridian's arms, holding him fast. "I want you to say it. This wasn't my fault."

Other images flashed about them: their mother refusing to leave her cell; their mother, mute as a stone; their mother staring vacantly past them, though Rayna begged her to look at them.

Something within Ridian wanted to hold on to all this weight, telling him he *deserved* to carry it. But now, he understood. None of this was his fault. It never had been. And with deliberate force of will, he let go of the guilt that had been choking him for as long as he could remember. As he did, the images blew away like smoke before a strong wind. Then an ugly, black creature that vaguely resembled a bat burst from his chest, fluttered a dozen feet and fell into the void.

A deep peace fell upon Ridian, and he found himself and Rayna in a sun-drenched wheat field. There was a lonely cottage, and was their mother, smiling at them from a distance. Feeling lighter than at any other time in his life, Ridian laughed—a bright, delightful sound that bubbled up from deep within him. Rayna joined in, and together, their laughter rang out over the golden crop. Then Ridian heard—no, *felt*—a strange music swirl about them. It was beauty. It was familiar. It was sweet. It was the Song of Silent Growing.

"You can hear that, can't you?" asked Rayna, knowing the answer. Her smile vanished as she glanced at the dwindling ribbon connecting Ridian's soul to his body.

"You have to go," she said. "Quickly, leave now and heal yourself. You can do it."

"What about you?" said Ridian. "I can't just—"

"Yes, you can. If you stay, you die, and then we're both stuck here forever. That won't do either of us any good. You already drive me crazy."

Ridian hesitated, thinking furiously. There had to be another way. But she was right. Of course, she bloody was. "I'll come back," he said. "I promise. I'll find a way to save you."

"No, don't promise that," said Rayna sternly. "Promise to stop Kyros. Promise that."

They looked at each other steadily. Rayna wasn't the little girl who was afraid of the dark any more. Indeed, as Ridian thought it, her projection morphed into three persons, each overlaid atop the other, each somehow shining through, visible. The first image was of herself, exactly as she was in the outside world. The second was of Valaria from the painting of the Elder Three—strong, defiant, unyielding as stone. The third was their mother, the very moment she said goodbye in the chicken pen, sacrificing herself for her children, though she knew the cost.

And seeing her thus gave Ridian the courage to let her go. "I'll stop Kyros, I promise."

Chapter 42

Ridian collapsed at the base of Hero's Tree, pain exploding through his stomach. Somehow, he knew hardly a second had transpired since he'd entered the Tree. *Heal yourself,* he demanded. *Heal.*

Silver was nudging him in earnest with his cold, wet nose. Some of Ridian's black-looking blood had smothered his wolf's luminescent fur, but Ridian barely noticed. He was too busy listening for the mystical song that he'd sensed moments earlier. The strange song with no sound—the Song of Silent Growing.

Bells still tolled from the Living Fort, and in the distance, people screamed.

Focus. You can't help if you're dead.

Ridian scrunched his eyes shut and really listened. Sure enough, the silent melody was there: resonating through every fiber of Hero's Tree. How had he missed it before? It pulsed in the roots, thrummed through the trunk, reverberated in the branches, and sang out into the leaves. Taken together from root to stem, the tree was an orchestra of pulsing, quivering energy.

Ridian slapped a bloody palm against the trunk and, with his mind, *pulled* –

The flow of Rava in the trunk was slow and ponderous, nudging only slightly towards Ridian. Ridian pulled with all his might, but the Rava slunk back into its normal rhythm with only a slight deviation. It was too hard to yield, like sucking cold honey through a straw. With his mind, Ridian quested farther up into the branches. Rava coursed quicker there, beating to a faster tune. He pulled again, and Rava stretched slowly towards him, only to recoil after a long strain on Ridian's mind. Frustration mounting, Ridian sought the leaves. They thrummed along to the quickest beat, almost vibrato. Ridian pulled, and Rava seeped out of the leaves and into him with palpable, thrumming notes, like the strokes of a violin. It was music alright—beautiful, delightful music—and Ridian sighed relief as the pain in his stomach dimmed.

Straining, he flexed his weak, atrophied mind, and the leaves yielded a little more Rava. He pulled till his head grew heavy. He pulled till it throbbed. He pulled till his skull felt full of crushed glass. And as he did, the leaves fell, only to dissolve midair into ash. The sprinkling fell on and about him like a soft, warm snow.

Finally, panting from the strain and the worst migraine imaginable, his gut was pain free. Gingerly, he curled up his shirt: beneath a smear of blood, he saw a new scar—a dash of white skin. Ridian laughed, drunk with relief and disbelief, and Silver pounced upon him and licked him. A miracle. He'd just performed a miracle.

Still, bells tolled, declaring disaster. Ridian shot to his feet, snatched the bloody knife that Kyros had plunged into him, and with a last glance at the sprawled dead Knights and the Tree that held his sister captive, he and Silver sped for the Living Fort. He tried drawing Rava from Silver, but his mind pounded, and he severed the link. He would need time to recover before he did any more magic—Soulcasting or healing.

Drawing closer, Ridian saw civilians pour into the outer gates, while Knights paced the battlements above. Ridian and Silver joined the crowd of civilians bottlenecked at the gate. People shoved their way forward like panicked sheep.

Ridian grabbed a woman by the elbow. "What's going on?"

The woman spun about wide-eyed, a squalling infant in her arms. "Kyrosians have broken through the northern gate." Then she dropped her shoulder and barged through the crowd.

Ridian felt like he'd been stabbed again. He could imagine all too well what had transpired. Kyros had marched up to northern Gate, hacked everyone to pieces, and opened the gates from the inside. Hector's disciples would have been waiting, Ridian knew. Perhaps they had followed Ridian and Rayna the moment they left Sky Island.

The onrush of civilians carried him through the gate like a strong flowing river, and before Ridian knew it, he burst into the bailey. People shot off along the street towards the hospital that would undoubtedly be used as a fortress, like it had of old. Families clung to each other. Parents cried for lost children; lost children cried. Knights shouted orders and were ignored. It was chaos. Then Kyros' vengeful dream flashed across Ridian's mind: men, women, and children tortured in a multitude of ways. Kyros making an art of it. Then he imagined the Thunderfells among the victims and a cold fear washed over him. *Surely, they can hear the bells. Surely, they're safe inside.* And if they were, where would they be? *Think, Ridian, think.* Then it came to him: *pediatrics.* Then Ridian ran towards the hospital and shoved his way through to the sweet water surrounding Fidic's statue. Despite the crowd, he managed to slurp a small handful, and the hospital glowed a silky green.

Inside, the front desk was overrun, and people who weren't pacing sat on the floor or slumped against the walls. Families huddled together, hugging their knees, biting nails, and sucking thumbs. The fear was palpable. Without delay, Ridian rushed up a bustling stairwell and then down a crowded hallway until he was inside the Pediatric Wing. Down the far end of the busy room, beside Ollie's bed was—

Everyone.

Theodor had his arm around Feya as they gazed down at a sleeping Ollie. Kess bounced Ella on her knee, while Kai tickled the toddler's ear, making her giggle. Felix sat on the bed, and Zeke perched on the windowsill. Though overjoyed, Ridian hesitated. The Thunderfells loved each other. They belonged to each other. Especially in this time of crisis. Surely his presence would be an intrusion. Maybe he should just slip away and—

"Ridian!" shouted Kai, seeing him.

Feya's eyes locked with Ridian's, sending his insides into a sickening free fall. A moment later, the family was crushing him in a massive, feet-off-the-ground embrace—all except Ollie, who remained asleep on his bed.

"You're back!"

"We've been worried sick."

"Did you find your sister?"

"Holy Fidic's Fiddle! You're covered in blood!"

The family stepped back and gasped at Ridian's blood-drenched tunic and pants.

"It's okay," said Ridian reassuringly. "I'm fine."

"You need medical attention," said Theodor. "Kai, help him into a bed—quick."

"No, don't." Ridian lifted his gore-clogged shirt, stopping Kai in his tracks. "See? Nothing's wrong. I'm not hurt at all."

Frowning, the family were on the cusp of asking a dozen more questions when someone shrieked, "They're coming!" And the room filled with terror and chaos as people raced to the windows.

Ridian and the Thunderfells followed suit. "There!" cried Kai, pointing out the window.

Seized with dread, Ridian crowded up amongst them. Birds of prey streaked through the night sky, flittering across the moon, while beyond the outer wall, figures emerged as they marched up the hill towards Last Stand Meadow: men and women, wolves and great cats. To Ridian's horror, he thought he saw a blood-splattered girl with blonde hair striding at their front, dual swords in hand. He shook his head. He was imagining it, surely, he was imagining it. Everyone trembled. Everyone except Theodor who wrapped his arms about them.

Feya slipped her hand into Ridian's. Her small, calloused hand was shaking wildly, and it crushed his fingers even as it sent electric shocks through him.

"What is it?" cried Ollie, who sat bolt upright in his bed. "What's wrong?"

Feya released Ridian's hand and was by Ollie's side in a flash. The boy looked terrible. Pale skin sagged off his gaunt frame, and dark rings circled his eyes. "What—what's happening?" Then he slumped forward, exhausted.

"Shhhhhh… it's okay," said Theodor, and together, he and Feya gently guided Ollie's head back onto his pillow. "Here. Drink this." Theodor grabbed a cup from the bedside and put it to Ollie's trembling lips. "That's it. All of it now… *Good.*"

Ollie slowly shut his eyes, and his shivering body relaxed into the mattress.

Feya placed her palm to Ollie's forehead. "He's burning up."

"It's just his body fighting," said Theodor, tucking Ollie in. "He'll be fine."

"He's lost so much weight," said Ridian, alarmed at Ollie's appearance.

"Oh, he's a good eater," said Theodor. "He'll plump up in no time." But Feya and Kess exchanged a look that said otherwise.

"Ridian," said Kai gravely. "What happened? They say Sevron and his squad were attacked at Hero's Tree by some girl. They say she single-handedly slaughtered everyone at the northern Gate. They say—they say…" He shook his head as if unsure how to articulate himself.

"They say she can sever a Soulcaster's bond," said Feya, struggling to mask her fear.

The Thunderfells all looked at him, all their fear and hope hanging on his answer.

What should he say? That Kyros' soul had been alive within Hero's Tree and had possessed his sister? That he had watched Kyros effortlessly murder a squad of Fidicia's finest? That the rumours were true? That Kyros was unstoppable? That Ridian was responsible? That with an army at their front and an unscalable mountain at their back, they were trapped? That they were doomed?

Collective gasps filled the room, drawing the Thunder-fells' attention away from Ridian and out the window once again.

"What is that?" said Theodor breathlessly, removing his spectacles.

Ridian followed their gaze, and what he saw filled him a terrible, indescribable feeling. Far in the distance, beyond the Ring Mountains, a pillar of fire shot into the night sky. Higher and higher, it climbed, swirling as it went, until finally, at its zenith, the fire spread horizontally into a giant, flaming T. The edges cascaded into a mesmerising, mushroom-shaped inferno. Most striking were the colours: *green*, *black*, and *gold* flames swirling together like a colossal flaming braid.

"What is that?" everyone whispered.

But Ridian knew.

It was Sunfire.

It was General Selkyrie.

It was her Sungazers.

They must have landed successfully upon Mirecross Castle and were celebrating. Hopelessness filled Ridian. Even if they could somehow hold out against Kyros—even if they could *defeat* him—the Sungazers would wipe them out as surely as sunrise. Who could withstand them? A single Sungazer could decimate an army, level a forest, scorch an entire plain.

Then with sudden, perfect clarity, Ridian knew what he had to do. It was a risky plan, and it would require plenty of luck, with a heavy price, but it was the only way. And so, while everyone gazed up at the blazing spectacle, Ridian slipped unnoticed from the room.

Chapter 43

Ridian and Silver ran down crowded corridors and bustling stairways, down into the very heart of the Living Fort—into Stonecrow Cavern. Candles flickered in the gloom, while dozens of devotees muttered prayers before the giant statue of Roki.

To Ridian's right, the Mural Wall stretched out in all its flawless artistry, portraying the legendary life of Fidic. Ridian approached the final chapter—the Last Stand. He ran his fingers over the rippling images: Kyros duelling Daegan; Fidic with his healing, outstretched hands; Valaria summoning a thorny hedge into being, trapping them within and protecting them from Kyros' rage-poisoned army. Ridian rapped a knuckle on the wooden mural. A secret tunnel lay on the far side, he knew. A secret tunnel that could take him to Madman's Falls and then—hopefully—safely out of Fidicia. He needed to get to it, but it would take days to cut through the Mural Wall with an axe, and that was if people allowed him to hack away at the sacred Valarian relic. No, he needed to try another way.

Checking to ensure he wasn't being watched, Ridian pulled his knife from its sheath. He gripped the cold blade, hesitated, then slashed the knife across his palm. Pain flared, and despite himself, he let out a gasp. He then slapped his hand against the wood and listened… Sure enough, Rava was pulsing through the Wooden Wall, begging to be drawn out.

Ridian pulled.

The slow throb of Rava deviated slightly, then realigned, unyielding. He pulled harder, flexing his mind, putting everything into it, and a single note of Rava sang out as it left the wall and flowed into his hand, healing him. Ridian opened his eyes: a grey blemish, the size of a plate, marred the wall. Ridian prodded it, and flakes of dead wood fell to the floor, crumbling into dust. He scraped at it and pulled out a handful of ash.

"Didn't think you were the religious type," said a voice behind him.

Startled, Ridian spun about. It was Feya, arms folded, eyes narrowed. She must have followed him. So much for his slick getaway.

"I'm not," said Ridian.

"So, what are you doing?"

In the dim flickering candlelight, Feya evidently couldn't see the mess he was making of the Mural Wall.

Ridian hesitated. Would she help or hinder?

"Come on," said Feya. "You know about that fire in the sky. You know what's going on. You have a plan. Tell me."

Ridian looked at Silver, aglow in a wispy, ethereal light. Silver cocked his head at him.

"Please," she said earnestly. "I want to help."

Ridian decided to trust her. "Okay, but one simple rule: no whinging, no whining, and no excuses."

Feya laughed at hearing her own words from the first

night of their training. It was an anxious laugh from a tight, nervous body. "That's three rules," she said quietly.

"Now who's the smart-arse?"

Somebody shushed them, and a few others were shooting harsh, admonishing glares. "People are trying to pray," whispered one sour-faced woman.

Ridian mouthed a 'sorry,' then steered Feya towards a dark corner. "I don't have time to explain," he whispered. "But behind this wall is a secret tunnel that leads to Madman's Falls."

"How do you—"

"Just listen. I need to get through this wall, get out of Fidicia, and get reinforcements."

Feya eyed the wall, confused and incredulous. "What reinforcements? We've already summoned every Soulcaster in the country."

"Soulcasters can't help us." Ridian visualized the Sunfire spiraling into the night sky, and General Selkyrie radiating heat as her eyes turned molten gold. If only he could point her limitless destructive force in the right direction.

"Then who can help us?" said Feya, voice rising and attracting more glares.

"I don't have time to explain. Listen. I'll show you how to get to Madman's Falls, and if all goes pear-shaped, get the family, take the secret tunnel, and get out of Fidicia."

"Shouldn't everyone know about this tunnel?"

"No. The family might be able to slip away, but not everyone. They'd be captured or killed before they made it down the hill."

Feya was shaking her head, struggling to comprehend everything. People continued to eye them with distaste.

Great, thought Ridian, *how am I supposed to get through without being seen now?* Then he looked at Feya and knew how. "Feya," he said. "I can get us through this wall, but I need darkness. I need you to blow out the candles for me."

She squinted at him. "Which ones?"

"All of them."

Feya's eyes widened in alarm as she understood. She shook her head and slipped her Windchaser hands under her armpits. "What if they see me?"

"Who cares?"

"If word got around?"

"You're a Windchaser. Big deal."

"Shhhh…" Feya hissed.

"The family accepts you," said Ridian sternly. "Soulcaster or not. Now quit being a baby and help me like you promised."

Feya bit the nail of her index finger, the very picture of anxious deliberation, before giving a reluctant nod.

"Good." Ridian pocketed a candle and a spare flint from a nearby bench, then returned to the dark corner where wood met rock. Hopefully it was an obscure enough spot and he wouldn't be seen. "Ready when you are."

Feya bit her lip as she clenched and unclenched her hands.

"You can do it," Ridian whispered.

Feya took a deep breath, raised her hands, and pushed as if straining against an invisible wall. Immediately, wind burst from Feya's palms, snuffing out candles and casting the room into sudden darkness, making Silver blaze all the brighter. People screamed as stale air wafted around the room. Amid the pandemonium, Ridian unsheathed his knife and sliced a scorching line across his palm. He slapped it against the cold wood and pulled. The stubborn wood resisted, but the pain provided ample inspiration, and after a few seconds of teeth-grinding effort, Ridian's palm no longer stung. He gouged away at the crumbling wall and hollowed out a bowl-sized crater. *Not enough...*

Ridian sliced open his palm again and repeated the process. It was harder this time. He could hear the Rava singing in the wood alright, but the part of his mind that pulled was weak from disuse, and his head began to throb. He scooped away the dead wood and found his arm could pass all the way through. But the hole was only big enough for a cat.

Near the statue of Roki, someone had re-lit a candle. People clustered around and extended their own candles to the flickering light. Soon, the cave would be alight again. Gritting his teeth, Ridian gripped the blade of his knife tightly, then slipped it through his palm with an uncontrollable cry of pain. Blood trickled down his forearm and off his elbow. He pulled, cut, and pulled again, until his head felt ready to split open. With the effort of pulling, he struck his forehead against the wall and barely felt it. It was hard to think. *Just Pull...*

At last, panting and with blood running down his arm, he pulled Feya through the narrow opening in the wall, skidding through the wood dust at their feet. Tugging her along, they passed the ancient box that had held Fidic's Lute. It reminded him of Rayna and Hector and Kyros. It reminded him of everything.

"Wait," hissed Feya. "I can't see."

Sure enough, though Silver's blazing coat illuminated the cavern for Ridian, Feya stumbled about, squinting, pupils massive.

"Hold this," said Ridian, and he handed Feya the candle so he could light it.

"How can you see in here?" said Feya, blinking blindly. "It's pitch black."

"I eat lots of carrots."

"What?"

"Never mind. Not funny."

Candle alight, Feya gazed about in wonder. "Wow. How long has this been secret?"

"This way." And Ridian led her out of the small cavern to the subterranean stream. Thousands of Looney Shrooms glowed their silver, eldritch glow, their reflection on the black water stretched and distorted from the flow.

"Left is a dead-end," said Ridian. "Right is Madman's Falls. Got it?"

"Right is right," said Feya, and on they went, silently walking along the narrow bank, accidentally dislodging the occasional wall-clinging Looney Shroom as they passed until the tunnel ended upon a circle of the night sky. Careful not to slip, they crept to the edge of Madman's Falls. Water shot off the edge and plummeted into the rumbling cauldron below, while water droplets whipped about and made them shiver.

"This is it," said Ridian above the roar. "Now, listen very carefully. If the Kyrosians break into Fidicia, do not surrender. Do not give up. The Kyrosians have no intention of keeping prisoners. They plan on killing everyone." It was a lie; Ridian well knew Kyros' sadistic plans. But it would serve. "You hear me? Do not allow yourself to be captured. And if the battle goes ill, bring the family here to escape.

Understand?"

Feya nodded, then peered down at the dizzying fifty-foot drop. "You want us to jump off here? Are you kidding?" Her dark eyes caught the light of Silver's blazing coat. They were so beautiful, and, with a pang, Ridian wondered if he'd ever see them again. He should say something, he knew. How he felt about her? What she meant to him? How her gaze made his stomach backflip? But he didn't know what to say, or perhaps he just lacked the courage.

"Well, we can't all fly," he said, and before she could utter a word, he jumped off the edge. His shirt flapped violently as the water rushed up to meet him, and he pinwheeled his arms wildly to stay upright. Then his feet and hands slapped the water, and he was engulfed in a freezing whoosh, a muffled roar pounding in his ears. He fought for the surface, mouth clamped shut, careful not to drink the poison water. Finally, he broke the surface with a gasp, paddled ashore, and heaved himself over the low retaining wall. Shivering, teeth chattering, he looked up. Feya was pointing at him and shouting, but her voice was drowned by the roaring water.

"What?" cried Ridian.

Feya shouted again, and Ridian cupped an ear to indicate he couldn't hear. She created a megaphone with her hands— still nothing. She appeared very insistent, and if it was indeed the last time he was ever going to see her, he had better know what she was saying. So, Ridian closed his eyes, embraced the feeling of death, split from his body, hurtled through the black, and merged his mind with Silver. In a flash, he was looking through his wolf's eyes atop Madman's Falls.

"Behind you! He's behind you!" screamed Feya beside him. She was pointing wildly.

With a bolt of fear, Ridian looked down upon himself: sure enough, a figure was creeping towards him. Ridian's blazing silver hair illuminated the man's face, and it made him panic even more. Without delay, Ridian slipped out of Silver and zoomed back –

Too late. Strong hands twisted his arm behind his back and locked his shoulder.

"Well, well, well… isn't this a pleasant surprise," the man hissed. His breath stank of boiled eggs.

Chapter 44

Ridian's shoulder screamed in pain. It riveted him to the spot, bent forward, staring at his feet.

"Lukas," said Ridian, wincing. "What are you doing?"

"I could ask you the same thing," said Lukas pleasantly. "You've been a busy little spy, haven't you? Spying away without a care in the world, up Madman's Falls of all places. Meanwhile, I've been stuck here, in disgrace, bored out of my brains and freezing my balls off." Lukas gave a little twist, and pain flared.

Ridian sensed Silver's desire to tear Lukas' face off, but Ridian held the wolf back. Given the circumstances, Lukas was an ally. Surely, he could be reasoned with. "Lukas, you don't understand. The Kyrosians are—"

Another twist—a big one—and it felt as if a white-hot knife had plunged, sizzling into Ridian's shoulder joint. It was impossible not to cry out.

"Oh, yes, you'll tell me all about your little friends. But first, the falls." Lukas was terrifyingly calm.

"Lukas, let me go. The Kyrosians—they're storming the Living Fort as we speak."

Lukas chuckled. "Bold lie. But it still won't stop me from snapping your arms and flinging you into the water."

Ridian looked out the corner of his eye at the poisonous water: it was churning at the falls, then swiftly flowed into a dark tunnel in the mountain that led to the aqueduct. From there, the water was dumped somewhere outside of Fidicia. Ridian was equal parts afraid and appalled. Lukas was willing to murder Ridian and discard his body. Ridian was about to draw Rava and try to escape Lukas' grip, when Lukas stiffened and spun them both around.

Six leering faces grinned at them, swords drawn, white streaks running through their hair. Ridian's stomach dropped, and Lukas almost let go of Ridian in surprise.

"Oh, don't stop because of us," said a sharp-featured youth Ridian recognized from Sky Island. "We were enjoying the show. Please, continue." His mates snickered, and a wolf bristled by the smug youth's heels. *He was a Soulcaster.*

Ridian resisted the urge to draw Rava or even to summon Silver while he sized up the situation. He was trapped within tall circular walls of stone, with only a single exit which the Kyrosians guarded. And they had swords, a wolf, and a Soulcaster. All he had was a knife and a confused Lukas twisting his arm. Surprise, for now, was his best asset.

"Declare yourselves and your purpose!" said Lukas, stepping back, taking Ridian with him.

"Draven, at your service," said Draven with an elaborate bow. "A pleasure, to be sure. Our orders were to clear the area. *Clear the area?*" he mused. "What does that mean? Round up prisoners? Or indiscriminate slaughter? I can't make up my mind, so I'll leave the choice up to you. Surrender or die."

Lukas shuffled back until his heel thudded to a stop at the retaining wall. "Stay back!" he cried, redoubling his grip on

Ridian's arm.

"Lukas, let me go," said Ridian. "I'm on your side."

A dark-eyed beauty sauntered forward and rested her chin on Draven's shoulder. "Oh, look at the poor boy. He's cute as a button. I want one." Her coy smile dropped. "Wait. That's Hector's boy."

The six Kyrosians squinted at Ridian to get a better look.

"Holy Crow, it is too," said Draven with a laugh. "Good spot." Draven kissed the side of her neck. "Can you imagine the trouble if we accidentally killed Hector's nephew?"

Ridian could almost hear Lukas' teeth grinding. "Hector's nephew, huh?" Lukas' knife hissed from its sheath and pressed against Ridian's throat. "Get back! Another step and I'll open his windpipe."

Instantly, the Kyrosians backed up, and Draven's cocky smile shattered as unmistakable fear shone in his eyes. "Easy, mate, *easy*."

"Lukas," said Ridian. "We need to work together."

"Shut up," spat Lukas.

"Nothing rash now," said Draven, raising a hand as if trying to calm a wild stallion. "Look. We're all putting our swords away. See? Let's just talk."

"There's nothing to talk about," said Lukas.

"No? How about a deal? Release the boy and we let you live. That's fair, right?" He looked between his companions who nodded their agreement. "A bloody bargain if you ask me."

"Piss off!" said Lukas.

The dark-eyed beauty slipped a knife out from somewhere on her person and pointed it at Lukas. "Or you both die, and we float your bodies downstream, and nobody need know—especially Hector."

Draven rested a delicate hand on top of the woman's knife hand. "My love. Diplomacy, please." She glared at Lukas, nostrils flared, before lowering the blade.

Draven flashed a winning smile. "Forgive her. She's impetuous by nature. Beautiful and dangerous, a truly irresistible combination."

"Stop," said woman with a little giggle.

"Can we get on with it?" said one of the Kyrosians, a bald brute with a bristling white beard, though he looked in his twenties.

"Aye, back to business," said Draven. "What say you, stranger? Life or death? Seems obvious to me, but what's your preference?"

The blade at Ridian's throat trembled. Lukas' eggy breath was coming short and sharp. Surely, Lukas didn't trust these Kyrosians. Surely, he knew they would kill him either way. Which meant he would surely kill Ridian as a final act of vengeance and patriotism. Internally, Ridian called for Silver and felt the wolf leap over the edge of Madman's Falls.

The woman pointed. "Did you see that? Something fell into the water."

"It's a wolf," cried the white-bearded brute, eyes widening.

"He's a Soulcaster!" said Draven, and they all re-drew their swords, and closed in.

Lukas glanced back to look at the wolf splashing through the water. The knife slid gently across Ridian's throat.

Wait, Ridian told himself.

Lukas turned again, and inadvertently, his knife nicked Ridian's skin.

Wait.

The Kyrosians closed in further, and Lukas pointed his knife at them. "Stay back!" he yelled.

Now!

Ridian spun and struck Lukas in the face with his elbow. Stunned, Lukas tottered and let go of Ridian's arm. Then, taking inspiration from Kyros—of all people—Ridian grabbed the hilt of Lukas' sword at his belt, and palmed Lukas in the chest, sending him toppling over the retaining wall into the water and unsheathing his sword in one motion.

The Kyrosians whooped in delight as a stunned Lukas trod water, blood pouring from a smashed nose. Silver paddled ashore and shook his silver-fire coat.

"Holy Crow, kid!" said Draven. "Hector's nephew, indeed!"

Ridian forced a smile. Now he just needed to lie and convince them to—

Something flew past Ridian with a whoosh and blew the Kyrosians tumbling away with a howling burst of wind. A moment later, Feya landed where the Kyrosians had stood, her palms outstretched, her wild hair billowing about her. Despite everything, Ridian swallowed. *Damn, she's beautiful.*

The blown-back Kyrosians finally slid to a stop and glared at her.

Draven snapped to his feet with a quick flick of his body. "The Windchaser's mine!" he cried, and he dashed at Feya with the quick, frenetic motion of a Soulcaster.

Feya launched skyward with a burst of air. Wind blew from her palms and feet, guiding her flight, and she landed gently upon tippy toes beside Ridian. "You take the Soulcaster, I'll take the rest," she said.

Draven skidded to a stop and looked from Feya to Ridian with sudden understanding. "Hector's boy is a traitor," he said in disgust. "Hector's boy is a traitor!" he said again with rage.

The Kyrosians closed in.

"I suggest one hundred percent," said Feya.

"Good tip."

A gale burst from Feya, and she shot towards a fallen sword, even as a man raced her for it. She landed in a roll, grasped the sword, and sliced the man's gut open in a single slick movement. Ridian saw no more. Draven was upon him, his sword flickering through the night. Ridian didn't think; he let instinct possess him. Drawing Rava in a panic, he dodged and darted. Draven pursued, relentless. He swung and slashed, his blade humming with a deadly tune. Ridian parried one fell blow, and their swords rasped off each other with a metallic shriek. Ridian returned a cautious thrust. Draven swatted it aside with ease and countered with a powerful overhead strike, his blade crashing down like a bolt of lightning. Ridian blocked—just in time—and Draven's blade lodged in the cross-guard, jarring Ridian's arms as he clutched the hilt. Draven wrenched the swords apart, and Ridian rolled away as Draven's sword whistled towards him.

As Ridian stood, he collided with the beautiful Kyrosian woman. She raised her sword. But she was no Soulcaster; she might have been stretching, or yawning, she was so slow. And Ridian hacked her arm off at the elbow with an effortless flick. Her sword clanked to the ground— amputated hand still holding on—and she screamed.

"NO!" cried Draven, and Ridian had to parry two ferocious blows in quick succession, their swords slithering off each other, before he could scurry out of range.

Ridian sensed Silver bounding after Draven and ordered his wolf back. The wolf was too vulnerable against an armed Soulcaster. Besides, if Silver died, Ridian would follow. He was utterly dependent upon the steady flow of Rava to fend off Draven's unremitting attacks. Unsurprisingly, with his girlfriend's arm cut off, Draven's ferocity intensified. His face was contorted as he rained down blow after blow, smashing with the force of a hammer. Ridian blocked and parried, trying to get away. But he'd backed himself into a corner, sheer rock at his back. Lukas capitalised and closed in. He struck, he struck, he *struck*—

And Ridian's sword snapped in half, the pointy end tinkling on stony ground.

Draven stopped before him, heaving as his face twitched in fury. "Watch me open him up and feed his guts to my wolf!" Behind him, the woman had sunk to her knees. She was very pale, and blood was pouring from her stump. She looked on the verge of passing out.

Ridian looked for Feya. She was busy contending with three other Kyrosians—flipping and flying above and about them.

Hoping to catch Draven unawares, Ridian summoned Silver to attack Draven from behind, and the wolf came running. But without looking behind him, Draven pointed his sword directly at the wolf, and Ridian called Silver to a sudden stop. No point in them both dying.

"Pathetic," said Draven. "Attacking from behind when I stand before you. That's why my Familiar always watches my back—for weasels like you." Sure enough, behind the Soulcaster, Draven's wolf growling at Silver, hackles raised.

Draven raised his sword for a final attack. Ridian only had one choice. He raised his own sword and flung it. Whirling, it flew straight past Draven and found its real target: Draven's wolf. It sank into the beast's flank and sent the wolf skidding away with a high, tortured yelp. As Draven's eyes widened in abject horror, Ridian covered the distance between them in a flash and kicked Draven across the side of the head in a brutal roundhouse that shattered his skull. Draven crumpled, limp as a jellyfish, his once sharp features mashed and unrecognisable.

Swords rang, and shouts echoed. Feya was hard pressed by two Kyrosians, while the white-bearded brute pinned Lukas to the ground with his heel, sword raised. Ridian scooped up Draven's sword and flew towards the brute. Too late. Even though Ridian sprinted with the speed of a hare, the man's sword plunged into Lukas' chest a split-second before Ridian cleaved the man in two. The man hadn't even seen him coming, and neither did the other two. Two brief sprints and two swipes later, they both lay dead.

With the threats neutralised, Feya floated slowly to the ground.

"Fey, you okay?" asked Ridian.

Feya didn't seem to hear. Without blinking, she was peering past him at the man she'd sliced open earlier, his guts spilling onto the ground.

Then, unreality washed over Ridian as he scanned the others. There were the two he'd just slain. There were more pieces of them than there should be. There was the white-bearded brute he'd cleaved in two. The dark beauty, face down in a pool of blood. And Draven, his mashed skull leaking brains, his dead eyes staring blankly from shattered sockets. Ridian looked at the sword in his hand. It didn't even seem like it was his hand. It felt distant and foreign, but blood was running off the blade and over his knuckles, warm and sticky between his fingers. His mouth filled with rancid saliva, and he keeled over to dry retch, eyes watering with the effort.

Finally, he joined Feya, who was washing her hands by the water. The water was freezing, which helped clear Ridian's mind. Feya's hands looked spotless, but she scrubbed vigorously over and over.

"Why would Hector's nephew kill his own men?" said Lukas, slumped against the retaining wall, blood spreading beneath him. His question was genuine. The last request of a dying man.

"They're not my men!" said Ridian with a burst of displaced anger, marching towards Lukas. "Hector betrayed me. He…" Ridian was going to say more, when a rising of silent music distracted him. The closer he got towards Lukas, the louder it grew. The louder it *called*. Instinctively, reflexively, without even meaning to, Ridian pulled with his mind, and all the ferns about him shrivelled and died. He pulled harder, and watercress, which bobbed on the surface of the water, withered and sank, while moss that clung to the slick rock walls blew away like dust. As Ridian sucked the life from these plants (it was much easier than from the Mural Wall), Rava sang out in a glorious harmony. More and more Rava filled him, and with no injury of his own, it had nowhere to go. Nothing to do. It became overwhelming, nearly painful. Ridian had the image of a dam. *He* was the dam. Then Ridian lay his hand upon Lukas' shoulder—

And Rava burst out of his palm and into Lukas in a great gush. It flowed into him, circulated through him, and began its work. The bruises around Lukas' eyes vanished. His swollen nose shrunk. Colour returned to his face, and within moments, Lukas sat up and blinked in bewilderment. He felt his nose: it was crooked as a dogs hind leg but no longer broken. He pulled down his shirt collar and fingered a new scar. "What—what just happened?" he asked.

Ridian sighed. The effort of holding Rava was immense, but letting it go was an effortless relief.

Feya walked cautiously towards them, her expression one of utter disbelief—like she couldn't believe what she was seeing. "You just healed him. You just healed Lukas."

"I know," said Ridian. "What was I thinking?"

But Feya didn't laugh. "How did you do that? You're like—you're like Fidic."

Silver sidled up to Ridian, and it reminded him of his haste. "Feya," said Ridian, "you think you can make it back up there?" He gestured to the top of Madman's Falls.

Feya pried her puzzled eyes off him to calculate the distance, then nodded. "I've harvested enough wind. I should have enough."

"Good," said Ridian. "Then do it. You'd better go before more come."

Feya nodded, then hesitated—chewing her lip as she always did when anxious and uncertain. Then, before Ridian knew it, she flung herself into his arms. "Don't die," she breathed into his neck. "Don't you dare die."

Ridian was buried in her hair. She smelt of leaves, grass, and wildflowers. She smelt of spring. He clung to her, amazed by how well they fit together. "I won't. I promise." He knew he couldn't promise that. But he meant it. He wanted to stay alive, and not just for his own sake. Feya's life was at stake. The Thunderfells' lives were at stake. But more than that, *thousands* of lives were at stake. And surprisingly, Ridian actually cared about the unknown thousands. He might not know them, but they had value nonetheless. And like Ridian, not just for their own sakes, but for the great network that they belonged to. Everyone, Ridian realised, was related to someone in some way. Whether they be somebody's child, sibling, father, mother, friend, or lover. Everyone had a unique connection to other people that no one else could fill. In that regard, it made everyone irreplaceable. Everyone mattered. Even Lukas, with his stupid, bewildered expression, mattered.

Arms still slung around Ridian's neck, Feya pulled back to look up at him with those dark eyes of hers. Her gaze terrified him, but it was impossible to look away.

"I love you," she breathed, then she pressed her lips against his, and there was nothing but her body, her mouth, and the smell of spring. It was a quick kiss: there and then gone, but Ridian was sure he would remember it for the rest of his life. Then she shoved him away and pointed a stern finger at him. "Don't die," she said sternly. Then she shot upward with a burst of wind, streaming through the air, and disappeared atop Madman's Falls. Ridian waited for a long moment, but she didn't come back for a lingering gaze, and despite the euphoria, a heaviness filled his heart, a heaviness he knew would not go away but only get heavier until he saw her again.

Ridian tore himself away. "Come, Silver. Time to go."

"Where are you going?" asked Lukas.

Ridian had momentarily forgotten all about him. Shivering and soaking wet, he looked so small and pathetic, a man sick with guilt. Ridian was amazed he had ever feared him, and somehow, he couldn't even bring himself to hate him.

"I'm getting reinforcements," said Ridian.

Lukas shook his head. "If the Kyrosians are attacking the Living Fort, they've already secured the southern Gate. They will kill you on sight." Lukas knelt on one knee and bowed his head. "Permit me to go in your stead. Allow me to atone for my transgressions, for I swear upon Holy Hero's Tree, upon Fidic's very grave, that I will not return until your will is done, Fidic's Heir."

Lukas was an even bigger religious nut than Ridian thought. "Lukas, get up."

Lukas obeyed, rising with the solemnity of a priest.

"You can't get the soldiers I'm after," said Ridian. "Stay and help if you can." Then he ran alongside the retaining wall, leapt into the freezing, swift-flowing water, and plunged into the tunnel.

Chapter 45

Utterly blind, Ridian felt the tunnel twist and turn before he was spat out onto the top of the aqueduct. Silver paddled after him, and, together, they let the current carry them speedily towards the Ring Mountains. They loomed slowly, and Ridian's teeth soon chattered from the freezing water. But he wasn't about to jump out. He'd been hardened in recent months with Tann's training, and besides, all Fidicia was at stake.

A long time passed. Silver shivered and whimpered in his arms, until, finally, they entered another tunnel that ran into the Ring Mountains. It swallowed them whole. Silver illuminated the cramped tunnel as it wound on and on beneath the million-ton mountain that bore down upon them. Many long, cold minutes passed, until the subterranean stream finally carried them to the far side of the mountain. They waded ashore, glanced briefly at the towering mountains behind them, then took off along the bank, leaving Fidicia behind.

***

Several hours later, Ridian and Silver stood upon the edge

of The Mire—right where Tann had sliced open Locke's ankle, severing the giant's tendon. It had been a rough trip. Ridian was bruised, scratched, and filthy, and mud almost completely covered Silver.

Ridian had forgotten how much The Mire stank. The reek was terrible, and yet there was still life. Reeds rustled with unseen creatures, and haunting bird cries echoed through the gloomy landscape of sick trees, black pools, and moss-covered boulders.

Where is the secret Waterway? Ridian probed the mud with a stick, and it sank with a squelch. Ridian poked again, and the mud gurgled. With Silver staring on, Ridian squelched around for another ten minutes, poking and prodding until he had an idea: summoning all his willpower, he Split, and entered the black Astral Plane. In this realm, all living things glowed with running, rivulets of light. Reeds shimmered. Moss glowed. Grass shone. Silver and himself were brilliant luminous networks. Their brains—the home of their Souls—were especially dazzling. Ridian willed his soul to roam. Here was a tadpole, there a frog. But most striking was the long, scintillating strip of light that shot out into the horizon—straight as an arrow: the secret Waterway.

Ridian shot back to his body, walked a few dozen paces and stepped upon hard Valarian wood, hidden just beneath the muck. He walked a few tentative steps and almost slipped off the edge. Then he picked up a stick, tapped the wood like a blind man, and shuffled forward. He needed to go faster; Kyros was attacking the Living Fort. Then he remembered: Locke had walked barefoot upon the Walkway. Somehow, the Arden druid had sensed his way across.

Ridian knelt and rested his palm against the lattice-like roots beneath… sure enough, a throbbing undercurrent of silent sound pulsed beneath his fingers, identical to the Wooden Wall. He tore off his filthy boots and slung them over his shoulder. Cold mud squelched between his toes, but he didn't care. Rava thrummed beneath his feet. Then he ran headlong into the fog, listening to the strange music humming beneath him.

Many misty miles passed. Silver skittered at his heels. Rotten trees and giant boulders came and went until he arrived at the abandoned island where Tann, Locke, and himself had passed long ago. Ridian pushed through the trees, into the clearing, and beelined for the same ivy-engulfed cabin that Rayna had supposedly camped in. He tugged the door open and collapsed upon the dusty rat's nest of a bed. A part of him wanted to keep going but he'd just had the longest, most exhausting day of his life: horse-riding, hiking, fighting, swimming, running… he was physically and emotionally depleted, and his poor abused feet would have been bloody stumps if he hadn't healed himself many times along the way.

Just a nap, he promised himself, as he closed his eyes. *Just an hour or so.*

Ridian awoke with a start, knowing instantly that he'd slept too long. Beams of late morning sun thrust through the ivy-covered windows. He jumped from the bed and groaned; his body was stiff and sore beyond belief. "Silver, come. We're late."

Sunrise had profound significance for the Sol, marking the resurrection of their god. And the Sungazers were infamously superstitious. Ridian had hoped to arrive by dawn to win their favour, but since he was late, he would have to arrive at the other most auspicious time of day—midday, when the Sun was at the height of His power. Sunfall was out of the question. That woeful hour would probably see him incinerated on the spot.

The rest of the journey was a slog of burning legs and searing lungs. His stomach growled and his lips were cracked, but worst of all was the anxiety. Almost everyone he knew and loved—including himself—was in mortal danger. Finally, he arrived at Mirecross Castle by noon. The ruinous fortress loomed, as it always had, atop a steep, rising island.

Ridian slowed to a walk. He knew how he would look: a stranger and a wolf striding across the water, emerging from the treacherous and fabled west. Given the many failed expeditions and the supernatural tales that had gripped Arden and Sol imaginations, those within the castle would be on the edge of paranoid. And Ridian needed to inspire trust. His whole plan, such as it was, revolved around it.

As he neared the muddy shoreline, a sentry spotted him from atop the perimeter wall. "Halt! Who goes there?" The man's voice was panicked and attracted two flustered soldiers who cocked crossbows and aimed them at Ridian, twitchier than mice.

Ridian stopped and raised his hands. "My name is Ridian Elderflower. I'm from Mudwall. I am a citizen of the Sol Empire, an adopted child of the Sun, and I claim his generous protection."

The sentries shot sideways glances at each other. They couldn't shoot him—not legally, anyway; the Sun's protection, once claimed, was sacrosanct. Only a priest or priestess could dissolve the safeguard. The soldiers didn't drop their aim, however. "What do you want?"

"Conference with General Selkyrie."

"Why?"

"I offer her a gift."

"What gift?"

"Safe passage west."

The soldiers consulted each other in whispers, until finally, the first sentry said, "Walk up to the gate and stay there. Any funny business and you and your mutt will be shot, protection or no."

Ridian walked slowly, mindful of the crossbows that followed him. He braced himself for the soldiers to lose their frail composure, to twitch a trembling finger—for the *twang* of a loosed bolt. But he made it ashore without a feathered shaft sprouting from his chest. A few minutes passed, then a dozen wary soldiers issued through the gate, hard eyes glaring behind the pronounced cheek-guards and almond-shaped eye slits of their bronze helmets. Half aimed crossbows, the other half pointed spears and hid behind large circular shields. They were all covered in mud, from their sandals to the collars of their red leather breastplates. Getting to Mirecross Castle had evidently been an ordeal for them.

"Kneel, hands upon your head," bellowed a soldier. His helmet had a bristling red crest that ran from ear to ear, symbolic of the rising Sun. It marked him as a Captain.

Ridian obeyed.

"Bind him," said the Captain, and a soldier advanced with a coil of rope.

Silver leapt forward and snarled at the advancing soldier,

snapping chunks out of the air. The soldier lurched back, and crossbows and spears swiveled to point at the wolf.

"No, don't shoot!" said Ridian.

"Then leash the beast yourself," said the soldier, flinging the rope at Ridian, who caught it.

The rope was coarse, and Ridian couldn't bear the idea of tying Silver up, so he calmed Silver with his mind, feeling his own anxiety bristle as he did. *Stay*, said Ridian inwardly. *I'll be fine.*

A minute later, Silver whined upon the muddy beach as Ridian was marched through the gate and up the stairs towards the castle. Ridian tried to send a wave of reassurance to his wolf, though he felt none himself. As they climbed, crumbling ruins loomed on either side, silent and desolate. Not a soul was in sight—only wary birds watching from hardy trees that had taken root in windows, rooftops, and cracks in the walls. A few twists and turns through the cramped street later, and Mirecross Castle appeared. It stood grim upon the hill with its shattered tower and fire-blackened walls.

An old bonfire smouldered before the large double doors, and as they drew near, Ridian was sickened to see a human skeleton resting upon the bed of ash. It was bleached white with black fracture lines. The yawning ribcage and grinning skull were large enough to belong to a cow. *So Locke did crawl all the way back home,* thought Ridian, feeling little sympathy for the cruel semi-giant.

Ridian's escort marched him past the bonfire, through the large doors, and into the Great Hall. Ridian barely recognised the place. All six fireplaces roared, filling the once dank place with red firelight and a moist tropical heat. And the elaborate wall-to-wall tapestry of The Last Stand Ridian had so admired had also been torn down, replaced with the Sol flag—a blood-red sun upon a black sky. Daegan's Sword had also been removed, though Daegan's oath, the Elderlion credo, remained etched into the wall: *Never shall the east touch the west.*

The place swarmed with soldiers who attended to every duty: butchering carcasses, tending fires, cleaning armour, reinforcing the collapsing minstrels' loft, tearing boards from the arched windows, and constructing bunks. If Ridian's plan failed, Fidician soldiers would be press-ganged into their ranks and shipped to some distant battlefront halfway across the world. Still, it was a better fate than Kyros indulging his perverse vengeance.

Through the commotion, Ridian was shoved towards the brightest fire where the dark-skinned Selkyrie glared with piercing, hawk-like eyes at three nervous-looking men.

"Unacceptable," she said, pursing tight, gold-painted lips. "I don't want excuses. I want results. Find the path back to Mudwall or you'll be finding a pathway westward—alone. Is that clear?" Her exotic voice was deep and rich and powerful.

The three men nodded. "Yes, General."

"Take the girl if you think it helpful." Selkyrie gestured at Kaisy Prillan, who sat hugging herself, blank-faced in the corner.

"It will be done." The men bowed and scurried away. One grabbed Kaisy by the elbow. She didn't resist. She hardly seemed to notice. Ridian felt a pang of sympathy for her. After her torment at Locke's hands, Kaisy had evidently made her way home, only to be forced straight back to

Mirecross Castle to serve as a guide.

Selkyrie strode to the table at the heart of the hall to loom behind a man who pored over a map. As she moved, the roaring fire she had stood besidesdwindled to a dull, flameless glow. "This whole section is blank," Selkyrie said, pointing at the map with a gold-painted fingernail.

"Well, General, given the heavy fog, it's impossible to…" The man faltered, withering beneath Selkyrie's menacing gaze. It was Jakeer, the creep who had ogled Rayna the day of Sunfall. He swallowed, Adam's apple bobbing up and down, and he ran his hand through his thin wisp of hair. "Forgive me, General. I will survey immediately and rectify the inadequacy." Flustered, Jakeer rolled the map and began gathering his cartography things—ink, quill, caliper, compass, and more.

"General," said the captain. "A prisoner requesting conference."

"Prisoner?" Selkyrie narrowed her gold, hawk-like eyes at Ridian, and fear seemed to reach out and grip Ridian by the throat.

"Yes, General," said the Captain. "He approached from the west and requested the Sun's protection, claiming to have a gift for you. Calls himself…"

"Ridian of Mudwall," interrupted Selkyrie. The air around her shivered with radiating heat waves, and Ridian felt another bolt of anxiety as the image of Locke's burnt skeleton flickered across his mind.

"I know you," said Jakeer, with an armful of implements. "You're the one in league with the outlaw Tann. General, he's the one I told you about. He's the one who—"

Selkyrie glared at him, and Jakeer snapped his mouth shut.

"I know who he is. He's the Caveborn bastard with a witch for a sister." As she approached, waves of heat rolled off her. "He helped murder Sol soldiers and even a sacred Sungazer." The statement was a verdict.

"We shall add him to the pyre," said the captain, and strong hands dragged Ridian towards the door.

"Wait," said Ridian, to Selkyrie's already turned back. "I can guide you across The Mire."

Selkyrie stopped mid-stride, and the soldiers halted. Ridian could feel others in the room turning to look. *That got their attention.*

Selkyrie turned to narrow her eyes at him. "You lie."

"He did approach from the west," the captain conceded. "It looked like he was walking upon water."

"A witch's trick," spat Selkyrie, face puckering in disgust.

"No," said Ridian. "An illusion. Nothing more. A pathway lies just below the waterline—strong, straight, and true. It will save you months of scouting and perhaps years of infrastructure trying to build a road across The Mire. Besides, seizing pagan structures is the Sol way."

"Do not lecture me on the Sol way," snapped Selkyrie, and the air around her quivered anew from a strong burst of heat that made Ridian shy away. "Even if there is a path, even if you take us across, *even* if it's everything you say, your life is forfeit."

"But I didn't kill the soldiers or the Sungazer—Tann did. Ask Jakeer."

Selkyrie rounded on Jakeer. "You said *they* killed our men."

"Oh, well. You know…" Cornered, Jakeer looked around the room for support. He found none. "He didn't land the blows himself, but he didn't stop Tann either."

"And you did?" said Ridian. "You pissed yourself and ran."

There was a terrible silence as Jakeer blushed in anger. Ridian was taking an awful risk offending him. Ridian's disrespect of Jakeer, a religious ordinand, might be perceived as disrespect for his adopted religion: an unpardonable sin. But Jakeer was career-driven—more interested in climbing social ladders than praying. Surely the keen, zealous eye of Selkyrie knew his false intentions, and Ridian was banking on harnessing her obvious contempt for the man. Besides, Jakeer *had* run away, and for the militant Sol empire, cowardice was an unconscionable flaw, to be treated with disdain.

Everyone waited for Selkyrie's response. At last, she offered the faintest smirk, and the soldiers around her sniggered, turning Jakeer's face a blotchy red.

"Look at me," said Ridian, taking advantage of the break in tension. "Do I look like I could kill Sol's finest soldiers barehanded?"

"And the Sungazer?" asked Selkyrie, eyes narrowed.

"Tann was an excellent fighter, but he was no match for the Sungazer. He was overpowered in seconds. But his wolf snuck up on the Sungazer and attacked the man unawares."

Ridian could tell by the way Selkyrie nodded her approval that this was the story she wanted: a Sungazer dying not in direct one-on-one combat, but by a cowardly trick.The story also had the benefit of being true. *But now for the first lie.* "I followed Tann across The Mire under a pretense of friendship. I learned valuable secrets—secrets I wish to offer you—and then I killed Tann as he slept, which is more than he deserved."

"So you say," said Selkyrie.

"It's the truth." Ridian's voice rang with a conviction that he did not feel.

"So, you've avenged our dead and can lead us across The Mire?" Selkyrie's voice was sharp with skepticism. "Sounds too good to be true. Why? Why help us? To atone for your sister?"

Now for the second lie. "No. My sister is a witch. I denounce her."

Selkyrie frowned, genuinely surprised. "Why would an edge-dwelling Mudwall bastard be so obliging?"

"Not just a bastard—a *Caveborn.*" Ridian glared about the room, showcasing his infamous silver-flecked eyes. "Yes, I know what I am: a child of darkness, a witch's son, a witch's brother. But it's because I was born into darkness that I so revere the light." Ridian looked about the room, pausing for what he hoped was a meaningful silence. *And now for the grand lie.* "I help because the Sun has purified me. I help because I revere the Sun. I help because I wish to join the Holy Order." Ridian knelt and bowed his head to the floor, hoping to convey the pious devotion of a believer—not the desperation of a prisoner. "I humbly ask for the privilege to help convert the pagans across The Mire to the All Seeing Sun."

"Outrageous," said Jakeer. "Letting a treacherous little Caveborn bastard—"

"Silence!" snapped Selkyrie, and Jakeer shut his mouth so quickly he might have chipped some teeth. Selkyrie stepped forward. "What do you mean, 'pagans across The Mire'?"

"Across The Mire is a fertile land with many pagan souls," said Ridian. "They are hungry—*starving*—for Sol Dogma.

Even through my pitiful teachings, many have converted. But when they saw the Sunfire spiralling into the sky last night, they all cried out for a fiery baptism." Ridian let his impassioned voice fall flat. "I could have harvested more souls, but I left before the invaders could cut me off."

"Invaders?" said the captain.

"Yes, they are being besieged as we speak by northerners called Kyrosians."

Selkyrie looked thoughtful. "These pagans are willing to convert, you say?"

"Oh, they are most eager," said Ridian, earnestly. He let his face drop. "Only, we're too late." Ridian was relieved nobody seemed to object to his deliberate use of the word 'we'. "They'll be wiped out in a matter of days. The invaders are a powerful warrior nation. Tann's people, in fact. They pray to some warrior god. For them, war is worship, killing a form of prayer."

"War is worship?" Selkyrie cocked an eyebrow, amused.

Ridian nodded. "Tann told me all about them. He said they have the strongest soldiers in all the world. That nothing could stop them, not even the Sol with all their spears and fiery gimmicks, as he said." Ridian wanted to say more, but he didn't want his story to be overwrought. He needed Selkyrie's pride to be pricked without rousing her suspicions. It was a delicate balance. She appeared deep in thought, until she finally nodded to herself as if making up her mind. "And what is the name of this warrior god?"

"His name?" said Ridian with a rush of panic. "The warrior god's name?" He'd thought his lies out in painstaking detail ever since he'd left Fidicia, but he couldn't think of everything. "Kyros," he said at last. "Kyros the Great, though his enemies call him The Terrible."

"Kyros the Terrible," said Selkiyrie with a sinister smile. "A good name… for a made-up god." She walked towards Ridian, and the heat radiating from her intensified. "You lie well, child of darkness. But the Sun sees all. Let me tell you what I see. There are a people at risk of annihilation from a foreign force. That is true. And you know how to cross The Mire. However, you greatly exaggerate these people's willingness to convert, and your devotion to the Sun is an outright lie. No. Some other motive brought you here." Selkyrie's eyes filled as if with searing, molten gold, and Ridian shrank from the sweltering heat bursting from her. When she spoke, her voice grated, harsh as stone upon stone. "It matters not. The Sun is good. He uses even lies and corrupt motives to fulfil his designs." She stretched a clawed hand towards the hearth, and a great tongue of fire leapt across the room towards her. Flames funnelled into her clawed hand and began to swirl into a flaming golden sphere. Then, with a crazed look of triumph, she raised her hand, and the revolving ball of fire ascended. "The Sun is good," she cried as the sun-like ball floated towards the ceiling, growing larger and hotter as it did. "Through lies, truth. Through treachery, opportunity."

Then the gold filling Selkyrie's eyes drained away, and the revolving sun winked out. "Captain, prepare to march at first light."

Chapter 46

The march to Fidicia took three days: a day to the abandoned island, a day to the western shore, and a day to get within sight of Fidicia's southern Gates. During those three stressful days, Ridian worried non-stop and answered a near-ceaseless battery of questions from General Selkyrie: *how many Fidicians are there? How many Kyrosians? How big are their armies? What weapons do they use? Describe the landscape. Describe the fortifications. Tell me about their religion. Their history. Their culture. Their system of government. Their export and import of goods...* Clearly, Selkyrie distrusted him. She made that plain by keeping his hands bound and by narrowing her eyes during her interrogations. And since she'd proved herself preternaturally shrewd, Ridian answered truthfully, only making the occasional omission, exaggeration, or embellishment to nudge Selkyrie towards attacking the Kyrosians with all haste. Thankfully, the General wanted to colonise Fidicia, which meant saving it first. In that, Ridian and Selkyrie were aligned, and that alignment allowed Ridian to sneak a few crucial lies in. When it came to telling truths, Ridian was especially careful to describe the location and cultural significance of Hero's Tree, knowing the Sol Way was to appropriate religious customs whenever possible. He was banking on this, hoping the Sungazers would preserve Hero's Tree and his sister's soul inside. He just hoped Selkyrie bought the truths and deceptions he thought essential to saving Fidicia.

Saving Fidicia... was that what Ridian was doing? The thought of a Sol-occupied Fidicia was grim: they would lose their religion, their culture, and their history. Many Fidicians would be conscripted or shipped off to colonize distant lands, and the Sol Empire would destroy or appropriate everything that made Fidicia what it was. It would be cultural genocide. *Still better than Kyros*, Ridian would assure himself, imagining the man torturing every man, woman, and child until death. He might not be able to save Fidicia, but he might save its people.

When Ridian and the Sol company finally arrived near the base of the Ring Mountains, the soldiers set up camp upon a bald hilltop with tremendous efficiency. Scouting, posting guard, collecting firewood, prepping food, cooking food, erecting tents—everyone knew their duty. Even Ridian, who allowed himself to be tied to a tree.

They were a small group: Ridian, General Selkyrie, three other Sungazers, and only forty soldiers. The forty were a rough, mean-looking lot, complete with scars, missing ears, and permanent scowls. No mere conscripts but career soldiers. Veterans all. But in the end, they were merely bodyguards. It would be the Sungazers who would decimate Hector and Kyros' Soulcaster army. One Sungazer was an imposing, muscle-bound man with piercing sky-blue irises. The second was a long-faced man with white irises that made his pupils seem tiny. The third was an impossibly tall woman with black irises that made her pupils appear massive. Ridian had never seen any of them smile.

And as their sacred sun fell behind the Ring Mountains, Selkyrie gathered everyone at the center of the camp. "Almighty, All-Seeing One!" she cried, arms raised towards the darkening western sky.

"You fall that we might rise!" chanted the Sol party as Ridian sat bound to a tree.

"Almighty, All-Knowing!" Selkyrie cried again.

"We know you shall return!"

"Almighty, All-Giving!"

"Please give and give again!"

"Almighty, Ever-Faithful!"

"You delivered on your promises!"

"Almighty, source of Light!"

"Punish those who summon the night!"

"Almighty, Greatest Fire!"

"GRANT US POWER!" With those words, the Sungazers extended their hands, and the unlit pyre burst into a sudden, crackling flame.

After dinner, the soldiers turned in for the night while Selkyrie and her Sungazers stayed awake. Stark naked and unashamed, they huddled about the bonfire, soaking up the flames. Ridian's eyes wandered over Selkyrie's flawless mahogany skin, shining in the flickering firelight. Dreadlocks cascaded over her firm breasts and lean shoulders; it was impossible not to look.

Eventually, Ridian fell asleep, only to wake with a start, his neck aching. Selkyrie and her Sungazers remained basking in the bonfire's heat as it crackled and popped and sent glowing motes drifting into the night sky. They conversed intently.

What are they saying? Ridian had a bad feeling. Selkyrie said they would attack tomorrow at midday—at the height of the Sun's power. Ridian had taken great pains to explain the layout of the Living Fort in relation to Last Stand Meadow, so no harm would come to the Fidicians. But doubt plagued him. What if there was some misunderstanding? What if Kyros had already broken through? What if Selkyrie underestimated Kyros' Soulcasters? What if Selkyrie stalled and allowed the Kyrosians to wipe the Fidicians out?

Unable to bear the uncertainty, Ridian reached for Silver with his mind. He sensed his wolf nearby. The wolf had successfully remained hidden since Mirecross Castle. Ridian then Split from his body and slid into Silver's. Immediately, the smell of moss, moist earth, fermenting leaves, and a dozen other fragrances of the forest filled his nose. Through Silver's eyes, Ridian peered about. The wolf was staring through a thicket at the firelit camp a little way off.

With a mental nudge from Ridian, Silver crept forward, silent as a shadow. Sentries were placed evenly around the crown of the hill, and Silver's keen eyes could see them all: pacing, slouching, or standing to attention. Ridian waited for one guard to stroll left and another to gaze right before urging Silver to slip past and into the row of tents to crouch between a pair of round shields balancing against each other. From there, Ridian could see himself tied to the tree. He looked asleep, his hair ablaze with a cold, silver fire.

Selkyrie and her Sungazers were breathing deeply and in unison. The flames of the bonfire pulsed with them, waxing and waning with each passing breath as if blown by a pair of giant bellows.

"We've overextended ourselves," said the blue-eyed Sungazer in a fathoms-deep voice. "Our supply line is non-existent. It places us in a precarious situation."

Selkyrie nodded. "True. Which is why a quick seizure is paramount. We require resources from both ends of The Mire."

"It's a good plan," said the white-eyed woman, the lean muscles of her long limbs flexing as she panted. "Only I wonder if sparing these Fidicians would prove more profitable. If we save them rather than exterminate them, perhaps their gratitude would make them willing subjects. Subjects that can be better utilised alive than dead."

Ridian's heart sank within Silver's chest. *No, I heard wrong. Surely.*

Selkyrie shook her head. "If you want control, fear trumps gratitude. Gratitude is fleeting and unreliable. Fear is dependable and permanent if well-maintained. Slaves obey the whip, not the master, as it were. Don't get me wrong. In another place, another culture, I might agree with you. Making allies and establishing harmonious footholds is essential for a successful campaign. But this Fidicia is the spiritual capital of this land. If we destroy this place, if we burn their temples, banish their false god, and kill all their holy men and women, we do more than destroy one city: we destroy that which unifies them—faith, culture, *belief.* It's not enough to control with fear alone. Sooner or later, seeds of courage take root, and the people will rise against us. But if we destroy who they are, their sense of self, their collective identity…if we abolish their songs, their stories, their history…if they forget who they are, they have nothing to fight for. Tomorrow these Fidicians will be vanquished, and in a year there will still be grief. But in twenty, there will be acceptance. And in a hundred years, from mind to marrow, these Fidicians will be Sol."

The Sungazers bowed their heads deferentially to Selkyrie and her apparent wisdom.

They're going to massacre everyone. Ridian could feel Silver's tucked tail and downturned ears. What had he done, bringing these living weapons here? What stupid pigheaded arrogance had made Ridian think he could control them? He couldn't let this happen. He couldn't.

Ridian guided Silver away from the bonfire and the talk of genocide. Slipping past tent openings and sleeping soldiers, Ridian saw himself tied to the tree. He urged Silver around the back of the tree and examined the rope that bound him, careful not to be seen by a nearby sentry. The rope coiled about Ridian's body a dozen times, then twice around the tree, before ending in a big, fat knot. He sank Silver's jaws over the knot and chewed. It was slow going, but the rope fibers began to fray and fill his mouth. Finally, with the knot half tattered, Ridian shot back into his own body and strained against the cords. Initially, it didn't budge; but he drew Rava, and the rope snapped with a little *twang*.

Ridian was shimmying out of his bonds when a sentry strolled into view. Ridian froze. Slowly, agonisingly, the soldier sauntered towards him. Silver slunk behind the trunk to remain hidden, while Ridian tried his best to remain inconspicuous, though he was certain the soldier would hear his hammering heartbeat. But no, the soldier barely glanced at Ridian as he past. All seemed well... until the soldier stopped abruptly and whirled around, eyes widening as he took in the loose coils of rope upon Ridian's lap. He went to shout, but Ridian leapt quick as silver and slapped a hand over his mouth. A moment later, Ridian's arm was about his throat. The soldier kicked and thrashed, but he was no match for Ridian's supernatural strength, and he soon dangled unconscious in Ridian's arms.

Letting out a slow, ragged breath, Ridian scanned the camp: guards stood or strolled; sleepers snored; and the naked Sungazers bathed before the sweltering bonfire, oblivious. Reassured, Ridian tied the unconscious soldier to the tree, and gagged him with a strip of the man's cloak.

Ridian grabbed the man's spear, and then he and Silver crept towards the bonfire. He couldn't allow Selkyrie to murder everyone. It was his fault for bringing the crazy bitch here in the first place, and so it fell to him to stop her. Crouching, they skulked along until they were within a dozen paces of the flushed and breathless Sungazers who luxuriated in the heat. Ridian's hands tingled as he imagined the next few moments: he'd throw the spear at Selkyrie and rush the nearest Sungazer, while Silver attacked another. From there, if he hadn't been burnt to a crisp, he'd attack the last Sungazer before anyone knew what was happening. Slowly, he raised the spear and aimed. He couldn't miss. If he did, he, Silver, and thousands of Fidicians would die. The Thunderfells would die.

Then, as he hefted the spear, a realisation struck him. If he killed the Sungazers, presuming he could kill them all—and he needed to kill them all—Kyros would still be alive. He'd still overthrow Fidicia, and the Thunderfells would still suffer a long, torturous, unspeakable death. A quick Sunfire incineration was probably better than that. But he had another idea, a desperate, risky idea, but still the best one at hand.

Ridian slunk away, and, after an intense Rava-fueled sprint, stood before the southern gates of Fidicia, hope and horror filling his heart.

Chapter 47

"Hey!" shouted Ridian.

The southern gate did not answer.

"Hey!" Ridian cried again.

Then an elderly, bleary-eyed watchman appeared upon the gatehouse battlements. "Who are you and what do you want?" he said in a disgruntled voice.

"I'm Ridian, Hector's nephew, and I demand you let me in at once."

"Hector's nephew?" said the old watchman with surprise.

"Open the gate! It's a matter of urgency."

The watchman leaned over the parapet to squint down at him. "Come closer. The moon's a hiding. Can't see a damn thing."

Ridian came within a few feet of the iron portcullis and gazed up.

"It's him," said a younger man, popping a head over the battlement. "That's Hector's nephew, alright."

"You sure?"

"Who else has eyes like that?"

The old man shouted an order, and chains clinked, gears groaned, and the portcullis began to rise. Ridian ducked beneath the rising gate and sped into the narrow canyon beyond. It was very dark, and it was only by the glow of Silver's coat that Ridian was able to dash through the winding ravine. Before long, the expansive Fidician valley appeared, and Ridian wasted no time plunging down into the fabled valley. At the bottom, down by Raven's River, the place was a mess. Windows were shattered, doors hung broken, and furniture, clothes, cutlery, books, and a hundred other belongings spilled out onto the street. A few Kyrosians rifled through the wreckage, scavenging for plunder. One shattered a plate against a wall; his mate laughed, then threw a stone through a window. Nobody noticed Ridian and Silver as they sped up the road to the Living Fort.

Soon enough, they passed the Thunderfells' home. It was dead quiet and looked gutted: belongings spilled from the open doorway and were strewn along the garden path as if the house had vomited up its possessions. There were Ollie's books, Kess' pots, Elle's toys, and a broken chair from the dining table. They were just possessions, he knew, but he was sad all the same. Whose chair had been ruined? Theodor's? Kess'? Kai's? His own? Whoever it belonged to, they would never sit in it again. He shook his head and ran on. *It's just stuff. It can all be replaced.*

At last, Ridian and Silver crested the hill onto Last Stand Meadow, and as Ridian slowed to a brisk walk, he beheld the Kyrosian camp. It was far larger than he imagined. It surrounded the u-shaped outer wall of the Living Fort in a great semi-circular barricade. There were thousands of Kyrosians. Hector must have emptied all of Sky Island to comprise this force. And though it was large, it was also a shambles. There were no neat rows or avenues to walk down like the tidy little Sol camp he'd just left, but a sprawling litter of makeshift tents and dodgy shelters.

To Ridian's tremendous relief, nobody was presently attacking the Living Fort. It's tree towers swayed gently in the breeze, peaceful in the night.

As Ridian approached the camp, he drew his hood over his eyes, just like he'd always done in Mudwall. Being Hector's nephew had been helpful at the southern Gate, but not now. Now, he needed to slip through unrecognised, and the last thing he needed was for his bloody Caveborn eyes to give him away. But as he drew closer, he realised he needn't have worried. There were no guards, not even a hint of discipline. If it weren't for the moaning injured, it might have been a festival. People drank and sang and danced about campfires. One man jigged atop a rolling barrel to the beat of a lively drum. Wolves gnawed on bones. Great cats stretched before fires. A woman ran past Ridian, shrieking with laughter, as a man chased her and pinched her backside. A hawk swooped over a barbecue and snatched a string of sausages to a chorus of drunken laughter. Indeed, nobody gave two spits in a can for Ridian and Silver. Everybody was too busy drinking, feasting, and making merry.

So far so good, thought Ridian, halfway through the festive barricade. Then his heart turned to ice as he saw Feya—

She was chained to a whipping post, arms shackled overhead. Asleep or unconscious, her bruised face rested against the rough wood of the post, and blood ran from her nose and all the way down her neckline. And her back was a bloody mess. Dozens of lacerations streaked across it as if some giant bird had been scratching for feed.

The sight of her hit Ridian like a slammed door. He

couldn't believe what he was seeing. She shouldn't be here. She should be safe atop Madman's Falls, inside the hospital. But then Ridian saw Lukas—in a similar state beside her—and the story became painfully clear. Kyrosians had attacked Lukas at Madman's Falls, Feya tried to save him, and they were both captured.

Anger and fear boiled Ridian's blood. It coursed through his veins and cleared his head. He scanned the area: there was no guards. In fact, nobody seemed to notice the half-dead Fidician prisoners. Everybody was too busy having the time of their lives.

Fists shaking, Ridian strode towards Feya, his concern for being recognised momentarily forgotten. As he drew closer to her, the trampled grass around him sang out, and what he did next was pure instinct. He *pulled* with a single, rage-fueled flex of his mind, and all the grass about him in a fifteen-foot radius died in a flash. Rava sang out as it left the blades of grass and flooded into Ridian, and then again as it re-directed itself into Feya. By the time he knelt beside her and laid a tender hand on her shoulder, the bloody grooves tearing across her back had healed into a patchwork of pale white streaks.

"Feya," he whispered. "You okay?"

Feya's groggy eyes fluttered open, then she jerked away with a jangle of chains in fear.

"It's okay," said Ridian, showing his open palms. "It's me. It's Ridian."

Feya peeped from behind her protecting arm and her terror slowly melted into confusion. "What—what are you doing here?" She glanced about like a furtive animal. "Leave, quick," she hissed. "Before someone sees you."

"It's okay," said Ridian. "Nobody cares." But as he said it, he noticed a man frowning at him from a nearby table. The man nudged the woman beside him and whispered something, and the woman looked up to scrutinise Ridian. They continued to whisper until the man pushed back his seat and began to rise. At the same time, a wolf crept out from beneath the table.

Heart lurching, Ridian stood abruptly. "You think you're better than me?" he shouted at Feya. "Huh? Do you? You Fidician whore!"

"What are you…" began Feya.

"Act scared," said Ridian, between his teeth, trying not to move his lips.

"What?" asked Feya.

"Act…" Ridian sighed. "Never mind." Then he slapped Feya—smartly, not savagely—with enough force to make his own palm sting. He felt sick, but it was enough to make the man stop in his tracks.

Ridian raised his fist. "You'll get my knuckles next if you don't learn respect. Cover yourself up, harlot!" And Ridian tied the back of Feya's torn shirt up as best he could.

The suspicious man snorted a laugh, sat back down, and clinked his goblet against the woman's. His wolf crawled back beneath the table to gnaw on a bone.

"Sorry," whispered Ridian. "Had to waylay suspicion."

"Hope it worked," said Feya, stretching her jaw. "At least it doesn't hurt as much as… wait. My back." She looked up at him with her big, beautiful, dark eyes. "You healed me? Wow. Are you going to heal Lick-Ass as well?"

"Don't worry about me," Lukas croaked, who looked on the verge of passing out. "Don't risk yourself on my account.

You're too important. Leave before it's too late."

"I think I preferred Lukas kicking your ass, not kissing it," said Feya.

Ridian snorted a laugh, then healed Lukas' injuries with decidedly more effort than it had taken to heal Feya. He had to reach further for fresh grass, and he was just so tired.

"Lukas is right," said Feya. "You should get out of here."

But Ridian wasn't listening. His eyes had been drawn to a man in a packed prison wagon walled with iron bars. The surrounding prisoners slouched where they could, but this man lay on his stomach upon the rough wooden floor, all four limbs bound uncomfortably behind his back.

It was Tann.

Already, his bruised face was thinner and reminiscent of the gaunt corpse Ridian had seen upon The Mire. How was the man still alive? Surely the other prisoners had snuck him water. The sight of Tann broke Ridian's heart, even though he had planned to kill Rayna. But had he, though? Was that just another lie from Hector? Regardless, Ridian was moved to pity. He went over and grasped the bars, onlookers be damned. "Tann," he whispered.

The sleeping Tann didn't respond.

Ridian tried again, and his mentor's eyelids slowly opened as far as his swollen face would allow. His eyes were bloodshot, and it took them a long time to focus. When they did, they were anguished.

"Go away," said Tann flatly, and he turned his head away, the only movement he could do.

"Tann, I'm…" Ridian stalled. He couldn't believe he was here again—saying sorry for abandoning him. But it was worse this time. This time, Tann felt betrayed, and Mal was nowhere to be seen. That could only mean one thing. No, saying sorry wasn't enough. And so, Ridian pulled Rava from the surrounding meadow grass with enormous effort. There was considerable healing needed; beneath the bruised skin lay many broken bones.

Tann turned back to look at Ridian. He blinked about in astonishment, his shocked face free of swelling and bruising. "What are you doing to me?"

"I'm saving you."

Tann snorted. "Nice try. But I won't be fooled. Not again."

He thinks I've drugged him the same as Tinker. Indeed, Ridian's words, 'I'm saving you,' sounded hollow even to him. Could Ridian save him? He looked at Feya, who was glaring at him to leave. Could he break them out and make a run for it? No. They'd never make it. Could he wait till the Kyrosians slept and sneak them out? No, there were dozens of Fidician prisoners—too many for a stealthy getaway. Besides, the Kyrosians looked ready to party all night. Ridian shook his head. No, he had to be smart, and he had to be bold. The time for sneaking around was over.

He went to a nearby trestle table, snatched an unattended waterskin, and passed it through the bars into the hands of an unsuspecting prisoner. "Give him some water," said Ridian to the confused woman. "Not too much at first, and just a little bit at a time, but keep him alive." Ridian met Tann's skeptical eyes. "I don't expect you to forgive me," said Ridian. "I certainly don't deserve it. But perhaps you can find it in your heart not to hate me."

"What the hell are you doing?" said the suspicious man from before. He stormed over, grabbed Ridian's shoulder, and spun him about. "Get away from him, and don't you dare give him some water." The terrified prisoner dropped the waterskin.

Ridian pulled his hood back, seized the man about the collar, and pulled him close. "Do you know who I am?"

Silver and the man's Familiar were at each of their Companion's sides in a flash, growling and snapping their jaws.

The man bristled, thrumming with a sudden inrush of Rava. "I don't give a spit who you are," he hissed, but then his eyes widened, and he wilted in Ridian's hand. "Forgive me. I—I didn't recognise you."

"Not just Hector's nephew," said Ridian. "The blood of Kyros. Where is he?"

The man swallowed and pointed a trembling finger at a giant pavilion some distance away. "That's his tent," he said. "Should be there."

Ridian flung the man away, and he and his Familiar scampered off. Tann's eyes remained narrow and wary.

"No tricks, Tann," said Ridian. "I was confused. But I'm not confused any more." Then he marched over to an astonished Feya and kissed her on the forehead. "It's going to be okay. I'm going to get you all free." He looked back at Tann. "I am sorry." Then he marched off to Kyros' pavilion, not daring to look back lest he lose his nerve. He passed campfires surrounded by drinkers, dancers, and singers— all red-faced and jolly. But as he drew close, he saw sober guards surrounding the pavilion. They were alert and stoic and totally at odds with the surrounding revelry. It made Ridian's heart drum against his ribcage.

Ridian was thinking through his plan when Chirpy fluttered in from nowhere. "Ridian?" cheeped the tiny bird as it fluttered before him. "You're alive! You're healed! You must have healed yourself! That's—that's great! That's wonderful!" The bird sounded sincere, and Ridian felt a tiny wave of affection for his uncle.

No, thought Ridian, steeling himself. *No manipulation. No mind games. Not this time.*

"Save it, Hector. We need to talk."

"What do you want to talk about?"

"I have a deal for you."

"A deal?"

"You want peace, don't you? Or was that a lie as well?"

"Of course I want peace."

Ridian snorted; the bloody bird had the audacity to sound offended. "Then let the people of Fidicia walk free and you can have Fidicia. You can have the valley. It can be yours. Just let the Fidicians go."

"Ridian," said the bird cautiously. "A deal like that can only be broached by the Fidician leaders. Besides…" Chirpy spun midair to glance back at the pavilion. "I'm not exactly in charge any more…"

Ridian didn't need to ask. He knew. And, heart thumping, he marched past the bird.

Chirpy fluttered back in front of Ridian to block his way. "Listen, Ridian. Kyros is single-minded and not to be trifled with. Trust me, he won't listen to you."

"Trust you?" Ridian laughed mirthlessly and went to swat the bird aside, but the bird dodged him quick as a fly.

Ahead, two Soulcasters and their wolves blocked the pavilion entrance.

"No further," said one guard, holding up a hand. "What's your business?"

"I come on behalf of the people of Fidicia. I wish to make a deal."

The guards looked at Chirpy. "This true?"

Chirpy hesitated before saying, "Yes."

The guard's face hardened. "You'll need to be searched, and no funny business."

"It's okay," said Chirpy. "He's with me."

The guard didn't budge. "With all due respect, Hector, we're not letting him in without a search."

Ridian spread his arms. "Go ahead."

The guards patted Ridian roughly down, leaving no part of him untouched. Once satisfied, a guard nodded at Silver and said, "And no Familiars."

Ridian looked down into his wolf's luminous silver eyes. *Sorry, boy. You'll have to stay.* The wolf could sense Ridian's rising anxiety and didn't want to leave. Nevertheless, with Ridian's insistence, Silver padded a few paces away and sat.

"Sorry," said Chirpy. "Kyros can be a bit…" But the finch glanced at the guards and said no more.

Ridian was following the guards towards the pavilion entrance when a strange thing happened: the slight trickle of Rava he'd been drawing from Silver suddenly vanished. It was as if the Rava had simply winked out. He could still sense Silver, he could still *feel* their bond, but the Rava itself was being stolen. Hardly able to breathe, Ridian stepped into the pavilion.

Chapter 48

A fire burned at the heart of the lavish pavilion, casting a warm light upon rich tapestries, plush carpets, and decorated pillars. Oil lamps hung from tasseled cords, and candles flickered in ornate candelabras. Refinery adorned every corner—the spoils of a sacked Fidicia. And the air was thick with tobacco, garlic, blue-cheese, lemon zest, peppermint, turmeric, and a dozen other fragrances. A pan flutist and two guitarists played a sultry tune, while a pair of scantily clad women danced along, bangles jingling on their wrists and ankles. Half a dozen onlookers lounged in idle comfort.

Hector sat behind an oak desk, its surface covered with maps and papers. He leaned heavily upon the tabletop to stand, grunting with the effort. He smiled broadly at Ridian, but it didn't seem to reach his eyes. "You may leave," he said to the guards with a nod.

The guards looked across the pavilion towards Kyros, who lay upon a scatter of pillows and gazed at the half-naked dancers. Ridian found it hard to look at him. He looked exactly like Rayna—only his bearing, his manner, and his presence were entirely different. An attractive woman lay at his side, and he patted a large wolf with a carefree hand.

Sevron's wolf, Ridian realised with surprise.

One of the guards whispered in Kyros' ear, and he dismissed the guards with a casual flick of the wrist.

Hector shuffled painfully around the table. "Ridian," he said with all the fondness of a doting uncle. "It's good to see you."

Again, Ridian felt a wave of unexplained affection for the double amputee, and he squashed it with rage and disgust. "I have nothing to say to you."

The music became upbeat and lively, and the dancers took turns leaping over the fire.

"Ridian…" Hector began.

"Actually," said Ridian bitterly. "I do have something to say. You are a liar, a manipulator, and a betrayer. And your words are nothing but sweet-sounding bullshit."

Hector's lips pressed together. "You have every right to be angry," he said in a restrained voice. "I lied to you, and I lied to your sister. It's true. I betrayed you both. But—"

Whatever was going to come out of Hector's mouth, Ridian didn't want to hear it. "I'm here to cut a deal, not listen to your drivel." And he turned his back on Hector. The man was no longer in charge. It was Kyros he needed to negotiate with.

The music jumped to double-time, and the dancers began twirling twice as fast. From the corner of his eye, he saw Hector drop his head, and his knuckles tighten around the head of his walking sticks.

Ridian felt a twinge of regret, then hardened his heart. *He's trying to manipulate you.*

The music stopped, and the flushed, breathless dancers froze in a final seductive pose.

Kyros leapt from the pillows to applaud in earnest. As he did, he knocked over a tray, spraying a bowl of fruit, bread, cheese, nuts and more over the carpet. He laughed at his carelessness and continued clapping. *"Enchanting!"* he cried. *"A feast for the ears!"* He bowed to the band, who bowed twice as low in return, and then he winked at the dancers. *"And a sight for sore eyes."*

The girls smiled bashfully. "We are pleased that you are pleased," one of them said.

"Most pleased!" Kyros slipped his arms around the dancer's bare, slender waist, then leaned in and smelled her hair. *"Indeed, the only deprived sense is taste."* He gave a mock frown and spoke to the room at large. *"Is there no wine?"*

"Perhaps you've drunk it all," said a man, to a chorus of easy laughter.

A servant poured Kyros a goblet of red wine. He drank deeply, then wiped his mouth with the back of his hand. *"Another!"* he shouted.

Ridian couldn't take his eyes off him. He was identical to Rayna, but he seemed taller, his gestures stronger, and his words were far more captivating. He had a gravity to him, an allure, a force of presence that demanded both attention and respect.

Hector hobbled towards Kyros. "My Lord, perhaps you've had enough. What if…"

"What if the Fidicians attack?" Kyros scoffed. *"Tell me, what do you sense from the Fidicians?"* Kyros' gaze did not waver. He pinned Hector with shrewd, uncompromising eyes.

Hector shuffled uncomfortably. "Fear," he finally grumbled.

"Fear," said Kyros. *"What a small, banal little word to describe*

their sheer reeking terror. No—they will not abandon their walls. Not when I can nullify their Soulcasters with a thought." Kyros' eyes fell upon Ridian, making his skin crawl. *"Ah, Ridian. You live. I am pleased. Seems you have the singular gift of accelerated healing, only it's not so singular. The minstrel, Fidic, was a healer, was he not?"* He then addressed the room. *"Leave us,"* he commanded, and everyone scurried out, leaving Ridian alone with Hector, Kyros, and Sevron's wolf.

"Pardon the revelry," said Kyros, gesturing vaguely. *"Most unbecoming in a leader, I know. But as you can imagine, being in a state of abject sensory deprivation for centuries gives one a deep hunger for carnal pleasures."* Kyros sank into a chair and kicked his boots up onto the table. He drew a pipe from a coat pocket and began lighting it. All the while, he scanned Ridian with his sister's familiar eyes, though they burned with a strange fire. *"So, you wish to broach a deal?"*

Ridian's throat was unbelievably dry. "Yes."

Kyros puffed amusedly on his pipe. *"You intrigue me, Ridian. You do. You have strong Kyrosian blood—indeed, my blood, which would afford you special privilege among us—and yet you align yourself with the Fidicians on the very eve of their demise. The way I see it, you are a man standing upon the safety of the shore, wishing to board a sinking ship."* He gave an exaggerated frown. *"Most bizarre."* Then he drew deeply on his pipe, only to cough violently and thump his chest. *"Your sister's lungs are far too dainty. I fear I will damage them before she gets her body back."*

"What?" Ridian looked at Hector, not believing his ears.

Hector nodded seriously. "Kyros has agreed to bring your sister back."

Ridian's head spun. "How?"

Kyros shrugged. *"I bond with the tree, form a link, and your sister flies out. Simple."*

Ridian fought against the frail hope rising within him. Surely this was too good to be true. "Why would you do that?" he asked.

"Because I'm in torment," said Kyros, favouring Ridian with a winning grin, though despair clearly lurked beneath the bright facade. And for the first time, he seemed more like Rayna. More human, less myth. *"I should have died long ago when the giant Daegan struck me down. I should have died, but I clung to life, dismal and bleak though it was, dreaming of reincarnation. Ha! And now that I live again, I'm still in anguish. Everyone I know is dead. Everything I built is gone. And no matter how hard I try, I cannot satisfy my lust for life. I thirst, and though I drink, I am never satisfied. I hunger, and though I eat, I am forever hungry."* Kyros' smile was now a sour thing, a slipping mask.

"You would go back into the tree that tormented you?" asked Ridian warily.

"I would ensure the Tree died the moment Kyros went back," said Hector reassuringly. "It will be cut down, uprooted, and burnt. Every piece of it. Without a vessel, Kyros' soul would carry on into the Great Unknown, and there, at last, find peace."

Ridian's mind whirled, and he dared to hope. "When?"

"My one remaining purpose—the legacy I wish to leave behind—is to provide my children, the Kyrosians, with a home," said Kyros, stroking Sevron's wolf as it sauntered past. *"That and dealing with the Fidicians."* He added casually.

Ridian's heart, so light with hope and possibility a moment earlier, sank. "What do you mean, 'deal with the

Fidicians'?" He asked the question, but he already knew. Rayna had shown him Kyros' dream. The screams, the horror. He'd seen it all.

"The Fidicians are responsible for numerous historical crimes," said Kyros matter-of-factly. *"They should be punished accordingly."* Kyros picked at his fingernails. He might have been talking about a special tax or asking the Fidicians to give an especially heart-felt apology. Not slavery and wholesale torture.

"Punishing people for the sins of their ancestors is not justice," said Ridian. "What if we struck a deal?" He was clutching at straws, and he knew it. "What if the Fidicians surrendered?"

"What if they did?" said Kyros with an amused chuckle.

"Would you let them go unharmed?"

Kyros looked levelly at Ridian. *"No."*

Hector shambled forward, seeming revitalised by the conversation. "My Lord, if we could establish peace, if it were possible, we should take it. We've buried enough of our own. Enough Kyrosian blood has been spilt." Kyros snorted, but Hector continued. "But Ridian, you have neither the authority nor the influence to make this deal. Surely you know this."

Ridian was being torn in two. If he warned Kyros of the imminent Sungazer attack and allowed him to sack the Living Fort, he would get Rayna back. But Tann, Feya, the rest of the Thunderfells, and thousands more would suffer. No, he decided. He would let Kyros burn, even if it meant losing Rayna.

"I have more authority and influence than you think," said Ridian, his voice growing hard with outrage. "Like you said, *uncle*, I'm a descendant of Valaria the Elderflower, Fidic's sister. Fidic's blood flows through my veins. That makes me his closest living heir, giving me both the authority and the influence. And if it's all the same, I'll have my family heirloom back." Ridian held out his hand pointedly to Kyros.

Kyros and Hector looked stunned, and for a moment, Ridian thought he'd overdone it. But Kyros slapped his thigh and burst into laughter. *"You might have Fidic's blood, but you definitely have my balls. You're gutsier than a rutting boar. Certainly, have it. It's nothing but a trinket to me."* And he tore the Elderflower Necklace from around his neck and flung it at Ridian.

Ridian caught the Elderflower and pocketed it. "Here is what I propose: if you let the people of Fidicia leave unharmed, you can have Fidicia. All of it. The Fidicians get to live, and you get Fidicia. It's a good deal. You get to give the Kyrosians a home—*without* any more of them dying."

Hector looked thoughtful. "My Lord, this is a good deal. We get all that we want and save many lives in the process."

"In a hundred years, everyone you know and love will be dead," said Kyros, dropping all pretense of mirth. *"In a thousand years, none of this will even matter. We will all be dust. Even our tombstones will crumble into nothing. Why, then, would I give up retribution? Why would I relinquish the one thing that might bring me satisfaction?"*

"My Lord," said Hector desperately. "If we could achieve a peaceful negotiation, if we showed mercy-"

"Mercy?" said Kyros, jumping to his feet, his face twitching with rage. *"Mercy to those scheming, conniving, backstabbing vermin? Never! I wouldn't spare one Fidician though it meant the death of a hundred Kyrosians."* Kyros glared at a dismayed

Hector before collapsing back into his chair. He closed his eyes and breathed deeply, calming himself. *"You're right, Hector, you're right... This is why I must go. This is why I must die. I can't be trusted. My mind is too twisted, too poisoned. I cannot see clearly."* He looked at Ridian, and Ridian sensed a great pain and struggle within his eyes. *"If the Fidicians surrender the Living Fort, I will grant them safe passage. I swear it."*

"And your prisoners?" asked Ridian tentatively, picturing Feya chained to the whipping post and Tann lying in his cage.

"I will keep them as leverage for now," said Kyros. *"But open the gates, and they too shall go free."*

Chapter 49

Ridian left Kyros' Pavilion, nerves thrilling. He was playing a dangerous game. Kyros had agreed to exchange the prisoners, Feya and Tann included, for the outer gate at dawn. And the Sungazers would strike at noon and incinerate everyone who wasn't safely underground, which, right now, was everyone. Noon the next day—that was his deadline. Ridian resisted the urge to check on Feya. There was no time. He needed to hurry.

Silver emerged from behind a tent, and together, they marched past the revellers towards the Living Fort. A loose string of guards protected the camp. They chatted and drank and paid no attention to Ridian and Silver as they slipped past. They were confident, clearly. And why not? They had Kyros the Terrible.

The ground between the Kyrosian camp and the Living Fort had been trampled and churned with heavy footfalls. Here and there lay a snapped spear, a dented helmet, or a broken shield. Closer to the Living Fort were fallen ladders and grappling hooks. With all the debris, it was easy to imagine the attacking Kyrosians screaming across the Meadow while the Fidicians gripped their weapons upon the battlements—full of reeking terror as Kyros had said.

Ridian sensed something and stopped mid-stride. "I know you're there," he said to the night sky, and from the night sky, Chirpy emerged. "What do you want?" Ridian asked.

"I want to say sorry," tweeted the bird.

Ridian scoffed and walked on.

The finch circled in front of Ridian and flapped along to keep up with his brisk strides. "I also wanted to say your father would be proud of you."

That made Ridian stop.

"Proud of you," Chirpy repeated. "Not of me. No. He'd be ashamed of me. He'd feel just as betrayed as you, probably more. And rightfully so. How could I do such a thing to his son and daughter? Especially after the promise I made." Chirpy shook his tiny head. "I thought Kyrosian freedom would be worth any individual sacrifice. And maybe it is. But I still can't bear it. That's why I'm manipulating Kyros' emotions."

Ridian narrowed his eyes.

"Why do you think he's agreeing to give up his life for Rayna?" said Chirpy. "Why do you think he's agreeing to let the Fidicians go? From a fit of mercy? No. He's unbelievably dangerous. His psyche is twisted and fractured beyond belief. One moment he's the insatiable hedonist, the next, he's wallowing in nihilistic despair, and then again, in the blink of an eye, he's possessed with sadistic impulses…" Hector did not elaborate, but Ridian well remembered the lashes crisscrossing Feya's back and wondered if it was Kyros himself who had held the whip.

"Why are you telling me this?" asked Ridian.

"I'm telling you because I can't restrain him much longer. Manipulating emotions influences my own emotions. If I inspire joy, I lose joy. If I suppress rage, I become enraged. And with Kyros… Well, it's exhausting. His emotions are so intense and so powerful that I'm struggling not to act upon them. His desire for revenge has been especially difficult to quell. It inflames my own repressed desires for retribution. I'm telling you this because soon I won't be able to trust myself. His emotions will become my emotions. And soon, we'll *both* want unrestrained slaughter." Chirpy sighed, swelling then deflating his little chest. "You need to convince the Fidicians to leave—and soon. If you don't, there will be a massacre. I'm sure of it."

You're not wrong, thought Ridian, imagining the coming firestorm. But Ridian was moved by the bird's sincerity. Was he being manipulated? He didn't think so. Not in any magical sense, anyway. Besides, Hector was merely encouraging Ridian to do what he already wanted to do, and, for a moment, Ridian considered asking Chirpy to come with him. He could use an emotional manipulator to convince the terrified Fidicians to open their gates and flee underground. But no. Hector couldn't know about the Sungazers.

"I'll convince the Fidicians," said Ridian. "Don't worry about that. Just have the prisoners outside the gates at dawn as promised. Do not be late."

"We won't be. You have my word."

Ridian scoffed. "Your word." Then he left the bird to approach the outer gate.

"Who goes there?" called a Fidician guard upon the battlements.

"Ridian of Mudwall, friend and Fidician Knight. I've struck a deal."

"What deal?"

"A deal to save all our lives."

The gate creaked opened, revealing dishevelled Knights with dark, sunken eyes.

"Who's in charge?" asked Ridian.

"Sevron," said the man. "You'll probably find him in Emergency."

Ridian took off across the bailey, drank from the water basin beneath Fidic's Statue quickly, and the Living Fort came alight with a hazy green glow. A cacophony of misery and wailing issued from the hospital. And inside was even worse than it sounded. The great hall that had been converted into the Emergency Wing long ago was full of injured. Everywhere, men and women groaned and clutched bloody bandages. Everywhere, Stewards bustled, frantically doing whatever they could to remedy the multitude of wounds. They'd even run out of beds. Patients spilled onto the floor or slumped against the walls. It was total chaos, and Sevron was nowhere to be seen. Nearby, a man screamed as he clutched a bloody leg stump. Stewards held the flailing man down. Theodor was among them.

"Theodor!" said Ridian.

"Not now," said Theodor, focused on pouring some tonic into the hysterical man's mouth. "Drink this. It will help the pain."

The wide-eyed patient managed a sip, then, almost immediately, fell unconscious. Theodor sighed and wiped his brow, smearing it with blood. His apron was soaked, his arms red to the elbows. "Take him to surgery," he said to one of the Stewards. "I'll be there soon."

"Theodor," said Ridian. "Where's Sevron?"

Theodor glanced at Ridian, then did a dramatic double-take. "Ridian," he said in astonishment. "Where the hell have you been?" Theodor swept him up in a massive hug, and Ridian grimaced as blood seeped into his clothes.

Theodor let go and looked at Ridian's now blood-stained shirt. "Whoops. Sorry." He retrieved a hanky from his pocket and began wiping Ridian down. It was a futile gesture.

"How's Ollie?" asked Ridian, dreading the answer.

"Ollie? Oh, he's fine, he's fine," said Theodor, though it only made Ridian more doubtful. Theodor scanned the room through his blood-flecked glasses. "Where's Feya, then? We haven't seen her since she ran off after you. You know Kess is going to wring your necks for disappearing like that. We've been worried sick."

"Theodor, I…" What could Ridian say? After a sigh, he decided on the truth. "Feya's been captured."

Theodor fell backwards against a bedside and clutched his chest as if he'd been shot with an arrow. "Captured!"

"She's fine," said Ridian. "I saw her not thirty minutes ago. She's not hurt." *Not now, anyway.*

Theodor looked utterly lost. "What… What…?"

Ridian grabbed Theodor's shoulders. "She'll be fine. I promise. I've made a deal with the Kyrosians. They're going to let her go, safe and sound." Ridian's voice rang with a confidence that he did not feel.

Cogs turned slowly in Theodor's mind. He blinked, unable to take everything in. "What deal?" he managed to say at last.

"Theodor, I've got to go. Where's Sevron?"

Dazed, Theodor simply pointed. "Post-Op."

Ridian left the devastated Theodor and the chaos of the Emergency Wing to enter the adjacent Post-Operative Clinic. Sure enough, Sevron sat slumped at the far end of the small room, a bloody bandage covering his eyes. A tense group stood arging before the blind commander.

"We have no other options," said a man heatedly.

"A surprise attack is madness," spat a woman. "We'll be slaughtered."

"But doing nothing will also get us killed," said another. "Even if we hold the wall, eventually we'll starve or succumb to disease."

"We should surrender immediately," said an older man. "Kyrosian mercy will wane with each passing day. The more we hold out—the more we hurt and kill them—the greater their wrath will be."

"You talk as if there's no hope."

"There is no hope!"

Everyone began shouting over the top of each other. Spittle flew as arguments raged. Prince Bevrik sat on the floor cross-legged, looking like the lost little boy that he was. Sevron remained silent and still through it all, until he finally thumped his fists against the armrests of his chair and roared, "Shut up, the lot of you!"

Stunned into silence, the group turned towards the heaving commander.

"We're going in circles," said Sevron. "The facts are clear: we cannot defeat them, and we cannot escape."

A man piped up. "If we attack them when they're not prepared—"

Sevron tore the bandage from his face to reveal one milky-white blind eye and a gaping socket of scabbed blood where his other eye had been. "I saw their secret weapon," said Sevron. "She's the last thing I will ever see, and I do not exaggerate when I say she could single-handedly wipe us out. And yes, we're running out of food, and yes, disease will soon run rampant. But we can't surrender. The Kyrosians have been very clear. They don't just want Fidicia. They want our lives—they want *revenge*."

The room was silent.

"So, what do we do?" asked a woman.

"We wait."

"But reinforcements are days away."

"Yes," said Sevron flatly. "And we'll probably be dead, but it's our only option."

That was Ridian's cue. "There's another way," he said. "A way we can all survive."

"Who said that?" demanded Sevron, somehow glaring at Ridian, though he had no eyes.

Everyone turned to look, and Prince Bevrik's face lit up with joy. "Ridian Elderflower," he cried.

"Ridian?" said Sevron, frowning. "You should be dead!"

"Yes," said Ridian quietly, kneeling at Sevron's feet. "I should." Then he placed his palm against the living wooden floor and leeched Rava from it.

People gasped and cried out as the floor began to rot away into dust. But no one was more surprised than Sevron when Ridian snatched his ankle and poured Rava into him. Ridian went to heal his old, blind eye—but couldn't. It was too scarred, too malformed, too dead. The damage had been done too long ago. Instead, Rava surged towards the fresh wound—the bloody, empty socket. The effort was immense. Ridian clenched his teeth and pulled with all his might. Even as he sank into the dissolving floor, he kept pulling, pulling, until the Song of Silent Growing finally ceased. Breathless, Ridian rose from the crater and stared up into Sevron's new, astonished hazel eye. "Listen to me very carefully."

Sevron did.

Chapter 50

Getting Sevron to understand the situation took some time. There was the imminent threat of the Sungazers, the secret tunnel to Madman's Falls, and, of course, Kyros' resurrection. Explaining Kyros' return had been especially tricky. But it explained why Sevron's Soulcasters were being sucked dry of Rava. Sevron also had a hard time digesting the news of Fidicia's imminent destruction.

"So Fidicia will be destroyed?" asked Sevron. "All of it. The Living Fort. The Valley. *Everything*."

Ridian nodded. "Yes. But its people will live."

"And we let ourselves be occupied by these fire-wielding Sungazers?"

"Perhaps. But we'll have to deal with them later. First things first. We need to get our prisoners back, and we need to get everybody underground."

A Knight ran breathless into the room and bowed before Sevron. "The tunnel's in Stonecrow cavern, just as described," said the man.

Sevron gazed at the floor, deep in thought. His decision balanced life and death and liberty for everyone—and everyone knew it. Those present stared at Sevron with bated breath.

"We have until dawn," Ridian reminded him again in earnest. "Before Kyros marches up to our gates with our prisoners. And we only have until midday to get everybody underground before everything above ground goes up in flames."

Sevron's healed eye locked onto Ridian, drilling into him. *You'd think that eye would be more friendly towards me,* thought Ridian.

Finally, Sevron stood decisively. "We surrender to Kyros, reclaim our prisoners, and evacuate to the caves," he declared. The room released a collective sigh. Ridian wilted with relief. Sevron then spent the next few minutes barking orders before he swept from the room. "Ridian, with me," he said. Out in the Emergency Wing, Sevron gestured vaguely at the multitude of injured. "Can you help them as you helped me?"

"I think so," said Ridian.

"Then do it."

***

A few hours later, the Emergency Wing was empty and quiet, and Ridian sat with his head in his hands, exhausted. Silver lay at his feet.

Lost gods, my head hurts, thought Ridian as he dug his knuckles into his eyes.

Ridian had healed many, but not all. He couldn't. Even when he drew from leaves and flowers—far easier sources of Rava than hard wood—he had limits. Healing was strenuous, mental labour. He needed breaks, and in the end, he had to be discerning. If the patient wasn't dying, he didn't bother. A broken ankle could mend itself, after all. He found partial healings helpful—restoring just enough to keep them alive, and no more.

With each healing, he learnt the parameters of his magic. It appeared he could heal tissue damage through cell regeneration, even restoring severed limbs and compromised organs like Sevron's eye—but only at great cost. It drained Rava and exhausted him. He found old injuries were beyond him, and he couldn't realign broken bones. One man's finger had to be re-broken, it was so crooked. And there were always scars. Some of them very ugly.

Thankfully, all the gawking spectators who wanted to witness yet another miraculous healing were gone. Ridian hated the attention and was grateful for the silence. There had been tears and handshakes and hugs and kisses and a thousand thank-yous. He would heal a brother or sister or son or daughter or whatever, and the whole family would gush over him. It was too much.

Just one more patient, he thought, forcing himself to climb a deserted stairway. Upstairs in Paediatrics, all the children were gone, all the beds empty—all except Ollie's. The sleeping boy lay like a sagging sack of skin, and he was deathly pale.

Theodor was there, stroking the hair from Ollie's face. He looked up excitedly as Ridian entered. "You're here! Excellent." He opened a satchel bursting with leaves and fresh-cut flowers. "This is what you asked for, isn't it? Is it enough?"

Ridian nodded wearily.

Theodor nodded out the window. "Not long now," he said soberly.

There was a lot happening outside the window.

Outside, Fidician soldiers were slowly leaving their posts, scurrying underground just as Sevron ordered and Ridian proposed.

Outside, Hero's Tree swayed with Rayna's soul trapped inside.

Outside, Feya remained chained to a post.

Outside, Kyrosians revelled, oblivious of their coming doom.

Outside—through the window—was a world waiting to be destroyed.

"Not long now," repeated Ridian, then he touched Ollie's cold, slender arm and waited for the call of Rava, for the soundless music, for the Song of Silent Growing… but it never came. Theodor beamed expectantly, looking between Ridian and Ollie, waiting for the miracle.

Ridian scrunched his eyes shut and listened harder: nothing. Still, Theodor beamed. *Bugger it.* Ridian actively drew Rava from the leaves and flowers in Theodor's satchel. They sang out as they shriveled and died, and he became filled with an overflow of Rava. He tightened his grip on Ollie's arm. But still, nothing happened. It felt as though there was nothing to heal. Rummaging in the satchel, he snatched a twig and scratched it along Ollie's shin, leaving a minor graze. A modicum of Rava poured out of Ridian and healed the shallow scrape. Ollie, so deep in sleep, didn't even stir.

"I don't understand…" said Ridian, turning his hands over to look at them. "Why isn't it working?" He drew more Rava. Theodor's satchel deflated as its contents wilted and died, but Rava continued to swell within Ridian with nowhere to go. He gripped Ollie tighter, trying in vain to force the Rava into him. Ollie groaned and began to stir.

Theodor placed a hand on Ridian's. "It's okay," he said in a flat voice. "I thought this would happen. Your magic… it only heals tissue. Regenerates cells." As Theodor spoke, his eyes were as vacant as the windows of a tumble-down home, as if his mind was far, far away. "The patient's condition is not a matter of simple healing. There's a more complex underlying pathology." He turned slowly towards the door. "We'd better go tell his family—I mean, the family." Then reality seemed to cave in on him, and his face contorted with grief. "My boy! My poor boy!" he wailed. "What do I tell the others? What do I tell them? How do I tell them he won't wake up this time?" Theodor doubled over and began to sob.

Ridian went to comfort Theodor. But as he went to place a hand upon Theodor's shuddering shoulder, his hand froze. He couldn't do it. He didn't know how.

Slowly, though, Theodor's sobs subsided. He sniffed, wiped his nose, and began cleaning his fogged glasses on his shirt. "Forgive me. I knew this day was coming. I know I didn't let on, but I knew. Deep down, I knew." He gave a sad smile.

Ridian couldn't bear to look at Theodor. Instead, he looked at Ollie, asleep and oblivious of his coming death. "Surely there's something else we can do?" said Ridian frantically, feeling his composure slip.

Theodor shook his head. "We've tried everything. Everything! Even magic." He gave a little laugh, his wet eyes twinkling, and it broke Ridian's heart. "Yep," said Theodor with a sigh. "Ollie's condition is beyond the powers of medicine and even magic. You heal with Rava, but for all we know, Rava could be driving his illness." He sighed. "Anyway, we'd better get him downstairs before…"

"What did you say?" asked Ridian.

"I said, we'd better get him—"

"No, the other thing. About Rava."

"Oh, only that it could be driving his illness. But that's complete conjecture, of course."

Something like hope—or at least mad desperation—filled Ridian. "Theodor, we haven't tried everything. Not yet." Then he closed his eyes, Split, and shot his soul into the black.

At first, everything was dazzling streams of scintillating light. Rippling, glowing threads pulsed through the surrounding walls, floor, and ceiling. Everything was alive and glowing. But then he discerned four radiant figures: Theodor, Silver, Ollie, and himself. Ridian sent his soul to hover over Ollie. Flowing strands of light pulsed through every fiber, every muscle, every tendon, every nerve of the young boy. Ridian could see them all. He drew closer, closer still, and passed unheeded through Ollie's translucent skin. He swam through the organs: the intestines, the stomach, the lungs, the heart. To his untrained eye, everything seemed as it should. Rava glowed and flowed. Soon, every major organ had been explored. Everything except the brain—home of the soul. It lay before him, aglow with brilliant rivulets of light, like a dense constellation of shooting stars.

Ridian shot towards Ollie's brain, infiltrated it for a brief second, and was repelled. An invisible, primal force reared from deep within Ollie's mind and pushed back with terrifying power. Ridian tried again, but Ollie's mind flung him out. He only burst through for a moment. Ridian then mustered all his willpower for one supreme effort, for a final assault. Ridian hurled towards Ollie's brain, and—perhaps due to the dying boy's failing health—Ollie's defenses faltered for the briefest of moments. But it was all Ridian needed. He broke through and shot up the spinal cord, past the brain stem, towards the front of the brain. He sped faster, aware of Ollie's unconscious mind closing in, hunting him down. As he sped, he looked. *There*! Amidst the thousand shooting stars, a bundle of light shone more brilliant than all the rest. Ridian shot a bolt of Rava, and the bright bundle devoured it—and grew. Then, Ollie's unconscious mind grabbed hold of Ridian and, with implacable, irresistible force, flung him out—

Ridian careened back into his body with a jolt.

"Ridian, are you okay?" Theodor was peering at him, puzzled.

Ridian felt his face break into a crazed, drunken smile. "I know what's wrong with him."

Chapter 51

Ridian pushed Ollie's bed down the hall at a run as moonlight streamed through the many rows of windows. He skidded around a corner, wheels squeaking on the smooth wooden floor.

"A tumour?" asked Theodor breathlessly for the seventh time as he guided the bed from the front. "You sure?"

"Yes. It was out of place. And it grew when I fed it Rava."

"It grew!"

"Only a fraction. I stopped as soon as I saw it was making it worse. I thought it might help." Ridian glanced at Theodor guiltily, but there wasn't a scrap of blame coming from the man.

"And you can pinpoint where?"

"Yes."

"Precisely? 'Cause if—"

"We get it wrong, Ollie will probably die. *I know.*"

Ridian turned another corner. The bed tottered upon two wheels, before clattering back down. Ollie rolled about on the bed, senseless from a large dose of anaesthetic. Felix stood at the foot of the bed like the ridiculous figurehead of a ship. Finally, at the end of the hallway, they entered the small operating room. With ritualistic efficiency, Theodor lit all fourteen torches affixed to the walls, filling the room with warm light, then prepped himself for surgery. He washed his hands, donned a fresh apron, and unrolled a leather bundle upon a side table, revealing surgical tools nestled in neat little sleeves. There were knives, clamps, pinchers, and saws of various sizes and styles. Theodor removed them. His hands trembled, but the familiar actions seemed to calm him. Finally, Theodor approached Ollie with a razor and began shaving the top of the boy's head. Soon enough, Ollie sported a large bald spot. Theodor blew the hair away, wiped Ollie's brow clean, and together, he and Ridian lifted the boy onto the surgical bed.

"Okay," said Theodor, staring intently at Ridian. "Exactly where?"

Ridian recalled the dark patch in Ollie's brain. He pictured it as clearly as he could, then pressed a trembling finger to Ollie's head: just off center, two inches from the hairline. "There," said Ridian. He held Theodor's gaze for a few long seconds before answering the unspoken question. "I'm sure."

To Theodor's credit, he didn't ask again. "How deep?" he asked.

Ridian frowned. He was less confident about the depth. "About this much." He made an inch-and-a-half gap with his thumb and forefinger.

Theodor pushed his glasses all the way up his nose, then leaned in close to glare at the gap for a long time. Then he nodded, grabbed a small saw, and hovered it over Ollie's scalp. His hand was perfectly still. Felix curled about his leg and seemed to hold his breath. "You might want to look away," said Theodor, his own eyes riveted.

Ridian did, then turned back. "Will this work?" he asked. "If you remove the tumour, will Ollie be alright?"

Theodor remained fixed on the bald patch on Ollie's scalp. "I don't know." The saw descended, and Ridian turned away, but he could still hear the horrible grating sound of the saw sliding back and forth over the boy's skull. Suddenly, Ridian was overwhelmed with a tremendous urge to heal. He held it back, but it was like holding his breath—the longer he held, the harder it got.

Ridian staggered away from the table. "Theodor, the magic is making me want to heal him."

"No, don't!" said Theodor in alarm. "Healing him now would be a disaster. Leave. I'll call you when I need you."

Ridian obeyed, stumbling out into the hall. With each step, the urge receded, and Ridian found relief, though anxiety coiled in his guts. What if Theodor cut too deep or too wide? What if the tumour was too big? What if he removed more than just the tumour? He paced the hallways and bit his nails, Silver loping alongside. And what about Tann and Feya? Would Kyros make the exchange? Would he deliver them as promised? And if Kyros delayed by even a handful of hours, Tann, Feya, and the rest of the prisoners would be incinerated along with the Kyrosians.

Tann, Feya, Ollie… everybody's lives were at stake, and for the moment, Ridian could do nothing about it. Silver whimpered, eyes wide with concern, and Ridian dropped down to cling to the wolf's neck. The hours passed very slowly.

***

"RIDIAN!" Theodor's call echoed down the hall.

Ridian awoke with a start, slumped in a corner with Silver's head resting in his lap. How long had he been asleep? He glanced out a window: the faint glow of the rising sun emanated from behind the Ring Mountains. How had Ollie's surgery gone? And were Tann and Feya going to be released at dawn as Kyros had promised?

Ridian sprang to his feet and shot down the hall towards the operating room, with Silver close behind. The room smelled of blood, and for good reason: it was everywhere. It clotted Ollie's hair, pooled about his shoulders, covered the surgical tools, spread across the table, and even trickled onto the floor where Theodor had trampled it all over the place. It was everywhere, but especially all over Theodor. From the tips of his fingers to the ends of his toes, blood covered his entire front. Most disturbing was the fleshy lump that sat conspicuously on the side table—the tumour, surely. The sight stopped Ridian in his tracks and filled him with a near-overwhelming urge to heal Ollie and throw up at the same time. Felix was in a far corner, as far from the gore as possible.

"Ridian, please!" cried Theodor.

Ridian dashed to the blood-soaked bed. With great concentration, Theodor delicately positioned the cut-out chunk of Ollie's skull back in place. The sight of the grotesque wound sent Ridian's desire to heal surging to a crescendo. He strained to resist the urge.

"Now?" asked Ridian through clenched teeth.

"No, wait," said Theodor as he fiddled with the loose bit of skull, jiggling it back and forward and side-to-side over the slippery bit of brain.

The tension within Ridian mounted. *"Theodor,"* he warned, scrunching his eyes shut and holding his temples.

"Wait... *Wait...*" The piece of skull clicked into place. "Okay, now!" said Theodor, holding the bone in place.

With relief, Ridian let go. He pulled Rava from the leaves and flowers in the nearby satchel with a burst of melody and funneled it into the small, lifeless, blood-soaked boy. Nothing happened, until it did. A sudden scab traced its way around the dislocated skull in a clockwise loop. The scab turned crusty, then flaky, then dark, then light, then peeled away, leaving a nobbly white scar—a month's worth of healing in a matter of moments.

Depleted, Ridian gave Theodor a weary nod. Theodor hesitated, then tentatively took his fingers away. They both leaned forward to stare at Ollie.

"Is he okay?" asked Ridian.

Theodor placed two fingers to Ollie's neck and counted under his breath. He then lifted Ollie's eyelids, one at a time, to peer at the unseeing pupils. Next, he placed his ear to Ollie's chest and listened to the boy's shallow breathing. During all this, Ridian barely breathed himself.

"His vitals are normal," said Theodor at last, "and he certainly looks better."

Indeed, beneath the trails of scabbed blood running down his face, Ollie's cheeks had some colour, and his skin looked like it actually fit him.

"Well, that's good, isn't it?" asked Ridian.

Theodor stared at Ollie for a long moment, before smiling at Ridian with a tight, toothless smile. "Yes, of course it's good. Thank you. You did very well. Amazing, actually."

Ridian peered at Theodor's inscrutable face. "What aren't

you telling me?"

Theodor stared at Ollie and said nothing.

"Theodor, what is it?"

"The brain is a very delicate thing," said Theodor, still looking at Ollie. "It controls every part of us—our eyes, our heart, our lungs… our personality. And I just took a chunk— a big chunk—out. And well, he might be a bit different if he wakes."

"What do you mean, 'different'? What do you mean *if* he wakes?"

"I don't know," said Theodor wearily. "I just don't know."

Ridian felt sick, and Silver's ears lay flat against his head.

"When will we know?" asked Ridian.

"People usually take months, sometimes years to recover from brain surgery." Theodor smiled kindly. "But we haven't had a magical healer since Fidic himself walked these halls. I suspect that, whatever cognitive deficits Ollie has, we should know as soon as he wakes from his potion-induced slumber. Indeed, how he is when he wakes will be how he will be for the rest of his life."

They remained in silence for a long moment before Theodor said, "Let's get him underground."

Ridian nodded, and together they lifted Ollie onto his old bed, wheeling him out into the hall. Windows slid past, pouring in the growing pre-dawn light. Through them, Ridian glimpsed a cluster of about twelve grey-clad Knights gathered before the outer gates. Ridian was sure Sevron was one of them. Theodor and Ridian exchanged a meaningful look. Would Kyros hand Tann, Feya, and the other prisoners over? He'd better—and soon.

At the end of the hall, Theodor pushed Ollie inside the

elevator, but Ridian stayed outside. "Ridian, you coming?" asked Theodor.

"Just a sec." Ridian dashed to the closest window. Silver followed, jumping onto his hind legs to see. Rays of crisp, golden sunlight shot over the Ring mountains, yet the gate remained closed. Ridian drummed his fingers against the window frame impatiently. *Come on. Where are they?*

"Ridian?" asked Theodor.

Ridian couldn't take his eyes from the gates. They needed to open. If they didn't, Tann and Feya would remain in the Kyrosian camp when the Sungazers arrived at Midday. They'd be burnt alive. "Can you and Felix manage Ollie by yourself?" Ridian called over his shoulder. "I want to watch and make sure."

"Sure, I can, but *Ridian,*" said Theodor firmly, making Ridian turn around. "If those fire people come, you leave. You hear? You're already a hero. Don't be a martyr." Theodor glared at Ridian with a severity he'd never seen before.

Ridian nodded. "I'll be down soon."

"Good." Then Theodor turned the winch crank, and he, Ollie, and Felix descended out of sight.

Ridian turned back to the window. More light was spilling over the mountains, and yet, still nothing from the gate. Ridian's guts churned as he had a terrible thought: what if Feya was still chained to that whipping post? What if Kyros had changed his mind? What if he decided to wait a day or two? Ridian needed to see what was happening. "Silver, come." They ran down hallways and up staircases, ascending the winding apothecary tower to its tallest room. As always, the room creaked as it swayed in the breeze and stank with a cocktail of smells—acrid, chemical, sweet, and sour. Breathless, he passed the lifeless furnace and the cluttered workbenches to peer out the window. From this dizzying height, Ridian could see almost all of Fidicia sprawling below. He could see the bailey, the outer wall, Last Stand Meadow, and even down into the Fidician Valley where tiny houses clustered along the banks of Raven's River.

Ridian saw a small cluster making their way across Last Stand Meadow towards the outer wall, and his heart skipped a beat. He scanned the group. The figures were distant and blurry, but he was confident it was the fifty or so Fidician prisoners surrounded by a Kyrosian escort, complete with prowling wolves, slinking cats, and wheeling birds of prey. A moment later, he thought he recognised Tann, Lukas, and Feya shuffling near the front of the prisoners, and a cold hand seemed to squeeze his throat. The exchange still needed to go ahead, and with tensions high, anything could happen.

As the party drew near, the gates of the outer wall opened, and Sevron walked through to meet and converse with the apparent leader of the Kyrosian party—a man Ridian did not recognise. Ridian looked for Hector and Kyros, and saw neither. Where were they? This exchange was paramount to both sides, and their absence made Ridian nervous. Surely, they would both want to be here to ensure negotiations went smoothly. Perhaps Hector was being cautious, sending disposable lackeys rather than their impetuous and bloodthirsty leader. But Ridian was dubious. Would Hector really entrust others to make such a vital trade? Minutes passed, and still, Sevron and the Kyrosian talked.

What's taking so long? Finally, Sevron made a gesture, and Fidician Knights dashed out to assist the prisoners while Kyrosian Soulcasters dashed inside to secure the gate. The exchange was happening, and the sight of it made Ridian almost collapse with relief. What's more, Feya strode forward lithely through the gate, assisting a stooped Tann, which meant she mustn't have been whipped again. Everything was going according to plan. The Kyrosians had fallen for Ridian's ploy. Even as Ridian watched, they were taking control of the guardhouse and allowing Sevron and his Knights to shepherd the prisoners towards the hospital, where the safety of Stonecrow cavern awaited.

Then Ridian gasped in horror and in awe—

Down in the Fidician Valley, a giant pillar of golden fire suddenly shot skyward. As it twirled, it seemed to cut the sky in two. Then swirls of black, blue, and white merged with the great golden flames. The colors chased each other, round and round, twirling faster, and then faster again, becoming a blur. It widened, taking the shape of a tornado, and began to roar. Just as Ridian thought his horror had reached its peak, the firestorm lurched forward, tearing ahead in a frantic, unpredictable zigzag.

This can't be happening, thought Ridian. *Midday. Selkyrie said they'd attack at midday. Not dawn. Not now.*

Below, Kyrosians and Fidicians stared, petrified, or clung to each other. Many fled. Silver cowered beneath a nearby table, cringing and whimpering like some pathetic stray dog. Below, Feya and Tann stood among the terrified onlookers. Ridian tried to scream at them to run, but couldn't. *He* couldn't even move. Down in the valley, homes were disintegrating as tiles, bricks, and beams flew hundreds of feet into the insatiable flames. Trees tore from their roots and were sucked into the flaming vortex. And still, the firestorm grew, roaring ever louder as it set everything ablaze.

What have I done? thought Ridian, only now fully realising the doom he had brought down upon so many. Ridian clutched the windowsill. It was solid. It was real. This wasn't some surreal nightmare. This was happening. The entire sky was shivering with heat as the Valarian Firetrees erupted into actual flame. Even trees far from the raging inferno burst asunder, a testament to its impossible heat. Even from where Ridian stood, a warm breeze dried his eyes.

Ridian blinked and looked down. There was Sevron, halfway across the bailey, waving everyone towards the hospital beneath Ridian's feet. There was Feya, frozen in the street, just as Ridian was frozen. And there was Rayna, dashing down the street.

Ridian did a double take. Not Rayna—*Kyros*. The man possessing his sister ran with supernatural speed—his hood blown back, his face twisted in fury. He flew past Sevron, dashed past the statue of Fidic, and disappeared into the hospital with the rest of the prisoners.

Then it clicked: Kyros had hidden in plain sight among the prisoners. Even as Ridian's mind whirled, Feya and Tann spun around and ran towards the hospital, and Ridian watched as they followed Kyros inside.

Chapter 52

Move, thought Ridian. But his legs remained rooted to the spot. *Move,* he demanded, as the Firestorm tore through the valley. The sun was blood-red behind a black sky—like the Sol flag, Ridian realised grimly.

Mere seconds had passed since Tann and Feya had followed Kyros inside the hospital. *Seconds*—yet they spun on and on, filling Ridian with a sick panic. Kyros would follow the crowd into Stonecrow Cavern and then into the secret tunnel. What monstrous deeds would he commit in that dark dead-end?

MOVE! Something clicked in Ridian's mind, and he managed to turn on his heels and sprint down the stairs. Down he ran, the windows letting in an eerie red light. He stopped partway down; Silver was nowhere to be seen. He reached for the wolf with his mind and felt the wolf trembling upstairs in abject terror. Ridian calmed the wolf, feeling himself grow in fear as a consequence. Emboldened, Silver followed, loyalty overcoming fear.

At the bottom of the staircase, people streamed past at break-neck speed. Ridian was surprised to see Fidicians and Kyrosians alike pouring into the Living Fort, all dashing towards Stonecrow Cavern, wide-eyed with panic. Though the halls were full of screams, the roar of the Firestorm could still be heard. Ridian peeped out a window: the swirling vortex of fire appeared larger—and closer. Ridian joined the panicked crowd. People jostled, the fast overtaking the slow, and as they got closer to Stonecrow Cavern, the hallway became congested. People pushed and shoved and barged past. Someone collided with Ridian, dashing him against the wall painfully. Ridian braced himself with Rava just as another man hurtled into him, the man ricocheted off him, stunned.

Ridian pushed forward, slipping between the gaps, all the while keeping an eye out for Tann, Feya and, of course, Kyros. What would the man do? His people were being massacred. All his plans were being thwarted. And Hector was not around to curb his worst impulses. And what was Ridian to do, come to think of it? Kill Kyros, and forever abandon Rayna to Hero's Tree? Even if he could, would he? Could he? It was unthinkable.

Finally, Ridian and the crowd poured into Stonecrow Cavern. In the confusion, it appeared Ridian was the only one who knew about the secret tunnel boring through Valaria's Mural Wall. While everyone else headed towards the back of the cavern near the statue of Roki, Ridian and Silver dashed for the dark opening and shuffled through. The far side was heavily congested. Knights, Stewards, disciples, Familiars, and regular townsfolk huddled together, eyes shining with candlelight, lamplight, torchlight, and fear. And for good reason: the walls trembled, pebbles bounced upon the floor, and dirt fell from the ceiling. The firestorm felt like a thunderclap that didn't end but only grew louder. People screamed, children cried, wolves howled, falcons screeched—every sound echoing through the chaos.

Someone grabbed Ridian's arm, and he whirled about in terror, fully expecting Rayna's grinning, leering face, fully animated by her psychotic possessor. But it was just a terrified woman.

"What's happening?" she shrieked.

"Earthquake," he lied, pulling free from her grip and marching to the main tunnel where all Fidicia had been ushered. People stretched along either side of the subterranean stream, sitting or standing on the narrow banks that hugged the slick, black water. Looney Shrooms glowed all about, though of course, nobody could see their glow except Ridian and Silver. Everybody else utilised candles, torches, or lamps. As Ridian passed further in, the rumble of the firestorm diminished until is disappeared.

"Feya!" Ridian shouted down the tunnel. "Tann!" he cried down the other way. But he could barely hear his own voice amid the cacophony of voices.

"Have you seen Feya Thunderfell?" Ridian asked a nearby family. "Or Tann. Or Theodor? Or any of the Thunderfells?" They shook their heads. Ridian asked another clump of people and then another.

"Aye," said a woman, clutching a crying toddler. "I think I saw Feya. She went that way." She pointed upstream, away from Madman's Falls. A dead-end, Ridian knew, and his neck prickled with fear. If he went down that way—and Kyros followed—he'd be trapped, as helpless as a hatchling.

All the Thunderfells would be trapped, he reminded himself, then pushed on downstream, Silver slinking behind. People clogged the narrow bank, forcing Ridian to skirt the very edge of the poisonous water and to leap across the stream a few times to make headway. As Ridian shuffled along, he shouted for Feya, for Tann, for Theodor, for Ollie, for all the Thunderfells. He examined every face, every turned back, each time expecting Kyros to whirl around and grin, full of predatory glee.

"Feya!" he shouted for the hundredth time into the echoing chaos, and to his astonishment, he heard a reply.

"Ridian?" Feya's voice echoed somewhere in the congested tunnel.

"Feya!"

"Ridian!"

And there she was, surrounded by her family: little Ella clinging to her neck; Theodor engulfing her in a hug; Kess cradling an unconscious Ollie; Kai looking on, his familiar perched on his arm. They were all smiling and crying, evidently celebrating Feya's safe return. But none of them were safe. Kyros was down here.

Ridian ran to them, overwhelmed by a mounting sense of urgency. Feya went to embrace him, and the others close behind—but Ridian shoved Feya off and held the others back. "We have to go," he said breathlessly. "We have to leave."

"What's the matter?" said a harsh voice. "Your plan not working out?" It was Tann. He was slumped against the wall and glowering at Ridian with hostile, unforgiving suspicion.

"Tann, I…" There was no time for more apologies. "Forget it. Let's just go."

"I thought we came down here to be safe," said Kess.

"Ridian, what's wrong?" said Theodor. His smile had vanished, and the often sleepy Felix was alert on his shoulder.

"There's no time to explain," said Ridian. "We have to—"

"Of course there's no time to explain," interrupted Tann. "It would take all day to explain how you betrayed us."

The words stung, and everybody looked from Tann to Ridian, bewildered.

"What are you talking about?" said Feya. "Ridian healed us. He helped us escape. He's the reason we're safe down here while that fire rages above us."

"Yeah," said Theodor. "He's a true hero. He's—"

"Hero!" Tann laughed. "You betrayed me, you betrayed this good family, and you betrayed every innocent soul in Fidicia."

"Tann!" shouted Theodor.

"Theodor, leave it," shouted Ridian, then he lowered his eyes, unable to meet Theodor's honest gaze. "What Tann says is true. I turned my back on you guys. I betrayed everyone. I was selfish. And I'm the one who's responsible for… for everything."

The family looked baffled. Theodor blinked behind his spectacles, Kai and his hawk glared, and a slow, dawning betrayal crept across Feya's face. It pained Ridian to see—though Tann's expression, at least, had softened ever so slightly.

"Ridian, what are you talking about?" said Feya. "You saved us. You *saved* us."

"It doesn't matter right now!" said Ridian. "Right now, we're in danger."

"I don't understand," said Kess. Ollie remained unconscious in her arms.

Other people had also taken notice. "Danger? What do you mean? What's happening? What's going on?" they asked.

"Guys, please," Ridian begged, checking over his shoulder. "If we're quick…" He groaned in frustration; nobody was moving. He knelt before Tann and looked directly into his eyes. "Tann. My sister. You were right. She *is* a secret weapon. Kyros has possessed her. He's inside her, and he's every bit as powerful as when he was alive."

Tann's face scrunched up dismissively, yet doubt flickered in his eyes. "Who is Kyros?"

"Who is Kyros?" said Ridian, beside himself. "Kyros the Great, but not yet the Terrible. You all know him. I know he died hundreds of years ago, but he's alive again, and he's controlling my sister—and he's down here."

Tann seemed swayed by Ridian's desperation and sincerity. Indeed, his eyes held a growing alarm as he stood up. "Theodor, get the kids and—"

Screams began echoing down the tunnel, cutting Tann off. Dozens of screams. *Hundreds.* All merging, all echoing into one great terrible shriek. Ridian's heart sank as he turned to look back the way he had come.

At first there was nothing to see. Just Fidicians clustered along each bank, looking down the tunnel with its flickering torchlight. Then a man came running around the corner, splashing through the knee-high water. He stumbled, kept his footing, and kept running. People called out to waylay him, to ask what was wrong. The terrified man ignored them all, and as the howling screams intensified, two wolves skidded around the corner and dashed along either side of the bank. A woman followed, only to fall on hands and knees into the shallow water. Almost immediately, a panicked crowd—a storm of flailing limbs—burst into view and trampled her into the stream. Dumbstruck, people watched as the whole tunnel became a broil of moving bodies. Everybody turned and began to flee, and those who tripped were trampled beneath the relentless stampede.

Ridian drew Rava from Silver, slung Ollie over his shoulder and yanked Kess to her feet—all in a blink. "Run!" he shouted. But he needn't have bothered—everyone was already scrambling along the narrow bank as fast as they could. The people ahead slowed them down, and within moments, the stampede crashed into them. And just like that, Ridian lost sight of the family. People barged past, pushing and shoving, heedless of anyone. An elbow struck Ridian in the face. He stumbled, stood on something—*someone*—and kept going. Another shove, and for a terrifying split-second, he almost fell into the stream, teetering on the edge before catching his balance. Falling into the water would mean the end of him—and certainly of the senseless Ollie slumped over his shoulder. Bodies crushed against him from all sides, the air thick with panic, but he kept his footing, pressing himself to the wall as the crowd shoved him along.

Even with Rava, Ridian struggled: running, jumping, weaving, stumbling. The tunnel narrowed, and the crowd crushed Ridian against the wall, grazing his shoulder painfully, tearing his shirt and scraping his skin clean off. Then suddenly, the wall disappeared, and he fell, tumbling into an alcove. Leaping to his feet, he dragged Ollie towards the back of the small cavern, no bigger than a tiny bedroom. His back to the wall and holding Ollie to his chest, he watched others stumble inside, and within moments, the small cavern was full.

People trembled and cried all around him, and still, the

crowd surged on, thundering past like a shrieking river of terror. He reached for Silver with his mind and felt the wolf's presence drift along with the crowd. He feared for Tann and the Thunderfells, but there was nothing he could do. At last—after a minute, or maybe ten—the torrent of people thinned, with only the odd figure blundering past. Those in the cavern hesitated before following the human herd upstream, some instinct urging them away from the unknown horror lurking downstream. But Ridian knew what lay down the dark, twisting tunnel. *They're all speeding to a dead-end. There's no escape.*

Ridian shuffled Ollie to the tunnel entrance and peeped out. It was dark. Dead candles lay like scattered bones, and only a handful of discarded torches remained burning on the ground. One steamed and hissed at the water's edge before guttering out, casting that portion of the tunnel into a deeper darkness. Looney Shrooms blazed all the brighter for Ridian, however, and from their cold, silver light, Ridian saw the carnage: the injured, the unconscious, the dead, the mangled. One woman limped past, whimpering as she clutched a handful of bleeding, broken fingers. One man pulled himself forward by his hands, dragging a pair of shattered legs. Many lay still, their bodies trampled into pulp. Many floated past, face down in the water.

A ringing clash of swords made Ridian start. The sound had come echoing from downstream, and Ridian held his breath and stared, transfixed, at the bend in the tunnel, terrified he would see his sister's lurching form. There came an agonised scream; then a wolf yelped in pain. A man cried for mercy, only to be cut short.

Ridian swung the limp Ollie onto his back and ran. He

didn't care that he was heading towards a dead end. What else could he do? Terror compelled him to run. Dashing, he leapt over and around the scattered bodies while others—more virtuous than Ridian—dragged the unconscious from the water, pumped their chests, and blew air into their lungs. Ridian sidestepped one injured girl, then stopped short—

The injured girl was Feya. She was crying and clutching her shin, which was severely broken in at least three places. Already swollen and purple, it looked like a giant slug. Unbidden, the urge to heal her possessed Ridian, and—without meaning to—he stole Rava from the surrounding Looney Shrooms. As they died, darkness spread across the ceiling and wall, and the stream turned black as ink. Rava swelled within him and surged to the point of release. But with supreme effort, Ridian held it back. If he healed her now, he realized, the misaligned bones in her leg would fuse improperly. She'd be crippled for life.

Pent up, the Rava yearned to fulfil its purpose. Ridian saw blood trickling down a nearby man's temple and unleashed the Rava with relief. The Rava whooshed out, and the man blinked about in surprise as he touched his healed head.

"Feya!" cried Ridian, kneeling by her side.

"Ridi–" Feya winced. "What happened? Why did everybody run?" She stared up at him with watery, pain-filled eyes.

Ridian didn't know what to say. His mouth opened and closed, and nothing came out. He couldn't think straight with all the panic raging through him. Some scared part of Ridian called for Silver. His wolf responded from upstream and began running towards him.

"Please, Roki, no!" screamed a voice downstream, followed by a cacophony of shrieks.

People were running again. Just a handful—only those who had stopped to help the injured, but their terror was immense. And Ridian saw why: a darting blur burst from around the tunnel, slammed into a limping man, and hurled him against the wall with a sickening crunch. It zipped past a woman, and shattered her skull in a spray of blood. The next straggler jolted to a stop and screamed as the blur materialised behind him and lifted him clean off the ground—

The blur was Kyros, a grotesque grin stretching Rayna's face. He was drenched in blood. Gore matted his hair, streaked his face, and soaked his torso. Only his fevered eyes and terrible white grin shone clean through the blood.

The man in Kyros' grasp kicked and screamed and flailed to no avail; Kyros plunged his fist into the man's back, and tore out his spine. The man flopped to the ground like a boneless sack of meat. Blood oozed over Kyros' knuckles as he looked for another hapless victim. All this happened in a matter of seconds, and Ridian watched as if it were far, far away—many miles and many years ago. But no. It was here. It was now. There was Kyros, stomping on a man's leg, shattering it. There was Kyros, grinding his heel and snapping the leg clean off. There he was, nudging the severed limb into the water with his toe and laughing in perverse amusement.

Searing pain licked up Ridian's calf. He had accidentally backed into a flaming torch, sending it rolling into the water with a hiss. The burning light died, and the silver light of the Looney Shrooms glowed all the brighter. He saw Kyros squinting as if in the dark, looking for another hapless victim, and Ridian remembered that only he can see by the light of the poisonous mushrooms. Stumbling along, he kicked another torch into the water. Torchlight dimmed, and silver light grew. But there were too many torches for Ridian to douse in time; Kyros was hurtling towards them with the speed of a galloping horse—from one victim to the next—and would soon be upon them.

And just as panic threatened to overwhelm him, Ridian saw Feya scrambling backwards, kicking off with her good leg and dragging her bad one.

"Feya!" cried Ridian. "Blow out the torches!"

Feya, sliding frantically on her backside, didn't respond.

Ridian ran and grabbed her by the shoulders. "Blow out the torches!"

Feya blinked up at him with terrified incomprehension just as another scream of pain echoed close behind.

"Use your magic, or we're all dead!"

Understanding dawned in her eyes, and for a fleeting moment, Ridian thought she was about to shake her head and say, 'What if people found out?' But she spread her arms and blew a powerful jet of air from each palm—upstream and downstream. Ridian was quick to jump out of the way while windblown torches flamed hotter, then blew out. Others rolled into the water. People leant into the gale, straining against it, arms protecting their faces, clothes aflutter.

And then, as quickly as it came, the wind died. One brief gust and Feya was clearly spent. She slumped forward, panting. But her efforts had done the trick. The tunnel glowed with Looney Shrooms, though Feya and everybody else squinted blindly. Even Kyros—a little more than thirty feet away—was blind and stumbling. He groped about, then unsheathed the twin swords from his back and tapped them against the floor like a blind man's canes. The blades found a woman crawling for safety, and Kyros stabbed her three or four times in quick succession for good measure.

Others were more fortunate. They remained quivering on the far bank or allowed the water to carry them safely downstream. The more able-bodied slid along the wall, passing Ridian and Feya with surprising speed, though they fumbled blindly. Ridian protected Feya's broken leg from the careless footfalls, nudging people aside if they got too close. Not far behind, Kyros moved with chilling calm. He found another groaning man and sank his swords into him until there was silence—just the sounds of rushing water and retreating voices. As Kyros moved on, his swords chimed a metallic *tink* as they rapped against the cold stone floor.

"Impressive display, my Windchaser friend," said Kyros to the tunnel in general. *"But know I have no qualms with your ancient and noble people. My grievances lie with the followers of Fidic. Cease forestalling me, and no harm will befall you."*

Tink, went the swords. *Tink, tink.*

He doesn't know Feya's all blown out, Ridian realised.

"Hey!" Ridian shouted. "Stay back! Or I will blow you away!"

"I'll say again, my Wrathwoli friend," said Kyros, advancing. *"You will not be molested. Just don't impede me."* There was a restrained threat in his voice.

Ridian mustered all his courage. "I said, one more step, and we will blow you away."

Kyros stopped. *"We? I thought you said 'I'?"* Ridian

couldn't quite see, but he was sure Kyros was smirking.

"Yeah, *we*." He cringed at the feebleness of his words, then nudged Feya. "Say something," he whispered.

Feya hesitated. "Yeah, you stay back or—or else."

Kyros' smirk grew into a wide grin. *"You're telling me there's more than one Windchaser down here?"*

"Yeah, heaps." Ridian bit down on his lip. He knew instantly he'd overshot the lie.

Kyros' teeth shone beneath a mask of blood. *"Heaps? Well, well, well... what are the odds? From what I hear, the Wrathwoli are a rare breed these days, and Windchasers, rarer still. Heaps, you say? Who would have thought? Heaps of Windchasers who will...? What was it you said?"*

"Blow you away!" Ridian meant to sound menacing, but repeating the threat only seemed to weaken it.

"Well then, Windchaser army of heaps... do your worst." Kyros' sword slithered and scraped along the stone floor as he crept forward, their tips *tinking* against every bump or divot. When no wind came, Kyros' maniacal grin only grew.

Ridian was just about to haul Feya up and make a hasty retreat when Silver burst around the corner, blazing like a silver lantern. The wolf reminded Ridian of Theodor, of Kess, of Kai, and of Ella. Of the dead-end. Of no escape. Ridian set his jaw. Upstream, people would have torches. Upstream, there would be light. Here, Kyros was blind. Here was his best chance.

"Take Ollie," said Ridian, dumping the sleeping boy into Feya's lap and ordering Silver to stay back.

"Don't leave us," said Feya desperately, holding Ollie to her chest.

Ridian put his mouth to Feya's ear and whispered, "I'm

not leaving. Trust me." Then he kissed her cheek. Why not? He might never get another chance. Then he turned and tiptoed soundlessly towards the approaching Kyros.

Ridian looked about for a weapon. No sword, knife, club, or stick presented itself, so he picked up a fist-sized rock with trembling fingers. It was smooth, cold, and heavy. It would do the job. Hardly daring to breathe, he crept into a small indentation in the tunnel wall and waited for Kyros. He was just in time. Kyros was a mere dozen paces away, swords slithering and scraping and *tinking* off the floor. Ten paces... Eight... Six...

Ridian raised the stone above his head and imagined the blow. He imagined how he would do it. How it would feel. The swing. The crunch. The collapse. He felt sick. It was his *sister's* skull he would be shattering. He couldn't do this. But he had to. He raised his arm higher.

Kyros was only a few paces away now. Ridian could see the congealed blood clotting in her eyebrows—no, *his* eyebrows. Ridian's heart thumped as he tried to remain perfectly silent. He held his breath.

Kyros stepped into range. *Now!* Ridian drew a burst of Rava from Silver, felt the energy course through his muscles and—

Two things happened simultaneously: the Rava vanished, and Kyros' head twitched in Ridian's direction, his eyes locking on him in alarm. Ridian swung but it was much, much too slow. With impossible speed, Kyros dropped a sword, seized Ridian's falling wrist, and crushed it so hard Ridian dropped the stone in a reflex of excruciating pain. Then Kyros snatched Ridian's throat with fingers strong as iron pincers, and pain shot through his windpipe. Gasping, he tried to pry Kyros' grip free with his free hand. Useless. Kyros' hold was unyielding.

Kyros lifted him off the ground with ease. *"Who might you be?"* he asked with mock politeness, before releasing the pressure on Ridian's windpipe.

"Windchaser… I'm a Windchaser," Ridian managed to wheeze.

"Really?" said Kyros with false interest.

Ridian couldn't hear Silver's pattering feet, but he could sense the wolf charging to his aid. Kyros must have, as well. As Silver leapt, Kyros gave Silver a savage kick. With a strangled yelp, Silver flew over the stream, slammed against the far wall, and fell into a twitching, crumpled heap.

"You are no Windchaser, but a liar," said Kyros. *"I can sense your bond. I can see it. Well, whatever's left of it."*

It was true. The link connecting Ridian to Silver was thinning out, dwindling, dying… Silver was dying, Ridian realised with horror.

"Anyway," continued Kyros, *"no more lies."*

With a squeeze, Kyros' fingers and thumb pierced Ridian's throat, and Ridian began choking and gurgling on warm blood. He strained, kicked, frantic to wriggle free, to breathe. But Kyros was simply too strong. Even Ridian's wrist began to make cracking sounds from Kyros' crushing grip.

"You think this is pain?" said Kyros. *"Pierced skin? Broken bones?"* He laughed bitterly. *"This is nothing compared to an eternity in hell. Never knowing relief. Forever mourning the loss of every good thing. Be grateful your end is swift."*

Then Kyros let go, and Ridian collapsed. He tried to breathe, but all that happened was blood spluttered out of the burning, finger-sized holes in his neck. Kyros fumbled in the dark, found his sword, and walked on as if Ridian's death meant nothing. *Tink, tink* went his swords as they quested in the dark and struck the stone wall and floor.

But *Looney Shrooms* were already dying by the hundreds and pouring their life into Ridian. And, as the silver light dimmed, so did the pain. Soon it vanished altogether.

Ridian coughed up a wad of congealed blood and gasped, filling his lungs with air. He coughed again, then gasped again, and by the time he'd composed himself, Kyros' swords were a few feet from a defenceless Feya and an unconscious Ollie. Ridian snatched up his fallen rock, aimed, and threw. It was a terrible throw—he missed Kyros completely. The stone skittered across the floor, ricocheted off the wall, narrowly missed Feya's broken leg, and plopped into the stream.

Kyros whirled around to face Ridian. He held his swords in guard position, squinting, unable to see.

"No more warning shots," said Ridian, thinking on the spot. "Stop or the next one goes through your face."

Kyros frowned in bewilderment and alarm. *"Ridian? Hector's nephew?"*

"That's right," said Ridian, picking up another rock in the dim light of remaining Looney Shrooms. "I can heal, but I can also *see*. And the next rock is going to smash right through your—"

Something burst from the water and clamped around Ridian's ankle. He recoiled from the wet, slimy grip. It was a man—but he drooled, growled, and hissed like a rabid animal. Mad as an outhouse rat, as Tann might've said. The madman crawled onto the bank and crouched, ready to pounce. The poisoned eyes were shining like a pair of scoured silver pieces, and they could evidently see just fine in the light of the Looney Shrooms. They were locked onto Ridian, and they were hungry.

The man lurched forward with animal ferocity. Resisting the urge to draw Rava from Silver, Ridian roundhouse kicked the man into the water, which carried him swiftly downstream. The man's reckless attack—wholly without regard for his own well-being—made landing the kick easy. But Ridian was shocked by the man's fury-fueled strength.

And his were not the only silver eyes gleaming in the dark. Those Ridian had thought dead or drowned moments earlier also began to rise: a dozen or so closed in on Kyros, while a smaller group dashed towards Ridian, full of fury and that wild, desperate hunger.

If they'd coordinated their attack, Ridian wouldn't have stood a chance. But they stumbled over each other in their rush to reach him. Two turned their fury on one another, wrestling, biting, and clawing like feral cats. Ridian front-kicked one into the stream, then dropped another with a spinning roundhouse.

"Ridian? What's happening?" cried Feya, her voice carrying above the snarls of the poisoned lunatics. Ridian glanced at her. She was looking around helplessly. Kyros was a mere few steps away, drawing the attention of the madmen and inadvertently keeping her and Ollie safe. Though blind, Kyros gave a quick kick, sending a woman hurtling through the air. He swung an elbow and crushed a man's skull like a soft melon. And his swords flickered, deadly as an executioner's axe. He made it look easy—and he couldn't even see.

As Ridian watched, a woman grabbed his sleeve. Ridian spun and palmed her in the face. She tottered, and Ridian kicked her, reeling, into the stream. Then three sets of hands grabbed hold. Then a third. Ridian tried to pull away but couldn't. They were the grips of famished men, clutching the last scrap of food. Their silver eyes closed in. Their jaws gaped open, then their teeth sank into Ridian, and hot pain blossomed across his arms, shoulder, neck...

Panicked, Ridian drew Rava from Silver along their thin, dwindling link. Strength flooded him, and with a powerful shrug, he flung his assailants away. Three swift, bone-breaking kicks followed, sending the three madmen flying. They struck the tunnel wall, slid down, and lay still.

Ridian realised his mistake too late. Rava vanished from within him, and a new dazzling pain flared. Kyros stood before him, grinning with triumph, his sword buried hilt deep in Ridian's shoulder. Whip-quick, Kyros snatched Ridian's other shoulder, and pain exploded as Kyros' thumb twisted and dug, inch by inch into his shoulder socket.

Ridian screamed and writhed, though he was barely aware of it. Everything was blind agony. It was acid. It was fire. It was a thousand knives. It went on and on until Kyros pulled his thumb out. Kyros' sword remained lodged, but it was nothing compared to the probing thumb. He opened his tear-filled eyes. It was very dark now. Only his wolf glowed, though he remained still upon the floor. And he couldn't heal any more; he'd sucked all the surrounding Looney Shrooms dead whilst Kyros tortured him. That explained the darkness.

"I should have known you were a deceptive little sneak," Kyros hissed, inches from Ridian's face. *"With a gift like yours, how*

could you not? A parasitic healer, just like Fidic. A liar of low cunning. A traitor to one's own family." There was murder in his voice.

"Traitor?" said Ridian, staring into his sister's face though it no longer belonged to her. "You're the one torturing your own descendant." And he surprised himself by releasing a hysterical laugh. "And parasite? You're the one infecting my sister's body. And *your* gift?" He brayed in Kyros' face, half in pain, half in a mad, reckless abandon. "You steal Rava. You desecrate a sacred bond. You—"

Kyros' thumb plunged into Ridian's shoulder, and he once again entered a world where only pain existed. When the thumb finally came out, Ridian was limp and shivering in Kyros' grasp.

"Thank you for this conversation," said Kyros, his voice cold as winter. *"You've sobered me. I'd lost control. If it wasn't for you, I would have killed everyone here quickly and efficiently. Everyone would have been dead by brunch. I would have robbed myself of my one remaining pleasure. Thankfully—thanks to you—I am now very much back in control."* Kyros smiled, and his bared teeth were white against his blood-covered face.

Beyond Kyros, Ridian could just discern Feya and Ollie in the dim light of Silver's coat. Feya was clinging to Ollie and sliding slowly away with her one good leg. They were so helpless. And they were next. He couldn't be sure, but he thought Feya was crying. And Ollie was finally waking up, staring around in bleary-eyed confusion. He was finally awake, just to meet some torturous end.

It was too much. He couldn't bear it, and a lump formed in Ridian throat.

"And another thing," continued Kyros, twisting his sword

a fraction to gain Ridian's attention. *"Up until now, I had planned on giving your sister's body back. Even though I've looked in the mirror and can plainly see she's the spitting image of Valaria, that treacherous, spiteful witch. But thanks to you, I've reaffirmed a fundamental truth: good fruit will never come from a diseased tree."*

Death was coming. Any moment now. Would Kyros make it quick? Or would he hurt him and hurt him until he drove Ridian insane? Kyros answered Ridian's unspoken questions by plunging his thumb back into Ridian's gaping shoulder.

Pain will set you free.

From somewhere, the words came to him. And on an impulse, he Split, knew instant relief, and launched his detached mind at Kyros. He had the briefest glimpse of Kyros' brain—a dazzling, illuminated network—before he slammed into the man's mental defenses and was flung back into his body. Pain and despair returned in full measure.

"How dare you?" said Kyros, sliding the sword out of Ridian's shoulder and flinging Ridian to the ground. *"How dare you desecrate the sanctuary of the soul?"* Kyros stomped on Ridian's hand. There was a wet crunch of a dozen—a dozen small bones snapped like twigs. Pain exploded up his arm like fire, fast and blinding.

"Hello?" said a familiar voice as Ridian's cry finally died. It was Theodor. The kindly Steward was rounding a nearby corner, fully illuminated by the torch in his hand. "Hello?" he cried again.

"Dad!" shouted Feya. "Come quick! Ridian's in trouble!"

Theodor ran towards them, torchlight stretching out before him. In that light, Feya's eyes latched onto Ridian—

and the blood-covered Kyros. "Ridian!" she cried. Then Theodor saw, and his face and posture changed instantly. Suddenly, he was nothing like the kindly Steward who cut the crusts off sandwiches. He was the wrath of all fathers.

Felix leapt from Theodor's shoulder, and Theodor sped forward in a blur, the torch a streak of fire in the dark. But no sooner had he launched himself than he came to a sudden stop. He looked baffled, but Ridian knew. Kyros had stolen his Rava. Nonetheless, Theodor continued his charge, though with the ordinary speed of a man past his prime.

"*Friends of yours?*" asked Kyros, tilting his head at Theodor, Feya, and Ollie.

"No, I don't know them," said Ridian, though his fear betrayed his affection.

Kyros stepped off Ridian's shattered hand. "*I'll be back. Feel free to watch.*"

"NO!" Ridian tried to grasp Kyros' ankle with his good hand and was easily shirked off.

Thoughts raced through Ridian's mind. He couldn't heal himself; there were no Looney Shrooms within reach. He couldn't draw Rava from Silver; Kyros would steal it all anyway. Nothing could stop him as he sauntered forward, clearly savouring the moment.

Ridian looked at Theodor, at the love that emanated as he ran. At Feya's loyalty as she cradled her brother. At Ollie, who had always been grateful despite his limitations and the tumour that—

Ollie's tumour! The one Ridian couldn't heal, only make worse. It flashed through his mind, and Ridian had a sudden, startling idea. He had no others, so he did it. He

Split—barely noticing his fear of death—and shot through the black towards Kyros. He would only have a second, Ridian knew. Less. A fraction of a second to infiltrate Kyros' perfectly protected, impenetrable mind. But not perfect. Not impenetrable. He would have a moment.

Ridian slammed into Kyros' mind and glimpsed the dazzling constellation of his brain. And for the briefest of moments—their minds were connected. There was a link. And in that brief moment—not having any plants to draw from—Ridian drew Rava from the only source left: himself.

He shot a bolt of Ravatowards Kyros. As it zoomed along, it sang out like a quick stroke from a fiddle. A single note from the Song of Silent Growing. It struck Kyros, and no sooner had it happened, than it ended. Ridian was back in the bloodied dirt, pain screaming in his weeping shoulders and in his crushed hand. Theodor was still sprinting. Only a moment had passed.

But Kyros had dropped his swords to hold his head as if suffering from a sudden, intense migraine. He turned to look at Ridian, eyes wide in shock and panic. *"What did you just do?"*

Ridian Split again, latched onto Kyros brain for another tiny moment, and shot another bolt of Rava into the exact same spot as before. Kyros grimaced, then lunged in Ridian's direction.

Ridian didn't stop. He Split again and again, each time depositing a small dose of Rava. A mere modicum, but each time he did, the newly formed bundle of light in Kyros' brain grew a little larger and a little brighter. Even as Kyros ran at Ridian, he staggered against the tunnel wall, eyes scrunched shut in pain.

The tumor was growing. It was working. But the Rava pouring into Kyros was also pouring out of Ridian. He was hungry, thirsty, exhausted, and in pain. His shoulders wept blood. His crushed hand was purpling and swelling. And his own swiftly mounting migraine felt like knives behind his eyes. It was killing them both, but he couldn't stop; Kyros was still shuffling towards him, closing in, nostrils flared in fury. The process was too slow, Ridian realised with despair. Kyros was a few seconds away. A few seconds, and Ridian would be dead.

At that moment, a corpse came to life on the far bank. Grunting with effort, it got to its feet, limped a few paces, and, with a great cry, leapt across the water and collided with Kyros, sending him crashing into the tunnel wall.

The corpse rallied first and grabbed the stunned Kyros about the legs, tripping him over. "Whatever you're doing, Ridian, keep going. It's working!" It was Tann. He was pale and bleeding and grimacing in pain, but he clung to Kyros' legs as if he had a thousand-foot drop beneath him. "Kill the son of a bitch!" he cried.

Tann's words were like a spur; Ridian redoubled his efforts. He didn't even try to aim now. He just poured as much Rava into Kyros as possible, flying into the Black the moment he was flung back to his own body. In this manner, he saw snatches of what happened over the next few seconds. Tann groaning with effort; then darkness. Kyros squirming to break free of Tann's grip; darkness. Kyros grabbing a stone; darkness. Kyros raising the stone; darkness. The stone descending; darkness. The stone crushing Tann's skull; darkness. Kyros kicking Tann's limp body away;

darkness.

Reeling with horror and grief, Ridian saw the flowing lights of Rava within Tann bleed from his body and gather into a single ball of light. The Rava bled and bled and bled, and then finally vanished. Just like that, Ridian's friend and mentor was no more. But he didn't have time to think about it. Tann's sacrifice had only given Ridian a second or two. Would it be enough? It had to be. He Split again, infiltrated Kyros' mind, and gave everything he had.

As Kyros crawled forward, Ridian could see his face in the growing light of Theodor's torch. It was slack-jawed, sagging, and hideously deformed. One eyeball was so swollen that Ridian was amazed it hadn't burst, and mottled tumours rippled over the face—disfiguring the nose and twisting the upper lip.

"*I goina kill you…*" Kyros slurred, still shambling on all fours. But just before he reached Ridian, his arm gave way, and he collapsed. He didn't even protect himself. He landed heavily on his chest, and his face plopped into the stream. Ridian waited for him to get up, but Kyros remained motionless. Only his head moved as it swished side to side in the current.

Theodor was only a few yards away by now, and Ridian Split again for one final attack—just to be sure. But as his soul hurtled through the Astral Plane towards Kyros, he saw something strange and stopped mid-flight to watch. The tiny, twinkling lights of Rava that trickled throughout every fiber of Kyros' being were gathering into a small, single ball of trembling light, just as Tann's had moments earlier. Surely this was Kyros' soul leaving Rayna's body. Surely, this was the moment that Soulsnatchers called the Reaping.

Somehow, Ridian knew he could snatch Kyros' soul at this moment: snatch it, consume it, devour it. He knew he could. A part of him even wanted to. Kyros would be trapped within him, just as he'd been trapped in Hero's Tree. He would suffer, and Ridian would know revenge. But as he looked, he saw that the little ball of quivering light was beautiful. That even Kyros' soul, such as it was, was precious. And as he thought this, the ball of light seemed to fall inward on itself—to fall and fall and fall until it finally winked out and was gone.

The moment it did, another ball of light hurtled in from nowhere and struck Rayna's vacant body. It was absorbed and assimilated in an instant, illuminating every muscle, tendon, fibre, and nerve in scintillating light.

Ridian slammed back into his body—into agony.

"Ridian?" said Theodor, rushing past the fallen Kyros to kneel above Ridian, his firelit eyes shining with concern. "Oh, Roki. You're bleeding."

Ridian ignored him and dragged himself to Rayna, who lay face down in the water. He tried to pull her out but lacked the strength. "Help her!" he cried, losing his composure. "Please! Help her!"

Though confused, Theodor pulled Rayna out. He put an ear to her mouth and listened. Dissatisfied, he pumped her chest and breathed into her lungs while Ridian watched on helplessly. He had to repeat the process three times before she coughed up water and gasped.

"Easy girl, easy," said Theodor, patting her back.

Cradling his shattered hand, Ridian crawled closer. He couldn't believe it. She was breathing. She was back. His shoulders were in agony, and his exhaustion profound, but he barely registered either. Somewhere in the background, Feya asked if Ridian was okay and was left unanswered.

"What—what happened?" asked Rayna groggily. Her face had been washed clean of blood, fully exposing the proliferation of tumours that disfigured her.

"Kyros is gone," said Ridian, his voice thick with emotion as he squeezed her hand. "He's gone, and you're free, and that's all that matters."

"Ridian?" Rayna was having a hard time staying awake. Her good eye kept shutting while her bulbous eye remained swollen open—rigid and dead. "I can't… I can't see very well." Her hand went to her neck. "Where—where is Mum's necklace?" Her breath quickened as she grew more and more frantic. "Where is it? Did I lose it again?"

"No," said Ridian. "It's okay. I've got it. It's right here." He fished the Elderflower necklace from his pocket and pressed it into her blood-covered hands.

Rayna's fingers closed over it, and she sighed as she clutched the necklace to her chest. "Don't let me lose it again, okay?"

"You're asking a lot," said Ridian. "You'd lose your thumb if it wasn't connected to your hand."

Rayna smiled faintly, and neither of them spoke as Theodor looked on, silent and solemn.

"Ridian," she said at last as if on the edge of sleep. "I think—I think I'm dying."

"No," Ridian said firmly. "You're not dying. I won't allow it. I'm a healer. I'm going to look after you. Nothing's going to happen to you. Not anymore."

Rayna's twisted lips formed a weak smile. "Don't… Don't you start your fussing."

Ridian laughed, though it was half a sob. "You know me. I'm worse than an old hen, remember…? Remember?"

But Rayna couldn't remember.

She was gone.

Chapter 53

Ridian swam up to the surface of a deep sleep and awoke upon the cold tunnel floor. At first, he didn't know where he was, then he found Feya staring intently down at him.

"He's waking up," she cried over her shoulder.

Everything came back in a flash. The loss of Rayna crushed him like a boulder, and he broke into uncontrollable sobs. He heard Theodor's soothing voice and Feya's. But he ignored them and retreated deep within himself. He closed his eyes and tried to block it all out, tried to push it all away. Then silver light blazed behind his closed eyelids, and he felt a cold, wet nose sniff his face and lick him with a rough tongue. Ridian clung to Silver's neck and sobbed all the harder. He wasn't sure how long he held on, but the pain in his chest lightened a little, and he somehow managed to stop crying. At last, he let go and opened his eyes.

All the Thunderfells—Theodor, Kess, Ella, Kai, Feya, and Ollie—were peering down at him. Ollie leaned in close. "How're you feeling? Dad said you had a seizure." His gaze was keen and sharp. He was his old self again. The surgery had worked.

Theodor pulled him back. "Give him space, son. He's been through a lot."

"Yeah, Mr. Haircut," said Kai. "Give him space."

"*Kai*," warned Kess, "Don't start. Not now."

Ollie fingered the bald spot on his head self-consciously, though he seemed to appreciate the familiar banter amid all the suffering. And indeed, there was suffering. Cries echoed throughout the tunnel, and families hugged each other for comfort as they wept over their dead. There were many.

"So, how are you feeling?" asked Feya. She bit her lip anxiously and crouched down upon two perfectly sturdy legs. It was only then that Ridian realised Silver was in perfect shape as well.

"How…?" Ridian began, frowning at her once broken leg.

"You've been healing in your sleep," said Feya.

"Hope you don't mind," said Theodor. "But we've been carrying the worst of the injured to you, along with whatever fauna we can find. The Looney Shrooms work a treat."

"Luckily, Dad straightened my leg before you healed me," said Feya. "How are you feeling?"

Ridian scanned his body. Besides the crushing grief in his chest, there was no pain. He felt each shoulder in turn: one had a neat little scar, the other had a nobbly, lumpy thing the size of a coin. No lasting damage. His hand though… it trembled and twitched, and most of the fingers were terribly crooked. Feya took it in both her hands and kissed the knuckles tenderly. Ollie and Kai raised their eyebrows at each other, and Kess gave Theodor a look that could only mean, 'I told you so.'

"Don't worry," said Theodor. "We'll fix your hand right up."

Ridian sat up with a sudden jolt. "Where's…"

"It's okay," said Feya reassuringly. "She's over there." She pointed to a covered body a few yards away. Rayna's feet stuck out from beneath the cloth. Beside her lay another shrouded figure—tall and lean. It could only be Tann. Tears burned Ridian's eyes, and he squeezed Feya's tough little hand till it hurt. Silver nuzzled into him.

Theodor stood wearily. "I'd better help out. Who knows how long we'll be down here."

"A while," said Kai. "The Firelords own Fidicia now. Whatever's left of it."

Everybody's head drooped with the despair of an unknown future that only held pain.

"At least we're all still alive," said Theodor. "We have each other. That's the main thing. It's more than many can say. We can always leave Fidicia and start again."

"Leave Fidicia?" asked Ridian.

Theodor shook his head and sighed. "We can't fight people who can harness fire. It would be suicide." He didn't look at Kai, and Kai didn't look at him, but an unspoken argument seemed to crackle between them. "I saw the flames and there's just no way—"

"You don't have to leave Fidicia and you don't have to fight," said Ridian.

Ollie straightened. "What do you mean?"

"The Firelords will destroy themselves," said Ridian.

Everybody looked at him.

Ridian's eyelids became very heavy. He was so tired. He just wanted to sleep, but an explanation was clearly expected. "I told them Madman's Falls was a sacred waterfall. That it was the very heart of the Fidician religion. I told them that drinking the holy water was the most profane and sacrilegious thing someone could do."

Ollie frowned, and he wasn't alone. "Why would you tell them that?"

Ridian yawned. "Telling them not to drink was the only way of making sure they did. Sungazers believe in the One who devours. Consuming religions *is* their religion." Ridian closed his eyes. *Just for a moment*, he promised himself, *just to rest them.* And he imagined General Selkryie and her cohort marching up the path to Madman's Falls, exactly where he told them it would be. He pictured them gloating in haughty triumph as they gathered by the water's edge. He imagined them drinking greedily. And finally, as Ridian drifted off to sleep, he imagined their growing confusion as their eyes began to glint with silver, just like a Caveborn.

Chapter 54

After winged Familiars scouted the region and gave the all-clear, the Fidicians dug their way through the warm cinders of the Living Fort and found their fertile valley transformed into a blackened wasteland. The path of the Firestorm had been erratic—its hectic zigzag could be traced by the eight-foot trench lined with swirls of polished glass—but ultimately, the Sungazers had been very thorough. Everything was scorched. Every tree, shrub, and blade of grass was ash. From the banks of the Raven's River to the tips of the Ring Mountains, nothing had been spared. Homes had vanished, the enormous hospital was a smouldering heap, and, if it wasn't for the occasional splash of metal or pale skeleton dusted with soot, it was as if the Kyrosian camp had never existed. Hero's Tree had certainly vanished. Only the stone foundation of the Lion's Den and the Outer Wall had been preserved beneath the ashfall. Daegan's stonework had been flung far and wide throughout the Fidician Valley.

Madman's Falls was unrecognisable. The ground and encircling stone walls had melted and been scoured by an impossibly hot fire, leaving sharp metallic grooves that spiralled up the rock face. General Selkyrie and her

Sungazers must have burnt each other and their troop to dust, for there were no skeletons. Whatever had happened at Madman's Falls, the Sungazers' fire had been too hot to leave even bones.

Only Sanctuary Forest, protected beyond the narrow canyon, remained intact. Many dispossessed Kyrosians had fled there and, without any leadership, surrendered unreservedly. Hector was not among the survivors, and no wonder, given his wooden legs. But Ridian did not believe his uncle was truly dead until he spotted Chirpy sometime later. The bird had flitted in from nowhere as usual, but the bird's eyes were bird's eyes. They possessed none of the gleaming intelligence that Ridian remembered, and he surprised himself by feeling a little sad. Despite the lies, manipulation, and betrayal, Ridian missed his uncle, or at least he missed the relationship they might have had some other time in another life.

Ash fell for days, smog lingered for weeks, and the Living Fort smouldered for about a month. During this time, Ridian kept himself busy. There were so many injured, so many burnt, and in their makeshift infirmary inside Sanctuary Forest, Ridian spent his days healing. His gift made the people of Fidicia love him. Everywhere he went, people kissed and embraced him. But many held him in awe. They would bow and avert their gaze as if afraid. He was Fidic reborn, he overheard someone say. Roki's chosen one, said another. Lukas was far and away his biggest proponent, singing his praises to anyone who would listen. "I was his first miracle," he would brag. "His first. Don't believe me? Look—" And he would show off his scar and crooked nose. Besides feeling extremely awkward, Ridian was unaffected. He was just grateful for the distraction of his healing duties. Without his work, he didn't know how he would have coped. Grief would strike like a hammer and often without warning. Sometimes the pain was unyielding, crushing the very air from his lungs. Sometimes, he would forget all about Rayna—until he remembered. That was the worst. The sudden stab was like a knife to the heart. And he kept seeing her everywhere: a glimpse in a stranger's face, an echo of her laugh, a flick of her hair. A treacherous joy would leap in his chest, then die mid-flight.

Thankfully, he was very busy. Even when all the initial injuries were healed, people had accidents and fell sick. Ridian found the illnesses far more interesting than the simple injuries. Injuries were easy. He drew Rava, channelled it, and the person got better. But in the accurate diagnosis and herbal treatment of illnesses, he found a passion he didn't know he had, and thanks to years living with Rayna, he found he was pretty good at it. Days were long and hard, and that was good, for it helped him sleep.

Sometime after the Sungazer attack, when the last of the smoke had been blown away, three Wrathwoli Windchasers—a wizened old man and his daughters— flew in from the north with news that the Wrathwoli were gathering at Sky Island once more. "To heal and become whole," the old man had said. When they heard of Tann's fate, a shadow fell over the old Windchaser's face. "Tannerion Sky was a great friend of the Wrathwoli. To do him honour, we shall burn his remains and scatter them above Sky Island." The Windchaser managed a smile. "We should not grieve for Tann but rejoice. He flies in the same eternal winds as his wife and daughter. At long last, his restless heart is at peace."

Ridian was saddened by this. He missed the grumpy arsehole—but he also felt a reluctant happiness. Ridian well remembered Kyros' soul falling deep into some other dimension, into some afterlife. Whatever happened when after death, it wasn't the end, and Ridian liked the idea of Tann being reunited with his wife and daughter. When his time came, Ridian promised himself that he would explore that dimension and find Tann, wherever he might be.

In late spring, Ridian guided a party across The Mire to claim Mirecross Castle, and without their Sungazers, the Sol garrison yielded with little resistance. Sevron then garrisoned Daegan's ancient home with Knights and ordered an immediate fortification of the walls. But Ridian shook his head. "Our greatest defence against the Sol lies not in sword or stone, but in the mystery of The Mire." He went on to suggest that Familiars should prowl and protect the border: "Monsters, not man, will protect us." To his credit, Sevron heeded Ridian's advice, and when it came time for Ridian to leave Mirecross Castle, Sevron took his hand and said, "Never shall the east touch the west."

Ridian returned the grip. "Nor the west, the east," he replied, hoping the words would prove true.

To everyone's delight, Kai married Sabrina in the first Summer after the great fire. Held upon the green-again Last Stand Meadow, it was a bittersweet event. Seeing their love exposed everyone's grief and yet inspired an even deeper joy.

As time passed, Fidicia slowly healed. First, the grass, then the leaves, and then new shoots sprouted from the stumps of Valarian Fire Trees and even from the Living

Fort itself, though what shape the Living Fort would take in the fullness of time was anybody's guess. And as the land healed, so did its people. Homes were rebuilt, plans for a new hospital were drawn, and people started to look to the future again. Smiles returned, and even laughter.

The Thunderfells adjusted to their new life well. Ella grew, learnt more words, and started climbing on everything, un-fazed by the destruction of her whole world. Most startling was Ollie's recovery. Not only did he fully heal from brain surgery, but with Ridian's magic, his legs straightened and grew strong, and under Feya's guidance, he learned Varki at a prodigious pace. Interestingly, he did not grieve for his burnt adventure books as Ridian had expected, but rather for Theodor's thick medical tomes. "I don't care about becoming a Knight any more," he said emphatically. "It's overrated. I want to become a Steward. I want to help people." He looked at Ridian then, eager for his approval.

He wants to be like me, thought Ridian with surprise.

Kai pulled Ollie into a headlock and knuckled his scalp. "Oh, no, Dad! You scooped out too much of his brain. He's lost his wits. He's gone soft in the head."

"Boys," said Kess in her trademark tone of warning, though she smiled.

"Yeah," said Theodor, frowning behind his glasses. "Ollie is a walking miracle. Who would have thought that neural adaptation could be so thoroughly optimised? Who knew the brain could heal itself so thoroughly? It goes against decades of established thought. I'm telling you, my book is going to be…"

"A great seminal work," everyone chimed in unison. "Yeah, we know."

Theodor didn't start his book for a long time, for one day after the destruction of Fidicia, Ridian brought Fidic's Lute for Ollie and Fidic's Journal for Theodor. At first, the relics delighted them both, but Ridian warned Theodor. "This journal is not a gift but a burden that will surely break your heart, but I can't keep its secrets, they're too big for me. Maybe you will know what to do with them." Indeed, Theodor was so shocked by the journal's contents that he was practically mute for the next two days. However, on the third day, Theodor came bustling inside with great enthusiasm. "Even if Fidic lied, our people have been praying to Roki for millennia. Roki is still our god, and we are still his people." Despite knowing the cultural impact and likely persecution, he exposed Fidic's lies and championed for unity between Fidicia and Kyrosia, insisting they shared the same faith and were all Roki's children. He also changed disciplines from Steward to Cleric and took Mother Asarah's place as Fidicia's spiritual Father—a role he didn't want but accepted when the people begged him to take it. And, through his influence, the Kyrosians were given their old lands back, and their tributes were lowered and eventually abolished. Thus, despite remaining bad blood, violence and the threat of war subsided, and Theodor became one of the most beloved and respected Elders in living history due to his great moral courage and commitment to the truth.

However, what moved Ridian the most in the days after Rayna's death was Feya confessing to Theodor and Kess that she wasn't a Soulcaster but a Windchaser. "I guess I should pack my room," she said, staring at the floor. "I should probably join the rest of my kin gathering at Sky

Island. I can't exactly stay here, can I?"

Theodor looked stricken. "But—but…"

"No, Theodor," said Kess, fighting back tears. "We made a promise never to hold our kids back. If she wants to go, she should go."

"Of course, I support her," said Theodor, quite beside himself, his glasses fogging over. "But she was my daughter before she was a Windchaser, and she can't just go traipsing off with any old stranger who blows in from the north Wind!"

"She can't stay here forever," said Kess sternly.

"Why not?!" demanded Theodor.

Feya flew into their arms. "I'll stay!" she cried. "I don't want to go if you don't want me to."

Seeing their unconditional love made Ridian shed a tear of joy. His first since losing Rayna—but not his last. For while Fidicia and its people healed, Ridian did too. And as he healed, the relationship between him and Feya grew. They snuck out most nights together, walking and talking late into the evening and often into the early morning. They would talk about the past—the good and the bad—and their future together. Sometimes, they sat in silence, holding hands and gazing at the stars. And, when they walked back home, Ridian would kiss her, and Feya would fly up to her balcony, only to linger at the window so they could stare at each other for a long time. When Ridian finally climbed into his own bed, he would think of her and wonder if she thought of him.

Epilogue

A man and a wolf dashed through a swaying wheat field. They moved impossibly fast, like sparrows in flight. Overhead, a woman flew like a bat, a great gale blowing from her hands and feet. The man and woman cast rippling shadows beneath the full moon. But the wolf blazed with a cold silver fire, like the moon made flesh, and cast no shadow.

At last, they came upon the Asylum. Leaving the wolf to prowl the grasslands, the man scaled the tall perimeter wall. He was very strong, and the scant footholds posed little trouble. The woman soared over the wall, coat aflutter, and landed lightly on the plush lawn.

Rows of trees stood guard. Flowers were closed in sleep. A fountain splashed in the courtyard. The man and woman strode past it all to the many-windowed Asylum: a place the man had once dreaded. The man climbed up a drainpipe and crept along the roof. The woman ascended with an elegant burst of wind.

At the centre of the building lay an open courtyard. The man lowered himself from the gutter and dropped four stories, landing deftly—though by all rights, his legs should've shattered. The woman drifted slowly down after him, gentle as snowfall. Inmates gasped and cowered and ran, scuttling away down dark corridors to dark cells. Only one woman remained. She sat in silence upon a bench, surrounded by her garden of closed Moonflowers. Her body was there, but her mind was not. She was far away—lost in a memory of long, long ago.

The woman who could fly hung back, while the man walked cautiously forward. "Mother?" he asked searchingly, with little hope of finding her, so deep was her silence. His hair and beard were streaked with thick strands of white, though he was barely twenty.

The silent woman didn't answer. She didn't even blink. She stared out from vacant eyes that seemed to see nothing. She was exactly the same as the man remembered. She hadn't aged a day.

He removed a vial from his coat pocket and uncorked it with a twitching, trembling hand. The fingers were crooked and still hurt, even after all these years. "Drink," he said, placing the vial to the silent woman's lips.

The woman drank reflexively—an automation. The man waited, afraid for the first time in a long time. Then a light began to shine from deep within those eyes. It shone, faint and from a long way away, but shining all the same. Slowly, then quickly, the light grew. It emanated outward, filling her eyes, then the rest of her face came alive.

Valaria, the Elderflower, blinked and looked upon her son, and as she did, Moonflowers began to bloom.

About the Author

Raised in rural Western Australia, Christopher Samuel Laundy escaped into his imagination at an early age—and never quite came back. Tolkien stole his heart first, sparking a lifelong love for fantasy.

Now a Sydney-based Clinical Psychologist, he's witnessed countless stories of pain, perseverance, and triumph. These experiences have deeply influenced his writing, infusing an authentic emotional depth into the page-turning action and adventure of his debut fantasy novel, *Elderflower*.

In his spare time, he writes songs no one wants to hear, prays, and daydreams of yet-undiscovered lands.

He loves making stuff up.

You can connect with me on:

🌐 https://cslaundy.com